Jill Gascoine was born in south London. Educated at Tiffin Girls' School, she was taught acting, singing and dancing at Italia Conti, and joined the theatrical profession at the age of fifteen. She is well known for the television series *The Gentle Touch* and also starred in *C.A.T.S. Eyes*. She has two sons from her first marriage, and now lives with her second husband, actor Alfred Molina, in West Sussex and Los Angeles.

ADDICTED

Jill Gascoine

CORGI BOOKS

ADDICTED
A CORGI BOOK : 0 552 14231 X

First publication in Great Britain

PRINTING HISTORY
Corgi edition published 1994
Corgi edition reprinted 1994 (twice)
Corgi edition reprinted 1995

Set in Monotype Plantin by
Phoenix Typesetting, Ilkley, West Yorkshire.

Corgi Books are published by Transworld Publishers Ltd,
61–63 Uxbridge Road, Ealing, London W5 5SA,
in Australia by Transworld Publishers (Australia) Pty Ltd,
15–25 Helles Avenue, Moorebank, NSW 2170,
and in New Zealand by Transworld Publishers (NZ) Ltd,
3 William Pickering Drive, Albany, Auckland.

Reproduced, printed and bound in Great Britain by
Cox & Wyman Ltd, Reading, Berkshire

To Fred and Francis
who both love me unconditionally

Acknowledgements

My thanks to all the women who shared with me so openly all their experiences; to Theresa Hyde for typing so long into the night; the general managers of the Swallow Royal hotels in York and Bristol for their comfortable rooms when I was touring while writing; to Gloria Hunniford for her invaluable help; and very specially to the Midhurst Writers' Group for their nit-picking, their constructive criticism and Bob Chandler's determination I would not stop writing until I finished.

Chapter One

Ignoring the previous night's overdose of vodka, Rosemary's internal clock went off as usual at seven a.m. Fifteen minutes before Ella's birthday gift to her had been set to go off. A Teasmaid, it sat like a small, compact power station on the lace-covered bedside table. Opening one eye, she regarded its smugness with trepidation, wondering what on earth possessed her flamboyant daughter to buy her such an extravagant, practical and sensible gift. Maybe her reaching fifty had something to do with it. Fifty.

'Hooray,' Ella had said, 'we'll have a party – it's a big-deal landmark.'

'What is? Why?' Rosemary hated parties.

'Being fifty, Mum. It's time to change direction. Do something different. Shake your life up. You're getting as bad as Grandma. Fifty close friends; you must have fifty close friends.'

'Ella darling,' *good God will she never leave home*? 'Ella darling, don't be facetious. Nobody reaches fifty with that many close friends. I cross off at least five names every Christmas. And not because they die.'

So it had been about thirty – twenty, in Ella's favour, depending which way you looked at it.

Rosemary's entertaining was well catered for these days. Media success had made her divorced life easier, and appropriately more comfortable. Divorced but not alone, not with a twenty-five-year-old, mostly out-of-work actor daughter who lived at home a good deal of the time, disappearing only when a job or lover spirited her away.

A light came on suddenly in the birthday present by the bed, and a dreadful cacophony of sound propelled Rosemary into a sitting position with her hands over her ears. Not just to block out the noise, but also to hold her head steady; it felt distinctly loose. Drink and middle-age were not good bed companions. She found herself looking forward to a cup of tea in bed. It had been a long time since someone had brought her one, apart from hotel staff. It was fifteen years since her acrimonious divorce. Fifteen years of tears, loneliness, struggling with difficult teenagers, and now, finally, success, confidence and real joy in being single.

Water boiled, the electrical invader fell silent and Rosemary reached across to pour the tea, quite pleased with her clever, thoughtful daughter. Plain boiled water splashed into the cup. She had forgotten the teabags in her drunken state of the night before.

'Oh shit.'

Now she would have to get up and stagger downstairs. By this time a cup of tea was a necessity. Not daring to attempt to comb through last night's lacquered hair, she found her dressing-gown and slippers, and headed for the hall in almost ferocious haste.

The house was breathtakingly quiet when she opened her bedroom door. A large, light, gentle house, she'd bought it five years ago when her television chat show had taken off with such miraculous success. One of the advantages of being famous: money in your pocket, the ability to acquire a home big enough to hide an instantly recognizable face. She had fallen in love with the house in Wimbledon more passionately than she ever had with a man.

She drew back the curtains at the landing window, revealing early morning and weak spring sunshine on a cold March day. Down the wide staircase, holding onto the bannister, legs shaky from last night's booze, she averted her eyes from open doors and the left-over mementoes of the party. Not her problem. Pat would be in later to clear it all up, sweep it away along with the mistakes and the hangovers. Once, long ago, housework had been the centre of her life. Now it was peripheral. Now she could afford a Pat to do it for her.

She opened the kitchen door. A man stood at the sink in front of the window overlooking the garden, silhouetted against the morning light as the sun struggled into strength. He was singing to himself, and washing cups under running water. Fear threw her heart into her throat, beating against the roof of her mouth, but only for seconds. He turned to look at her, a blue-checked J-cloth in one hand and a china mug in the other. The water from the tap behind him continued to run into the white ceramic sink. A first impression indelibly stamped.

'Morning.' His voice was soft for such a large man.

'I'm sorry,' she said, apologizing needlessly for her intrusion. 'You must be one of Ella's friends who stayed.'

He came forward, mug still in hand, forward where she could see him better, away from the back-lighting of the window. She could see brown eyes and a melancholic smile.

'We met last night,' she said.

'Ben. Ben Morrison.' His voice matched his smile. 'Hello again.' He turned back to stop the running tap. He brought the mug to the kitchen table in the centre of the room. Rosemary felt small and vulnerable in her early morning déshabille. Overwhelmed by the size of him, she sat down and looked up at him. Tall, dark and handsome; nice to have in your kitchen at seven-thirty in the morning the day after your fiftieth birthday. Smiling to herself, she smiled at him. He looked young and wicked, with fathomless eyes.

'D'you want tea?' he asked, looking down at her from

his well-over six foot height. 'Hope you don't mind, I helped myself. Made some, I mean.'

'How wonderful. Yes please, I'm desperate for a cup.'

He turned and picked up another mug from the draining board.

'I'd like a cup and saucer.' The words were out automatically.

His eyes all but disappeared into his thick hair at the authority in her tone. He picked up a cup and saucer and began to dry them. 'I bet you won't drink champagne out of plastic either, will you?'

She laughed before she replied. 'No you're right. Nothing but the best crystal.'

Smiling, he began to pour the tea, made, to her surprise, in a teapot. He had made her feel patronizing and she didn't quite know why. She usually worked so hard to accommodate the feelings of others.

Moving to the fridge, she said, 'I've only skimmed milk, is that all right?' Holding it up for him to see, the cold air from the fridge caressed the thin material of her nightdress. She shivered.

'My mouth has no tastebuds this morning,' he said. 'It'll be good whatever. My teeth itch.' He looked round at her. 'Where d'you keep the sugar?'

'Would you like an Alka Seltzer?' She'd taken the sugar bowl and placed it on the table with the milk she'd already put into a small, matching jug. The flowered crockery sat close and neat. A set piece.

Ben Morrison laughed at the sight. 'Perfect.' Then, 'No thanks, no seltzer. What I really need is a nice, thick layer of tannin round the innards.' He sat at the table. 'Drink tea with me,' he said, 'we don't have to talk if that's how you like your morning.'

She sat opposite him and put milk in her tea. He had spilled some in the saucer. Taking a tissue from the pocket of her pink housecoat she laid it carefully under the cup. She took a sweetener from the same pocket and pressed one into her tea.

He watched her, sipping from the mug held to his lips, steam from the hot liquid dissolving the contours of his face. The clock in the hall chimed a quarter to eight.

'You found the Earl Grey and mixed it,' she said. 'That was clever of you.' Silence. And she found him staring at her.

His mouth was held slightly open so that she could see the pink end of his tongue. He watched her mouth. Not wanting to meet his stranger's eyes, she shifted her gaze out of the window and onto a bird feeding at the plastic container which Ella had stuck to the outside of the glass. It needed filling, and she added it mentally to the list in her head under the heading, 'Saturday. Things To Do Today.'

The unshaven young man in her kitchen seemed to find it totally unnecessary to utter a word, which she found most disconcerting and vaguely irritating. She would have liked to be alone, to get on with her lists and her day. Compelled to break the silence, wanting to move the atmosphere, she said fatuously, 'That's the best morning tea I've had in years.'

'I should be here every morning.'

Her eyes on his face now, her thoughts tumbled in a direction alien to the order of her day. 'My God, he's flirting with me. Damn cheek; I'm old enough to be his mother.' The cliché locked itself into the banality of her mind.

His smile grew wider, his eyes surprisingly distant, as if he'd used the same 'chat' before, and it was well rehearsed. 'Did you enjoy your birthday?'

She found his habit of watching her mouth most disconcerting. 'I'll think about it,' she said, 'and let you know.' Brown eyes into grey ones. Momentarily locking into an unfulfilled pledge. She poured herself more tea,

13

forgetting the strainer in her sudden confusion, and watching, with annoyance, the tea leaves float to the surface.

'Shit.' It was out before she'd thought. And he threw back his head and laughed. Then she remembered him. Both from last night's party and from something else. 'Does Ella talk about you, or have we met before?' she asked.

'Ella and I were lovers. For about – oh I dunno. Not for long. We're better at being friends.' He paused. 'Sorry, that was a bit blunt. My mouth's not in the same gear as my brain until noon.'

He was vulnerable then, and she warmed to him, realizing that some part of him wanted to see if she was shocked by his explicitness, or even by her promiscuous daughter. But shock was not what she felt. She had grown accustomed to Ella's ex-lovers drifting in and out of her daughter's life. Ella collected them: like a hobby. As if she believed in sleeping with everyone, boy or girl, before she could be the very best of friends; childish in her naivety. Rosemary's prudent nature wouldn't allow her to dwell on anything so alien to her own stifled upbringing.

So Ella's circle of friends widened every year. Occasionally, for old times' sake, she would sleep with one of them, though Rosemary often suspected they had long since ceased to be exciting to her. It was as if she felt obliged to keep the friendship going in this bizarre way, finding comfort in the cosiness of familiar sex; enjoying the laughter more than the passion. It all seemed much too casual for Rosemary, but at least Ella kept to an accustomed circle, which these days hopefully was safer than dissipation. Rosemary loved her audacious daughter, accepted her strange way of loving, and reluctantly minded her own business.

So, Ben Morrison was one of those 'lovers-become-friends'. For how long and when? Last night? The

14

thought crept in to check the beds before Pat arrived. His eyes were on her, as if he knew what she was planning. She said quickly, 'You've had some success with a film recently, haven't you?'

'Right. Have you seen it?' Suddenly young and eager, he wanted to impress her. She reeled from the rapid change in his demeanour.

'Not yet.' All at once, she hated to disappoint him. 'But we reviewed it on the show two weeks ago, and I seem to remember they raved about you.'

The smile lit up every feature of his face. Like every actor she had ever met, praise was as necessary as food and sex. The advantage was hers. She savoured it, feeling intuitively that moments like this were rare with this young man. A thought entered her mind through the keyhole of a long-ago shut door: *I've never been in love with an actor. It must be hell.* The morning was taking on a very strange shape.

'Do you want some toast?' she asked. She was hungry. Something was needed to soak up last night's alcohol.

'Great. I'll make it.' He stood up noisily, the chair scraping tooth-edgingly on stone-tiled floor.

She moved quickly. 'No, I'll do it. I know where everything is.' She smiled, obvious in her desire to keep him seated and not messing up her kitchen. He watched her, again in silence, drinking his tea noisily. Wholemeal bread cut thick stood in a china toast-rack, beside butter and the home-made jam that she'd picked up on one of her forages with Ella into a WI stall when she'd opened a fête one summer afternoon. She went for plates, but Ben had found a knife and was buttering his toast straight onto the still-grubby-from-last-night table. Plate in each hand, she hesitated before self-consciously placing one in front of him. It teetered against the crumbs from the toast.

'Oops, sorry.' He grinned, amused at her propriety. Brushing the crumbs heedlessly onto the floor, he threw his toast onto the matching plate with a certain amount of acerbic ceremony.

Rosemary remained standing; awkward, as if the kitchen were not her own. He ate as noisily as he'd drunk his tea: with concentration and obvious felicity.

From upstairs a toilet flushed and the whisper of bare feet padded down the stairs and towards the kitchen. The door opened aggressively, as only Ella could open a door, and her daughter bounced into the quietness that had been theirs. Brown tousled hair over the same grey eyes as her mother's, eyes still swollen with too little sleep.

'I smelt the toast. Is there tea? Morning Mum. Christ, Ben, you're eating again.' Words tumbled out while she fetched mug and plate, accompanying the abrasive clatter of cutlery while she looked for a knife. Kisses on Rosemary's cheek in passing, a snigger and a prod of the finger at Ben who laughed with his mouth full of toast. Her daughter had erupted into the day as usual. This time spoiling – what? Silly even to think about it.

'Morning Ella, don't make too much mess.' The request was automatic. The reprimand natural, coming as it did from mother to daughter, alike in their looks, but not in their ways.

The mood in the kitchen, whatever it had been, was now irrevocably broken. Rosemary had been effectively and abruptly moved from centre stage. It seemed now that she was the odd one out. Ben and Ella chatted easily together. She could find no way into their banter.

Putting down her empty tea-cup she said, 'I'll get dressed. Ben, thanks for the tea, do help yourself to anything.' *Except my daughter,* crept unbidden to the front of her mind.

He stood up as she left the room, chair scraping noisily once again. She winced, then smiled at him. He was altogether old-fashioned in his politeness, and it touched her, because it was surprising in someone who had seemed so much the modern, aggressive occupant of the late twentieth century. She left the room, still smiling at him, while Ella's words, 'God Ben you're such a toady,' followed her upstairs.

Once back in the bright, perfume-heavy bedroom, her familiar morning ritual began. She slipped easily into the preferred order of her day: bed aired, naked body toned and stretched for fifteen minutes, oil-scented bath in which to luxuriate, perfectly ironed denims only worn at weekends laid out on the chaise, shirt to go with the jeans, and all chosen this morning with more than her usual care.

She liked the pattern of her days, enjoyed the tidiness of it all, hated to be jarred or hurried into the day, preferring to greet each one with stealth and gentleness. There had been a hiccup this morning. And there was a small knot of disturbance in the pit of her stomach that she couldn't erase. Make-up applied, she tied her blond hair back from her face and steeled herself to go back downstairs. She had heard Pat arrive some time ago and then the sound of the vacuum cleaner in the sitting-room. The kitchen door opened and shut and sounds of laughter and Ella floated upstairs.

'Mum,' a cursory knock on her bedroom door before entering. 'Mum, did you know Pat's here? What's she doing here on a Saturday?'

'Did *you* want to clean up?' Irritated, Rosemary dabbed perfume behind both ears, wondering briefly if Chanel was too powerful for early morning.

'Don't let her do my room, Mum. It's chaos.' Ella left, crossed the landing to the said chaos and shut her door.

Rosemary had forgotten to check where Ben had slept. Telling herself she needed to know exactly what the day held for her in the way of mood, she moved rapidly to the two spare bedrooms. One of them had been used. Not pleased with herself, she nevertheless felt relief.

The sound of Ella's noisy teeth-cleaning competed with the vacuum cleaner, Jazz FM and Radio 4 that Pat had switched on automatically when she arrived.

Ben Morrison stood, solitary, in the kitchen and stared out across the well-groomed garden, sparse with March plants. Bulb leaves showing energetically, one daffodil, brave in its solitude, a week too early for its peers. Spring waited with bated breath to burst from the still-frozen ground.

There was something about the house, an almost forgotten experience of order from his childhood that he found dangerously seductive. The fading smell of toast, the competitive background of two radio stations, a bath running upstairs, the sound of a shower starting. A family home beginning its day.

It was a harmony basking in complacency; asking for destruction.

Unable to move, standing by the window, not wanting to blemish the small aura of quiet about him, he watched the birds on the terrace outside. The rabbit that scuttled up from the lower level and found itself nearer the house than intended and bustled away again, chased suddenly by a black cat who, up to that moment, had been busy trying to get the goldfish out of the ornamental pond.

'Is the moggy yours?' he asked Rosemary when she came back into the kitchen.

'Yes. His name's Ben.'

They laughed, in the way people did at things not funny.

'My son's favourite film when he was younger had been about a rat called Ben,' Rosemary went on, 'and as I refused point-blank to let him have one for a pet, we got him a cat to stop the tantrums.' She paused, remembering. 'Anyway, he called the cat Ben instead.'

'Ella never talks about her brother,' Ben said. 'Only that she has one. Is he older?'

'They don't really get on. He's almost thirty and everything that Ella seems to despise, I'm afraid.'

He searched her face as she busied herself with the crumbs on the kitchen table. 'What does he do? Is he in our business?'

'Good God no.' Rosemary laughed at the thought. 'He's in insurance. Successful, too. Married. One child, little girl. Nice, tidy wife.' It was hard to keep the disappointment out of her voice when she talked about her eldest child.

'So you're a grandma?'

She laughed again, and to her dismay she began to blush, as if being a grandmother didn't sit easily with the thoughts she'd been having when around this young man. 'Yes I am. But I see very little of them. They live in Birmingham.' She went on, 'We all steel ourselves at Christmas. I dread it every year.'

Ben smiled and turned back to the window. Rosemary started to fill the dishwasher with the breakfast crockery. Why on earth had she opened up so much to a stranger? Unlike her, a private person. It was the only characteristic she had in common with her son. She had only been an instant away from telling him what a difficult teenager John had been, far worse than Ella.

He'd been fifteen when his father had gone, leaving a house that seemed to him full of crying women. He was his father's son in every conceivable way; Rosemary had admitted that to herself a long time ago. Sadly, she had always been uncomfortable with him as soon as he had started growing up. From a spoilt, but well-loved little boy, he had come to disapprove whole-heartedly of his mother: blaming her for the divorce, believing her to be so dull that any man would leave her. Later, her television success, her strength of purpose and direction, had surprised him. But by then it was too late for them ever to be easy with each other. Rosemary had only the memory of a blond baby she had adored to hang onto when she wrote the loving messages on the birthday and Christmas cards.

'Is it too soon to offer you coffee?' she asked Ben. 'I have to make one for Pat.'

'No – I mean yes – I'd love one.' He turned away from the window. 'I love your house, Rosemary.' He was awkward in his praise.

'We've been happy here.'

'It shows.'

She looked up at him and the expression in his eyes, unmasked with the directness of her gaze, took her completely by surprise. There was an open longing and desire which she couldn't have imagined. It disappeared as quickly as it had arrived, and as soon as he knew she'd seen. As if he'd been caught with something that didn't belong to him: an alien emotion. The kettle boiled through their silence. He turned back to the window and she noticed his shoulders hunched down and forward, making him smaller, less brash-looking. She made the coffee, apologizing automatically because it was instant. Needing, not wanting, to make conversation, she said, 'Are you waiting for Ella?' Without waiting for a reply she moved restlessly to the door and opened it, calling, 'Ella! Pat! Coffee!'

The sound of cleaning stopped. Upstairs was full of silence. Ill at ease, Rosemary smiled quickly at him, distant in her edginess. He drank his coffee. 'Ella's probably in the shower,' she said. 'She won't be long.'

Pat came in cheerfully, moaning as usual about the smell of dirty ashtrays, said she'd already been introduced when Rosemary politely presented Ben, sat down, and a sprinkling of small talk bounced between them.

Ella eventually came down, hair damp and curly from the shower and, without much effort, Saturday morning began to take on more or less its usual shape. And Ben

Morrison remained. Ella asked him if he'd like to stay for the day. If he had 'nothing better to do'. He said he didn't, and he would. They could go to the pub at lunchtime.

'You come, Mum. Do you good.'

'I'll be recognized.' But she knew she'd go with them. The local Saturday market was fun to visit, as well as the usual weekly buy-up at their favourite deli.

Ben attached himself to them and the routine with perfect ease. He clowned and made them laugh. Rosemary was enjoying herself. They made a list for shopping and Ben added some items. It was as if he'd been part of the household for a long time, so easily did they and the house embrace him. So comfortable was his insidious arrival into their way of life. It crossed Rosemary's mind that it was unusual for a young man to be at a loose end on a Saturday. He made no phone calls to tell anyone where he was. But her curiosity remained stifled and the questions unasked. He was there; attached to them, untied for the moment from whatever was the rest of his life.

They took Rosemary's car – Ella in the back – Ben beside Rosemary in the passenger seat. He asked if he could put a tape on, which he did, almost before she'd said 'yes'. Rifling through her neat and organized line of cassettes, he found a Miles Davis.

Itching to straighten the tapes he'd left in some disarray, she smiled in acknowledgement that they liked the same music.

Rosemary, aware of the ease with which Ben manipulated and amused both Ella and herself, uneasy as she was in the seemingly contrived threesome, went reluctantly along with it all until, somehow, the whole situation became disturbingly exciting. It was everything left unsaid that pushed the slumbering fertility of her mind in directions where she had long ago lost the compass.

They parked the car and went to the delicatessen. They drank capuccino from plastic cups and bought exotic tastings that fed their sensual longings. Food, to Rosemary, had always fed more than one appetite.

Ella grew bored early on. 'I need the library. Let's meet in the pub at one, OK?' And she was gone.

Two full carrier bags later, warm Italian bread broken off and tasted by Ben, she paid for the food and he took the bags in one hand to lead the way out of the shop. As he stood back, holding the door for her, the strap of her bag slipped from her shoulder and his hand was on it, pushing it back firmly, carefully, casually, as if their acquaintance was already old. Their eyes met, momentarily, shifting away quickly in the sudden and unbidden heat of discomposure. His hand stayed on her shoulder, pressed with the feeling of ownership on the back of her neck as they left the shop. And to her enormous dismay her stomach lurched in a very ancient and familiar fashion.

Her heart sank, and a little piece of her brain sighed and acquiesced with some misgiving. *Oh Christ, not that. Not at my age, not with his age. Not NOW.*

The day went. Ben stayed for tea. And then for supper. They ate the food they'd bought from the paper it was still wrapped in. Rosemary opened wine. They sat long into evening, round the table in the kitchen. Too stimulated to move to another room in case whatever it was that held them breathless would vanish, never to manifest itself again.

And then it was midnight and once again Ben was too drunk to drive his car home and once again Ella asked him, 'Why don't you stay the night? Make a weekend of it. We've nothing planned.'

And in her head, Rosemary was back to the question that began her day. Was something going on with him and Ella? Something that in her excitement she had refused to see? She stood up, shaky from too much sitting and too much wine, eager for solitude and the gathering in of a little propriety.

'Can you two kids sort yourselves out? This old lady needs more beauty sleep than both of you, and I think I'll start now.'

Ella, affronted by the word 'kids', turned and looked up at her mother, who bent to kiss the surprised look on her daughter's face. Rosemary only glanced briefly through the confusion in Ben's eyes at the patronizing tone in her voice. It had been intentional on her part.

Let's squash this here and now, her cursory glance had said quite plainly. *Whatever it is, whatever you want. You've had your flirtation with both of us; we've all enjoyed it, and here it stops.*

He stood up as she walked to the door. Large and powerful in the disrupted kitchen.

'If you've gone in the morning,' she said, *and dear God, I hope you are,* 'I'm sure we'll meet again. Ella's friends are always welcome.' She left the room, resisting the desire to turn back to him, knowing he was standing there in boyish politeness. She thought to herself, *I should kiss him good night like a small child.* But she didn't trust being near him or touching him. Tomorrow she'd be back to normal, tomorrow, hopefully, he'd be gone, taking with him that compulsive charm that had filled her house and her day. Tomorrow she wouldn't care where he'd slept last night, or where he'd be tonight. Tomorrow. And as she walked upstairs she looked forward to Sunday almost as much as she'd enjoyed Saturday. Almost.

Chapter Two

When Rosemary ventured downstairs the next morning it was ten o'clock, and to her surprise both Ben and Ella had gone. They'd left dirty crockery, toast crumbs on a tea-stained table, and a hastily scribbled note in Ella's handwriting explaining that Ben had wanted to go to Petticoat Lane, so she'd gone with him, and not to worry if she didn't get back because she was partying that night and would stay with friends in Stepney. She had an audition first thing Monday morning. There was a postscript, obviously in Ben's handwriting: 'Thanks again – see you soon.'

She tidied and cleaned the kitchen, half-listening to the radio, her mind busy with her own thoughts, dipping in and out of the angst of the radio soap characters as the programme drifted on in the background. And she worried about Ben and Ella. And as Sunday went on, so did her agonizing. The thought and the image took root in her mind and grew, and stayed, and dominated her all day and well into the early evening. Increasingly upset and angry with her obsessional imaginings, she kept herself even more than usually busy. She was alone all that Sunday. Even her mother for tea would have been a welcome invasion into the bedevilled silence that seemed to surround her all day. A phone call to her parent was unanswered, ringing out endlessly at the other end into that small, terraced, sterile little house in Streatham. She let it ring twenty-four times, standing, counting in her hall, watching the sudden hailstorm pelting at the pane of stained glass in the front door.

She lit the fire in the sitting-room and made a pot of tea. Wanting comfort, she toasted crumpets and spread butter so thick that it dripped through her fingers.

She sat upright on the long sofa and tried to read the Sunday papers. And the hail, turning to sleet, went on pounding into the now-sodden lawn. She found some music she liked and put it on. It seemed to induce an inexplicable melancholy in her, reminding her too much of a time in her life that was long ago.

Unable to concentrate on reading, she tried the television. A black-and-white film on Channel 4 sprang into life, and for a while she watched Joan Crawford in *The Women*. But it was useless. Ben Morrison crowded into every tidy compartment of her brain. He invaded her peace of mind – and she resented his presence.

She watched her own show, the one she had recorded the previous Thursday, and envied herself in that earlier state of being forty-nine and as yet unchallenged by any male intrusion into her chosen solitude. But Ben was there now, immovable in his charm.

The telephone remained silent. She watched the sleet and rain, and only moved to take the tray back to the kitchen, and then stand at the large window, mesmerized by the puddles forming on the uneven stone terrace. As the downpour began to ease and it was evening, she found a half-finished bottle of wine in the refrigerator and sat on the floor in front of the fire. Using the television as background, the murmur of actors' voices inexplicably alleviated a sudden loneliness that had crept up on her. She allowed the wine to relax her, and her thoughts opened, unhindered by self-imposed prudery: the feel of his hand on the back of her neck; his eyes on her whenever she turned in his direction; the smile that hovered continually when their eyes met and held; the promises in his looks; the suggestions in his hands when he brushed past her; the way he made her laugh; the ease with which he'd slipped into her weekend. And most of all, she felt again that sensation in the pit of her stomach travelling through and into the sensual and erotic part of her that she had believed was sealed for ever.

How many times had she told her friend Frances, 'my libido is gone for always, thank God.'

'Don't believe it,' Frances had said. 'It'll turn up again. Always dose. Usually uninvited. And causing the usual havoc. Even worse when you're old and sensible.'

Rosemary had laughed, not believing her. Now, damn it, here it was, back after God knows how many years. And unless she could stop it now, it would cause mayhem. He was, what? Thirty-two, three? An actor. He and Ella had been lovers. It got worse and worse, and these were only the things she knew about him. Maybe it had only been one-sided, just in her imagination. Maybe she'd never see him again. But somehow, she knew. No man had moved so thoroughly into her head as this one. Not for twenty years. And this one was trouble.

She'd had one affair during her sixteen-year marriage. Her husband had never known. No-one had, except Frances. But then John had scarcely noticed much after the first few years of their marriage, and less than nothing once Ella had been born. Her affair had lasted only six months and she had felt quite wonderful, even through the guilt. But the man, the lover, had grown tired of her. He'd left, without explanation. She had kept her tears to herself. But infidelity did not sit easily in her make-up, and her marriage began to crumble more rapidly. They staggered on for a few more years in increasing futility and eventually it all fell apart and into the hands of the lawyers. It had been acrimonious, but both their lives got quickly better when they lived separate existences. Eventually they were friends. Occasional friends anyway.

And that had been it for the last fourteen or so years. As far as men and serious romance was concerned, anyway. There'd been a couple of what Frances had called 'brief encounters' – even one of Erica Jong's 'zipless fucks' one drunken night while waiting for the decree absolute, but nothing else. And now the peace and eventual security she had found for herself in celibacy was far too precious to be ruined by falling in love, or letting any man into her life again. She enjoyed being on her own, forcing herself in her late thirties into a strange sort of chastity. But it became curiously seductive as the years went on.

'It will have healed over,' said Frances, staggering blatantly from one affair to the next with her usual enjoyment. But Rosemary stuck to her guns. She loved her life. She found ambition, and her work, that started as a mattress to save them all from the erratic payment of alimony, became a career. And suddenly from working as a television journalist behind the scenes, somebody gave her a radio show and eventually a networked television chat show. And she was there. Arrived. A smile on the face of her patient and supportive old friend of a bank manager, a new home and even less time and energy to fit any sort of lover into her life. She felt no desire for any kind of disruptive male influence, knowing finally that women in charge of their own lives close the gap of a manless existence with more ease than they are led to believe.

'But it's so dull without men,' wailed Frances over the years.

'When I'm bored I'll tell you Frances.'

'You won't recognize it. Your life's too tidy. It's not a rehearsal you know. This is it.'

But Rosemary smiled, kept men as acquaintances, and stayed at ease with herself. Until Saturday. Until the day after her fiftieth birthday. Until her daughter's lover, ex-lover, friend or future foe, had dropped into her kitchen, her spare bedroom, her life, and hung around long enough to remind her of a mis-spent youth. Memories of moments 'behind the bike-shed', when she hit her teens, puberty, and boys, all at once.

'You'll end up on the streets,' had been her mother's constant and furious warning. But it was mainly bomb sites and allotments in the summer and bus shelters when it grew colder. And not as much girl-guiding and church youth-clubbing as her mother had believed. Just a lot of heavy petting. 'Ants in her pants', as the song says, were now back with her again. Making her feel like a middle-aged teenager.

And that wicked, melancholy smile of Ben's stayed with her as she wandered aimlessly that evening, drinking wine, staring out of every dark window in every lonely room of that large and silent house. He sank with her into the bottle of her favourite claret and eventually into her bed and stayed as she slept restlessly and woke with her, and her headache, on a bright, cold Monday morning.

Her secretary, Jennie, always arrived promptly at half-past nine. She was employed for just two mornings a week to see to fan letters and other requests by mail, and to make the phone calls that Rosemary hated making. They worked together in the small light room off the main hall that Rosemary had made into a study for herself. Monday's work was appointments, and refusals with regrets. The phone began to ring constantly as soon as offices everywhere started to function.

Jennie was in her early thirties, divorced with two small children, and delighted to find any sort of part-time work when her marriage finished. She had been with Rosemary for the last two years and they got on well. Both private people, they seldom delved into each other's personal lives, and talked fervently and mainly about gardens and supermarkets. A pretty and tiny woman with features as neat as her clothes and her mind, she fitted into Rosemary's life with no difficulty.

That Monday morning, with all Rosemary's inner

turmoil, Jennie was exactly the tonic that was needed. Everything seemed to fall into perspective, and for a blessed few hours Ben Morrison took a back seat in her mind. Yet, at half-past one, when Jennie said, 'I'll see you tomorrow,' and left to catch the bus home via Sainsbury's, Rosemary was disturbed to find herself alone in the house with all of Sunday's thoughts and images crowding in on her again. Pat had left by twelve, bearing articles for the dry cleaners and a list of things to bring for tomorrow. Frances was away for the week in Paris, where the cosmetic company she worked for was running a promotion. She phoned her agent, but he was out at lunch. There was nothing else to do except sit with a sandwich and a sherry in the conservatory and let Ben move into the channels of her imagination, just for a brief while.

She had made a list of things to do this free Monday afternoon. Phone calls, a visit to the garden centre and finally and reluctantly, tea with her mother who had been feeling neglected since Christmas. Rosemary's mother: Betty Dalton. A divorced and later widowed woman, who had lived seventy-nine unfulfilled and mediocre years. Her only interest and somewhat dubious joy in life was complaining bitterly about her long-dead husband whom she had divorced. She never realized, when relating the stories about him, how the listener always sympathized with *him*. Wanting pity more than companionship, it seemed she would pretend to laugh derisively at the 'silly things he did', never sensitive to the atmosphere she created.

They had been married twenty-five years when he walked out. She had planned a silver wedding party at a local hotel. After all, it was what one did. As far as Betty was concerned, she had been a good wife. Twenty-five years meant a successful marriage, however lacking in love that union had been. They'd invited twenty guests, including the newly married and pregnant Rosemary and her husband. They had eaten the inevitable half melon with port and chicken breast with grapes and white sauce, expressed loud delight at the dessert trolley and the cake with the silver paper frill and edible, heart-shaped bells, and were finally on the port for the gentlemen and the Tia Maria with cream for the ladies.

Bill Dalton, Rosemary's quiet and depressed-looking father, rose from his chair, a little out-of-focus after an unusually large consumption of wine, and raised his glass to his wife at the other end of the table. The guests, some of them damp-eyed with pretended sentimentality, hushed each other and looked with expectant smiles at their host. Bill cleared his throat. He looked at no-one except the woman at the other end of the table, who smiled with her mouth only, pleased with the effect of the whole evening.

'Betty,' his voice had been strangely loud and firm. 'Betty Dalton. My toast is to you. For giving me first of all my daughter, the very best part of everything I've ever had. And secondly,' he swallowed, pausing. His wife's eyes were suddenly suspicious at the new-found strength in her husband's voice. 'Secondly,' confident again, his eyes never leaving her face, 'for giving me the worst fucking twenty-five years a man could ever have.' Silence, and nobody moved or even breathed. 'This seems to be the time for me to go, before you confiscate the rest of my life.'

Without another word he drained his glass, kissed his daughter, stroking her cheek as he left, shook the hand of his gaping son-in-law, clicked his heels to the speechless and suddenly sober guests, and walked out of the dining-room, the hotel, and Betty's life. For ever. Leaving everything behind, including the bill for the party.

It was an unforgettable night, etched for ever on the memories of the friends he had left sitting there. They slunk away from their swooning hysterical hostess, now being consoled by a tearful daughter, disappearing into the night, turning over in their minds the events of an evening that they would remember and talk about for the rest of their lives. Probably the only one they would never have to embellish.

He had prepared his exit well. A solicitor dealt with the aftermath and Australia and a new life had welcomed a father she had never known again, except eventually through loving and frequent letters which were always kept secret from her mother.

And Betty continued to complain about and worry at the memory of that desperate man, even after the news of his death some years later. He had never re-married, but Rosemary knew he had at least enjoyed his final years. She never blamed him, and grew to like him at a distance more than she had ever done as a child.

Her mother remained in her life. Rosemary tried hard to please her, to make her comfortable with material things, phoned her regularly, and had her to the house whenever she had the energy to cope. They disagreed on almost everything, but Rosemary had learned over the years to keep her opinions to herself.

She picked up the phone at two-thirty. After her mother's habitual cheese-and-biscuit lunch and hopefully before her afternoon sleep.

'Hello Mum. It's me.'

'The boiler's gone again.'

And *hello to you too*, thought Rosemary, her heart sinking at the familiar whine in her mother's voice.

'We'll have tea here. I'll come and get you.' Rosemary forced an edge of enthusiasm that she had perfected over the years.

'Your father messed with that boiler just before he deserted me.'

Rosemary resisted the urge to wonder if the events

were related. 'Mum, that's thirty years ago. You can't possibly have the same boiler.'

'He was useless round the house. We always had to get a man in.'

'I'll pick you up in about an hour. And I'll phone a plumber. All right?'

'It's a new boiler I need again. Things don't last any more.'

'Christ, Mum, be reasonable, nothing lasts for ever.'

'Don't blaspheme Rosemary,' Betty lowered her voice at the other end of the telephone, 'you know I hate it. Especially from a woman of your age.' This came from an agnostic who never stepped inside a church except for funerals.

Rosemary sighed. 'I'll be over as soon as possible. You can even stay to supper if you like.' She was an only child. She had grown to suspect her parents had managed sexual intercourse only the once, and she had been the result. Her mother, she had been told relentlessly, had had a difficult pregnancy culminating in a long labour.

'Why would anyone want to do that twice?' Betty had asked again and again whenever friends had second or third children, filling her growing daughter's head with dreadful future imaginings.

On Betty's return from the Brixton nursing home, ('Streatham Hill' she had corrected primly whenever Brixton was mentioned, 'Streatham Hill you were born'), she had moved her husband's clothes and small amount of personal toiletries into the box-room on the first landing of the two-and-a-half bedroomed terraced house she and her husband had rented since the beginning of her marriage before the Second World War. It was a small and neat little house and garden that she had insisted on staying in all these years, the one that Rosemary had finally bought for her at a greatly reduced price just a few years previously. She had set up the second-hand, newly painted cot in the double bedroom at the front of the house which she had, up to then, shared with the then meek little man who was her husband.

Thinking the box-room was to have been the nursery, Bill had returned home from special leave in the war-time army when his baby was due, and while his wife remained in the nursing home he worked day and night to wallpaper and paint with loving care that little room which he believed would hold and shelter his first born. But it was he that slept there without complaint in a small divan bed in that pink and white bedroom with the teddy bear wallpaper. And there he stayed. Until Rosemary left home and he moved into her room opposite Betty's, with the bathroom in-between.

According to Betty, he had stayed solitary in the smallest room on the first landing, set apart from the women in his life, silent in his isolation. Ostracized. But Betty said, often, he had 'never bothered me again, thank God', as if it had been the only decent thing he'd ever done. Alone in that room, surrounded by teddy bears, who would ever know what dreams he'd had? What plans he'd made. What desires had been dashed. Sex had never enticed his wife, let alone delighted her. Rosemary had never dared to ask why they'd married. It was all so long ago, and emotions were long since buried and forgotten. So Rosemary had grown and ripened in that sterile and loveless house until she had met John Downey soon after leaving the grammar school, and married him quickly and far too young, just to get away, and, knowing the 'heavy petting' of her teens, was ready to move on, and there was nowhere else to go in those days but a marriage bed.

By three o'clock she was on her way to her mother's, dreading the advancing afternoon, but driven by the one so-called virtue that had been hammered home to her so often as an only daughter: duty. Once again, filling her free time with other people's desires.

Her mother was waiting in the front room when Rosemary arrived. Hat on, her coat by her side, 'I'm ready for the off,' she said, as usual. Her daughter automatically kissed the dry, much-powdered, and offered cheek.

'It's lovely to see you looking so well Mum, despite the boiler.'

'I don't feel it. But I appreciate you coming, this house is freezing and it's got right inside my old bones.'

Rosemary smiled. 'Do you want to stay with me until you get the boiler fixed?' Rosemary crossed her fingers behind her back as she helped her mother out of the locked, bolted and barred house and into the large, sleek expensive car which, in her confused state of arrival, she had forgotten to lock.

Betty paused and looked carefully at her daughter before struggling with the seat belt. 'No, I'd never see you. And I can't bear that Pat woman. She's so familiar.' And the small, dissatisfied mouth pinched in even further at the memory of Pat once daring to call her Betty. Rosemary sighed inside herself, lifting her eyes skywards, and wondered at the snobbery of the lower middle class.

They stopped on the way back to Wimbledon to buy some cake for tea. Lemon sponge, the kind her mother loved. And the kind Rosemary loathed. The sometime weekly tea ritual had begun. During the late afternoon Ella came home, throwing herself through the back door like a volcanic teenager, shouting at the top of her voice, 'I got the fucking job! Mum?' And bursting into the living-room she saw her grandmother sitting by the burning log fire, with a mouth on her like a small round sour grape at the four-letter word that had sprung so easily from her granddaughter's lips.

'Christ,' said Ella, making it worse. 'Oops, sorry Gran.' She bent to kiss the upright and bristling little woman on the top of her tortured, over-permed grey hair and raised her eyebrows in mock panic to her mother sitting on the other side of the fireplace.

Ignoring the expletive, used to it and not finding it personally offensive, Rosemary said, 'Wonderful. Where? What?'

'Three plays in Nottingham. Good parts. Good plays –'

'No money!' they said together.

'When do you start?' Rosemary poured a third cup of tea and winced as Ella flung herself onto the draped sofa, untucking the tapestry covering and squashing the carefully placed cushions.

Betty said, 'You never could sit on a couch properly,' but she smiled. Ella had always been her favourite. It was normal to be drawn to this confident, take-me-as-you-find-me young woman. Betty refused to confront or even believe anything even slightly 'bad' about Ella, and saw only what she wanted. Ella took the tea and grabbed a piece of cake, ignoring the plates. Rosemary watched the crumbs disappearing down the side of the sofa.

'I start rehearsals next Monday,' Ella replied. 'I think someone must have dropped out at the last minute. Bit of luck for me, really. I'll go up to Nottingham next Saturday and find some digs.' Her mouth was full of cake for the next sentence and Rosemary had to ask her to repeat it. She did. 'Did Ben phone today?'

Rosemary's throat closed in panic. 'There were no phone calls for you at all,' she managed to get out, amazed at how normal her voice sounded.

'He said he was going to phone you, to thank you, and can he come again? I think he fancied you, Mum.' Ella flung the words quite casually in the general direction of her mountingly tense mother, but Rosemary knew that they were said to provoke some kind of reaction. Ella's eyes and the expression in them belied the ease of tone in her voice. And Rosemary didn't disappoint her.

She blushed, briefly, like a schoolgirl, and Ella saw. She straightened her back just slightly, smiled like a sphinx and touched her top lip with her tongue – a habit she'd had since childhood, whenever she felt particularly pleased with herself at some mischief she had consciously provoked.

'Who's Ben?' asked Betty looking sharply, from mother to daughter, not too sure of the sudden change of temperature in the room, but not too old yet to be unaware.

'One of Ella's friends, Mum. He stayed for the weekend. A young actor.' She found herself stressing the young. 'She's teasing me. Do you want some more tea?' The room re-focused, Ella laughed, and the moment was gone.

The afternoon developed into a cold and suddenly snowy evening. Betty had to stay after all, tetchy at not sleeping in her own bed, but too terrified to let even her sensible daughter drive her home on icy roads. Ella could take her back in the morning once Rosemary had left for the BBC studio, where she had a radio quiz show to record. A hot water bottle was placed in a spare room bed, a borrowed nightdress put to warm in the airing cupboard, Rosemary prepared an early, uninspired supper and the three of them ate it in front of an even more uninspired television soap opera that Betty refused to miss.

Ella, buoyant with the prospect of work, was full of the best part of being an actor – being offered the job. She kept up a spirited conversation with her grandmother, thereby leaving Rosemary to the dubious but delicious wanderings of her sub-conscious which she finally allowed to surface and linger. Ben Morrison. And then, at ten o'clock, just as the news began, and Betty had begun to make noises about bed time, the phone rang. Rosemary knew beyond a shadow of doubt who it was.

'Hello?' She had gone into the hall to pick it up, away from her parent's scrutiny.

'Rosemary?' He actually sounded nervous.

'Yes?' Putting a query in the word, she couldn't bring herself to admit to him that she had immediately recognized his voice.

'It's Ben.' A pause, and a moment's silence from both ends. He said again, 'Ben Morrison.'

'Oh, hello Ben. D'you want to speak to Ella? I'll get her.'

'No.' His reply came quickly, overlapping her last few words. 'I wanted to thank you for the weekend.'

'I'm glad you enjoyed it. Ella must bring you again.'

'Great.'

Politeness crackled through the line and filled the long pause. She waited, unsure of the game. Whose move now?

Ben's tone became one of intimacy. 'Why don't we meet for a drink somewhere?'

'A drink?' Like a schoolgirl, she was wondering if he could hear the thundering beat of her unsophisticated heart.

'I'm finding this difficult,' he laughed. 'Help me out here, lady.'

A pause again. She pondered the word 'lady'. Then, 'Ben, why don't you come in for a drink with Ella after the show on Thursday?'

'Is that it? With *Ella*?' he sounded peeved.

With him unsure of his direction, she felt the power in her corner. Back in control she laughed. 'I'll leave two tickets. It'd be lovely to see you again. Hang on, I'll get Ella.'

'You're the boss.' His voice smiled at her across the wires.

She laughed, and repeated, 'I'll get Ella now and you can make the arrangements. See you Thursday.'

'I'll count the hours.'

She put the receiver down on the table in front of her.

She called her daughter without moving from the spot. 'Ella, it's Ben. For you. He'll explain.' And she turned and walked into the kitchen to boil the milk for her mother's Ovaltine. Three days until Thursday. Three days. And something had already begun. Something unstoppable, if the memory of her youth was reliable. He was what? Confident, rather arrogant, exciting, and *young*. That was the word she brought out from the back of her mind and placed at the front of her thoughts. Once started, as she knew it had, what the hell would they have in common? And did that matter anyway? It wouldn't last, didn't have to last, she could walk away when that first undeniable itch had been more or less satisfied. Surely she was old enough to recognize that moment by now, to know when it was getting dangerous and get the hell out. Life wasn't a dress rehearsal, as Frances had said. And she wanted him. Once and finally and absolutely admitted. Christ, she wanted him. Shaking knees and a certain dampness accompanied the Ovaltine-making which, if they could have been stirred in with the sugar, would have given her mother a very uncomfortable night.

Drink supped, mother put to bed, avoiding actual eye contact with her daughter, Rosemary disappeared upstairs early with a new library book. And after reading the same paragraph six times she turned off her light and buried her head into the pillow along with the brown and bottomless eyes of Ben Morrison. And the bubble of panic and confusion that had been part of her since Saturday morning took on the definite shape of erotic and exciting movements and ideas that became the sure caresses of hands and tongues and filled her head until she fell into a dream-filled sleep.

Chapter Three

Recording day took a long time to arrive that week. Three days of undeniable anticipated excitement. *Oh God*, she thought as she opened her eyes on Thursday morning, *Oh dear God, I feel like sixteen again*. And she remembered clearly that whatever they tell you as you try to propel your teenage self towards adulthood, there are very few good moments of being sixteen.

She fell out of bed immediately, not wanting the sex-filled dreams she'd been having for the last few days to follow her through the morning hours yet again.

Eventually, dressed and groomed, she sat downstairs over tea and toast in the quiet of the kitchen, with only Ben the cat for company. He had lovingly laid a small field mouse at her feet when she was pouring her tea, having dragged it through the cat-flap with great delight. She thanked him profusely and, unable to touch the creature, even dead, she moved and sat round the other side of the table where that other Ben had sat last Saturday morning. Pat, afraid and disgusted of nothing, would remove the dead offering.

Rosemary was on the road to the hairdressers by nine o'clock in the limousine the studio supplied on recording day, having left a note for Ella about meeting her in the hospitality room after the show. And perhaps Ella could book somewhere for dinner at nine? *That's probably a mistake*, she thought, *we'll end up in Joe Allen's, and the world and his wife will be there*.

Hair done, smoothed, heightened and lacquered, 'Why

does it look like a blonde football?' Ella always asked. She sat back into the limousine, full of and feeling a little sick with hairdresser's coffee. The car manoeuvred its way expertly through London traffic and deposited her in front of the studios just before mid-day.

From the producer, there were the flowers, as usual, in her dressing-room. Her dresser brought two sets of clothes for her to make a choice. The decision seemed beyond her.

'I don't know May – you choose.'

May said, 'I'll press them all, you decide later. Do you want coffee?'

'No thanks, too much already.'

She was left alone for a while to go through the script for the evening's recording. Two guests, one from the States, a new popular chart-winning group and the usual reviewers made up the forty-five-minute weekly show.

At lunchtime she went to the executive restaurant to eat and chat to her producer, Derek Smyleton and the director, Anne Jefferies, and, as always, Derek dominated the conversation. Anne, an ineffectual woman in her mid-thirties smiled and nodded at everything he said, a duty she had learned well, and which had secured the job she was now settled and bored with. Rosemary had always found the situation between Derek and Anne fascinatingly awful. They had been lovers for about ten years. Anne had been his secretary, then his PA, and finally he had manipulated the studios to put her into the position of staff director and kept her on the show he now produced. Twenty years older than Anne, married, he had not the slightest intention of changing any aspects of what had become his well-oiled life.

The whole set-up was such a cliché, and Rosemary by this time was well used to the frequency of Anne's 'will he never get a divorce?' What really crossed Rosemary's mind when she was with them was *where do they do it these days? The back of the car? In his office at the studios? And just how awful is Derek in bed?* Looking at them both, averting ·her eyes from the continuous mastication of Derek's mouth, she remained fascinated by the unattractive image of these two panting bodies in the throes of passion.

'I have two guests tonight Derek,' she interrupted, wanting to get away, 'Ella and a friend. Could someone look after them?'

'Of course, of course dear girl. I'll put it in motion.'

Rosemary went to make-up and, leaning back in the chair with her eyes closed, let the make-up girls' chat wash over and around her. Years ago somebody had told her it was from these sort of rooms that tabloid newspapers got their gossip. And Rosemary believed it. It was delightful to listen to, dangerous to join in.

She wandered to the studio, her script, pen and notebook in her hand. The floor manager ran through the running order with her, and May, hovering, brought her coffee. The music group began to rehearse and Rosemary and Annette, the researcher on the programme, disappeared to the still-quiet hospitality room for last minute suggestions.

'They're both quite easy this week,' said Annette. 'Just keep off Gene Hyman's first marriage – the only touchy area.'

'And the most interesting,' said Rosemary, not looking up from the pages in her hand.

The girl laughed and groaned at the same time. 'Isn't that always the way?' she said.

Tea-break came and went. The studio got busier, louder, more crowded as people began to arrive and move about, preparing for the show ahead of them. The two guest reviewers that week were from a long-running television soap opera and a new quiz show. The actress from the soap had hated the play she had been sent to review.

'What the hell do I say? If I tell the truth I'll get hate letters from the actors.'

'Castigate the director,' said the young quiz show host.

The actress groaned. 'Then he'll never employ me.'

Rosemary commiserated with her. Criticizing shows in public as an actress was a dodgy thing to have to do; integrity was often best kept to the privacy of one's home.

At six-thirty both guests on the show had arrived, with spouses and entourage, and were firmly ensconced in the hospitality room with everyone except Rosemary, who sat alone in her dressing-room with the small whisky and water she allowed herself at every recording. She made a point of not meeting people before the show, in case they 'chatted themselves out'.

At seven-fifteen the warm-up man began his act to the seated audience in the studio, and Rosemary stood behind the set, listening, wondering whether Ben and Ella had arrived. She turned to May. 'Did someone find my guests, d'you know?'

May whispered, 'I'll find out,' and disappeared before Rosemary had time to tell her not to bother. Right at that moment Ben was the last person she needed to clutter up her mind.

'Stand by,' called the floor manager, and Rosemary looked round for somewhere to put her now redundant notes.

'It's OK. Ella and her boyfriend have arrived,' May whispered and disappeared again after a tweak of Rosemary's skirt and frantic grab of the script out of suddenly clammy hands.

'Silent studio, please.' And the countdown began. 'Fifteen seconds to recording.' Now was the moment she wished she'd worn lower heels and a not-so-tight skirt. 'Ten seconds,' – the walk to her chair on the set got longer every week – 'five, four, three, two – ' The signature tune swelled, an out-of-vision voice boomed, 'Ladies and gentlemen, would you welcome, please, your Sunday evening host, Rosemary Downey.' And she was on. Her mind cleared. Her smile was real. This part of her life was untouchable, and all her own.

The show, thankfully, was one of the smooth ones, meaning that the guests remained sober and stuck to the subjects that had been researched. Dull, but safe. That particular evening it was all that Rosemary wanted. Without even a technical hitch, the musical quartet played out the final chord, the audience applauded and they stopped recording. Then a necessary wait for some minutes to check the tape was clean and the stills photographer appeared to get shots of Rosemary and the guests. Once cleared, the audience began to depart, Rosemary smiled for the camera, chatted to the American guest, who by now was talking more interestingly than he had in the interview.

Nothing changes, thought Rosemary, her eyes by now sweeping across the moving and departing people. She saw him immediately. Sitting at the very end of a row half-way up the block of seats, Ella beside him, Rosemary took in her presence and moved her eyes quickly and firmly back to Ben. He sat slouched, head and shoulders forward, a bear of a man, imperturbable amongst the people milling round him. He stood up suddenly to let someone past, his eyes on Rosemary. He smiled slightly and inclined his head. Ella waved and gesticulated to her mother that they would see her upstairs for a drink. Then they both left, Ella hanging onto Ben's arm. He, unprotesting, still smiling, a backward glance, held for a moment, photographed for memory in a corner of Rosemary's mind.

Back in her dressing-room, changing her clothes, hands

quietly trembling trying in vain to re-do her lipstick without putting it up her nose, she half-listened to May chatting on as usual.

'Handsome young man Ella's with. Serious at last?'

'I doubt it.' Out loud and serenely she said it – to herself, *please God, no*. Dismayed at the self-acknowledgement, excited at the prospect, she dropped earrings through shaky hands, sprayed on too much perfume, thanked May, and over-tipped her as always. Silent now in her dressing-room, she washed her hands yet again, wanting to be at home. All the people in the hospitality room loomed ahead of her. Ben was somewhere there. Waiting.

When she got upstairs, she made a slow, talkative progress across the crowded room to where Ella and Ben were chatting to Derek and the hovering Anne.

She stood at last beside Ben, looking up at him, tiny, diminished, despite the height of her heels. He, powerful, sure of himself, smiling at the sight of her, bending to kiss her on each teenage blushing cheek, delighted at her discomfiture.

'Hello Ella's mum.'

'Ben, how good to see you again. Thanks for coming.'

'Nice show, Mum,' Ella said, with strong emphasis on the nice. Then, abruptly, 'I booked at Joe's for 9.30. OK?'

'Fine.' Rosemary turned out of politeness to Derek and Anne. 'D'you want to join us? Both of you?'

The pair looked quickly at each other. Her eyes pleading, his dead. 'No.' Derek spoke quickly. 'Anne and I have made other arrangements. People to meet.'

'What a shame,' Rosemary lied. 'Thank you both, once again. Nice smooth show.'

'And boring,' muttered Ella as they said their goodbyes and pushed their way back through the room.

Derek appeared again by the door as they attempted

to leave. Cornering Ben, still dead eyes and smiling lips. 'Some little bird's just told me we ought to have you on the show some time. Up and coming, I hear, young man? D'you want to do one of the reviews one week?' Derek prodded Ben in the chest playfully, with one pudgy finger, and Rosemary closed her eyes with irritation.

Ben said, 'Well, thank you, Derek. I guess somebody should call my agent.'

A sigh of relief issued from Rosemary, and Derek, pleased with himself, disappeared back to the other guests. Ben smiled at her and shrugged gently.

'Patronizing shit,' hissed Ella, loudly through her teeth and smiling.

'Ssh,' said Rosemary, 'he's my bread and butter.'

'Doesn't make him a nice person.' They went down in the lift to the front reception, Ella still irritated. 'Christ, Mum, you work with such wankers.'

And again in the restaurant, twenty minutes later, studying the menu, like a terrier, she wouldn't let it go.

'How d'you go on putting up with that man week after week?'

Ben was quiet, choosing his food, mother and daughter familiarly abrasive with each other.

'Ella, don't irritate me. I *have* to work with him, you don't. Be grateful.' *If she spoils this evening I'll kill her*, thought Rosemary, wondering what to order when all desire for food had left her, only Ben's presence at the table filling the space and energy nearest to her.

Ella, like a moth, banged away at the invisible barrier around her mother and Ben that she understood and didn't like and butterfly-like, she fluttered from table to table and back again.

Alone, briefly, their order taken and drinks in front of them, Ben and Rosemary looked at each other and smiled.

'You're quiet,' she said.

'Who needs to talk when Ella's around?'

'I'm sorry. She's in an abrasive mood tonight.'

'Why are you apologizing? And I don't mind anyway, I'm used to it. She has a low tolerance level. Doesn't bear fools gladly.'

'In our business you have to.'

'Sometimes.'

They drank in silence. Rosemary waved to some familiar faces at the other side of the crowded restaurant.

Ben said, 'I wouldn't have chosen this place.'

She looked carefully at him. 'You should have said.'

He smiled. 'It's Ella's evening. She seems to be pulling the strings.' There was a long pause.

'Should we let her?' asked Rosemary, pushing him to make a move.

'There's plenty of time, Rosie,' and briefly and quickly he covered her hand with his. Her drink spilt as her hand shook, but he steadied it, his eyes not leaving her face. 'D'you mind if I call you Rosie?'

'No-one does. Not since I was a child. But no,' a smile in her voice, 'no. I don't mind. Makes me feel like a girl.'

Ella came back. Their meal arrived. Rosemary and Ben ate very little. Ella's hamburger came with chips. Ben had ordered red wine.

He didn't call her Rosie again, not in front of Ella. The three of them played out the evening each in their own way. Ella provoked, Ben stayed sure and patient, Rosemary wanted to be alone with him. Wanted his hand on her again. Ella stayed at the table. Then, after midnight, tired of the game-playing, she stood and said, 'I need the loo, Mum. I'll get the cab.'

Ben said, 'The bill's mine. And don't argue. But you can drop me first in the cab if you would.'

Ella went to the cloakroom, and Ben leaned across to Rosemary. 'Can we do all this again, just us next time?'

'Yes.' There was no hesitation in her voice, only fear that Ella would appear again too soon.

'When?' His voice determined. Pinning her down. Cornering her.

'Phone me.'

'Tomorrow?'

Suddenly, out of breath, throat closed, she merely nodded. She could feel her heart beating, fearful excitement through her whole body.

'I'll phone you tomorrow morning at ten,' Ben said quietly as he saw Ella approaching. 'Sleep well Rosie. And don't fret.'

And there was nothing more to say. Ella came back, and they had more coffee while waiting for the cab. A kind of peace settled on them both. Rosemary had passed that brief moment of being able to stop, and turn, and walk away. There was only one way to go now. There was in her a sudden and unusual wilfulness that Frances would have been proud of. *God, I wish she was here*, thought Rosemary. *I need someone to talk to.*

The cab arrived. They dropped Ben at the end of his road. He touched the back of her neck as he left the car and said 'Good night.' Ella fell asleep on the way home. Conversation was blissfully absent. It started to snow. The evening was over.

The snow fell all night, and by the morning it lay thick and innocent over the garden. Ernie, her twice-weekly and couldn't-be-sacked seventy-year-old gardener would arrive at nine, look around and shut himself in the greenhouse with his seeds and his sandwich lunch, which he would eat at ten.

Rosemary, eyes and mind alert long before his arrival, lay in bed as the clock by the front door struck seven. She listened to the stillness surrounding her for some moments, then she went downstairs into the quiet heaviness of a house surrounded by snow.

She stood by the kitchen window, her mug of tea in her hand, where Ben had stood that first morning. A robin was beating frantically at the white, blanketed ground, the worms confident under the protection. The cat threw himself through the cat-flap as if the hounds of hell were at his heels, breaking her reverie and the silence in one great clatter.

'Good God, Ben,' nerves shuddering and jumping with fright, spilling tea into the saucer in her hand, 'cats are supposed to be graceful.' She put down his breakfast, which he ignored. Looking at her with disdain and incredulity, as if she alone were responsible for the snow and the chill on his paws and the underside of a too-low belly. Forgetting, as always, the other winters in his fifteen-year-old life.

She, restless with anticipation for the morning to pass stood, and then paced, and finally sat in her neat and clean kitchen, unable to plan her day ahead for the first time in years.

Ten o'clock came and went. Every phone call became an invasion when it started to ring. Seated in her study, she hurried everyone she spoke to through the call, not daring to admit to herself the fear that he would find it engaged and not try again. Unable to move him from her thoughts or plans.

Pat made coffee, talked at length about window cleaners who disappeared and gardeners who shut themselves in sheds. Rosemary smiled and nodded, shifting her mind around, looking for an exit to push the image of Ben through, wanting something, anything, to stop the obsession which was too new for her to cope with. Lust makes idiots of us all.

At noon Pat left. Hunger now making her feel sick, she stood up from her desk to go to the kitchen and make toast. The phone rang. This time, or so it seemed, louder than all morning. She jumped involuntarily, an intake of breath, the chair at her desk knocked to the floor in her sudden flailing panic. *I can't bear this*, she thought, her hand stretching to pick up the receiver, silencing the jangling that unsteadied her heart, knowing all at once it was him.

'Rosemary?' He was out of breath. A long pause crackled between them, through his breathing and the beating of her heart in her ears. 'Rosie?' Urgency now in his voice.

'Ben, is that you?' Lying easily, hanging on to the shreds of an old dignity.

'I'm sorry, Rosie. Our phone's out of order. I walked for miles before I found one that worked.' More answers to questions not asked were in that explanation. She knew it and ignored it. He was there. Here. His breathing touchable. His voice putting the image of him in front of her.

'It's all right. I realized something must have come up.' Calm now, obsession and panic forgotten at the sound of his telephone voice. 'Rosie,' he called her.

'Are you busy tonight? Come and eat with me. Some-where special.'

'All right. Where?'

'The American Bar at the Savoy at seven-thirty. Would that be good? Or shall I come and get you?'

'No, I have to be in town this afternoon.' *And Ella will be here*, she thought quickly. 'I won't finish at the BBC till seven, so I'll come straight on.'

She heard Ella outside her closed study door, newly and late woken, pounding as usual down carpeted stairs, heard the noisy entrance into the kitchen, wait-ing for the word 'Mum' to call through the house.

She lowered her voice on the phone. 'Where are we going? So I know what to wear.'

'Wear whatever. You'd look good in a sack.'

She smiled, relaxed with his clumsy compliment. Feeling his boyishness wash over her, giving her confidence suddenly in this new power struggle of a relationship. 'Ella's awake, Ben, I'd better go. I'm not sure quite about her involvement in this.'

'She isn't. Ella and I are good friends. She's a big girl now.'

Me too, she thought, *big enough to know better*.

She replaced the receiver and made her way to the kitchen as Ella yelled, 'Mum, I'm in here! D'you want tea?'

Excitement had replaced the sick feeling and her hunger had disappeared again. Her daughter, dishevelled, was busy messing up what had been Pat's cleaned kitchen.

'Ella, for God's sake use the bread board.'

'Sorry. Listen, I've packed. I'm going up to Nottingham today. To check the digs. Is that OK?'

'Yes, of course.' Wonderful, the decks were cleared and she didn't have to mention her date with Ben. Ella, for now, wouldn't have to know. Hugging it to herself at this moment felt right. She would phone Frances next week. Things could change so rapidly.

At four that afternoon mother and daughter stood in the drive by the car to say their goodbyes.

'Get in touch with Jonathan while you're up there,' pleaded Rosemary.

'I will, I will – but I can't stay with him, not even at weekends.'

'I know darling. Let me know where you are. I'm out tonight, but you can leave a message on the answerphone.' She got into her car and as she turned on the ignition, Ella bent down and tapped at the window, holding herself against the spring wind, and shivering in the brisk air, hair untidy. Rosemary, without turning off the engine, pressed the button to release the window. 'What is it darling? I'm going to be late, and you'll get cold.'

'Are you going to see Ben?'

Rosemary cleared her throat. 'Yes,' she managed, across the secure sound of the car engine that would take her quickly away from any confrontations.

'When?' Ella's voice, sharp and all at once actressy with definition.

'Really Ella, don't use that tone of voice with me.'

'I'm not. It's just – oh I don't know. You're so naive.'

Words unspoken hung obviously in the air, not ready for any kind of verbal formation. Grey eyes met square on and Ella looked away.

Then, as the car window began to ascend, 'Mum, be careful.' And she turned and walked back into the house. Head bent against the cold, one arm raised in 'goodbye'. Rosemary watched her go for only seconds, then put the car into drive and moved quickly away without asking herself or her daughter any more questions.

She had decided already what to do with her immediate future. She wanted, maybe needed, an adventure. It was a pity that Frances wasn't immediately around, but listening to other people's advice was a silliness she had long since forsaken. She pushed 'be careful' to the back of her mind. Fifty should not be an age for caution, too much of that had gone before. A new, childless and free life ahead of her beckoned, full of suspected delights and maybe miseries. But with wilfulness she wanted it.

The sun came out, glistening and sparkling onto the white trees. The snow would melt, dropping like soundless crystals from the trees on either side of the avenue where she lived. The busy rustling preparation of spring was in her loins as well as Nature's, and it felt good.

The doorman at the Langham smiled his recognition, took her five-pound tip and whisked the car away God knows where, to keep until she returned. Derek sat reading the Evening Standard and drinking tea in the front lobby of the hotel. He stood and kissed her on the cheek.

'Rosemary, I have good news.'

They sat, poured tea and Rosemary smiled. 'Are they going with the show again?'

'Certainly they are. Finish these final two, then a break until September. We should be celebrating.' He raised his cup to her, delighted with his own cleverness.

'Where's Anne?' she asked. 'She should be here for this.'

Derek shifted uncomfortably. 'Well my dear, that's why I wanted this meeting. Sad I know, but it's time we moved on, and Anne understands. New director, new style of show for the autumn. Must think of the future. What d'you think?'

Rosemary looked at his smug and satisfied face and controlled a strong desire to head-butt him. Not that Anne was particularly talented or inventive as a director. It was just that, quite obviously, he had finally, after years of pussyfooting around with her emotions, decided to dump her. Maybe his wife had at last put her foot down. Rosemary, cowardly, said only, 'It's your show Derek, I'm sure you know what's best.' Hating herself for such wimpishness she went on, 'But I'm thrilled we're going again.'

'Shall we have champagne?' Derek, excited now that he had got away so easily with the departure of his mistress, moved into the new Anne-less era ahead of him with ill-concealed delight.

'Too early for me Derek, and I have a radio to do.'

'Of course, of course. We'll go out next week. Discuss ideas and directors. I'll bring Margaret.' His voice softened with deceitful warmth as he spoke his wife's name. And Rosemary felt the bile rise in her throat and

Ella's words 'you work with such wankers Mum' drifted and lodged in her mind. But she smiled at him and ate one of the tea-biscuits to abate the sick feeling.

The Savoy was full of an American tour group when she walked into the lobby that evening, at just after seven-thirty.

'Evening Miss Downey, nice to see you again,' the familiar top-hatted doorman saluted her vaguely, and smiled through a momentary harassment while he dealt with several loud New Yorkers wanting cabs all at the same time. On reflection, it might have been an irresponsible place to meet, she realized. She was well-known here. And this first evening with Ben was upon her now, too late to go back, too early to avoid a dangerous and public future.

She turned left in the lobby, walked past the Grill Room and up the thickly carpeted steps into the American Bar. Ben was sitting on one of the curved soft seats in the centre. He rose quickly when he saw her. Black-suited and unsmiling, a nervousness about him taking her by surprise. His hair gelled straight back from his heavy brows. *Robert de Niro or Al Capone* flashed through her mind. He took her hands and then he smiled. Intense and wordless, and the moment held a shade too long to escape embarrassment.

She said, 'Ben, am I late?' knowing she wasn't. 'I'd love a drink; it's been a pig of a day.'

'I was early.' A nod to the barman who hovered and then stood by their side.

'Miss Downey, how nice to see you again. It's been a long time.' He smiled down at her, a middle-aged Lebanese waiter she had known at the hotel for years, and placed more olives on a plate at the table in front of them.

'I've been busy,' she smiled. 'Are you well? And your family?'

'Would you like your usual Miss Downey? The family are very well, thank you.'

Ben, beside her, sat down, awkward and out of place. He said, 'What's your usual?' The waiter had gone to the bar.

She leaned forward and touched his hand. 'Sorry, it's just that everyone knows me. Is that horrid for you?'

'I'll get used to it.' He turned their hands around so his covered hers.

She said, 'I always have martinis in here. They're the best in London. Vodka. What are you drinking?'

'Whisky.' He was put out. His jaw had tightened. His smile belied the look in his eyes. *Wrong-footed*, thought Rosemary. He had planned the script for the evening, and her momentarily-forgotten fame had thrown him off-course.

She gave a cursory look round the room. 'Is this your local?' she asked, smiling. 'Or are you slumming?'

He laughed, relaxing, stroking the top of her hand with his thumb. 'I'm between well-paid films. I always behave like a millionaire in the circumstances, just like any other working class boy. Anyway,' he leaned across to her, staring now at her mouth, taking her breath away with the promises in his eyes, 'you seem like a Savoy lady.'

The waiter brought her martini. Their hands pulled apart and they picked up their drinks.

She wished she still smoked. Being nervous, she wanted as usual to eat. Instead, she drank the martini too quickly and began to feel light-headed half-way through it.

'Where are we going to eat?' she asked, succumbing to one of the large green olives.

'The Ivy.'

'I warn you, everyone will know me there.'

'Me too. I did a short-lived play that was on in St Martin's Lane, and used the place too frequently for my wage packet.' *I wonder*, thought Rosemary, *does he parade all the women in his life into the same restaurant?*

The evening seemed to have begun rather badly. Rosemary suddenly wanted to be at home watching *Coronation Street* instead of sitting with this too-young man, drinking vodka martinis, and knowing full well the evening would lead to somebody's bed. Her life began the eruption gently in a direction she couldn't control and she was unsure she could gather back into herself any of the frayed edges. But when, just after eight that evening, they stepped into the taxi to go to the Ivy, he placed his hand once more on the back of her neck in that proprietorial fashion of his, to her uncomfortable but tremulous delight, she was lost again.

Spun with charm and experience to trap even the most difficult of prey, his web was delicately strong. And by the time she was at the Ivy, she capitulated completely and handed over to him the agenda for the evening, even to the ordering of her dinner.

As he grew more sure of himself, the ground beneath her feet grew softer. She, with a nervousness that hinted of hysteria, felt herself drowning in the mindless meandering gossip that escaped from her as conversation. He stared at her mouth as she talked, and her mind flooded with the promise of that hand on the back of her neck.

Middle-aged innocence closed in on her, watching with frightened fascination the pinkness of his tongue between his open lips, not daring yet to meet his eyes square on she let her fingers, clammy and hot, rest passively between his two bear-like hands. 'Ben,' she began, but found no words to finish the question in the air.

He spoke for her. 'What are we going to do?' His question was a statement. His eyes moved from her mouth to her throat, her breasts and then into the greyness of her gaze. 'There's panic there,' he said.

'I know,' she whispered, and moved her hand further into his. 'I feel silly at my age. All this. You make me feel like a young girl again. And I think I'm scared.'

'Don't be.' A gentle answering pressure on her captured hand. 'Leave everything to me.'

Weeks, months later, she could remember every detail of that first evening, imprinted for ever on a mind eventually unable to throw out any peripheral debris. She was to take out and examine each sentence, each look and touch until the mental images tumbled over each other in a medley of confusion.

Acquaintances drifted past their table all evening, arriving or departing, even just table-hopping, constantly cutting across Rosemary's and Ben's highly-charged conversation. None of the sexual tensions that seemed to hang like a blanket of fog around the pair of them touched or penetrated the friends who stopped to say 'hello'.

His youth bludgeoned her repeatedly in the face whenever he introduced her. No pearl-studded earrings and diamond-covered fingers among the people he knew. Only anarchic hairstyles and knee-torn jeans, and bright young female eyes passing over and through her briefly and without question. 'Good old Ben – must be a friend of the family.'

She, on purpose, managed to dictate the length of the evening, spinning it out, postponing the inevitable, knowing the last vestiges of whatever small amount of power she had were rushing and slithering through the fingers of her desire for him. Enjoying the last hours of flirtation, she clung on and played the game until only the silence of resignation remained between them. Their hands across the table, touching and stroking, his eyes hungry.

Desperate and shaking for consummation, they rose from the table at midnight and taxied to Rosemary's car, still standing where it had been parked in what now seemed another lifetime ago. She drove, too full of alcohol to be safe, and without question she made her way to Wimbledon, taking for granted their destination.

It started to snow again as they parked the car, and she fumbled with the house keys. Through the garage, in through the back door and fingers shaking towards the lights over the kitchen units. Ben holding her free hand, taking her bag from her shoulder, her coat from her back, beginning to kiss her mouth half-way through. 'Would you like a coff . . .' Pushing her out into the dark hall, surprisingly and suddenly aggressive in his need, persuading, his mouth and hands on her face and neck. Taking off his jacket, unbuttoning her shirt, fumbling and breathless. Articulate in emotion, wordless in speech, they were on the carpet, hungry for everything the evening had promised. Wanting too much of each other this first time, trying to find the way into the mind through each other's body.

They lay still at last, finished, ungainly and un-romantic, her head uncomfortable against the first step of the staircase. The light from the open door of the kitchen spilled out across the dark hall, picking out the scattered pieces of their clothing and their half-dressed bodies. *This is the worst bit*, thought Rosemary, *the breaking away and the picking up of the knickers. This is the part that never sits easy.*

She cleared her throat, unable to deal with the lack of familiarity of his large body looming over her. Wanting to say with ease that comes with knowledge, 'Christ you're heavy. Get off for God's sake.'

Ben, insensitive with the timing of his silence, moved away and put his head back onto one of the stairs, his eyes still closed. She saw, through the suspended dust of the kitchen light, that he was smiling. Unprepared for what seemed the smugness of that smile, she found herself inexplicably near to tears as she started to gather the scattered pieces of her clothing. Desperately wanting him somehow, someway, to go, disappear, never-to-have-been, she pushed past his body, stumbling briefly over one very large thrown-aside male shoe, and ran up the stairs.

Sitting up at last, his eyes opened, the smile wiped from his face, 'Rosemary, where are . . . ?'

'Go into the kitchen. I'll be down in a minute. Make some coffee.'

Looking at the flushed face in the mirror of her dressing table she fought back the tears. Not wanting now to go down and face him. Feeling her age and belated sensibility for the first time in a week. Frenetic carpet coupling belonged in the loins of the young. Too late now. It was done. Lust had brought her to this point. Life's wisdom would have to get her out of it.

Making her way downstairs, the house now flooded with all the lights she had put on, feeling safe in the electric brightness, she half-hoped Ben wouldn't be there, standing once again in her previously unusurped kitchen. But it was two o'clock in the morning. With a drowning heart she knew he would want to stay the night.

He had made coffee and was sitting comfortably at the kitchen table, large feet planted and rooted, his smile greeted her. 'D'you want coffee?'

'It'll keep me awake.' She spoke without thinking, the words from her mouth automatic.

His smile widened. 'That's the intention.'

She sank without trace into the chair opposite him. Sapped of strength of any sort of purpose, she managed at least to say with a sort of spirit, and quickly before she lost the courage, 'Will you sleep in the spare room?'

There was a pause. The clock was loud in the hall outside. He searched her face but her eyes were on the cup of coffee he had placed in front of her. When he spoke, the gentle Ben appeared again. 'Yes of course. If that's better for you.'

Maybe then, if he had continued to brutalize the evening, she would have turned away from him for ever. But he chose to recognize her distaste for the feeling left in her after their discordant lust. He treated her like an old friend and she began to warm to him once more. Putting aside her disappointment of the evening's finale, remembering again her anticipation of the days before, she forgave his crassness, and without any sexual tension she eventually smiled at him across the kitchen table.

They sat until three that morning, and talked of everything except their intimacy. Too early in the relationship for analysis. Eventually Ben stood and said, 'OK ma'am, which room?'

'I'll show you.' She rose and left the kitchen, with Ben following her, leaving the empty mugs on the table. Ben's vacated chair was pushed out and left where he had stood.

He kissed her lightly on the end of her nose before he shut the door of the spare bedroom – his hands at his sides so as not to touch her, sensitive now to other needs. Grateful to him, and without desire, she went into the sanctuary of her own room, and, without removing her make-up for the first time since her teens, she climbed into bed, teeth unbrushed and hair still stiff with lacquer.

She woke two hours later, the morning light white with falling snow hitting her tired eyes and went to the bathroom to wash. Then again, back to bed, she fell once more into a thankfully oblivious sleep.

Chapter Four

Early spring sunshine struggling through morning fog trailed its way under Rosemary's eyelids, accompanied by a tentative knock on her bedroom door. Ben was in the room, a cup and saucer in his hand. A towelling dressing-gown found on the back of the bathroom door, stretched itself over his large, uncompromising frame. He stood still in the room, cup rattling slightly in the saucer, tea spilling. The door closed behind him.

'I brought you tea.' His voice was quiet out of respect for the morning.

'Thank you. That's nice.' Only banality came from her mind and her mouth, both foul from the memory of last night. She lay still, and Ben moved towards her and the bed. Tea placed by a library book, he loomed and looked down at her. Eyes at last meeting, acknowledging, knowing each other's discomfort, and they both, surprisingly, smiled. Her hand came from under the duvet and reached to him. He took it, and sat down, still tentative.

'Rosie, I'm sorry. Badly judged and badly timed.'

'I'll blame it on your youth.'

His hand stretched out and touched her cheek. Stroked it. Gentle fingers round her jaw and outlining her mouth. Trembling, she held her breath in the stillness as he bent to kiss her, wanting him again now, feeling powerful in her vulnerability. Face naked, hair dishevelled, mouth and tongue still tasting last night's mistakes.

They met at last. This time with their minds as well as their bodies. Waiting for each other, their insistent tenderness turning together into a passion that was well matched. Forgiving and forgiven. Taking and taken. All the promises fulfilled and lengthened. Fantasies touched on and discarded without need. Images into reality. The cat scratched demandingly at the bedroom door.

'Go away Ben, only two can play this game.' And then, 'Not you Ben, the other Ben.' Words were kissed from her mouth. Smiles and laughter, quiet and secret, passion wrapped round them, duvet pushed and pulled, bodies watched and touched and held. Cup parting from saucer at sudden movement of an arm towards bedside table and tea dripping unheeded onto discarded dressing-gown. *I'll wash it later* devoured from her thoughts. Desires touched and tormented and then finished, waiting only moments and then caressed into re-awakening. Morning into mid-day and then a gradual slow delivery into stillness and closeness, they lay finally, his head on the once crisp pillow, incongruous against the small flowered pattern, hers against his chest. Their breathing even and together. Then his hand under her chin lifting her face round and towards the smile in his eyes and on his mouth.

'Rosemary Downey,' his voice soft, 'Rosemary Downey.'

'What?'

Their mouths a breath apart, their eyes watching.

'You surprise me.' He kissed her nose, the corner of her smile.

'I've surprised myself.'

Hungry for every detail of each other's face, they lay watching in silence, hearts loud in their beating.

She pulled away at last and looked at the clock. 'Good God, it's lunch-time. I'll get some coffee.'

'I'll come with you. You're all mine today. I'll not let you out of my sight.' Smiling, she began to dress. His voice stopped her. 'Don't—'

She looked up. 'Don't what?'

'Dress.'

Standing and thinking, thoughts of coming pleasures washed through her, leaving her trembling and out of breath. He stood now beside her and she reached to touch his smile with her fingers. 'All right.'

They made coffee. Fresh and bitter-sweet. Filling the kitchen with warmth and clatter along with his kisses on the back of her neck. 'Don't Ben, don't, I'll drop something.' Said with laughter and responses, hands full of toast-making and jam-finding. And then, crumbs left on the floor and table, plates empty and used, pulled once more into passion, they took their coffee and moved upstairs, disabled in their walking with their lust. Into the tousled and once virgin bedroom, coffee spilling on the pristine bedcover, and her words disappearing into his open mouth: 'I feel, oh God Ben, I feel . . .' And the morning fell into the afternoon.

Later, hungry for food, they raided the larder and the fridge as the evening began to take over the sky, and the time of day for depression and the football results became a Saturday night for lovers.

She left the phone unanswered, hearing the disembodied voices of unmet messengers clicking and stuttering out of the answerphone into the empty rooms downstairs, as they lay in quiet moments on the tumbled bed. 'Leave them,' Ben had said, holding her close, constraining, when she felt guilty as Ella's voice for the third time held tinges of panic in 'Where the hell are you Mum?'

By nine that evening, too late to dress and too awake to sleep, they went finally downstairs for food, music, anything outside the craving for each other. And also to feed a disgruntled and hungry cat who not only promptly turned his tail up at Ben's stroking hand on the base of his spine but, showing them the intestinal remains of some hapless small mammal he had brought in, he left them to dispose of it by shooting out through a madly swinging cat-flap as if the devil or God knows what was after his tail.

'Not mad about cats,' said Ben, his nose twisting as he watched her clean up the sordid remains of her pet's alternative dinner.

'That means he'll not leave you alone,' laughed Rosemary, kissing his disgruntled look away, and putting the gentleness back into his eyes.

They listened to jazz, sharing the same passion, and ate smoked salmon with home-made garlic bread. Home-made by Ben, that is, rummaging in her refrigerator without asking, and finding a French loaf. They lay together on the rug before the fire she had lit and listened to the provocative sounds of Art Pepper and Charlie Parker.

Saturday became the early hours of Sunday and, leaving the littered living-room, they went again to bed. This time to sleep. His arms around her, her head uncomfortable on his chest, but not wanting to move away, only turning aside from the awkwardness of their need in the solitude of their separate sleep.

Then the morning, nine o'clock. Sunday papers being pushed noisily through the too-small letter-box stirred Rosemary to leave the warmth of the man's body lying beside her, content as she was to have him there, in that place so used to celibacy.

He slept on his back, serene, unlined and unstressed: the sleep of the young. Hands above his head, the resting position of a baby, or even a beach worshipper trying to catch the sun in all those awkward places. Powerless he was in his 'little death'. He did not stir. And on that Sunday morning, as the cat began to scratch at the bedroom door, demanding attention and breakfast, Rosemary all at once and in that moment fell in love with the stranger in her bed. His breathing deep and even in his sleep, he didn't know the sudden widening of her heart. He didn't see the drowning in her eyes as her soul went out to search for his. So how was he to know that when she left him to make tea downstairs, a part of her remained entwined in him? Because that's the bondage of falling in love. Not being alone. Not for a moment. Putting the water to boil and wondering if he had turned in his sleep. Placing leftover pieces of smoked salmon down for a surprised and delighted cat, not finding the kind of energy to open a can of Whiskas, and wanting the kettle to boil quickly so she could go back upstairs. Watching the cat eat his salmon too rapidly with one eye on Rosemary in case she changed her mind, she stood in heart-beating silence as the steam started to come from the kettle. Afraid to miss any part of his waking day. Afraid to lose the look in his eyes when he opened them to greet the morning. Afraid not to be the first and only thing he looked at that Sunday.

She carried a tray of tea and orange juice up the stairs carefully, slipping easily and without thought into a role she had believed discarded for years before, along with her marriage. She opened the bedroom door, went inside, and pushed the door shut behind her with her foot. Ben stirred in his sleep, opened his eyes, saw her, and for the first moment there was no recognition in his look.

'Ben? Sorry, did I wake you too quickly?'

'Rosemary? Rosie – sorry,' he sat up. 'Christ, I was dreaming, couldn't think where I was for the moment.' *In my bed*, thought Rosemary, *dreaming of God knows who while I was downstairs busy falling in love with you.*

He smiled at her and she brought the tray of tea across the room towards him, placing it precariously on the lace-covered table by the bed. She sat down beside him and he put his arms round her without a word. She knew at that moment, now she had fallen in love, that all the power had finally shifted into his corner. She sat in his arms and let him rock her, his mouth against her hair, no words between them for a moment while he struggled completely into wakefulness. Then, into her ear, he said, 'Is it Sunday?'

'Yes.'

'Do you have plans today Rosie, or are you still mine?'

She pulled back to smile at him. 'Still yours. What do you want to do?'

'You mean apart from what we've been doing?' Teasing her, he stroked her face, outlining her cheeks and lips.

'We could talk. Find out about each other.' She handed him the orange juice.

'Nothing about me to know, Rosie. You get what you see. There's nothing else.' He put his finger into the juice and placed it against her lips, then kissed the sweetness from them.

An hour later, while she showered, and Ben used the other bathroom, she realized how well he had side-stepped her suggestion. *My God*, she thought, *how quickly being in love has made me paranoid.*

The sun shone on the fast-melting snow that Sunday, and after breakfast they wrapped up and went for a walk. Ben borrowed a long scarf he'd found in Ella's room and a pair of matching mittens which covered only the ends of his large hands. He declared it was better than nothing, and made her laugh as he struggled to keep his cold fingers covered. The desire to play the clown was strong in him. And she wondered what it hid.

When they got back to the house Ben lit the fire and she made some coffee. They sat again to listen to music, and silence fell around them as they began to plough through the Sunday papers. Ben's face, concentrated, frowning, bent over the latest reviews, stamped itself into her memory. She put out her hand to reach his face as she sat opposite him, and without looking up or breaking the silence he kissed her fingers one by one absent-mindedly. The phone rang.

'Who's that?' Ben jumped and looked fierce at the interruption. It made her laugh.

'I don't know. Let me get at it.' Reaching across him to where the telephone sat, she picked up the receiver. It was Ella. 'Mum, at last. I've been phoning and phoning. Did you get the messages?'

'Yes, but you left no number. Everything OK?'

'Fine. I got digs but I can't use the phone there. Are you OK, Mum?'

'Yes of course darling.' She mouthed to Ben that it was Ella and he shifted in his seat, giving her more room. Then he put his finger to his mouth and shook his head, indicating for her not to mention him. She frowned and shrugged.

Ella said, 'Did you see Ben?'

'Yes.'

There was a brief silence, then Ella, snappy at the other end of the phone, 'Well?'

'Well *what* Ella? Don't play games with me.'

'Mum, it's *you* that's playing the games. I want to know what's going on.'

'Ella really, it's not your business.'

Ben shifted suddenly, getting up from the chair and moving to look out of the window. She watched his back. Tension invaded the room. Her daughter's voice in her ear, so loud, that Ben must have heard it.

'Mum, is he there? Has he been there?'

'Ella, this is silly. We should have talked before.'

'Jesus Christ – oh hell – look – oh shit, shit, shit. What's he playing at?'

Ben turned and walked out of the room. Rosemary, alone now, confused, angry, spoke quietly into the phone. 'Look, I don't know what went on or is even going on with you and Ben, and I'm not sure I want to, but now I need to know. Was the affair with you serious?'

'Nothing's serious with Ben. Just his ambition. Look, *make* him talk to you. If you can. He and I, there's only an old friendship there, but as lovely as he seems to be, there's another side to him, one you couldn't handle. Please believe me.' Pleading in her voice, Ella finished up the conversation. 'I've no more money. I'll phone tomorrow from the theatre and give you the number there. Just try and make him *talk* to you.' And she was gone, and the dialling tone was heavy now in Rosemary's ear. She replaced the receiver and sat for a moment.

Then, 'Ben,' she called, and saw through the french windows that he was standing, hunched, in the garden watching the birds feeding on the bag of nuts swinging from one of the bare branches of an apple tree. She tapped on the window and he turned. And he smiled at her. She beckoned and mouthed, 'Come in.' But he stood a moment longer and watched her face close to the window. She felt anxious and unsure. Suburban Sunday morning traffic was the only sound that invaded the space around him. Inside, Rosemary turned down the stereo and waited. Ben moved at last and came back into the house, cold and blue-faced from the March wind.

'Talk to me Ben. What is it with you and Ella?'

'Nothing. I told you. She's being over-dramatic.' He sat forward in the chair, eyes blank, not looking at her.

'She said we should talk.'

'Look Rosemary. Ella and I were bedmates. For about a month. It was never serious, she was in love with someone else. Not that that mattered. Not to me. It was just a bit of fun.'

'Why is she so horrified about us? Apart from the fact the whole situation is slightly bizarre to *me*. I wouldn't have thought it could affect Ella like this, not with her track record.'

'She loves you. She's frightened I'll hurt you.' He looked at her at last.

'Will you?' She hardly dared ask the question.

'Probably. I hurt everyone.'

They fell into a silence that Rosemary found unable to break.

Ben leaned across and took her hand. 'Rosemary, I'm thirty-three and very ambitious. I have no time to fall in love. Ella knows that. She also knew from the start that I wanted you.'

'Why? Why me?'

'I don't know. Christ, does it matter? You're so *still*. I wanted you. You looked untapped. It intrigued me. This is stupid – do we have to discuss this *now*?'

'I don't understand. I thought we'd just met, were attracted, made love and it was all that simple.'

'Nothing's that simple.'

'Not with you, anyway.'

'Not with anyone. Anyway, Ella obviously thinks I made up my mind to get you and I did – get you I mean. And she doesn't like it. That's all.' He stroked her hand. She knew without doubt it wasn't 'all', as he said. But she'd heard enough. She had been a challenge for him, set up it seemed, unsuspectingly by her daughter. No wonder Ella was upset, confused. Her mother had fallen into the trap just like any other woman, and so quickly.

She said, 'Now what?'

'What?' He smiled at her.

'Do we continue? Is this it? Weekend over, affair over. You *got* me, that was the word wasn't it? *Got* me? Didn't take you long. You made your point. D'you all plot like this?'

'All men, d'you mean?'

'All *young* men.'

'I don't know Rosemary.' Irritated, restless, he took his hand away. *God he hates being cornered* she thought. *Any minute now he's going to say 'this is getting heavy'.*

'This is getting heavy,' Ben said, as he leaned back in his chair.

And Rosemary laughed. 'Oh Ben, why are you all so predictable?'

'Don't patronize me sweetheart. Don't patronize me.' He stood up as he spoke, voice raised, his head down, eyes intense and hot on her, anger sudden and explosive barely contained in his whole presence. She sat back with surprise, speechless at the sudden fury in his voice, on his face, her throat closing with panic. He stood for seconds then walked to the window.

Rosemary said eventually, 'I didn't mean to patronize you. I'm not sure what's happened here.'

'We're bothering what other people say about us, that's what's happening.' Ben spoke without turning, his voice now steady. He put one hand on the window pane and scratched to the cat outside, attracting his attention. Man and animal stared at each other through the glass. The silence in the room between them remained. Only the faint sound of Sarah Vaughan's singing came blissfully from the stereo's speaker on the bookcase.

'Ben. Talk to me. I can't bear this.'

He turned at once and came to her. On his haunches in front of her chair he took her hands in his and looked once more at her mouth before they kissed. There was no resistance in her mind or body. She felt as if some part of herself was forever lost to him and the disturbance between them turned to passion as he pulled her without ceremony onto the floor in front of the fire. Kissing, stroking, pushing away all the unanswered questions that hung between them, and only the feel and smell of him filled the spaces around and in her until he

69

was all the answers she would ever need. They spoke no more about Ella's phone call. He became again the lover, the gentleman, the clown who made her laugh, and by teatime it was as if nothing but harmony had ever been present throughout the weekend.

Early that evening they watched the television: the show that Rosemary had recorded the previous Thursday. Ben said as it finished, 'It's all so safe isn't it?'

'What d'you mean?' She was sitting between his legs, on the floor in front of his chair.

'Safe – no dangerous questions. Pap television.'

Frowning, she looked round at him. 'It's just entertainment,' she said. 'Is that wrong?'

He shrugged, said no more, and continued to stroke her hair. She went later to the kitchen to make sandwiches and get something to drink. He followed her, and opened the bottle of wine she had placed in the fridge.

Ben said, 'I must go after this, Rosie.'

'OK.' She smiled up at him.

They ate the sandwiches and drank the wine in front of the fire and the television, watching some mindless programme masquerading as a situation comedy. Ben's comments were funnier than the script. Just before nine he said, 'I'll get my coat.'

'Can I take you?'

'No, I'll walk to the Tube.'

'It's miles.'

'Oh all right. D'you mind?'

She got up quickly. 'Of course not. I'll take you home if you like.'

His reply came quickly, almost drowning the last words of her sentence. 'No, the Tube is fine.'

In the car he kept his hand on the back of her neck while she drove, his fingers gentle against her skin. They scarcely talked, and she wondered why on earth she found it so impossible to simply say, 'Where d'you live?' She pulled up outside the station and turned off the engine.

'Don't get out,' he said, restraining her, 'it's Sunday. I'd hate for you to wait around.' He bent towards her, and taking her chin in his hand he looked into her face, then kissed her without passion on her lips. Briefly, so that she had no time to close her eyes. And Ben's gaze, open too, looked without expression into hers. She shivered suddenly, unreasonably afraid. Still close to her he said, 'I have had a great weekend. We must do it again some time.'

'Yes. We must.' Her mouth moved into a small smile, copying his.

'Rosemary Downey,' he spoke again. 'You've got yourself a lover.'

He got out of the car. She bent forward, her voice stopping him as he was about to close the door. 'Ben . . ?'

He leaned down and smiled at her. 'I'll give you a bell, Rosie. OK?' And he was gone. Turning once more before he disappeared into the entrance of the station, and waving both hands and blowing kisses to her. She laughed at him as he clowned into vanishing round a corner and finally out of her sight.

She sat for a moment before turning on the ignition, disturbed and unsatisfied, and unable to pin down the feeling. She drove home with the car radio switched to a chat programme, but she heard not a word. Tired now, and unable to get him out of her mind, she left the living-room as it was and went upstairs to bed. She found in her bathroom cabinet some sleeping tablets once prescribed and never used. She took one, went carefully and thoroughly through her usual preparation for bed and finally fell exhausted under the duvet that was still crumpled and smelling of Ben.

The telephone woke her suddenly, confusing her with its shrilling, and she put out her hand and looked at the clock. One o'clock.

Ben's voice across the confusion in her drug induced sleep. 'Rosie? Did I wake you?'

'Ben? Is that you?'

'Who else calls you Rosie?'

'Is something wrong?' She tried to struggle into wakefulness.

'I just wanted to say good night.' He spoke so quietly she could scarcely hear him. She couldn't speak, struggling as she was to keep her eyes open. Giving in, she shut her lids and leaned back on the headboard of the bed, the receiver cradled into her shoulder. The bedroom felt cold, the heating had gone off at midnight, and she pulled the duvet up to her chin.

He said, 'Are you still there?'

'Yes.'

'I wanted to make sure your dreams were pleasant, and all about me.' His voice caressed, seduced her.

She smiled. 'They will be.'

'Good night my darling,' he said, and his phone went down.

She fell immediately asleep again, but this time beguiled by his words and voice with a feeling of peace. *There's nothing wrong*, she thought, *just beginning pains*. And out loud to herself, as if to test the words. 'I think I love you, Ben.'

The weekend was over.

Chapter Five

She opened her eyes on Monday morning and found she had overslept. It was almost eight o'clock. The sleeping pill, along with Ben, had given her turbulent dreams, and she was still trying to shower them away when she heard the phone ring and Pat arrive downstairs at almost the same moment. She dripped her way to the phone, pulling the towel round her and taking the shower cap off to shake her hair loose. It was Frances.

'You're back!' said Rosemary, pleasure obvious in her voice.

'I am. I am. How are you? Did I miss a wonderful birthday party?'

'Good God Franny, that seems a lifetime ago. I've so much to tell you. When can I see you?' Her words tumbled from her mouth almost too fast to make sense. She felt again like an adolescent.

Frances said, 'You mean something happened in your life that was eventful? I know, Ella left home.'

Rosemary laughed, overwhelmingly pleased to have her friend back. 'No, you fool. But she *is* in Nottingham for three months doing theatre.'

'London's McDonald's will be destitute.'

'It is *so* good to hear your voice. When are you free?'

'Shall we meet tonight? In town? The Ivy?' Frances suggested.

'No,' Rosemary said quickly, 'somewhere else.'

'I see. What happened at the Ivy?' Frances' voice dropped inquisitively.

'I'll talk when I see you.'

'Maybe we should make it breakfast.' Frances came back quickly, and Rosemary laughed again.

'I just need to say it face to face. And I'm running late. Pat's here already and I'm not dressed.'

'You're not dressed! And it's eight o'clock! Now I *am* curious. I know, there's a great little Italian place opposite Drury Lane Theatre. The San Francesco. Don't bring your car, and we can get drunk. Are you dieting?'

'No I'm not. And yes, that'd be great. Can we make it seven-thirty?' Rosemary ticked off in her mind the things she had to do.

'I'll count the minutes. Have a good day,' said Frances and rang off.

Downstairs Rosemary hurried into Monday. Forgetting where Ben had slept on the Friday night, she looked up surprised when Pat called down from upstairs, 'Shall I change this unmade bed in the spare room?'

'What?' She had been shuffling through the mail while eating her toast, and looked up through the open kitchen door towards Pat's voice, her eyes unfocused over the top of her reading glasses.

'One of the spare rooms was used. Shall I change the sheets, or are they coming back?'

And she remembered. 'No Pat, change the sheets. And you can give Ella's room a good going over. She's away for three months.'

'Oh I'll leave that until I've got more time. I've not been inside that room since God knows when. There'll be all sorts under the bed, no doubt.' And Pat's voice faded away into the airing cupboard as she located the clean sheets and went on muttering to herself.

Rosemary left her second piece of toast and poured herself more tea before carrying the cup through to her study to wait for Jennie.

* * *

Most of the calls that morning were business, about the forthcoming Thursday show or otherwise. Much to Rosemary's surprise, her mother rang at about eleven. She usually left it to her daughter to make contact.

'Rosemary?'

'Mum. What a surprise. I was going to phone you this afternoon to see when you're free this week.'

'What do you mean, *free*? I never *go* anywhere. I'm ringing you because I haven't heard from you for days and wanted to see if you were all right. You seemed harassed last time we met.'

'Did I? No, I'm fine. I've been busy. The weekend I mean. Sorry.'

Betty sounded peeved. 'Has Ella gone?'

'Yes. She went last Friday.'

'Were you away for the weekend?'

Rosemary paused. 'No. I had a friend here.' She hesitated over the word friend, but any other description would have thrown her mother into confusion. She went on, 'Is the boiler OK? Did you ask them to send the bill to me?'

'Yes, it's working very well. And yes I did. I couldn't understand the time clock, but Mrs Drewett next door came in for coffee and kindly explained it all to me. I don't know what I'd do without her.'

Rosemary wondered how her mother had perfected the art of making her feel guilty of neglect. The urge to apologize hovered needlessly over so many of their conversations. She said again, 'Which is the best afternoon for you, Mum? I'm busy today and obviously on Thursday.'

'I'm going to the Bingo twice this week. You phone me when *you're* free. And give my love to Ella if she calls. I hope her show goes well.'

Exasperated, and not quite sure why her mother called, except perhaps to remind her daughter unnecessarily of her existence, Rosemary heard the receiver go down at the other end.

She visited the supermarket in the afternoon, standing at each aisle holding on to the trolley and wondering what to buy with Ella away for so long. *Shall I go on a diet?* She threw some Lean Cuisine and Weight Watchers frozen meals into the trolley and walked determinedly past the biscuits, realizing that for the first time in years she had brought with her no shopping list.

She later went to the delicatessen she had stood in with Ben that first Saturday, and smiled to herself as the memories came and brought a sudden heat to her face and body. She grabbed some things from the shelves, and then went very quickly home, in case he had phoned. Four messages on the answerphone. All about the show on Thursday. Nothing from Ben.

Disappointment came and sat with her as she made some tea and ate the last two chocolate biscuits in the tin. *I'll be back on course tomorrow*, she reassured herself, and left the used cup on the kitchen table when she went upstairs to get ready for the evening. Frances was in the San Francesco when Rosemary arrived at quarter to eight. She had ordered a bottle of Frascati, was already drinking, and the inevitable cigarette was held aloft while she talked enthusiastically to an attentive waiter.

'It is *so* good to see you. I missed you,' Rosemary said as she sat down.

'I've gathered. Will this wine do, darling? Drink some immediately and catch me up. It'll loosen your tongue and I can hear all your news.'

The waiter poured her some wine and handed them both a menu. Frances raised her glass. '*Salut*, cherished one. Forgive the cigarette. I started again. Don't be cross.'

Rosemary laughed and then said, 'Oh what the hell, give *me* one.'

'Good God.' Frances lit her friend's cigarette from the candle on the table, then spoke again. 'Let me order. Are you hungry?'

'I've hardly eaten all day.'

'Good.' Frances raised one arm to attract the waiter. '*Alfredo, per favore. Per incominciare il tonne e fagiole, e doppo, pasta alla carbonara, grazie.*'

Food ordered, they were left in peace at the small table downstairs in the corner of the restaurant.

'Now,' said Frances, 'what the hell is going on in your sedate little life all of a sudden?'

Rosemary smiled. 'I've met a man. Well, I don't know. Almost a boy.'

'What have you done? Got yourself a toyboy?'

Rosemary recalled the person that was Ben. 'No, you couldn't call him that by any means.' She laughed at the thought. 'And I met him at my birthday party. He is, was, a friend of Ella's. A week later, he asked me out and I went. Mainly because I hadn't been able to get him out of my mind all week. Anyway, to get to the point, we spent the weekend together. At my house. Most of the time in bed.'

'I am speechless.' Frances took her friend's hand across the table. 'Was it good? Are you OK? So it hadn't healed over after all.' They laughed together, then Frances said, 'How old is he? What does he do?'

'He's thirty-three. Very handsome. *I* think he is any-way. Handsome I mean. I *know* he's thirty-three. And I'm afraid to tell you he's an actor.'

'Good grief my darling, you don't do anything by halves do you?' Frances sat back in her chair and lit a new cigarette with the end of her old one. 'Now let me get this straight. After a couple of meetings you invite this young good-looking actor to spend the weekend at

77

your home, in bed. Anything else? Not bad going from someone who vowed to be celibate for the rest of her life.'

Rosemary said, 'There's a problem. With him. And Ella I think. I don't know. He's a bit of a mystery.'

Frances looked carefully at her, screwing up her eyes against the smoke from her own cigarette. 'What's with Ella?'

Rosemary poured more wine. Then, at last, 'He's an ex-lover.'

There was a pause, and then Frances started to laugh. Rosemary stubbed out her cigarette, aware now that some of the other diners had turned to look at them. Recognition of *her* and the sound of Frances' raucous laughter.

'Ssh,' said Rosemary, but started to smile.

Frances said eventually, 'I always knew you had it in you. Have you really stolen one of your daughter's lovers?'

'No, no. It's over, they both said so. It's not quite like that.' Rosemary lowered her voice. 'It just feels so bizarre, Franny. I kept thinking to myself, is he comparing us?'

'You mean,' Frances whispered back, 'am I as good as Ella?'

'Don't say that, for God's sake,' Rosemary said quickly. She could feel the wine going rapidly to her head, assisted by the unaccustomed nicotine. She took what must have been her fifth or sixth breadstick from the jug on the table and without thought buttered it thickly before eating.

Frances looked at her and then lifted the butter dish out of reach and gave it quickly to an obliging waiter who was passing by empty-handed. She said, 'What are you doing? D'you want to be fat *and* fifty, treasure?'

Rosemary said, 'I suspect that Ben, that's his name, I suspect he likes the idea of mother and daughter.

And I know nothing about him, except that Ella has more or less warned me off.'

'Screwing someone as ladylike as you after Ella must have been quite refreshing,' commented Frances.

'Franny you're incorrigible.'

'D'you think she uses all her dreadful language in bed as well?' Frances was relentless. 'You must ask him next time.'

'I don't know when or if there's going to be a next time,' said Rosemary. 'He simply said, what was it now? oh yes – "I'll give you a bell." Then he phoned later to say good night. I'd been asleep for hours, I thought I'd dreamed the whole thing. I took a pill.'

'Why are you in pieces so quickly?'

'God knows.' Rosemary pushed her half-empty plate away and took and lit another cigarette from the pack on the table. 'You see Franny, for some childish and adolescent reason, I'm infatuated with the man. I think I've fallen in love. And I'm horribly out of practice.'

'I don't know what to say to you. Except that you're being premature. You're seeing only disaster ahead. Let me meet him. I'll look him over for you.' Frances laughed now at her own presumption of wisdom. 'Not that I'm exactly an authority on Mr Right.'

'I don't even know where he lives,' said Rosemary, 'not even his phone number.'

'You mustn't phone, anyway,' Frances said. 'And no more pills. That way you'll fuddle your brain, sweetness, and it sounds to me like you need to be clear-headed. Here's your food. Drink and eat and thank the good Lord I came home when I did.'

Thursday came and there had been nothing from Ben. Rosemary had lasted until Wednesday night and then succumbed and taken another sleeping pill. She was still drowsy when she got into the limousine and then the hairdressers the following morning. She sat sipping black coffee and staring at herself in the mirror waiting for her usual stylist.

'You're quiet this morning,' he said when he eventually appeared.

She looked up at him in the mirror and smiled. 'I was contemplating all the new wrinkles,' she said.

'Can't see *one*. But you *are* a little puffy round the eyes. Not sleeping?'

'I'm fine. Slept too heavily, Martyn, with exhausting dreams.'

'It's the spring. Once April rears her pretty head the sap rises in us all. I swear it's the month for erotic dreams. I could write a book, or even a mini-series.'

Rosemary laughed at him. 'Who mentioned mine were erotic?' She didn't mind his familiarity. They had known each other a long time.

'So what else is exhausting when you get to our age?' He raised his eyebrows at her and started to brush through her hair. 'Now, the usual darling? Or has the sap gone to the head as well?'

She stared at herself in the mirror. Ella's voice came unbidden into her ear: 'Why d'you always make your hair look like a football helmet?' – she spoke quickly, 'No Martyn, do something different. What d'you fancy?'

'Oh my goodness. Now you've thrown me. D'you want to cut it? Take years off you.'

That did it. 'Yes. Give me – what did we used to call it? I know, an urchin cut.'

'I'll not be that drastic. You might sue. Leave it to me. Raquel Welch will be green, darling.'

Two hours later she was in the studio. May said, 'My goodness you look different,' and took Rosemary's choice of clothes for the recording away to be ironed.

The security man had saluted her as he opened the

door and said, 'Lovely Miss Downey, makes you look like a girl.'

'Thank you George. You're very clever, because that's why I did it.'

The make-up girls were enthusiastic and she was only momentarily thrown when she saw three others in the room with the same hairstyle. Not that it mattered, only they were all about twenty-three.

Oh what the hell, she thought. *Who said mutton couldn't masquerade as lamb anyway? Probably a man.*

She lunched with Derek, but not Anne. 'A few problems this week,' he confided. 'She sends her apologies, and will talk to you at teabreak.'

Rosemary, controlling an urge to push him face-down into the sweet trolley, smiled at him with dead eyes over the top of the menu. He didn't mention her hair.

At teabreak Frances phoned her and they put the call straight through to her dressing-room. The sudden ringing broke her concentration while she had been going through her notes for the show, and sent her heart beating into her throat. She picked it up, believing, hoping it was Ben. 'Yes?' She was slightly breathless; excitement quivered in her voice.

'It's me, honey face,' Frances said. 'I can tell by the way you answered that'll be a disappointment.'

Rosemary laughed. 'No it's not. Are you still coming tonight?'

'Yes. Shall I sit in the control box with the obsequious Derek?'

'Fine. I'll tell him. He'll be delighted. He harbours an illusion that you find him attractive.'

'Sweet Jesus, the man's arrogance knows no bounds! I'd rather bed Ella.'

'Franny, you get worse.'

'I know my love, it's my age. Forgive me. Have you

81

heard from that young man? Or don't we talk about it?'

'We don't talk about it. I feel sillier every day. And I'm beginning to hope he won't appear again.'

'No chance. He won't be able to resist. Just when you start to feel normal again, he'll phone. They always do. It's the power game.'

'I'll see you later Franny. Reception is expecting you, and I'll meet you in hospitality after the show. Did you book a restaurant?'

'I will, right now,' said Frances cheerily. 'See you later, angel.'

Standing behind the set, ten minutes before the recording began, Rosemary watched the warm-up man on the monitor beside her and remembered how she'd felt the week before. She felt changed and vaguely distraught, wishing now that she had made other decisions about Ben in her life. Even the professionalism in her was conscious of what seemed like a small, black cloud hovering at the very back of her mind. May came up and stage-whispered in her ear.

'Your friend's in the box, and Derek's got her a drink. Have you finished with your notes?'

'Thanks May. Yes, here you are.' She handed over the notes and put her free hands up nervously to feel the back of her new-shorn hairstyle.

'I'm getting used to it now,' said May. 'Quite like it. Good for you.'

'Thanks.' Rosemary smiled at her. May turned to leave her, then swung quickly back as the floor manager called, 'Five minutes to recording.'

'Oh yes,' said May, 'I nearly forgot. Ella's friend turned up and Derek took him into the box as well.' And May walked away.

Rosemary's legs buckled, and she held on quickly to the top of the monitor beside her.

'May!' she called out, as loud as any whisper could be. 'May, come back here. What friend?' But her dresser had left the studio. Wendy, the make-up supervisor, fiddled with the back of Rosemary's hair. 'Don't do that!' Rosemary barked, irritated.

The girl took a step back with surprise. 'Sorry. It was sticking up.'

'Forgive me Wendy, I'm a little on edge. Just nervous. Have you got a mirror?'

'You look lovely.'

Rosemary stared at herself in the small hand-mirror and saw the eyes of the same expectant woman who had stood in the same place the week before. She knew it was caused by the presence of Ben in the control box. The evening stretched ahead of her. The show was a small mountain she had first to climb.

It did not go well. She fluffed her lines more than once and they had to stop recording each time and start again. The auto-cue broke down completely, and Rosemary was left without her notes, trying to remember some of the prepared questions for her guests. She floundered badly, and Derek stopped the show while Anne came out of the control box to talk to her.

'D'you want to wait for another auto-cue Rosemary?' Anne asked.

'How long?'

'I'm not sure.'

'Good God woman, you're hopeless. Tell May to bring my notes to me. I'll manage.' Anne scuttled away in panic, surprised and near to tears at the unfamiliar scorn in Rosemary's voice and on her face. Rosemary could have bitten her tongue out.

That's right girl, she thought to herself, *hit the poor woman when she's down.* She scribbled a memo to herself in her mind to remember to send flowers, with an apology, to Anne the following day. The studio audience, restless now, shifted in their seats, and some left for the lavatories. Derek sent the warm-up man on to settle them down and came out of the control box to talk to her. Wendy re-touched her make-up.

'All right Rosemary?' Derek said. 'Just a few hiccups. Nothing to worry about.'

She put her hand over the radio-mike that was pinned to her dress. 'Derek, out star guest will be getting drunker by the second. For God's sake tell somebody to watch him. I know the man from way back.'

'Will do.'

'And please tell Anne I'm sorry. I didn't mean to snap. A little panic creeping in, I fear,' she joked to him as he turned to walk away. He smiled back at her and put his thumb up to confirm he understood.

The show continued. When the final guest was announced and the music began to play him in, Rosemary's heart sank. She knew from long experience he was well on his way to being too drunk to manage. She stood to greet him and put out her hand, waiting for the quartet to finish playing.

'Tony, how lovely to see you again. Welcome.'

He stumbled briefly up the one step to the podium where the sofa and chairs were placed for the interview, and Rosemary hastily put out both hands for him to grab and steady himself. 'Whoops-a-daisy, girl,' he said. 'Who put the fucking step there?'

The show began to slide disastrously into hilarity from then onwards. The audience gasped, laughed and held their combined breaths during the last minutes of the interview with the middle-aged actor, who was as well-known for his drinking as for his performances. Rosemary knew the colourful language would be bleeped out at the editing, but it was appallingly hard work to get coherent words out of the man at all. It wasn't the first time she had had a difficult guest, and she knew it wouldn't be the last.

A few minutes before the final music, the floor manager began to make signals for her to wind up the interview. The actor was meandering through a tale which seemed to have lost its thread. She leaned towards him.

'Tony darling, I can't tell you how wonderful it's been to talk to you again. I'm sorry we can't go on like this all night, but you've been so fascinating that the clocks have caught up with us rather drastically.' She put her hand out to cover his. He turned and stared through her with bloodshot, unfocused eyes.

'Jesus Christ, I hate broads who interrupt me.' He snatched his hand out from under hers and stood up, swaying dangerously. 'Who do you have to fuck to get a drink around here?'

The audience gasped unanimously, and in the box Derek yelled to the vision mixer, 'Get the fucking camera off him! Get it off him. Play the bloody music.'

And the quartet came up loud and hurried, the pianist trying to hide his mirth under loud chords. Rosemary stood and ripped the radio-mike off her dress and walked off the podium and out of the studio into the control box. The warm-up man was pushed on to chat and send on their way the highly excited audience, while the floor manager and his new, trembling girl assistant helped the confused and drunken guest to his dressing-room. His voice faded into the distance, obviously delighted with the devastation he'd left behind.

Anne was pale and shaky. Rosemary looked at her. 'Where's Derek?' she said, calm now, professionalism hiding her remaining anger.

'Coming,' said Anne quietly.

The vision mixer had one hand across her mouth. Rosemary suspected a hidden smirk, but the funny side of the situation was escaping her for the moment.

'Derek, what happened? Did someone just give him a bottle and leave him to it?' she said.

85

'I'm so sorry, Rosemary. I'll look into this straight away. We can salvage something in the editing, I'm sure.' He put out his hand and touched her. She flinched.

'Just get him out of the building,' she said and walked out of the control box and headed for her dressing-room. Once there, she poured herself a whisky and sipped it as she dressed.

May shook her head while she helped her. 'What a dreadful man. Are you all right?'

'I'm fine. Do you have a cigarette?'

'Not *on* me.' May looked surprised.

'Never mind. It was just a thought. I'll see you next week.'

'Last one. Couldn't be worse than this, anyway.'

Upstairs, the hospitality room housed the usual crowd. Only the inebriated Tony and his entourage were conspicuously absent. Rosemary headed directly for Frances and Ben, who were standing with drinks in their hands, listening to Derek.

'Darling heart,' said Frances, loudly as usual, as Rosemary arrived at the group. 'Get this woman a drink, someone. She needs it. D'you want a ciggy as well?'

The two of them kissed, and Rosemary smiled at Ben over her friend's shoulder. 'Hello Ben.'

He bent and touched her cheek, his moustache rough against her, flooding her with weekend memories. 'Hello Rosie. Did you mind me just turning up?'

'No – no – not really. You picked a good night for it, I must say.' She took a whisky from someone's outstretched hand and spoke to Frances. 'I think I'll take you up on that offer of a cigarette.'

'There you are my flower.'

Derek sprung eagerly forward with a light.

He said, 'Nobody seems to know where that dreadful man got the drink from, my dear. But please, you were magnificent as usual.'

Frances mouthed something behind his head. Rosemary said, 'Did you book somewhere Franny?'

'I certainly did. I've asked Ben to join us. I'm devastated that your attractive producer has to hurry home.'

Derek turned to her and kissed her hand. Rosemary and Ben smiled at each other. Their eyes held for a long moment. He put his hand out and touched her arm. His fingers against her skin were familiar and electric. The days of anxiety and doubt disappeared. He was here now. The night waited for them.

'Let's go and eat,' he said quickly, as if he wanted the preliminary part of the evening over and done with. For the first time in the twenty-five years that Frances and she had known each other, Rosemary wished her friend was elsewhere. They all said their goodbyes and left for the Caprice, taking Rosemary's hired limousine. The three of them sat together in the back, Frances pushing Ben to sit between them. Slightly drunk already, teased into a certain light-headedness by the cigarette, Rosemary let her hand lie discreetly in his, feeling again his touch stroking her thumb and twisting her rings round her fingers. She counted the hours until bedtime, and wondered at her audacity.

Chapter Six

Once again there were three at dinner. Once again it was a crowded restaurant, full of people who knew them.

As soon as they had sat down Ben had said, 'Now that really was some kind of show tonight, Rosie.'

'We loved it.' Frances waved to the waiter for wine.

'A nightmare,' said Rosemary. 'I half-expect it every week.'

Ben laughed, 'Come on now, it was great. I've heard of rough theatre but never rough telly.'

'Anne was no help,' said Frances. 'How the hell does she keep her job? Still got her legs in the air for that creep?'

'Derek went back properly to his wife. Anne's off the show in the autumn.'

'Poor cow. They were so suited, as well. Can't imagine either of them heaving their limp parts into other people. Yuck, the thought's disgusting. Enough to put anyone off sex for life.'

'Try to ignore her, Ben,' said Rosemary. 'Her mouth usually ends up in the gutter as the evening goes on. But she means well and I love her.'

Ben said, 'Don't mind me. I love a woman to talk dirty.'

He and Frances smiled at each other, and Rosemary would have felt jealous if she hadn't known her friend so well. Ben was still an unknown quantity in that field, and the image of Ella was still strong in her mind.

They ordered their food, and drank wine while they waited. Ben said, 'I need the john, will you ladies excuse me,' and left, stopping on the way to talk to a young, pretty and animated girl at another table. Rosemary watched him with hungry eyes, and Frances watched her.

'You're too obvious, gentle heart. He knows he's got you.'

Rosemary turned her face towards her friend. 'I'm besotted, aren't I? D'you like him?'

'He's utterly charming. Is that enough? But I'm not in love. They're different creatures when you're under their spell.'

'You make it sound dreadful.'

'Just dangerous. You trust too much. Keep something back.'

'I can't. I don't know how, and I think it's too late.'

Frances leaned across and took her hand. 'Sweetheart, you've pulled your life around you from bits and pieces. Don't let it all dissolve so quickly. Not until you know him better. Find out what he's after.'

'I know it won't last, Franny. I'm not stupid. There's seventeen years between us, what the hell kind of future is that? Anyway, I just want a fling.' She took a cigarette and lit it quickly. 'I think that's what I want, anyway. I don't know. I'd forgotten this feeling. I can't wait to feel his hands on me again. What do I do about that?'

Frances looked seriously at her, then laughed. 'Oh go for it, girl. You'll always pick up the pieces. You're stronger than any of us. Anyway, *you* might be the one to get bored. What d'you talk about, the two of you?'

'We haven't talked a lot. He seems to like sex, food and silence. In that order.'

Frances laughed even louder and a few people looked in their direction. 'Well, my angel, that would suit me, so all I can say is, if you can get some sort of perspective about it all you'll probably be all right. He's desperate to get into your knickers tonight, so let's not linger.'

'You romantic little soul,' said Rosemary. 'I would have put it differently.'

'Make yourself indispensable to him.' Frances lowered her voice. 'It's the only answer with men like that.'

'Men like that? Men like what?' She spoke quickly, frowning, wondering what her friend had seen in Ben that she had overlooked.

'Try to remember the first impression you had of him. A basic instinct. It's seldom wrong, and you're usually a wise old bird.'

Frances put a finger to her lips and Ben came back to the table, touching Rosemary's still-outstretched hand as he sat down. He put the pink end of his tongue just slightly out towards her and looked coolly and secretively into her gaze. She realized he was sure they had been discussing him, and he was delighted at the thought. Rosemary withdrew her hand and looked down at the oysters that had just been placed in front of her. She felt suddenly sick, and not at all hungry in the face of such charming arrogance.

By one o'clock Frances said with her usual authority, 'I want no arguments from either of you. The evening's on me.'

Rosemary protested. Ben thanked her and held tight to Rosemary's hand under the table.

'I'm going to get a taxi,' said Frances, who lived east of London.

Ben said, 'Can you drop me? I'm in Hackney.'

Frances paused and stared at him. Rosemary's breath seemed to stop still in her body, her heart beating too fast and, she was sure, out loud. 'Are you going home?' asked Frances.

Ben turned to Rosemary. 'I want to pick up some things. I've an interview early in the morning. Can I come on to you after that? I'll pick up my car. Could you leave a key out for me? Under the mat or something. I won't be long, I promise.'

Rosemary could feel Frances staring across at her. Ben leaned towards her and, oblivious of anyone else in the emptying restaurant, kissed her briefly on her slightly open mouth, touching her quickly on her lips with his tongue.

Frances spoke. 'I need the loo. I'll order the cab. OK?' She left them alone and went across to the ladies room, looking back briefly in their direction as she opened the door.

Ben said, holding both her hands, clammy now as they lay in his, 'I'll let myself in like a mouse in case you're asleep.' His voice was low, seductive, sure of her as she trembled under his pressure.

'Ben—' she began, finding her voice at last.

'I know it's a bit out of order Rosie, but if you say no I'll have to go home. And I'm filming next week. In Spain. And it'll be too long before we can be together again.'

It was useless. All strength gone at the thought of weeks without him she fumbled under the table for her handbag. 'I have a spare front door key,' she said. 'I'm sure I'll be awake, but just in case.' She handed over the single key she always kept in her bag. For a brief moment they each held it, then it disappeared into his jacket pocket. She watched and felt her independence diminishing before her eyes. She reached out as if to get it back and he took hold of her fingers and kissed them, putting each one into his wet and inviting mouth.

'Delicious you are, my Rosie. All mine for ever.'

She shivered then, afraid of her weakness, wary of his strength, not knowing where her life was going.

He said, 'I could put *you* in my pocket as well, and take you to Spain with me. Would you come?'

'I have another show next week. How long are you away for?'

'Three weeks. Come out when you've finished. I'll pay your fare.'

She smiled now. 'I'll pay my own fare, if you don't mind. Leave me with some strength of purpose for God's sake.'

He beamed. 'I want you to have none as far as I'm concerned. Keep it for other people. You were wonderful tonight.'

'What d'you mean?' She frowned, forgetting the beginning of the evening in her obsession for him and the present.

'In the studio. When you got mad. I'd never seen the show so exciting. First time it held my attention.'

'You've said something like that before. D'you hate what I do?'

'Not in bed.' He stared at her mouth in his usual way.

'You know I didn't mean that.'

'I'm not interested in your show. Just in you.'

She was annoyed. Irritated. Wanting him gone and wishing she hadn't given him her key. Frances came back from the cloakroom and there was no time to answer him. She and Ben left in the taxi. Rosemary had asked her limousine to wait and she fell unhappily into the back seat, huddled into a corner, wanting all at once never to have set eyes on Ben Morrison. He had made her feel inadequate. Good only for a plaything, and she had been unable to find the words to answer him back. She toyed with the idea of putting the bolt on the front door, but realized he'd probably knock loudly for her to let him in. Maybe she was tired and had read too much into his remarks. Why should everyone think the show and she were wonderful? Maybe he'd been joking? She remembered his hand on her arm, her fingers in his mouth and knew she still wanted him.

'I think I'm in real trouble,' she murmured to the cat when she stood, at last, in her kitchen. Ben's namesake padded across to her purring loudly and brushing roughly in and out of her legs as she stood there, still in her coat, unable to make a decision about whether to go straight to bed or wait up for Ben. She poured herself a brandy and rummaged in the top drawer of the kitchen dresser where she kept all miscellaneous junk, to see if by any remote chance there was a cigarette. The search proved fruitless. She opened the biscuit tin and found only Ella's beloved Jaffa Cakes lurking in the bottom. 'God, I hate Jaffa Cakes,' she said to the cat, who by now was trying to climb up her leg. She took out three biscuits and sat at the table drinking her brandy and eating, her coat still on, the purring animal now lodged firmly in her lap, clawing at her tights through the silk material of her dress.

The hall clock struck two. She decided to leave the lights on for Ben and go to bed. Closing the biscuit tin and pushing it into the centre of the kitchen table, she stood up. The cat fell, protesting, off her lap.

'Sorry darling,' she muttered to the back of his upright and furious tail. 'But I have other fish to fry.' She went upstairs, leaving her coat thrown across the bottom of the banisters. Cross with herself for eating the biscuits, she undressed and peered at her back view in the long mirror by her wardrobe. Ben had said that first weekend, 'I've never known a woman with such beautiful dimples in her arse.' She had smiled over her shoulder at him, confident in her nakedness after their lovemaking, and had not mentioned cellulite to spoil his innocence.

She brushed her hair back from her face and removed her make-up, enjoying this freedom to prepare herself for a lover in unplanned solitude. She put on a clean white nightdress smelling of fabric conditioner, and slipped

93

between newly ironed sheets. Feeling beautiful against the frilled white pillowcase, she left the table light on at the side of the bed where Ben would sleep. She put out her hand and touched the smooth, head-free pillow, wanting him there quickly. The clock downstairs struck three and she struggled to stay awake. Giving in at last, her eyes tired from resisting, she fell without tranquillity into a dream-filled unconsciousness. The bedroom door, not quite shut, drifted open a few inches, and the cat padded in quietly, waiting to be sent back as usual to his own basket downstairs. But Rosemary, asleep now, lay still, her breathing even in the cold and silent room. He jumped stealthily onto the bed and manœuvred himself in the dip of the duvet where her legs were curved. His purrs, loud at first, grew quieter and, not believing his great good luck, he too fell asleep, smugly pleased with himself and his own deviousness.

She was awakened by Ben's voice as he got into the bed.

'Christ Rosie, you're sleeping with the bloody moggy.' And with one swift lift of the duvet, the unfortunate cat was propelled onto the floor. The animal stared with distaste at the large intruder in his mistress's room and, with a furious protesting squawk, raised his tail and tripped quickly to the door. Ben got once more out of bed and opened it, raising one foot to push the offended animal on his way.

Rosemary said sleepily, 'I didn't know he was here. He crept in quietly.' Then fully awake, 'Don't kick him Ben.'

'Sorry darling. Didn't think.' He smiled disarmingly and came quickly back to bed, hurrying his nakedness into the warmth of her body and pulling the duvet round them both. They stayed 'spooned' together, Ben kissing her gently on the back of her neck and touching her breasts with his cold hands.

'God you're freezing,' she said.

'Warm me up then,' and he placed one of his hands between her thighs. She held it close, ready quickly for him.

'What time is it?' she asked.

'Our time, Rosie.' He turned her round into his arms and began to kiss her mouth, leaving his bedside light on to flood her face and force her to close her eyes against the glare.

They made love in silence. She, tired and lazy with only a gentle passion, he, taking her with an arrogance she found both exciting and disconcerting. So quiet he was that she was unsure of his orgasm. And then he was asleep, and she too, before any questions were formed in her head.

He woke her again at six the following morning and made love to her once more in that strange and silent way. By seven she was showering, the water refreshing against her tired body, soothing her and waking her up at the same time. Ben, stirring now when she pulled her dressing-gown round her still-damp skin said, 'Put the telly on Rosie. I can watch the news.'

'What side?'

'BBC. The others irritate me.'

She switched it on and threw him the remote control before she went and sat at her dressing table. He said, eyes on the screen at the bottom of the bed, pillows piled up behind him, 'What are you doing this morning?'

'Talking to Derek. Post-mortem about last night's show. Why?'

'I have an interview in Kensington at ten.'

'A film?' she asked.

He nodded. Then, 'D'you want lunch?'

'I can't. I must leave myself free today. In case they want to re-shoot anything after that disaster last night.'

He turned his head to look in her direction and their eyes met in the mirror. 'I go to Spain on Monday. This is the last day I'll be able to see you.'

She frowned. 'Can't you come for the weekend again?'

His eyes shifted back to the morning news. 'I'm busy this weekend.'

She said nothing, not knowing how to question him. Then he smiled and turned his face again to see her confusion in the mirror. 'Just a few loose ends to sort out Rosie,' he said, 'before I go away, and to leave the coast clear for us when I come back.'

'Am I allowed to ask what?'

He stared at her, but his smile remained. 'Just trust me.'

'What if I can't?'

He pressed the remote control, flung it onto the duvet and swung his legs over the side of the bed to sit up. 'That's tough,' he remarked, blew her a kiss, and went, still naked, into the bathroom.

She applied her make-up with trembling hands, annoyed with herself and his arrogance. He called out, 'I'm going to shower. Is that all right?'

'Ben,' she said, going to the open bathroom door. He looked up from the lavatory where he was sitting. 'Sorry,' she backed away.

'It's all right you fool,' he laughed. 'I'm not shy.'

'Well I am,' she protested. 'I've never met anyone quite like you.'

He flushed the toilet and came to her, his hands untying the belt on her dressing-gown, and pulled her body towards him, holding her tight, laughing at her prudery. 'Meet me later Rosie. Tell Derek to get lost. He got you into that débâcle last night, let him get himself out of it.'

'You're leading me astray, Ben Morrison.' His breath was hot on her neck as his tongue probed her ear.

'Oh all right,' she said, 'I give in. I'll get out of it somehow. Where shall we meet?'

He laughed, delighted with his victory. 'If you were taller Rosie, when I hold you close like this all our bits would fit.'

'I'm not fitting any of your bits again this morning,' she murmured, pulling away from him, smiling. 'Pat will be here any minute now and I've masses to do before Jennie arrives.'

'Get dressed woman,' he slapped her suddenly and playfully on her bottom and she cringed. 'Oops,' he said, 'mistake!'

'Have your shower,' she retorted quickly. 'I'll see you downstairs when you're dressed.'

By nine o'clock Ben had gone, driving off in an amazingly dirty old Metro.

'That's an awfully small car for such a large man,' remarked Pat as she and Rosemary stood at the front door, watching him disappear. 'He must drive with his knees in his ears.'

Rosemary went to her study to wait for Jennie. Derek phoned at ten. 'We could re-record this afternoon Rosemary,' he said. 'I can edit quite a bit out but, if we cut it leaves us about two minutes short.'

'What's your intention?' She was terse with him, not wanting to cancel her lunch with Ben.

'We have organized Jerry and the boys to do a number,' said Derek. 'And we will just need you to introduce it and tidy up the end of the show.'

Rosemary closed her eyes at his unimaginative idea of using the regular and rather dull musical quartet to fill the gap. 'That'll be cheap anyway Derek,' she said sardonically. Then, 'What time were you thinking for me to come in?'

'About two?'

She sighed. 'I can't – four o'clock is when I'm free.'

'Oh dear,' he murmured, almost to himself, and feigned a patience that Rosemary knew was not in his nature.

She spoke again, abrasively, and with a certain amount of guilt. 'Four o'clock Derek, take it or leave it. Last night could have been avoided by anyone with an iota of imagination, and you know it.'

'I've spoken to Anne, my dear,' he said patronizingly. 'She realizes someone should have stayed with Tony in hospitality.'

Rosemary toyed with an Ella-type reply and then dismissed the thought; *That's your job, you useless wanker*, stayed where it was, on the tip of her mind. She replaced the receiver and turned back to Jennie. 'He gets almost more loathsome every day,' she muttered.

Jennie looked up, surprised at the vehemence in Rosemary's usual gentle tones. But she said nothing. Her employer's new hairstyle had quietly confused her, let alone this sudden lack of charm and serenity.

Ben had arranged to meet her in a small rather obscure Italian restaurant that sat in one of the roads running from Wardour Street to Berwick Market. He had said twelve-thirty, but when she arrived only ten minutes late, there was no sign of him. Recognizing her, the head waiter manœuvred her into a seat at a small window table so that half of her faced the street, and she could also be seen by the other diners. Without thinking she sat, and then began to feel rather silly as she caught other people's stares from each direction. She had for a long time worked out a sometimes successful method of dodging autograph hunters and over-enthusiastic fans: never, ever catch anyone's eye in public. Look ahead when you're walking and always have something to read when you're sitting down in a public place! The menu, thankfully, was extremely lengthy and she pored over it with much pseudo concentration. She ordered mineral water and sat longing for a cigarette. Every two minutes she looked at her watch.

At one o'clock, one of the other diners and Ben arrived at the table together. Ben stood behind the autograph hunter, a smiling and talkative middle-aged woman who was 'only in London for the day, just shopping and going to a show, you know Miss Downey, so excited to see you, you're the second celebrity in the last hour. Jeremy Beadle was in Covent Garden. Such a nice man, isn't he?' She got her autograph, written on the back of her cheque book, which Rosemary knew would be discarded as soon as she wrote her last cheque and turned to find Ben smiling down at her.

'Oops, I'm sorry young man. Another fan for you, Miss Downey.'

'I'm her lunch date actually,' said Ben.

The woman turned again to Rosemary. 'Is this your son? I know you've got one, read all about it in *Woman's Realm*.' She took Ben's hand. 'You must be so proud of your mum. So much pleasure she gives us all. I do hope you enjoy your meal. You've made my day!' She wandered back to her table and the three other women who broke into excited chatter as she sat down, queen of the moment as she was.

Ben exploded with laughter and bent to kiss her. 'Mum, you are looking as sexy as ever. Sorry I'm late.'

'I could kill you,' she said, trying hard not to laugh, because the four women were still eyeing her up and down, locking into their day's memories every detail of her grey suit and expensive shoes. 'Where were you?' she asked as the waiter gave him a menu.

'They didn't see me for an hour and I had to go see my agent. Look Rosie, you sit here, you'll have your back to the room and I can hide the front of you. I keep forgetting how famous you are.' They changed seats with a lot of shuffling and scraping of chairs on the wooden floor and when they sat again he reached across the table and held her hand.

'This'll confuse them,' he whispered wickedly.

'We'll be front page of the tabloids if you're not careful,' she murmured back. He took his hand away.

'Christ, I didn't think of that. I'm not ready to go public yet.'

She stared at him. His eyes were on her mouth. 'What do you mean?' she said.

'Darling Rosie, my life has certain complications at the moment. It'll be sorted when I get back from Spain.'

'Are you living with someone? A woman?' she found the courage to ask him.

He hesitated. And then, 'Yes.'

Her throat closed. 'I see. I don't know what to say. I'm confused. Where does she think you were at the weekend? How long have you been involved?'

'She doesn't ask questions.'

'Meaning that I mustn't?'

'No.' He smiled at her now, with all the gentleness, she remembered, which had first attracted her. 'You're different Rosie. *We're* different. I'll sort it out. Trust me.'

'That's twice you've said that.'

'Then I must mean it. What d'you want to eat?'

No longer hungry, she ordered salad. She said at last, as Ben began to munch his way through the bread sticks placed on the table, 'Our affair seems to be constantly held in bed or restaurants.'

'So?'

'I don't know. Where are we going? I think we're heading for disaster.'

She felt his foot under the table as he manœuvred it between her legs. 'Don't give me a hard time, Rosie. Gill and I called it a day almost six months ago. I just haven't found anywhere else to live. Her flat, you see.'

She didn't, but said nothing.

The pause hung between them. She remembered, for the first time that morning, that he still had the front door key. She couldn't and wouldn't say what she felt he wanted to hear. It was too early. Too new. And as infatuated as she had so quickly become, the privacy of her life was uppermost in her mind.

He said, 'Will you come to Spain for a while? I want you there. It's important.'

'All right.' Her smile was quick. A small moment of vulnerability had crept into his eyes, giving her confidence and knowledge of his desire.

He smiled back. 'You're the best thing that's happened to me, Rosie. I don't want to lose you. I promise, I won't let you down.'

And she believed him.

Chapter Seven

After a compassionate coffee in the studio with a contrite and apologetic Anne at the end of the afternoon, she made her way home within an atmosphere of gloom that had suddenly fallen upon her. The idea of a solitary weekend all at once filled her with dread. She phoned her mother, looking for comfort in a barren place, and in a rash moment asked her to stay and keep her company.

'It means giving up my Bingo,' said Betty. Then before Rosemary could change her mind, 'But I don't like you on your own in that big house, not on these dark nights.'

'Clocks go forward on Saturday,' said Rosemary. 'That's tomorrow.'

'Is it forward or back?' said her mother. 'I can never remember.'

'Spring forward and fall back.'

'That's clever,' Betty said, and Rosemary tried to count how many times over the years they had had the same conversation. Clichés and banalities loomed ahead of her for the next two days, and for an instant she almost drowned in the sudden depression of being without Ben.

'I'll fetch you in the morning, Mum. About eleven. Is that OK?'

She regretted the idea almost immediately she put the phone down. A whole weekend: a tough hurdle. Sighing with exasperation at her inability to stop accommodating other people, she opened some wine and poured herself a glass. It crossed her mind she was drinking too much. She'd finally given in and bought a packet of cigarettes that afternoon, and she sat now to read the evening paper while she drank her wine and smoked. The cigarettes would have to be hidden while her mother was in the house. It would be easier to succumb to that little subterfuge than explain why, after all these years, she had lapsed once more into what Betty called 'that disgusting and filthy habit'.

It was eight o'clock when Frances called. By that time Rosemary had eaten her way through two bowls of chocolate ice-cream that she had found lurking at the back of the freezer, and which only Ella would know how long had been there, two slices of bread and butter, and a piece of very runny brie cheese. She'd also succeeded in finishing off most of the wine which had led her into thinking over everything Ben had said and done to her in infinite detail. By the time the phone rang she was feeling confident, young, and glowing with memories of words and caresses that were hers for ever.

Frances said, 'Darling heart, it's been a pig of a day. Are you on your own?'

'Yes. Ben's off to Spain on Monday to film. I'll not be seeing him this weekend.'

'Are you drunk?' A note of amusement was in Frances' voice.

'I am a little. Feel rather good actually, Franny. Am I mad?'

'I don't know. Are you? Did you get your key back?'

Rosemary hesitated. 'I forgot,' she said. 'He does carry me away a little.'

'Shall I come for the weekend, precious?'

'My mother will be here.'

Frances laughed. 'I'd better come then. You really pile it on yourself at times. Is this "let's drive Rosemary to a nervous breakdown weekend"?'

'It's to assuage my guilt,' Rosemary replied.

'I'll come over tomorrow.' Frances was still amused. 'I'll handle the old biddy, and you can wallow in thoughts of that young man.'

'It would be nice to get him out of my mind for a while. Get on with everything else in my life.'

'He has you exactly where he wants you.'

'He said I was the best thing that's happened to him.'

'Believe it.'

'I did.'

Frances said, 'You'll do. Have you heard from the dreaded offspring?'

'You mean Ella?' said Rosemary. 'Not Jonathan?'

'Good grief, not him, he's almost worse. How did anyone as nice as you manage to get two kids like that?'

'Good God, Franny they're not that bad! Anyway, they take after their father.'

Frances laughed again. 'You're getting quite bouncy in your old age.'

'It's sex.' Rosemary smiled as she spoke.

'I'll be over tomorrow afternoon. You can tell all while the wicked witch of the west is nodding in front of the wrestling. She of the crimped hair and the similar mind. It's years since I can remember sex of any kind making me feel as good as you obviously do. Mind you, I still think you should have got back that key. See you tomorrow. Put champagne in the fridge.'

And Frances was gone. As if she'd been in the room and left, silence fell around Rosemary, joined by the beginnings of a headache. She went into the kitchen and put the kettle on for tea, and drank two glasses of water in quick succession to ward off any hangover symptoms in the morning. She realized now that she hadn't heard from Ella since last Sunday, and after the somewhat disturbing conversation they had had while Ben was there, she felt surprised. Her daughter was usually good about keeping in touch, wanting to spread all her news when good things were happening to her. Silence usually occurred when her life got complicated. A jot of worry lodged itself in Rosemary's mind. She went to her study and found the number of the theatre in Nottingham.

'Is she in the play on now?' the stage doorkeeper's voice was brusque.

'No, she's rehearsing I think.'

'She won't be here then. They finished at six. I can take a message. She'll get it tomorrow. I'll leave it in the rack.'

'I wondered if you knew where she was staying?'

'Can't give that out, I'm afraid.' Pomposity echoed loudly in her ear, heavy with the authority of someone who knew the rules. 'It's more than my job's worth.' Rosemary mouthed the words with him as the cliché bounced with a fascist-like quality out of the phone.

'I'm her mother,' she said firmly, her voice drawing itself up to her full five-foot-two inches.

'Still can't, madam, unless I see your credentials.'

Does he mean stretch marks? thought Rosemary, irritability beginning to get the better of her.

'I can give you the director's phone number,' the man went on. 'She might know.'

'Well give me that. Many thanks for your help.' She wrote down 'Joanna Tristram' and the number he gave her, and replaced the receiver.

It seemed all at once quite silly to start chasing her daughter all over Nottingham. Ella could well be a little put out at finding her mother had gone to so much trouble to track her down. Drinking her tea, she put the television on and stood in front of it, scarcely listening or watching the picture in front of her, hearing only the canned audience laughter. She wondered what to do. Unable to make a decision whether or not to move again to the phone, melancholy fell on her once more, but this time only lightly, like a bad taste in the mouth that could be easily brushed away. It was as if Ben had always been in her life, and two weeks without him was suddenly unthinkable. She still had no idea of his phone number. No way of hearing his voice, seducing her once more into a feeling of unjustified complacency. Would it always be like this whenever he disappeared for a while? Had the rest of her life slipped so quickly through her fingers and into his control? Maybe these two weeks would be good for her. Time to get straight again. Put him where he belonged. An affair. A fling. Exciting, rejuvenating, delicious. The gloom left her as rapidly as it had descended. Suddenly she was looking forward to the following Ben-less weeks. Even the weekend ahead with her mother didn't fill her with too much dread, now that Frances would be there to see the funny side.

The telephone cut across her thoughts and her voice was firm and cheerful. 'Hello, Rosemary here.'

'Mum.'

'Ella darling. I wondered where you were. Everything OK?'

'Everything more than OK here, Mum. What about you? Is it still Ben?'

'Yes,' Rosemary answered firmly, defying any query from the other end of the phone.

Ella hesitated. Then, 'As long as you're all right.'

'I am, darling. Frances is back and coming for the weekend. Along with your grandmother.'

'Don't tell me Ben's included with that bunch of hysterics?'

Rosemary took a deep breath. 'Listen, young woman. I won't interfere with you if you don't involve yourself in my life. Wasn't that the bargain when you moved back home?'

'Yes. And you're right.' Ella laughed. 'D'you want my phone number up here?'

'Please. And the date you open.'

Ella gave her the number and the date. She spoke briefly about the rehearsals, how she was enjoying it and what a great company it was. She sounded excited and happy. Rosemary, relieved, listened to her chattering on, feeling deliciously selfish at the prospect of being able to concentrate on herself during the weeks ahead.

Finally Ella said, 'I've got to go, Mum. Some of the others are coming round to do lines. Don't worry if you don't hear from me. Just look after yourself. Oh yes, you'd better give my love to your weekend guests.' She rang off, leaving the sarcasm heavy in the air. Rosemary smiled to herself and went to put the telephone number in her address book. Writing it next to the one marked 'Joanna Tristram', she realized they were the same. She was glad Ella had found friends to stay with. Spring and summer stretched ahead of her: freedom, independence, chosen solitude and a love affair. Life was suddenly perfect.

She picked up her mother the next morning, arriving cheerfully and promptly at eleven, her car boot full of things to eat to please her parent.

Betty was in a good humour. 'I've turned everything off,' she said as she opened the door to Rosemary.

'Don't turn the heating right off, Mum, in case we get a frost. Pipes might burst.' She picked up her mother's overnight bag and took her arm as they walked to the car.

'It'll save money,' Betty replied weakly.

'It'll be more expensive to call a plumber. Let's just turn it down.'

They drove back to Wimbledon and Rosemary told her

about Ella phoning and how happy she'd sounded.

'Did she send her love?' her mother asked sharply.

'Of course, Mum. She always does. And very disappointed she was that she would be missing you.' The small lie was worth it when the pleased smile brightened Betty's face. Rosemary felt a sudden rush of affection for her and squeezed her mother's arm quickly, steering the car deftly with one hand. 'It's lovely to have you for the weekend.'

'I'm glad I could manage. I don't like the thought of you being lonely.'

Rosemary smiled to herself, allowing the generosity to be taken from her. 'Frances is coming as well,' she said.

'Oh that's lovely. We can have a good old gossip. She always knows what's going on.'

And what she doesn't know, thought Rosemary, *she makes up.*

Her mother sat in the kitchen with her and watched the preparation of their lunchtime salad. Rosemary poured them each a sherry. A sweet one for Betty. 'Like syrup of figs', Ella always said, grimacing at the thought of that middle class apéritif. Her daughter's inverted snobbery was clinging on well past her adolescence. Chopping the tomatoes, Rosemary listened with only half her senses to her mother's chatter about neighbours and their noisy dogs and dirty children.

'Don't put any cucumber in mine,' Betty said quickly. 'Not unless you take the peel off. Gives me indigestion.'

Rosemary peeled the cucumber in sections down each side, the way her mother liked it. They ate in the kitchen, watching the sky darken with the oncoming rain. Betty complained at great length about the weather, as if it had been sent as a personal affront on her person.

After lunch, Rosemary sat her in an armchair in the

living-room and stoked up the fire. Ben, the cat, damp from the sudden downpour, settled on the old woman's lap, and Rosemary turned on the television. 'Wrestling or a Kenneth More film?' she asked her mother, flicking over the pages of the *TV Times*.

'Ooh, Kenny More would be nice. Can I have some tea as well?'

Rosemary smiled and bent to kiss her on top of her head, amused at the excitement in her mother's voice at so simple a pleasure. Going through to the kitchen to load the dishwasher and put the kettle on to boil, she wondered if the limits of delight would ever shrink as drastically in herself. Thoughts of Ben joined her as she watched the kettle. She had half-hoped he would ring, but the telephone remained silent. She would have loved to be able just to dial his number, wherever he was. To hear him say 'Rosie'. But somewhere out there, with the rain probably beating on his window, he was more than likely saying 'Gill'.

She made the tea and pushed him resolutely out of her mind. Frances arrived at five, with arms full of Harrods greenhouse flowers, smoked salmon and chopped herring in polystyrene tubs. Betty held her face up to be kissed. The cat protested at the rain from Frances' coat as she removed it and threw it over the sofa, and jumped from Betty's lap to find a place nearer the fire. The television stayed on, background for a house suddenly alive with loud voices and laughter and a champagne cork leaving the bottle.

'D'you want a glass, Mum?' Rosemary called from the kitchen.

'It's a bit early,' Betty said dubiously.

Frances brought one through for her, and Rosemary carried the bottle and two full glasses. 'Go on,' said Frances, placing the crystal glass into Betty's reluctant hand. 'It's just us girls! No-one to disapprove. Rosemary, put the bottle back in the refrigerator. I detest warm champagne! I'm starving – no lunch. Harrods was packed, and I bumped into everyone I knew.'

'D'you want some salad?' Rosemary asked.

'No, no; some of the herring on crackers. We'll eat later. "Chopped herrin'",' she mimicked. 'Isn't that wonderful? "Chopped herrin'." That's what the girl in the food hall called it. Nobody says the g's any more. Have you noticed?'

Rosemary envied her friend's enormous appetite for everything that life had to offer, wondering at her ability to eat continuously without putting on weight. 'Do you exercise a lot?' somebody had once asked Frances, watching cake and ice-cream disappear into her pencil-slim body. 'Do you use a gym?'

'Only if it's catered,' Frances had said, lighting a cigarette and washing a dessert down with a glass of wine. She lit a cigarette now. In the front room, falling into the chair opposite Betty, she offered the pack to Rosemary, who made frantic signs of refusal behind her mother's head. Betty went on smiling. Somehow she never seemed to mind Frances' habits. Along with Ella's foul language, she was able to ignore in them most of the things she usually found offensive. Rosemary wished Betty was as tolerant about her own daughter.

Saturday evening deepened into Saturday night. So excited was Betty with Frances' masterly gossip that she forgot to watch her favourite quiz show on the BBC.

'Let's eat on our laps,' said Frances when it was time for supper.

'D'you mind, Mum?' Rosemary knew her mother had always considered it 'a lowering of standards not to lay a nice table'.

'Of course not.' Betty was affronted at the question,

as if the thought had never crossed her mind.

Rosemary eyed her mother accepting the third glass of champagne. 'She'll be in bed by nine,' she whispered to Frances. 'We'd better not eat too late.'

'That's the idea,' her friend whispered back. 'I want to talk to you.'

Rosemary put the trays out and found linen napkins. The crystal glass shone in the light as she lifted it to her lips. She was full with an excitement of fulfilment that wasn't only caused by the champagne. Memories of Ben, along with Frances' jubilation of life in general, had generated a feeling and an atmosphere in the house that had been absent for some time. *Falling in love*, she thought, putting food into the microwave, *is something I should have done years ago.*

Her mother's eyes began to droop just after nine that evening. Flushed with a more than usual intake of alcohol, she enjoyed her meal without once complaining of indigestion.

'I've put you in Ella's room, Mum,' Rosemary said as she helped her upstairs. 'I've put the blanket on for you.'

'Those things frighten me. Can't I have a hot-water bottle?'

'I'll turn it off before you get in.'

Betty put her hand up to her daughter's face as Rosemary tucked her into bed. 'You're so good to me,' she said, 'I've had such a lovely day.'

'Sleep well, Mum. I'll bring you tea in the morning.'

She was asleep as Rosemary left the room.

'She's quite human when she's pissed,' she said to Frances as they settled in front of the fire with coffee and brandy.

'Sometimes,' said Frances, offering her a cigarette, 'I catch a glimpse of the girl she once was.'

'I wonder. She made my father's life a misery. God

knows why she dislikes men so thoroughly.' Rosemary pondered on the thought.

'Did she have a father alive when you were young?' Frances asked. She bent forward and switched off the television.

Rosemary shook her head. 'I never knew him. He left my grandmother when Mum was a baby. She never talked about him.'

'Aah well, that explains it. Now, heart face, what's happening with that cunning young man you're bedding?'

Frances remained silent while she talked. 'So he'll phone you from Spain and make arrangements?' she said eventually.

'That's the idea. Barcelona.'

Frances said, 'It'll be all round the business by the time you get home. You know what film crews are like.'

'I know. I think I'm prepared to go public, if that's the expression.'

Frances lit another cigarette. 'He's still got your front door key.' It was a statement.

'I forgot to ask him.'

'He wants his feet under your table, darling heart. What about you?'

'He must be uninvolved first. I've said that. More or less said it, anyway. He's promised he'll sort it out.'

'Poor what's-her-name. Gill isn't it? Wonder what she's like.'

'Young.' They both stared into the fire. Rosemary broke the quiet of the room. Her voice soft against the spitting of the logs. 'I want him, Franny. I have a terrible feeling about it all. But I want him. D'you ever remember me this wilful?'

Frances shook her head. 'No. But you've never been weak. You're always determined to get what you want and you usually get it.'

'And this time?'

Frances stared at her. Her face was unusually serious. 'I don't know, my lovely. There's just a feeling, a tingling behind my ears. I wish you'd get your key back.'

The evening ended quietly, drifting away into other conversations, leaving Ben to re-surface later, when Rosemary went to bed.

Chapter Eight

The weekend passed. Thoughts of Ben came and went in Rosemary's mind. Her moods swung from body-hugging joy to despondency brought on by confusion and the desire to know what he really was all about. She had half-hoped he'd ring, regardless of his situation, but as much as she willed his voice to be there whenever she answered the phone, it didn't work.

Frances drove Betty home late on Sunday night. 'Go to bed and read,' she said to Rosemary after she had settled her passenger into the car and supplied a rug to wrap round her knees. They kissed on both cheeks and held each other briefly. 'Try to enjoy whatever it all is, dearest heart. Don't make fires where there's no smoke – you're a big girl now. And I'm certain he's besotted with you.'

'Thanks Franny. I don't know what I'd do without you.'

'Get yourself in monumental messes my lovely one. As soon as my back was turned last time, look what happened!!'

Rosemary laughed and hugged herself against the cold.

'Go on,' said Frances, moving round to the driver's door. 'Don't wait here. You'll freeze. Phone me if you hear about Barcelona. I'm in Birmingham till Wednesday. I'll phone then if there's nothing from you.'

Rosemary waved, blew a kiss to her mother and ran back into the house, rubbing her arms now against the March wind. Next week, April would arrive. British Summertime had begun. The first buds would appear on the early flowering cherry trees and there was only one more show to record before she could relax. Spain beckoned. She would have to think of telling her mother about Ben before the news hit the tabloids. *I'll think about that later*, she thought, getting ready for bed and feeling suddenly, ridiculously, like Scarlett O'Hara and sixteen years old.

She slept badly and woke at seven with her eyes puffy and red from tiredness and the consumption of alcohol at the weekend. 'Franny never seems to get red eyes,' she muttered to herself in the mirror while finding the blue eyedrops in the bathroom cabinet, 'and she drinks like a fish.' She threw herself into a quick and short frenzy of exercise as if to propel Ben out of her thoughts via her body. Showered, made-up and dressed, she faced the morning. *No breakfast*, she thought, feeling the all-too-familiar padding at the back of her waist beginning to build up after the indulgence of the past two weeks. Black coffee and orange juice began her day. Pat arrived, and Jennie came punctually as usual at nine-thirty. They took coffee into the study.

'Don't give me biscuits at eleven,' called Rosemary over her shoulder to Pat. The too-full cup of coffee lapped and spilled a little as she carried it through the hall. 'Shit! Pat, I've spilled something on the carpet. Only a bit. Catch it before it settles. And I mean it about the biscuits. I'm on a diet.'

'There's only Jaffa Cakes left,' said Pat.

'Good. Remind me not to buy anything else.'

Derek phoned at ten, confirming the guests for the final recording on Thursday and asking if she'd enjoyed the show the previous night. Rosemary realized for the first time that she had forgotten to watch it. So had Frances, and even more surprisingly, so had her mother.

'Derek, I'm terribly sorry, I haven't seen it. Had to go out. Was it all right?'

'Wonderful. We left just enough conflict in to titillate. Go out and get the tabloids. You've come out really well. One said you're the best interviewer we've got.'

'I've got the papers here. I'll ring you back when I've read them.'

She was about to hang up when Derek said, 'There's something in the *Sun* about you and that young actor. What's his name? Ben – Ben Morrison. Someone saw you in a restaurant.'

Rosemary's heart dropped to her groin. 'Oh dear.'

'Good publicity, dear girl. Don't panic. Shall we squeeze him into the show on Thursday?'

Over my dead body will he ever *be in the show*, thought Rosemary. She said, 'He's in Spain, Derek. Look, let me read it. I'll speak to you later.' She replaced the receiver and turned to her secretary. 'Jennie, go through the papers for me. They're still in the hall, on the table I think. And ask if Pat's got the *Sun* on her, and has she read it?'

Jennie hurried out of the room. The phone rang again. It was Ben.

'Where are you?' she said.

'I'm at the airport. Are you OK?'

'Yes. Why?' she asked nervously.

'We made the gutter press.' His voice was expressionless.

'I know. I'm sorry. It was probably Friday's lunch.'

'Don't worry, Rosie. I'd already sorted everything. You can tell the world.'

Her heart lifted once more. 'Are you going to tell *me* what's going on with you?' she said, smiling at him into the phone.

'In Barcelona. I'll phone when I get there and tell you where I am. When can you come out?'

'Any time after next weekend. I have a game show for television to do next Sunday. In Manchester.'

'God, how boring. Can you get out of it and come on Friday?' She hesitated, and before she could speak he said, 'My money's running out. I'll be in touch. Don't forget me.'

'How could I?' she said, but he'd gone. And the drawn-out tone from the disconnection whined in her ear.

It was just a few lines in one of the columns of the *Sun* newspaper. Pat had missed it and, furious with herself for not being able to bring the news personally that morning when she arrived, she read it out now, loud and slowly with mounting irritation. 'Rosemary Downey, fifty, was seen holding hands in an intimate restaurant late one night with up-and-coming actor Ben Morrison. Hard to imagine she was interviewing him for her show.'

'Oh dear,' said Jennie.

'Bloody cheek,' said Pat. 'Why do they always mention your age?'

'It was lunch,' Rosemary remarked banally, ignoring Pat's fury. She read the piece again and tried to re-member who had been in the restaurant. It couldn't have been the Caprice because Frances had been with them. 'Definitely lunch,' she said, and threw the paper onto the kitchen table. 'Tomorrow's chip-wrapping,' she remarked to the two women she now left standing in her kitchen as she made her way back to the study. 'Can I have some more coffee Pat. Black. I must phone my mother. She always reads the *Sun*.'

But the telephone was ringing as she headed towards it.

'Rosemary?'

'Mum.'

'Have you read the newspapers yet?'

'By newspapers, d'you mean the *Sun*?'

'Of course I mean the *Sun*. I get it for the Bingo.'

Rosemary waited for the next question.

'What young man?' Betty asked. 'And were you hold-ing hands?'

'Mum—' Rosemary sat down. 'He's a friend of Ella's. They've got it all wrong. They always do. I've told you before.'

'Mrs Drewett came in and told me. I hadn't read it yet.' Betty was furious she had got the news from a neighbour. 'You must sue them, Rosemary. They make it sound like you're having an affair.'

Rosemary sighed. 'I can't sue them. They haven't said anything dreadful or anything untruthful.'

'Well, they've insinuated.'

'You can't sue for insinuation.'

'It looks so bad. Everyone knows you don't bother with men. This makes you look silly, written down on paper for everyone to see.'

'Only those who read the *Sun*, Mum.'

Rosemary managed to get her off the phone eventually and settle down to some work with Jennie. The reviews for her and the show were good. No more phone calls came about the mention of the lunch with Ben. She rang her agent and told him she would be going to Spain the following week. He didn't seem perturbed about the newspaper article. She didn't cancel the Sunday appearance in Manchester. Now was the time to hang on to any remaining common sense she had left. Her agent had taped the Sunday show and offered to bike it round for her to see.

'You came out well, Rosemary. The negotiations for the autumn series should go ahead without too much conflict about money.'

'Don't waste your time biking it, Michael. I can get a tape when I'm at the studios on Thursday. Are you coming for the party afterwards?'

'Yes. I'll be on my own. One of the boys has come down with 'flu, and Barbara doesn't want to leave him with a baby-sitter.'

Surprise, surprise, thought Rosemary when they'd said

goodbye. She turned back to Jennie who had come back in with two more cups of coffee. Rosemary had been with her agents, Michael Dawson and Associates, for ten years and she had never known him go anywhere without his wife Barbara. After twenty years of marriage they still seemed delightfully involved with each other and their four children of various ages. *One of the boys, must be the youngest*, thought Rosemary. Joshua Dawson, was born just three years ago to his forty-three-year-old mother, who had not planned for any more family, but who very quickly became infatuated with her new and latest son. More infatuated than maybe Michael liked or wanted. Rosemary pondered the thought.

The days leading up to the final show of the series on Thursday were good ones for her. Relaxed for the moment about her relationship with Ben, pleased with his phone call from the airport, knowing he was working out of the country and away from any entanglements he might have at home, she felt he was more completely hers. Her usual compassion for any abandoned woman refused to surface over the subject of the mysterious Gill in Ben's life. She had convinced herself the affair was over long before *she* had come on the scene. The knowledge that he had probably been sleeping with Ella, however casually, while he was living with Gill, she refused to think about. Maybe he had been unhappy at the time. Wasn't that the usual reason that men strayed? Her knowledge was small, her innocence unchallenged by her advancing years.

Now, at last, she felt happy to be so thoroughly in love. She spent one day in Harrods buying underwear for her Spanish trip. She dieted vigorously and lost, too quickly, seven pounds in weight in only a few days; acknowledging to herself she was doing all the things women were told they do when in the first flush of infatuation.

On Wednesday night, Rosemary went to a first night.

Arriving with Michael at the Aldwych Theatre, the press photographers sprung forward as soon as their limousine drew up.

'This way Rosemary, look over here, smile now. Thank you. This way, up here, show us yer teeth!'

She paused for only moments while they snapped away. Michael stood apart from her, leaving her alone in the glare of publicity. Finally, one arm raised to signify she'd had enough, she moved again to his side.

'Where's the young man?' called one photographer, scribbling in a quickly produced notepad.

Rosemary froze and nudged Michael. 'Think of something,' she whispered. 'Confuse them, for God's sake.'

He laughed and, putting an arm around her shoulders, he bent and kissed her on the cheek.

'That'll just confuse Barbara,' she hissed back at him. And they both laughed.

They skipped the first-night party. Glad of the excuse of a show to do the following day, she even refused supper at Joe Allen's. Michael dropped her home by eleven.

'Give Barbara my love. I hope Josh is better soon.'

'I'll see you tomorrow Rosemary. If Barbara changes her mind about coming, I'll give Derek a ring.'

They kissed quickly on both cheeks. Air kisses, fashionable now with sets of friends, even those without the worry of lipstick marks left on powdered cheeks. Feeling hungry, but delighted with the reappearance of her hip bones, she avoided the kitchen and headed straight for her study and the answerphone. Four messages. Frances, Ella and two from Ben in Barcelona.

'Sorry to miss you Rosie, although I do – badly. I'll bell you later.' And then, the fourth message on the machine. 'Where are you Rosie? Why aren't you at home? I'm at the Comtes de Barcelona. When are you coming? The bed is too small, but I need you in it. I'll ring you tomorrow.'

She rang Frances, knowing her friend never went to bed before midnight. 'How was Birmingham Franny?'

'Just like Birmingham. What else do I say? Are you well?'

'Wonderful. Michael's coming on his own tomorrow; you could have an escort.'

'Nice one,' said Frances. 'He can keep me out of the deadly Derek's clutches. When d'you hit Spain?'

'I'll go on Monday.' Rosemary cradled the phone under her chin and lit a cigarette with her free hands. 'Ben seems to be missing me. I'd better get out there before he goes cold.'

Frances said, 'Any repercussions from the *Sun* article?'

'Not really,' Rosemary hesitated. 'D'you think I shouldn't go to Barcelona?'

'You won't be secret any more.'

'He doesn't mind. Ben I mean. He said so.'

'Never mind about his permission. What about you?' Frances said. 'Sweetheart, *you're* the one who's famous, *you're* the one who'll get all the stick. Don't dance to his tune. What do *you* want?'

Rosemary stubbed out the unfinished cigarette into the ink-well on her desk. The combination of the nicotine and her empty stomach was making her feel sick. Beads of sweat on her top lip, and the sudden clamminess of her body, had brought her dangerously close to fainting. She closed her eyes, not wanting to look at a room that had suddenly gone out of focus. 'Franny darling, I've got to go. I feel frightfully unwell suddenly. We'll talk tomorrow.' She hung up and bent forward to place her head on her knees.

'God you're stupid,' she muttered to herself, feeling the water rising like bile into her mouth from the acidity of her empty stomach.

'This is teenage behaviour, woman.' It had been many years since she'd starved herself through vanity.

Moments later she stood in the kitchen and cut bread to toast. The food was scarcely chewed before swallowing, her hunger so desperate for appeasement. She poured skimmed milk for herself. Still in her coat, she stood and devoured the almost midnight feast. There was little else in the fridge, and she was too hungry to cook. She was behaving like a fool. Wanting a man's approval. Wanting Ben's approval. Desiring a young body to keep him with her, uncomfortable in her middle years with a feeling of lost beauty. Insecurity washed over her. Where had she gone so quickly? Wasn't the Rosemary he'd met and wanted enough? He hadn't complained, so why was she behaving like this?

She went to bed, longing now to be as she had been before her birthday, and knowing it was too late. Silly with desire for his touch, she fell asleep caressing herself, crying silently over her own stupidity and the memory and the loss of her twenty-year-old self.

Thursday came and with it as always were hairdressers, limousines, dressers, make-up chatter and researchers' questions. Lunch was taken as usual with Derek, and for this last show, the head of programmes for the company. Anne sat at another table in the executive restaurant, lunching with the vision mixer, her eyes wandering inter-mittently towards Derek. Rosemary felt ashamed that she hadn't supported her emotionally in some way during the course of the series of shows. Abandoned now as Anne was, in her private and public life, Rosemary thought the very least *she* could have done was to have shown some sort of female solidarity. No-one deserved the kind of casual betrayal Derek had so easily thrown out to his long-time mistress.

Rosemary smiled across the room and watched for a moment a small crumb of cheer flicker, then fade into the sadness of Anne's face.

God I pity her, thought Rosemary. *Where does she go inside that head of hers?* She shuddered and turned back to her lunch companions.

'Don't take the world on your shoulders, lovely one,' Frances would say. 'You survive first, then share out any strength you have left over.'

I don't know where mine's gone, thought Rosemary, and sipped at a glass of distinctly unpleasant warm white wine. Her jaws clicked and she swallowed and pushed the glass away. The lunch remained on her plate. Hunger eluded her.

'Cheese and biscuits and coffee,' she said in answer to Derek's query about dessert, and forced herself to eat when a large piece of sweating Cheddar shuddered on the plate in front of her.

Dress rehearsal out of the way, and alone in her dressing-room, she managed to contact Ella at the theatre.

'Can't chat long, Mum. We're in teabreak.' Ella sounded cheerful.

'When d'you open darling?' Rosemary asked. She put a hand up to her forehead, feeling the beginning of a headache.

'I told you. Shit, you're getting like Grandma; she never listens either.'

'Don't shout at me Ella. I've got a terrible headache.' Rosemary's voice remained calm. 'My diary's at home and I've forgotten the date.'

'April 13th, and I didn't mean to shout. Are you all right?'

'Yes darling.' Her heart sank. April 13th. She would be in Spain.

'Are you coming up for the opening, Mum?'

Rosemary hesitated and then, 'I can't Ella. I'm going away on Monday. To Spain.'

The line crackled through the brief silence. 'That's

OK. You deserve a break. You going with Frances?'

Why is she suddenly being so sweet? thought Rosemary, *and why this unbelievable cheerfulness during rehearsals? Very unlike Ella.* 'Ben is filming in Barcelona. I'm going to join him.'

'Aah.'

There seemed no more to be said, and before the conversation fell into danger they said 'goodbye' and rang off. Rosemary couldn't remember ever missing one of Ella's first nights. May came in and Rosemary sent her off for Nurofen.

After the recording, at the end-of-series party at the top of the studios, Frances said, 'You look awful, my darling. Aren't you enjoying this romance of yours?'

'I am when I'm with him.'

'That's not often.'

'It seems enough at the time.'

Frances stared at her and then bent forward to take her hand.

'I take back what I said about going for it. You're unhappy. There's no point. What the hell are you getting out of it, darling?'

'If I could be sure of him,' said Rosemary unhappily.

'It's only been two weeks for God's sake.'

'But he blows hot and cold. He seems so inconsistent.'

Frances gritted her teeth and put a cigarette in her friend's mouth and offered her a light from her own. 'Rosemary, I'm serious, get out *now*. He's delectable and sexy, but it's supposed to make you feel good for longer than the odd five minutes a day.'

'What's he done to me?'

'Knocked you off balance. That's all. Don't go to Spain. I promise you'll forget him in a week.'

'Forget what? I don't know who or what he is. Just that I'm not myself any more.' She felt the headache of the afternoon returning now with a vengeance, and she fumbled in her bag for the Nurofen. 'I don't like being in love today,' she said.

'Did you yesterday?' smiled Frances, amused at the petulance in her once-practical friend's voice.

Rosemary looked at her. Then, realizing her childishness, laughed. 'Yes I did. I am so *silly*. Will it get better?'

'Only if *you* make it. Don't wait for him. I'm not too sure that he isn't playing games.'

'Perhaps this is what Ella meant when she warned me off?' Rosemary frowned at the memory of that Sunday afternoon such a short time ago.

'Have you asked her?' said Frances.

'No. We both promised not to interfere in each other's life.'

The evening was long and Rosemary drank too much champagne, inducing a gaiety she was far from feeling.

As she fell asleep at about three in the morning, she reviewed the picture in her head of Frances and Michael talking somewhat intensely for a long time. Had she been the topic of their protracted conversation? It seemed likely. Her life, it seemed, was in everyone's hands but her own.

Chapter Nine

Next morning she called Ben's hotel in Barcelona.

'I'd like to leave a message for Señor Morrison. Could he phone Rosemary tonight? He has the number.'

She had felt almost like her old self when she had woken on the Friday morning. She threw herself into a frenzy of activity, clearing all the jobs she had left unfinished in her moments of depression and immobility during the previous day. Jennie organized her air ticket for Monday afternoon. Rosemary rang Michael and said she would be away at least a week and gave him the hotel number in Spain.

'I'd better warn you, Michael. I'm going to see that young man. Ben Morrison. I'll keep away from the film set, but it's bound to leak out that I'm there. Can you hold back the tabloids for me just in case?'

'Are you being wise, Rosemary?' Michael spoke without expression in his voice. She had never known him do anything but sit on the fence when it came to the escapades of his clients. He seldom judged, only rarely offered advice, and then only when it was asked of him.

'Probably not,' said Rosemary. 'But it has to come out sooner or later.' She knew she sounded unusually terse, but the memory of him and Frances with their heads together the previous night sprung into her mind. It was all she could do to stop herself reminding him that it was her life and therefore her business. Wilfulness sat on her, a cloak she was beginning to wear rather frequently.

'Is all this serious?' Michael's voice was tentative. He

was beginning to be faced with a Rosemary he had never previously encountered.

'Yes,' she answered. And there was nothing else to be said.

That evening she sat by the phone and waited for Ben's call. Frances rang, and Rosemary said, 'I can't speak for long Franny, I'm waiting to hear from Ben.'

'When are you going?'

'Monday afternoon. I'm in Manchester on Sunday, just for the day. I'll drive myself up and back. Are you around tomorrow?'

'I think I'm away for the weekend.'

Frances offered no further details and it wasn't until she had rung off that Rosemary realized how strange it was for her usually ebullient friend not to discuss her plans more openly. There had just been a certain tone in her voice that Rosemary couldn't put her finger on.

'Phone me as soon as you get back,' Frances had said. 'And do try to enjoy yourself. Don't get heavy.'

'You sound like a man,' retorted Rosemary.

'You know what I mean. Play it by instinct and not your mother's training. You don't *have* to fall in love with every man you fancy, darling heart, in spite of your Fifties' morals.'

Rosemary mused to herself as she went through the clothes to take to Manchester on Sunday, whether she really had only talked herself into falling in love with Ben. A foolish thing to have done with anyone so capricious. Fortifying herself with a glass of wine, she phoned her mother. 'I rang to say I'll be away next week, Mum.'

'Oh. Where are you going? Anywhere nice?'

'Spain.'

'What a lovely life you lead. What for?' A note of envy bordering on irritability crept into Betty's voice.

Rosemary panicked for a moment, unable to think of

any kind of convincing reason for her departure. 'I'm going to Barcelona. With Michael. It's business.' She knew her mother wouldn't question her, knowing very little about the world of television; only the glamour and immediacy of the actual camera image fascinated her. Rosemary could probably have said Siberia and her mother would have accepted it. Excitement, to Betty, was every place in the world except Streatham. Secure in the knowledge of getting away with one lie, Rosemary told another. 'I can't see you this weekend, Mum. I go to Manchester tomorrow. Saturday. And I'm not back until late Sunday night.'

'Ooh. Well, I know how busy you are. It's nice of you to fit me in like you do.'

Rosemary winced. *Does she really think I don't know she means it nastily?* thought Rosemary as she hurried her mother through the remainder of the conversation and eventually left the telephone clear once more. She had longed for years to bring the conflict between herself and her parent out into the open.

But Betty Dalton had been brought up in a different era. One even more restricted than the Fifties. Things unpleasant were best left undiscussed. A show of polite affection in families was compulsory, even if a natural hatred bubbled dangerously near the surface. 'Your mother is always your best friend,' she'd said often, along with, 'If he's good to his mother, he must be all right.' Thoughtless platitudes that led young women into deep waters; in the Fifties, anyway, when they were churned out to many a girl battling her way through adolescence. Rosemary still wondered about 'a man only wants one thing and when he's got it he loses respect for you!' She always suspected it was grounded in some basic truth but now, in the Nineties, enlightened as women were supposed to be, she kept the unliberated thought to herself. The Fifties of her youth pursued her with dogged determination. It had all seemed so simple then, those days when everyone had a rôle. The last era of the innocents.

Ben eventually phoned at midnight. She was in bed but unable to sleep. He said immediately, 'Why didn't you come today Rosie?'

'Ben darling, I can't just cancel work at a moment's notice. I wish I could. I'd much rather be with you.'

'When *are* you coming then?'

She could have sworn for the moment that she was talking to her son Jonathan when he had been in the worst years of his juvenescence, so petulant and put-out did Ben sound. She swallowed the smile she was afraid would bubble into her voice, knowing from experience he needed careful handling. 'I'll be there Monday.' There was silence from the other end of the phone. She said, 'Are you still there?'

'Yes. I'm just disappointed.' His voice now was low.

She felt light-headed with a sudden surge of joy, sure of him in that instant. She said gently, 'Forgive me Ben. I did what I thought best. And I'll be with you on Monday. I'll be at the hotel when you finish filming.'

'Go to the bar. I'll come straight there.'

She hesitated and then said quickly while her courage remained with her, 'I'm counting the hours.'

'Me too. Good night.' And he was gone.

She fell asleep immediately, hurrying herself into her dreams, which filled every erotic longing. Monday would take for ever to arrive.

She arranged flowers to be sent to Anne the following day and, thinking ahead, some white roses to arrive for Ella on her opening night. She wasn't sure enough of the language of flowers to know which colour meant 'I'm sorry', but Ella would understand her guilt and laugh at her.

Driving to Manchester on Sunday she wondered if she should have given her mother the hotel phone number in Barcelona. She rang Betty from the car. 'All right Mum?'

'Where are you phoning from? It sounds like you're in a tunnel.'

'I'm in the car. On the way to Manchester.'

Betty said, 'I thought you went yesterday?'

'Something came up, I had to postpone.' Guiltier than ever, she went on without thinking, hoping now that her mother wouldn't suspect her lie, knowing she would never hear the end of it, 'D'you need my number in Spain?'

'Well yes. Michael's with you, so I can't phone him if I need to. And I am feeling unwell. Just in case. You know I won't use it unless I have to.'

'Have you phoned the doctor?'

'Oh, I don't want to bother him. Anyway I can't get to the surgery. Mrs Drewett's away and he won't come here.'

'What's wrong?'

Her mother dropped her voice. 'My stomach is sore. Same old trouble. But I don't want to complain. You expect it when you're eighty.'

Rosemary bit back the desire to remind her she was still only seventy-nine. Her mother had begun to add that extra year since her last birthday, feeling as she did that the older she was, the more attention she got. Sympathy had become more important to her than any other emotion she could rouse in people. Commiseration from others seemed to make her feel special. Rosemary did now feel sorry for her, realizing how sad it must be to reach an age when the most exciting things in your life were your ailments.

'Mum,' she said, 'you're not eating properly.'

'I can't be bothered. Wait until you're old, then you'll understand.'

The outskirts of the city of Manchester loomed ahead of her and Rosemary wound up the conversation before pity turned to irritation.

'I'll give you a ring tomorrow morning. Make yourself a hot-water bottle and something to drink. D'you have any brandy?'

'I can't afford brandy.'

'Hot milk then.' She said 'goodbye' and switched off the phone, but not before she missed the correct turning in the road and had to go round the one-way system again. It started to rain heavily, as if she needed to be reminded she was in Manchester.

Her mother was always pleading poverty. It took all Rosemary's patience not to constantly remind her that money was paid into her account on a regular basis from Rosemary's own bank. Betty also had over £10,000 in a post-office account which she refused to touch, but its very existence barred her from any sort of income support from the state. Ella would say, 'Why don't you spend it Gran? Have you figured a way of taking it with you?'

Betty's mouth would tighten into a thin line. Discussing money, a surfeit or a lack of it, was something ladies did not do, even in the family. 'That's for a rainy day. Your grandad left it to me. His way of making up for all the pain he caused me. As if all the money in the world could do that.'

'Darling Gran.' Ella was relentless. 'Darling Gran, this *is* a rainy day. It's your old age, enjoy it.'

'Ella, that money is for you and your mother when I go. Which won't be long.'

Nobody could ever top that remark. It was always guaranteed to stop any conversation in its tracks. Useless to explain to her mother that she didn't need ten thousand pounds, and Ella would probably spend it all anyway. And she understood her parent's need to leave the small inheritance. An old-fashioned and genuine gesture that Ella would never comprehend. So Rosemary sent flowers to her mother every Friday, paid her bills and gave her two hundred pounds a month, and neither of them talked about it. It was simply given and accepted. Betty's due, and Rosemary's duty. This materialistic transaction also helped cover the lack of real love that existed between them.

Frances had once asked, 'Why d'you feel you owe her so much, treasure face?'

'She's my mother.'

'*She* owes *you*. That's the way round it should be.'

'That's Ella's thinking.'

'Good grief, have we actually got something in common?'

Rosemary had laughed and poked her friend in the ribs. 'Why do I put up with you hating my daughter?'

'I'll love her when she leaves home. Children should be away by sixteen.'

'I'm not surprised you never married, Franny.' Rosemary went on, 'My mother's had a lonely life. It's good to make up for it a little.'

'Nonsense, you innocent creature. She *adores* being miserable. Your generosity puts her street credibility for depression back years.'

They both knew that Rosemary would never change. It was one of the reasons she had always had Frances' respect, if not her complete understanding.

Once her day had begun in Manchester, she enjoyed herself. There was an old acquaintance on the quiz show they were recording. Cathy was a journalist she had liked and trusted for years who, because of her media critiques, had become a celebrity, and was now a regular on this particular show. They bumped into each other coming out of the dressing-rooms and went together to the hospitality room. They sat over coffee and chatted about work.

'I loved the show on Sunday,' Cathy said, 'specially the way you handled the well-known drunk. What an arsehole!'

'Used to be a lovely man.' Rosemary frowned at the memory of the middle-aged Tony, who had once been young and easy.

'You came out well, girl!' Cathy leaned towards her and lowered her voice. 'Do we talk about Ben Morrison?'

Rosemary laughed. 'I'd rather we didn't.'

'Well if you do, or even if you don't and find you have to, make sure it's me you bell. OK?'

The show's director came in to explain the quiz game to them and to run the tape of a previous show. Casual conversation could wait until after rehearsals.

The recording was over by nine that night, and Rosemary had no desire to hang around for any sort of idle conversation.

Before she slipped away, Cathy said, 'D'you have my number still?'

'Yes.'

'We'll do a piece for one of the magazines. It's been ages. Can you phone me tomorrow?'

'Cathy, I'm on holiday tomorrow. I'll phone you when I get back.' Rosemary went for her car to begin the long, wet drive home on the motorways. Her mind was now in Spain, wanting the hours to go quickly, forgetting to begrudge the wishing of her life away as she had so often told her children when they had counted the days until the school holidays. Wanting only to live the special hours with Ben, feeling that other moments of her existence were merely a filling of the gaps.

Monday came. Pat arrived, and Rosemary gave her reminder lists.

'What to do when I'm away, especially feeding the cat.'

'D'you need more cat food?' Pat asked.

'There's plenty. I got the small expensive tins. His favourite. In case he feels neglected.'

Pat raised her eyebrows. 'Shall I sit and talk to him every morning?'

'Don't tease me. He hates being on his own.'

'Why don't you get a kitten?' Pat asked, putting a cup of coffee down on the kitchen table in front of Rosemary, where she was beginning her list for the gardener.

'A kitten? He'd never stand it.'

Pat shrugged, and leaning now against the sink she sipped her coffee noisily. 'You'd better leave your number,' she said.

'I will.'

Everything to be done before her departure was completed and crossed off her list. Phone calls made, letters answered, two appearances at charity lunches cancelled and several appointments she'd forgotten left to be dealt with by Jennie.

'Contact Michael if anything else comes up. I'll let you know when I'll be back.'

Alone by lunchtime, she went upstairs and changed for the journey. She'd ordered a car to take her to the airport, and it arrived fifteen minutes early. Forgetting lunch, she left immediately in the early cab, deciding to enjoy the wait at Gatwick. She would use the first-class lounge in the North Terminal and buy some expensive perfume in the Duty-Free. Liberated and anonymous she would be, as soon as the plane left the ground. Still not blasé about air travel, the adventure always began as she left her own drive.

Avoiding all eyes by wearing dark glasses and averting

her gaze, she got through to the lounge without signing one autograph. If luck went with her, English holiday-makers would be scarce in Barcelona, and her days with Ben would be undisturbed. Determined to use this time to cement and clarify whatever relationship they had found, she waited for her flight feeling better than she'd done for the last few days, her carry-on bag full of duty-free cigarettes, perfume and even more extravagant cologne for Ben.

They were delayed for an hour-and-a-half and it was almost six-thirty before the plane landed in Barcelona. By the time she got some pesetas and found a taxi to take her into the city, she was feeling tired and irritable. But Ben would be filming probably until early evening and hopefully she would be in the hotel, unpacked and showered before he appeared.

At half-past seven she stood at reception in the Comtes de Barcelona. 'My name is Downey. I believe Mr Morrison booked for me.'

'Aah yes. Señor Morrison. He's in the bar. He says you can meet him there.' The girl behind the desk spoke English with only the slightest of accents. She smiled abruptly at Rosemary and summoned in Spanish one of the porters. 'I will get your bags taken up to your room. Will you want a morning call?'

Rosemary winced slightly at her manner. She'd for-gotten the disinterest of well-manicured young women, when to them you were unknown, and because of your age, no threat.

'I'll let you know,' she said to the girl, who immediately left her to deal with another arrival.

Rosemary stood and looked round for the bar. She had wanted to be more old-fashioned in her reunion with Ben. Had looked forward to at least a couple of solitary hours of primping before they met. By now her make-up was patchy, her breath unpleasant from the cigarettes and champagne of the journey and she longed for a cup of tea. She went to a ladies room to attempt some repairs on the ravages caused by air travel. Her eyes were puffy and beginning to redden. She turned on the tap, and screwing her face against the taste of chlorine, she scooped water into her mouth with her hand. The attendant sitting knitting in the corner of the room looked across at her and said something in Spanish. Rosemary smiled at her. '*No hablo español.*' It was one of the few Spanish phrases she knew. Languages at school had been her weakest subject, and she had in her early years been too lazy, and later too busy, ever to rectify what could only these days be thought of as a disability. The attendant shrugged and continued to knit. The mirror above the washbasin threw the reflection of her tired face back at her without mercy. She had wanted to be beautiful, now the week without proper food showed plainly on her fifty-year-old face. Once she could have gone hungry for days and still be bright-eyed and hipbone-slender at the same time.

'Maybe the lighting's bad,' she muttered to herself, and turned away. The chic and expensive-looking middle-aged, obviously Spanish woman standing next to her glanced up and smiled.

Heavily accented she said, 'It is.'

They both laughed, and Rosemary went back into the lobby, putting some pesetas into the saucer by the knitting attendant who murmured '*Gracias*' without glancing up and only pausing briefly between counting stitches. She walked to the entrance of the cocktail bar, her high heels loud on the marble floor. It was a busy hotel in a busy city, and the lobby was alive with excited and quick Catalan voices mingling with mainly English and German. The bar was quieter. In Barcelona it was not yet time for even pre-dinner drinks let alone dinner. Most people were at work until after seven, and then they would head for a local *tapas* bar before going home.

She hesitated at the entrance to the cocktail bar and looked round quickly for Ben. She saw him across the bar and stood for a moment to catch her breath. He sat in a corner with two other people. A young woman and an older man. The girl, dark-haired and olive-skinned, was laughing and looking down at papers in her hand. Ben was speaking close to her ear. Rosemary watched as the girl squealed suddenly and started to slap Ben vigorously with the papers still in her hand, loud with her delighted protests. She said something back to him, in Spanish, quickly and sure of herself, and Ben threw his head back and laughed in such a suddenly familiar way that Rosemary, standing nervously now by their table, was filled with a warm longing through her entire body.

He saw her, and the laugh became a smile. Standing up quickly, he put his hands towards her, unable to move round the small table to get to her, hemmed in between the two other people. 'Rosie! Rosie, you're here!' He pulled her off-balance and towards him, kissing her nose and mouth quickly and passionately. Rosemary saw the other man at the table stand up, smiling at her, the girl still seated, looked surprised. Rosemary realized they were English, and recognized her. 'Darling.' Ben held onto her hands. 'This is Gerry. He's in the film. And this is Betsy. She *is* the film. She's the runner.'

The girl smiled now. *Nervous*, thought Rosemary. Introductions over, Ben waved towards the bar and called something in Spanish.

'I've ordered champagne,' he said. 'The Spanish one is very good,' and sitting down again, pulled her round Gerry to squeeze her in beside himself. He kept his arm round her shoulders, touching her neck and her hair.

Gerry said, 'Sorry if I seemed surprised at the introductions, dear lady.' Rosemary recognized him now, old-fashioned charm and patronizing manner familiar on several television plays. He went on, 'All young Ben said was that he was expecting Rosemary. No mention of Downey. Very quiet about that.'

Betsy said, 'I'd better go. Give everyone else their times for tomorrow.' She stood up, dropping schedules and call sheets onto the floor. She bent and fumbled for them under the table.

Ben said, 'Stay and have some champagne.'

The girl, upright now, papers rescued, blushed and muttered, 'Thanks, but I'd better not. The car'll pick you up at seven. From the lobby.' And she scuttled away, falling briefly against a passing waiter and saying her apologies in Spanish before disappearing.

Rosemary frowned momentarily. She recognized Betsy's embarrassment and that look of a frightened rabbit. Young enough to have a crush on someone unobtainable. Someone like Ben, but he didn't watch her go, too busy as he was stroking Rosemary's arm and holding her hand.

'Stay and have a drink Gerry!' Ben was expansive in his obvious delight at seeing her. She relaxed and felt again the excitement and joy of being with him.

Gerry stayed, unable to resist Ben's invitation, and a very noticeable interest in the relationship taking place before his eyes.

'This is my lady,' Ben had said when he had introduced her, and Rosemary was glad she hadn't seen what must have been the forlorn look on Betsy's face.

'I thought Betsy was Spanish?' she asked him later, trying to see some reaction in his expression at the mention of the young girl's name. But Ben, busy ordering dinner for them both, scarcely looked up from the menu.

'She's *half*-Spanish. Born in England. D'you want fish or meat my darling?'

'I want *you*.' Her voice, bold now with new-found security, brought his face up towards her.

He smiled. 'I'm all yours Rosie.'

Chapter Ten

And all hers he was, that first night in Barcelona. Emotionally exhausted as she was with the sheer anticipation of sensual pleasure, she toyed with the food he'd ordered and left the wine. She wanted her mind alert to savour each moment of passion that waited for her in that too-small Spanish bed at the end of a long hotel corridor. Her body was his, her mind possessed with the longing to say, 'I love you Ben Morrison.' But later that night, full of him at last, she lost the courage. Afraid he would draw back, take fright. So she fell asleep in his arms feeling young and wanted and beautiful – and out of control.

He had left when she was merely stirring the next morning, kissing her on lips closed firmly against morning breath.

She woke again at eight and saw the crumpled and empty place beside her, a note on the pillow, and the smell of the cologne she had bought him lingering still. She sat up to read the note, scribbled almost illegibly in pencil and in haste on the hotel telephone pad.

'Rosie, the bad news is we're scheduled until eight tonight. The good news is I have tomorrow and the next day free. Have a great day. See you later. P.S. you look beautiful in your morning face.'

She read it three times, and finding nothing between the lines, she folded it and put it in her handbag. He'd been in a hurry for God's sake, what was the man supposed to do?

At last, later than she could ever remember lying in bed, she pulled herself into the shower and let the water pound on her face and body until she was completely awake and the smell of their love-making driven reluctantly from her skin.

She remembered now the restaurant of the night before, and the way she had sat back with contentment once again and let Ben take control. It came to her suddenly while she dried her hair, that he had read and ordered from the Spanish written menu with no difficulty, his command of the language sounding perfect to her untutored ears. She smiled to herself, and wondered how many more surprising talents he would display before she grew bored.

Outside, on the streets of Barcelona, the sun shone.

At breakfast the waiter suggested many places of interest for someone new to Spain. Where to eat, places to take coffee, and which bars it was safe for her to visit. The weather was warm, and the solitary day ahead of her with Ben to look forward to at the end of it beckoned invitingly.

Ignoring the yellow-and-black taxi cabs touting for business, she made her way on foot down almost the whole length of Las Ramblas, taking the breakfast waiter's advice. She behaved like any other tourist. No-one recognized her, nobody asked for her autograph; she was merely a woman, like millions of others, filling the hours before her lover came home.

Somewhere along the way she came across a market, and the smell of food and the lunchtime emptiness of her stomach drove her inside. She bought sliced salami and ate it out of the paper bag, standing at a counter drinking strong black coffee. She drank a glass of rough red wine in a dark little bar the same waiter had recommended, and it reminded her of Paris. *One day*, she promised herself, *I'll take Ben there, to the most romantic city in the world. If he sticks around that long.*

In the afternoon, the film in her camera finished for

now, she sat on the terrace of the restaurant of a big department store that overlooked the Plaza de Catalunya and drank coffee and watched the crowded streets in the square below. She smoked, and lingered and, mesmerized by the lilting abrasiveness of the Spanish voices, she dwelt on Ben, and all the possibilities that could be theirs if he fell in love with her.

It was childish, and she knew it. But the sun, and being so far from everything that made her sensible, had made her silly instead. Time enough for practicality when she got home. Now it was a holiday romance that, like all such affairs, momentarily convinced her it would last for ever. She watched the hands of her watch, counting the hours, the minutes, almost the seconds, as they crawled towards eight o'clock and the taste and the feel of the man that obsessed her would belong to her once more. Her skin tingled at the memory of him. Thinking of the days ahead when she would have him and Barcelona and anonymity, and all those nights that would be theirs to share. Alone in this addictively indestructible bubble.

At six, she was back at the hotel and trying to decide what to wear that evening. The choice was limited. She had never quite managed to shop for clothes that travelled well, and most of them arrived at their destinations with 'more wrinkles than prunes', as Frances had once remarked, eyeing her friend hanging the dishevelled garments up on the less-than-perfect hotel hangers that were always found in holiday wardrobes.

'You always look so pressed,' Rosemary had moaned at the time.

'Just practice, sweet face,' her friend had answered. 'My love life is spent in hotels, and who has time to hang things up at times like those?'

She chose at last a black chiffon silk dress that looked passably uncreased and one that Ella had said made her 'look sexy'. She was unable to choose for Ben, having no idea of his taste in anything except sex and food. Her day had been so perfect so far that she was disinclined to brave the Catalan housekeeper and request an iron. Maybe Ben would translate for her tomorrow. She touched herself with the expensive perfume she had bought in the Duty-Free: '1000', by Patou. This she would now always keep for him, and knowing where he would touch her that night, there she lingered with the spray.

The telephone by the bed rang and she went across to answer it. A girl from reception said, 'Señora Morrison?'

Rosemary hesitated to work out the 'Señora'. Then, tentatively, 'Yes?'

'Señor Morrison left a message. He is here early now. Eight o'clock.'

Rosemary looked at her watch. It was half-past seven. 'Thank you. I'm to expect him at eight? Is that correct?'

'Si, gracias.'

'Gracias.' Rosemary replaced the receiver and smiled at her reflection in the mirror. Now who did they think she was exactly? His wife or, God forbid, his mother? Aah well. Glossing her lips and checking herself from every angle, she was aware she liked the feeling of belonging. She pulled her stomach in and remembered, with a degree of sadness, the youthful days when that particular part of her anatomy was concave without any effort. Turning from the mirror, she picked up her handbag, left the room and made her way to the lift.

Stopping at the ground level, she narrowly missed colliding with Betsy getting in. The girl was crying, visibly, but trying to stifle dry sounds. 'Are you OK?' Rosemary put her hand out anxiously to touch her arm, but Betsy turned her head away, and pressed a button for the lift to ascend. The door closed before Rosemary could say any more. She stood there rather foolishly for a moment, and then walked towards the lobby.

Ben was standing at the reception desk, talking on the phone. He raised one hand when he saw her and pointed towards the bar. She missed his usual smile and felt strangely and irrationally uncomfortable.

Gerry stood in front of her, a glass of wine in his hand. 'Dear lady, come and join me. I'm in the chair. What would you like?'

'I'm in Spain, so I guess it's about time I had a sherry.' Rosemary began to concentrate on Gerry's loud actor's voice telling her about the horrifying delights of the day's filming. Ben arrived at her side, carrying a rather battered and well pencilled script in his hand, and frowning. He bent and kissed her on the cheek absent-mindedly.

'All right Rosie?' Before she could greet him in any way he went on. 'I'll put my script upstairs and have a shower. Wait for me here. Have you got the key?'

She handed it to him. 'Are you OK Ben?'

He nodded and patted her on the arm. 'Gerry, be a love and order me a lager. I'll not be long. Entertain Rosie for me.'

'Certainly dear boy. Very pleasant task.'

And Ben disappeared. Walking quickly, head down, the frown still heavy on his brows.

Forcing herself to stop watching and pondering his mood and quick departure, she turned and smiled at Gerry. Artificial in her well brought-up charm, wanting only Ben's company at this moment. 'A bad day then Gerry? For everyone?'

'Ben was as controlled as ever, dear lady, a joy to work with. No, no, just tension with a less than able director, and a rather dramatic crew. The Spanish brigade, I mean, of course.' He laughed. Leaning towards her as if about to impart some enormous secret, he lowered his voice, 'The little runner, my dear. Betsy somebody-or-other. In tears all day. Very difficult to work without some sort of self-control from assistants.' He drained his glass and put his arm up to attract the attention of the barman. 'More sherry, dear lady?'

Rosemary shook her head, covering her glass with her hand. She said, 'Is Betsy ill? I bumped into her a moment ago. She seemed upset then.'

Gerry shrugged. 'Obviously man trouble, or should I say *boy*?' He laughed. 'She's a child, my dear. A mere child. Barely twenty-two. Remember the misery we put ourselves through at that age? She'll get over it. Just wish we didn't all have to share it with her, whatever it is.' He straightened up and raised his voice. 'Always happens, my dear, when you're filming. Everyone gets bored and sleeps together. Now then, where's young Ben going to whip you away to tonight?'

The traumas of Betsy were dismissed, and Rosemary shrugged them away. None of her business. As much as she enjoyed gossip, it was always more enjoyable to delve into in the company of women. Men seldom seemed interested enough unless they were gay or personally involved. Frances said once, during a particularly long and talkative ladies only lunch, 'The exquisite selfishness of the male manifests itself in a total disinterest in other people and their affairs.' Rosemary had questioned the assumption, remembering her gay friends, but Frances had gone on, 'Believe it my angel.'

Ben joined them after thirty minutes, and Rosemary was relieved to see that he was now smiling. He kissed her hand and held onto her fingers, gently pulling her towards him. 'I missed you,' he murmured, while Gerry turned away and ordered him the lager.

She smiled up at him and touched his cheek. 'Bad day?' she asked. 'Gerry's been telling me some tempers got frayed.'

Ben didn't answer but turned instead to pick up his drink and raise his glass to Gerry.

They dined later at a fish restaurant not far from the hotel.

'Shall I order?' Ben asked, holding her hand across the table.

'Where did you learn such perfect Spanish?' she asked, when the wine had been presented and served, and they were waiting for their first course.

'It's Catalan I speak,' he said, and turned his head across the restaurant to watch some people arriving and settling.

'All right,' Rosemary was amused. 'Where did you learn Catalan?'

He turned back to her and looked down at the glass in his hand. What had been merely a conversational remark had suddenly become important in the pause that followed. 'My mother's from Catalonia. My father's English.'

Rosemary watched his face settle into an expression she had noticed before, and one she found totally unreadable, bordering on blankness, as it seemed. 'Are they still alive?' she asked, wondering briefly if the mention of his parents conjured up some tragic memory, so tight were the muscles now in his face and neck.

Ben said, 'They live in Spain. My mother came back to take care of my grandmother when she was dying three years ago, and they never returned to England.' It was the first time he had mentioned any part of his family.

She said quickly, not wanting to lose his unusual openness, 'Whereabouts in Spain? Will you get to see them while you're here?'

Ben poured more wine. She waited. It would be unwise to push.

'They're here.'

Rosemary stared at him, slow to understand. 'D'you mean they actually live in Barcelona?'

'The suburbs. Badalona.'

'Have you seen them yet?'

'No.'

'Don't you get on?'

He looked carefully at her, 'D'you want to meet them?'

Thrown now, she laughed. 'I don't know, Ben. Well, yes, if you like. Oh dear, you've taken me by surprise. Have you been in touch? Why the mystery?'

He said, 'My mother phoned the hotel tonight. I did an interview with a local journalist and she read it in the paper.'

Questions filled her mind, but the look in his eyes held no encouragement. She remembered him leaning over the reception desk in the hotel, talking into the phone. Unsmiling, he watched her intensely now from under his eyebrows.

'Don't you want to talk about them?' she asked, aware that she was being gentle, as if getting a secret from a child.

'No,' he said. 'I want to have dinner and take you to bed.'

Knowing she was beaten for the moment, she shrugged. 'All right.' She took his hand, kissed it, and watched the confidence come back into his eyes. 'All right,' she said again.

The waiter placed fish soup in front of them and Ben, relieved at her sensitivity, started to ask about her day.

The questions that filled Rosemary's mind that night at dinner were not asked. And Ben didn't mention his parents or the possibility of her meeting them again during the entire meal. She waited for an opening, but he gave nothing away. Her curiosity became a hunger. She had asked him about Betsy at one point during the evening. 'She looked a little emotionally battered,' she said.

Ben shrugged. 'She's over-dramatic.'

'Is it man trouble?'

'Who knows? Who the hell cares? Don't get involved.'

'You sound like Ella.' She laughed across at him.

'How dare you,' he joked. 'I've not mentioned "fuck" all evening!'

'Now *you* sound like Frances,' she retorted. They touched each other, hands across the dessert, filling her with a hunger not to be quenched by the food on her plate.

'I wanted to take you to a little bar I know, but I think I want you more,' he said. 'Let's go.' He paid the bill, not allowing her to argue, and they took a taxi back to the hotel and the yielding Spanish bed.

Chapter Eleven

They awoke late to overcast skies the following morning. Ben ordered breakfast and coffee on room service, and they stayed in bed, listening to the rain against the window and then laughing as he translated the newspaper to her over the croissants and teased her about her Spanish accent. The fallen crumbs from their breakfast eventually drove them uncomfortably from the bed and into the shower.

Wrapped in towels, she said, 'What shall I wear? Where are we going?'

He was trimming his moustache and he looked at her through the mirror in front of him. 'What time is it, Rosie?'

She looked at her watch, abandoned on the bedside table during the night's love-making. 'Eleven-thirty.'

'*Tapas* time.'

'Sex over,' she said, 'now it's food.'

'So what's new?' He grinned at her.

'I'll wear my track-suit.' She turned away and began to dress. 'If we go on like this it'll soon be the only thing that will fit me!'

They had coffee downstairs in the hotel. She saw Betsy come in behind Ben's back and sit alone in a corner. She looked miserable still. Rosemary waved to her, and the girl raised one hand in recognition.

Ben said, 'Who are you waving at?' and turned to look.

'Shall I ask her to join us?' Rosemary asked.

'No. We'll never get away. D'you want a drink?'

She looked at him. 'Too early for me. I don't have the Spanish stamina.' There was a feeling that affected the hairs on the back of her neck that she couldn't quite place.

They drank their coffee and silence fell between them. Ben read his paper, his face hidden, and Rosemary cast glances over his shoulder at Betsy who sat with her head back against her chair, her eyes closed, the coffee in front of her untouched. Irrationally and suddenly Rosemary felt depressed.

Ben said eventually, looking at his watch, 'Let's go and eat. Are you hungry?'

'Yes,' she said, the lie coming easily to please him.

They passed Betsy on the way out. Her eyes touched briefly on Rosemary and settled with unmistakable misery on Ben. And then Rosemary knew what the feeling at the back of her neck had been. Only another woman would have recognized and acknowledged that look in Betsy's eyes.

Ben said, 'Hi Betsy. OK?' He had stopped his journey to the lobby and Rosemary closed the gap between them, her hand coming up to touch his arm, conscious of the possessive quality of her action.

Betsy said, 'Hi. I'm fine. Going somewhere nice?'

'It's raining,' Rosemary said unnecessarily, wanting to break the invisible but atmospheric thread that kept the other two looking at each other.

Betsy glanced at her and smiled weakly. 'Some of us are going to the movies. Busman's holiday on our day off.' Her eyes shifted back to Ben. 'Shall we all meet up later?' she asked.

Ben said, 'Where'll you be?'

'In the bar. About eight?'

'OK. Might see you. Have a good day.' And he bent to kiss the young girl's cheek, his hand holding onto Rosemary, keeping her rooted to the spot, her discomfort giving way to a feeling of nausea.

They got a taxi to a bar that Ben seemed to know. It was full of locals; all men. He ordered what seemed an enormous amount of different dishes, and they sat in a corner, high on stools around a table just big enough for two. The air was thick with smoke and conversation. The wine he'd ordered was red, and Rosemary drank her first glass too quickly, hoping to relax herself out of her misery.

Ben seemed to notice no change in her demeanour. He was confident, cajoling her to try each dish, refusing to acknowledge her lack of appetite. She had no desire for anything except an explanation from him of something nebulous she felt, but couldn't understand enough to put into words. He remained his charming self, more than usual. Or so it seemed. Was that her imagination? She remembered the way he had held her hand as he bent to kiss Betsy. Who was he trying to placate? Her or the girl? Either way it confused her, Betsy as well, if the look in her eyes as they departed was anything to go by.

Over coffee Ben said, 'Shall we go to Badalona this afternoon?'

She had forgotten his parents. 'I'm not dressed,' she said.

Ben threw his head back and laughed. 'Oh Rosie I do love you. You're so middle-class.'

'Do you?' she said.

'Do I what?'

'Love me.'

He smiled at her. 'I must do. How else could I put up with your out-dated sense of propriety?'

She said, 'Have you slept with Betsy?' She was shaking as she asked the question, not wanting the answer, but unable to face the rest of the day without it.

He stared at her.

'No-one said anything,' she said hastily. 'I just know.'

'It's not important,' he said.

'What isn't?' He'd confused her again.

'Sleeping with Betsy. It's not important.' He sounded irritable.

'It is to me.'

'Why?' he said, drinking his wine.

'What d'you mean? Why is it important to me, or why isn't it important you slept with Betsy?'

'Same thing.' He shrugged, and glanced away from her for a moment. Then he said, 'D'you want coffee?'

'Is that all I'm getting?' she asked, feeling a certain hysteria creeping into her voice.

'You can have more wine as well if you like Rosie,' he joked, laughing at her anger. She felt she was beginning to lose touch with her own sense of reality. He leaned across the small formica surface of the table and took her shaking hand in both of his. Gentle now, he said quickly, as if to bring her loud voice down to his level, 'Betsy's not important.'

'I don't understand. Why did you sleep with her?'

'Why not? Now *I* don't understand. Why are you in such a state? For Christ's sake Rosie, why the fucking questions? You sound like a wife.' He dropped her hand as his anger took over, but his voice, intense and harsh, remained low.

She felt foolish, cornered, unable to explain her confusion and unhappiness.

He stood up and sighed. 'Women,' he muttered.

'I want to go home,' she whispered. 'I want to go home.' No-one in the bar around them even glanced in their direction. 'You said, "I love you Rosie",' she whispered.

He sat down again. He touched her face and quite suddenly she began to cry. Like Betsy. Like a child. Like a silly girl. *Make it better Ben*, she thought, as the tears rolled silently down her cheeks in that noisy,

polluted *tapas* bar on a rainy afternoon in Barcelona.
'Make it better Ben,' she whispered out loud. He went
on stroking her cheek and watched her cry. No-one
looked at them. They were isolated in their embarrassment. An island for two. A sea of noisy conversation
battering at their little drama.

'Don't Rosie,' he said at last. He waited until the tears
stopped, then he leaned across to wipe the smudges of
mascara from under her eyes. 'Why d'you women wear
that stuff?' he said.

'Let me do it.' She pushed his hand away and found
mirror and tissues in her handbag.

He said, 'I didn't realize you'd be so upset. I didn't
promise to be faithful did I? How did we get to that point
so quickly?'

Her voice steady at last, she said, 'I apologize. I'm
behaving appallingly. I told you, I haven't had an affair
for years. I'm out of practice. Especially with being in
love.'

'*Are* you in love Rosie?' He smiled across at her.

'Yes.' She put her compact away and took a deep
breath. 'Right,' she said, 'where to now?'

'You won't go home will you?' Ben asked.

'No, I won't, unless that's what you want?'

'And I'll be good,' he said, putting on a silly face. They
both stood. 'Badalona?' he said.

'God yes, I'd forgotten.' She took another deep breath.
Then, looking up at him as they waited outside the bar
for a cab, sheltering from the rain under a shop awning,
'Who am I, if your parents ask?'

'You're just Rosie. The rest will be obvious. There's
no-one else. Believe me.' He kissed the top of her hair,
damp from the rain and put his hand on the back of
her neck as they got into a cab.

She asked no more questions, not even of herself.
She wanted him, it seemed, even more than her own

self-esteem. Behaving like Betsy could have scared him away. It had been her sensibility that had first attracted him. The ugliness of the incident had been her fault. She had much to learn.

Letting him hold her close in the back of the rattling cab, feeling his mouth on her hair, his fingers stroking her back and shoulders, she forgave him and his youth. Promising herself she would never again let him see her so vulnerable and exposed, she didn't stop to understand how much he'd enjoyed the whole performance.

She stood by his side and waited for the blue-painted front door of his parents' sixth-floor apartment to open and reveal his background to her. They stood in silence and she felt his tension, saw the familiar frown on his face, that look of almost blank misery or anger that fell on him at moments of confusion, or was it panic? The rain splashed indiscriminately onto six floors of geranium-filled balconies, uniform and suburban.

'Municipal flats?' asked Rosemary, looking around her.

Ben shook his head. 'They bought it two years ago. Depressing, isn't it?'

The blue door opened. 'Hello Dad.' Ben smiled at the man standing in front of them in shirt sleeves, one hand on the open door, plaid slippers on his feet. Tall as Ben, and thin, his eyes peered through reading glasses, then lit up at the sight of his son.

'Ben my boy, how wonderful to see you! Come in, come in. Your mother's resting. We expected you later. But this is wonderful. Come in, come in.' He pulled his son into the narrow hall and Rosemary followed awkwardly. The door closed behind her, and the two men hugged, kissing each other on both cheeks, smiling, his father removing his spectacles, his eyes damp with pleasure.

'This is Rosemary.' Ben turned and pulled her forward.

'With a friend as well my boy? What a surprise. Wonderful. Hello Rosemary. Come through, come through. I'll wake your mother.' He pushed, pulled, coaxed them through into an austere and square, formal-looking room, furniture big and dark, looming in a space too large for the small windows, the layered blinds closed against the grey skies outside. The room smelt of polish. 'Sit down my dear.'

Rosemary sat on the dark leather couch, the cushions, yellow and plump in each corner, untouchable in their neatness, forced her down into the very centre. Ben pushed her over as he lowered himself beside her. 'Move over,' he hissed, 'I know it's difficult to believe, but you can sit down on it.'

His father had left the room to go and rouse his wife. Rosemary looked around her. She said, 'It's so dark in here.'

Ben got up and went to open the blinds. 'My mother believes the smallest amount of sun fades the carpet.'

'Good God,' Rosemary whispered. She would have loved to smoke, but no ashtray was present in the room. There was a glass coffee table in front of her, a newspaper, obviously discarded with haste when the doorbell had rung, lay beside a short glass vase that held a bunch of plastic roses, dust-free, and standing, unbelievably, in water. 'Good God,' Rosemary said again.

Ben turned from the windows and laughed. His father came back into the room. He had put on a pale blue, hand-knitted cardigan, his name, 'Jack', embroidered in a darker blue on the pocket. He said, smiling, standing close to Ben, one hand holding his son's arm, 'Rosemary my dear, would you like some coffee?'

'Thank you. Yes. Thank you Mr Morrison.'

'Call me Jack.' He turned to Ben. 'Your mother's coming. She's getting dressed.'

Ben said, 'Is she unwell?'

'No. Oh no son. *Siesta*. You forget.'

'Christ yes. Sorry Dad.' Ben looked at his watch. It was three-thirty. 'Open some wine Dad.'

Jack Morrison looked doubtful. 'Well, I don't know son, your mother—'

'Jack Morrison, open some wine. My son is here.' The woman's voice from the doorway was loud and confident, the accent heavy. It was all Rosemary could do not to stand up.

Ben's mother stayed where she was, framed by the light behind her, which had been switched on in the dark and window-less hallway. A large and imposing, dark-haired woman, brows and eyes like Ben's, a mouth thin and tight, discontent etched deep into even her smile as she looked at her son. He moved across to her. They kissed. Tension showed visibly with every movement that Ben made.

He said, 'Hello Mum.' Rosemary met the woman's eyes over Ben's shoulder as he bent to kiss his mother. Imposing as she had seemed at first sight, she was smaller in height than Rosemary had at first presumed. In every other detail, every physical attribute, Ben could only have been *her* son. He said, 'This is Rosemary, Mum.'

'Oh this is nice, he seldom brings friends.' Magdalena Morrison (Rosemary had seen the name embroidered on the footstool by the electric fire and assumed that it could only be the lady of the house) walked majestically towards Rosemary and the couch. Only three steps, and it was like a parade. Unable to stop herself, Rosemary stood up, feeling foolishly like a teenage acquaintance of this awesome, broad-hipped lady's son. She put out her hand.

'Mrs Morrison. How nice to meet you. You have a lovely home.'

The banality of the remark was out before she could stop herself. She cursed her upbringing. Behind his mother Ben smirked. And to her horror, Rosemary blushed. Magdalena's smile widened at the compliment. Rosemary had said the right thing, and found herself being kissed formally on both cheeks. She thought, *I prefer the Italians when they kiss. At least they seem spontaneous.*

Jack Morrison had brought in some red wine and carefully placed a glass each in front of them on small, silver-plated coasters. The four of them sat. The room was dark with the rain outside. Magdalena held court, one hand reaching across to Ben. She had placed herself beside Rosemary and both women sat upright, one with terror, the other with territorial confidence.

Biscuits and fancy cakes were brought in by Jack. Small plates were given out, a laced paper napkin folded tidily on each one.

'Mum we've eaten,' Ben groaned.

He and his parents began to converse in Spanish, their voices strident, their laughs brisk and short-lived. Discomfort sat heavily in the air, and as if a bad charade was being played out for her benefit, Rosemary felt embarrassed, out of place, unable to find any sort of composure. So she ate, almond-scented biscuits, each one a mouthful, eaten quickly, afraid the crumbs would drop onto the spotless coffee table. *My God*, she thought, *she's worse than my mother. Shit, she's worse than me.*

At last Ben's mother turned and spoke in English. 'You are in the film work with my son, Rosemary?' Her eyes, as fathomless as Ben's, rested without passion on her nervous guest.

'No, no, Mrs Morrison.'

'Please call me Magdalena.'

'Magdalena. Thank you. No, I'm, I'm—'

Ben said, 'She's come to see me.'

His mother turned to him. 'But I know Rosemary's face. She is an actress? Yes?'

'No, Mum. She has a show on television in England. You probably remember her.'

Magdalena turned back and stared at Rosemary. 'Yes, yes. Father, you remember?' She prodded Rosemary and threw the remark across to her husband.

Ben's parents stared curiously at her. Then Jack said, 'Of course. We remember. Well, well. A celebrity in our midst.'

Ben groaned, 'Christ. Me and my big mouth. They'll have the neighbours in in a minute.' Rosemary laughed, relieved to be part of the group again. Jack poured more wine.

Magdalena said, 'You are on holiday, then, Rosemary?'

'Yes.'

'Where are you staying? Somewhere nice?'

Rosemary glanced across at Ben who had picked up the discarded newspaper from the table in front of him. He didn't look up. His body language said, quite plainly, *you sort it out. I can't be bothered.*

She said, 'I'm at Ben's hotel.'

There was a pause then Magdalena turned to her son. 'How is Gill?'

Ben looked up at his mother and smiled grimly. 'She's fine.'

Mother and son stared at each other. Then the woman spoke again. 'And the boy?'

The pause was longer this time and Rosemary watched Ben's face. He said, 'He's fine too, Mother. Why don't you phone them some time and ask for yourself?' He spoke through gritted teeth and Rosemary felt a scream beginning to build within her.

Magdalena turned to her again. 'You have met his boy? My grandson?'

Rosemary lifted her chin and stared thoughtfully at the only slightly older woman. The mother of this man she had fallen so drastically in love with. The two women's faces held nothing but challenge. 'No,' said Rosemary, 'but Ben's told me all about him. I look forward to meeting him soon.' She had won that round by mustering up the last remnants of a dignity which seemed to be getting buried deeper every day. Ben's look showed pride when it settled on her, but she turned away from him, feeling only a desire to slap him hard. To throw her into a situation as grotesque as this was unforgivable. Twice in one day she had been confronted by something about him that other people had thrown at her. First Betsy, with her lost lovesick eyes, and now this. Not just Gill he lives or lived with. Now she learns he has a son. Was he totally unable to tell her anything himself? Had he brought her here on purpose, knowing this was a way to lay his past in front of her?

They stayed until half-past five in that coldly clean apartment, and when Ben ran out of conversation and the desire to even try, he suggested they made their way back to the hotel. The four of them stood awkwardly at the front door – Ben and Rosemary outside and his parents pushing against each other as they kissed him 'goodbye'.

'Have a pleasant holiday Rosemary,' Jack kissed her cheek and shook her hand at the same time. 'Will we see you again?'

'No Mr Morrison, I'm going home soon. But thanks for your hospitality. It was nice to meet you. Both of you.'

The women nodded at each other, wary, knowing the small battle that had ploughed its way through the afternoon. 'Come back and see us, son.' Magdalena held tightly to Ben's arm, tears springing suddenly down her cheeks. 'Come back soon.'

'I'll phone Mum. OK?'

Ben and Rosemary walked in silence down six flights of concrete stairs, unable to summon the elevator, which was stuck somewhere between floors. Ben slouched ahead.

She followed, shivering against the rain when it caught her unawares on the open corners of the stairway. They had phoned for a cab and it was waiting for them.

'Comtes de Barcelona,' Ben said, and held the door for her.

They rode back in silence. Ben stared morosely out of the window. Rosemary got angrier and angrier. He said, 'Are you mad at me?'

'What d'you think?'

'I think you're furious.'

'Then why ask?'

Still not looking at her, he said, 'I'm sorry.'

'Are you? Isn't it what you intended? You write the script and we all perform for you.'

He turned and tried to take her hand. 'She knows Gill and I are finished. I told her. But she won't accept it. There's my son you see—'

'Ben, for Christ's sake, why didn't you tell me you had a son? Why make such a fool of me? Why do you insist on being such a mystery?' She pulled her hand away, irritated with his inability to explain himself and angry with herself for even trying to reason with him. Then, 'Tell me about your son.'

'He's four years old. His name is James. That's all.'

'What does Gill do?'

He hesitated, and then quickly, as if it had just occurred to him, 'She's a teacher.'

'What d'you intend to do?'

'I don't know.'

She stared at him. He looked so miserable and young that she put out her hand by instinct and touched him. 'God Ben, you're impossible. I don't know where I am with you. But I don't want to go home and behave like a spoilt girl. I want to enjoy my holiday.'

He smiled. 'You were great.'

'With your mother?'

'Yes. With my mother. Isn't she monstrous?'

'Where the hell did you come from amongst all that?'

He shrugged. 'Dad's OK. Just scared.'

'And *very* clean.'

He laughed, the way his mother had laughed, and Rosemary shuddered involuntarily. 'D'you hate her?' she asked, drawn with compassion to his obvious vulnerability now laid before her.

'Probably. She's a monster, you know. Couldn't you tell?'

She said nothing, unable to find the absolute ruthlessness to agree with him.

He said, 'I have a half-sister. My father's daughter by his first marriage.'

'Really? At home?'

'No.' A silence fell and then he said, 'My mother turned her out of the house when she was seventeen because she was pregnant. We've never seen her since. Her name is Janine.'

The cab deposited them at the hotel and they ran for cover and into the reception. 'Shall we have a drink?' Ben suggested. 'I'm going to shower and change.'

They ordered wine on room service, changed into towelling dressing-gowns and sat awkwardly in the bedroom, waiting for their drinks to arrive. Unable to touch each other, they stayed silent until the floor waiter had pocketed his tip and left them alone. 'Drink to us?' said Ben, still unsure. His hair, damp from the shower, hung untidily onto his forehead, his eyes begging for reassurance.

'To us,' she said. 'If you're sure that's what you want.'

'What are you getting out of this affair Rosie?'

'Everything I've never had, and nothing I ever thought I wanted.'

He laughed then and pulled her towards him. 'Are you in love with me Rosie?' he asked.

'Yes. Are you in love with—?'

'You'll be hurt,' he said, before she finished the question.

'I'll risk it.' In her foolishness she felt more confident than she had for ages. Just knowing more about him had made him more accessible. 'Has your father seen her since?' She asked the question suddenly, lying in his arms, close and without passion for once.

'Seen who? Janine?'

She nodded.

'I've never asked. She'd be forty now. We never talk about it. Not even my mother.'

'Poor Janine.' She put her hand up to stroke the hair from his eyes.

'Poor Dad.'

'Poor Ben.' She reached again to touch his cheek, his evening beard was beginning to show. 'I love you Ben.'

'Let's enjoy ourselves. No more paternal visits,' he said.

'OK.' She shivered. 'What an awful day it's been.'

'Wednesdays are always pissers. We used to have woodwork at school.' He smiled at his memory. 'I hated woodwork.'

She groaned. 'We had needlework.'

'Thursday'll be good.'

'That was country-dancing day,' she said. 'Only slightly better.'

Chapter Twelve

They stayed alone that Wednesday evening, avoiding the bar and the film crew. They ate much later in a nearby restaurant. Ben was relaxed now, once more his totally confident self. Rosemary still fought with her doubts about him, but decided to enjoy the rest of the week, determined, if possible, to keep the affair light-hearted.

He talked at length about his mother and eventually, to her relief, about his son, James, and his five-year affair with Gill. He had left home suddenly at the age of sixteen, to live in a squat with friends from the Catholic school he had attended since he was eleven. His fights with his mother had been horrific at the time, and his memory was strong about the scenes that had taken place years previously with his young, pregnant half-sister. His father's inability to put his foot down had eventually stirred Ben into a violent streak which led to him smashing his way through his parents' obsessively neat North London home, leaving the debris behind and running away. He'd been just two months past his sixteenth birthday. His friends from school, two other boys and a girl, had joined him by getting into a boarded-up old mansion flat in Albany Street. And he had felt reasonably in control of his young life for the first time.

His mother was horrified to discover that, in law, she had no power to get him home. Seldom attending classes, he was eventually expelled from school and signed on as unemployed. He smoked a little grass, when he could get hold of any spare cash, and a few times he had tried cocaine, but he had never been tempted by heroin. 'Too much of the survival instinct in me, I guess,' he said to Rosemary, now listening with open-mouthed amazement to his story. Her own life had been so orderly and what could only be called 'well-mannered' by comparison.

'How did you ever get into acting?' she asked.

'Joined a youth club. Not many left these days. Thatcher government put paid to that. God knows where I could have ended up.'

'Did you work?'

'In bars. Odd jobs. More of those around in those days as well.' Ben waved his hand for the bill.

'Go on. What about your parents? How did you, well, start talking again?'

'Youth club leader. I auditioned for drama school. Got a scholarship. My O levels hadn't been that bad and he persuaded me eventually to take at least one A level at night school.' Ben paused, then, 'I had to go home when I went to college. Couldn't afford anything else. I was nearly nineteen by that time.'

'Did your mother welcome you with open arms?'

Ben laughed. 'Afraid so. I was once more in her power. Me *and* my father. Two years I had of bowing to her every whim. Made more bearable, I must admit, because of college. Acting was my salvation, you might say. God I hated her. All those dreadful hand-knitted jumpers she made me wear. I'd take them off on the Tube. Preferred to shiver even in the heart of winter. They were all pale blue and yellow, and I was big in those days.'

'Fat?' asked Rosemary, surprised.

'Fat. Believe me. I was shaped like an avocado. My mother is relentless with her cooking. I think she works on the theory that if she makes everyone fatter than her, she'll look dainty.'

Rosemary burst out laughing. 'Your Dad's thin.'

'Dad's sick. Has been for years. He has an ulcer.'

'Oh.'

He took her hand across the table, taking a cigarette away from her and stubbing it out into the ashtray. 'You smoke too much,' he smiled at her.

'I only just started again.'

'Why?'

Rosemary shrugged, not wanting to explain the turmoil he had caused in her life.

'What about Gill? Will you tell me about it?'

Ben looked down at his empty coffee cup and motioned to the waiter for refills. He held on tight to Rosemary's hand. 'You ask too many questions.'

Rosemary said, 'Do I have no right to? What is this affair? I don't think I want to make love with a man who's sleeping around. Not these days.'

'You and I work. Isn't that all that matters?' he asked.

'Betsy?'

'It just happened.' He leaned closer to her. 'Listen. You have to take me or leave me. I'm besotted with you, I want to be with you when I can but I can't and won't promise anything else. Rosie darling, I'm only coming this way once.'

She tried to pull her hand away but he held onto her.

'Lighten up, Rosie. D'you want me?'

'Yes.'

'Then take me. This is all there is.'

'What about Gill?'

'It's been over for the last six months. I just need to move out. She's fine, but James is my son and that's my business. It won't affect you.'

'Oh Ben, I don't know, I'm not good at casual affairs.'

'Nothing casual about us. I'm yours. Believe me, trust me. Right now you're what I want. That needn't change.'

'Why me?'

'You asked that before.'

'Tell me again.'

'You're strong. You're different. You seem uncrushable.'

Rosemary fell silent, knowing the one thing she wasn't was uncrushable. The dilemma that was him sat before her like a challenge, and unable to resist the idea of changing him, she smiled across the table and succumbed. 'And you're impossible, Ben Morrison. I think what I have to do is make sure I'm enough for you.'

Ben smiled. 'Well now, there's a thought.'

They made their way back to the hotel at midnight and passed the bar on the way to the elevator.

'Nightcap,' Ben said.

'Everyone's in there,' remarked Rosemary. 'Will you cope?'

'Try me.'

They went in and Ben led her across to a group at one of the tables. Betsy was sitting in the middle of a small sofa between Gerry and a man that Rosemary learned was the second assistant. She said 'hello' to the director, two other actors and a middle-aged actress. The director, Robert, pulled two chairs across from an empty table beside them and Rosemary sat down. Ben disappeared to the bar with his order then came back to the table and sat beside her.

'They'll bring it over,' he said. 'Was it a good movie?'

'James Bond dubbed into Spanish, dear boy,' Gerry replied. 'I've seen better films. And Jessica slept through it.'

The middle-aged actress laughed. 'I always do.' She turned to Rosemary. 'You do when you get to our age don't you, darling? I'm useless after nine-thirty at night.'

'Mornings are better for me as well,' Rosemary smiled.

'Comes with the denture fixative and nostril hair,' said Jessica. The rest of the table groaned.

'Shut up Jess,' Robert pushed her sideways on her chair. 'You'll be wanting a zimmer next.'

'Funny you should bring that up.'

Rosemary watched Betsy, while Betsy watched Ben who stroked Rosemary's hand. They sat until almost one-thirty when, a little drunk, they all dispersed to various bedrooms, laughter and voices carrying down the hotel corridors.

Rosemary and Ben fell into each other's arms, too exhausted to do anything but sleep. Tomorrow was Thursday. 'Country-dancing day,' murmured Ben into her hair just before he drifted off.

The sun brought in Thursday, which meant they could wander and graze all day. In fact, do what most of the population of Barcelona seemed to do. Eating was without doubt the local pastime.

'If we work it right we could have five meals today,' Ben said over coffee in one of the local bars at about ten that morning.

Rosemary pushed away half her croissant. 'I'm going to be fat as a pig by the time I get home.'

'You're lovely,' he said, 'just the way you are. I like my ladies voluptuous.'

'Oh thanks.' Rosemary kicked him under the table.

'Ouch. Violent now are we? Is it the hangover?'

They wandered and took photographs of themselves and the architecture until almost noon and then, tired still from the late night, they fell into the nearest *tapas* bar.

'How do people eat like this? Do they all grow enormous in later life?' Rosemary asked. She remembered his mother.

'The sensible ones work it off.'

She looked at him. He was smiling. 'I think I'm asking for trouble,' she said, 'but OK, I'll buy it. How? How do they work it off?'

'Sex and conversation. Noisy and horny. That's the Spanish.'

'Which side of the family do you get that from?'

He put both hands out and pulled her towards him. They smiled long and hard at each other. 'Are you getting cheeky?' he whispered. 'Do you need putting to bed for the day?'

'I just lost my appetite for *tapas*, Ben Morrison.'

By eight o'clock on Friday morning he had left for filming. On the pillow beside her was a note with the address of the location. 'Get a cab and join me for lunch.'

She sat down at the telephone in the bedroom at ten that morning to make some phone calls.

'Franny? It's me.'

'Darling girl, are you having a wonderful time? I miss you.'

'On and off. Having a wonderful time, I mean.'

'Well now, you *could* ask for more I suppose. How's Ben?'

'He's well, and I'm eating too much.'

'That sounds ominous. When are you coming home?'

'I don't know. I must phone Michael. I think I have some radio dates next Tuesday. I'll be home Monday night if that's the case.'

'Shall I pick you up?'

'I'll let you know.'

'I need to talk to you.' Frances sounded serious, unlike her usual self.

'What about? Ben?'

'No, you idiot. There are other people around, you know.'

'Sorry. Is it you? Are you all right?'

'Yes. But I'm afraid I'm messing on my own doorstep. I doubt you'll approve.'

'Shit.'

'Exactly.'

'Darling, I'll phone you at the weekend. We'll talk when I get back.' Rosemary replaced the handset and immediately lifted it again to phone Michael.

'He's out of the office,' she was told.

'When am I working next week?' Rosemary asked his secretary. 'I know it's not like me, but I forgot my Filofax.'

Michael's secretary sounded surprised. 'No, it's not like you. Do you want me to phone Jennie and tell her to get in touch?'

'It'll be in Michael's diary,' Rosemary said. She waited while Sue put her on hold. 'The Dream of Olwen' flooded the telephone line, and she held it away from her ear. 'You're hosting a charity lunch in Reading on Wednesday,' said Sue eventually.

'Nothing on Tuesday?'

'Radio at five. Oh hell yes, Michael wanted to have lunch with you on Tuesday as well. Something about the new series.'

'I'll phone him tomorrow. I'm going out now. Try to walk off the three tons of food I've consumed since I've been here.'

Sue laughed. 'Enjoy,' and rang off.

Rosemary put on her trainers for the third consecutive morning and left the hotel to walk until lunchtime.

She arrived on the film set just after one-thirty, and everyone was already either eating or queueing at the large buffet table laid out with various salads. Ben was nowhere to be seen. The second assistant put one hand up to her across the open-sided large canvas marquee that was the lunch area. 'Rosemary, come and sit. I'll send someone to fetch Ben.' She made her way across to the large wooden table. He pulled a chair towards him with one outstretched foot, and introduced her to everyone who sat near. It was obvious that at least the English members of the crew recognized her.

'Hello Derek,' she sat next to the second assistant. 'I always feel such a sponger at these affairs. Not being a worker, that is.'

'Nonsense, I'll get someone to bring you food.'

'Just a salad.'

'Where the fuck's Betsy?' Derek shouted across to a young girl helping herself to a glass of what looked like sangria.

The girl looked up. 'She took food to Ben's trailer half-an-hour ago.'

'Fuck.' Derek stood up. 'Hold on Rosemary,' he said, 'I'll go get him.'

'No, don't – it's all right—' But Derek had already bounded across to one of the group of trailers a few yards from the marquee.

Jessica, sitting opposite her, smiled and Rosemary wondered if she'd only imagined the embarrassment in the look that the woman shot across to her. Rosemary found herself unable to make any sort of conversation. It seemed suddenly to her that everyone was avoiding her eyes; conversation tumbled over itself all around her. Her mouth felt dry but she longed for a cigarette. 'D'you mind if I smoke?' she said.

Jessica leaned across and offered her a local brand and then a light. 'D'you want a drink, darling?' she whispered.

'I'd love one. Is it sangria?'

'Wait. I'll get it. Salad?'

'No thanks. Just the drink'll do.'

The actress, a lighted cigarette in her own hand, went across and returned with two glasses in her hands. 'I suspect it's not strong, darling. Fear of drunken actors, I believe.'

'And unfocused close-ups probably.' The man who spoke, the focus puller, leaned towards them and took a cigarette from Jessica's pack. She slapped his hand.

'Ask. Anyway, I thought you'd given up.'

'I have. I just never buy any of my own.'

Derek appeared with Ben by his side. 'Rosie – sorry, no-one told me your cab got here.'

She looked up. He was smiling, unflustered. Somehow Rosemary had expected some air of impropriety about him, some feeling of embarrassment at being discovered in his trailer with Betsy. There was none, and she wondered if she had imagined the atmosphere round the table. She felt paranoid and wanted to be anywhere but where she was. She was uncomfortable, displaced, unsure. Betsy was nowhere to be seen.

'Are you eating?' Ben said.

She shook her head. 'I'm not hungry.'

'I've eaten,' he bent forward and kissed her cheek.

'I know,' she said.

And to her dismay he shifted his eyes away from her and she knew immediately her first instincts had been right. Not even Ben's fathomless eyes could shut down quick enough to hide his sudden guilt. She had no idea how to handle the situation. What to say or what to do. So she sat and smoked and drank her sangria, asked for a refill and lit one of her own cigarettes. Jessica talked and Rosemary laughed.

Ben remained silent and still. 'D'you want coffee?' he said eventually.

'No. Thank you.' She was unable to look at him. Fury rose inside her like a sickness. When Jessica was called to make-up and people began to disperse she said, 'Had a good morning?'

'Not bad.' He seemed relieved at the normality of her conversation and bent forward to try to take her hand. She held tight to her cigarette.

He said, 'Is something wrong?'

'I'm afraid I have to get back,' she said, still not

catching his eyes, as hard as he was trying to make her look at him. 'Back to London I mean,' she went on.

'Shit.'

She turned now. 'Is that all you can find to say?'

He shrugged.

'Just get me a cab Ben. I'll organize the plane ticket when I get back to the hotel.'

'Don't go.'

'You must think I'm stupid. I have never been so humiliated in my life, and if I don't get out of here now I'll humiliate you as well.'

'What are you talking about?' He pushed his face into some semblance of innocence.

'I know you're a wonderful actor Ben,' she said. 'Right now just don't perform for me. Just organize a cab. OK?'

He stood up and moved away from her and across to one of the trailers. People were beginning to drift back to the set. Actors to the make-up trailer, crew to their various occupations.

Jessica joined her. 'Amazing how little they have to do to make me look old these days,' she said as she sat down.

Rosemary smiled across at her, glad of her reappearance, consoled by her presence because it halted the flood of tears that were threatening to engulf her.

'Are you staying around?' said the actress.

'No. Ben's getting me a cab. I came to say goodbye actually. I have to get back to London tonight.'

The other woman paused and looked carefully at her. 'Very wise, darling. We need nurturing at our age, not violating.'

Betsy appeared behind Jessica. 'You're wanted on set, Jess.'

'I can remember the day when they called me Miss Damien,' she said as she stood up. She took Rosemary's hand. 'Have a safe trip back darling. With any luck it'll piss down over here all week and we'll all have a thoroughly miserable time.'

She left, and Betsy smiled at Rosemary. 'Hello,' she said.

'Hello Betsy. Are you feeling better?'

To Rosemary's immense delight the girl blushed, nodded, and ran back to the set.

Ben came back. 'Cab's on the way. Well, about twenty minutes.'

'Fine. Any of that sangria left?'

'Are you sure?'

'Ben,' she said, her voice low, 'I'm a big girl now, I know when I want a drink and I know when I want to go home. And shouldn't you be on set?'

'Not in the first scene. We're behind schedule.' He went to get her a drink. 'Shall we go to the trailer?' he asked, sitting now beside her.

She reeled at his lack of sensitivity. 'I find that idea extremely unpleasant.'

He tried again to take her hand and she ignored him.

Most of the actors and crew had left the area, and the caterers were beginning to clear up the debris. Just two prop men sat across at another table playing cards. They were unaware of Ben and Rosemary.

'Rosie, are you going to talk to me at all?'

'What about?'

'Anything. Why you're going home. Why you're so mad. Nothing's changed. Not me. Not the way I feel about you.'

'I find I can't cope, Ben. Not with the way you obviously are. I know it's not been long, but I'm in too deep and it's too uncomfortable – and what's more, I'm too old for all these teenage shenanigans.'

'Look—'

'No, you look. Just let me walk away. You don't need someone like me. You're a single man. In every way. Enjoy it. But not with me. It was a mistake. Ella was right.'

'Fuck Ella,' he said, loud and furious, frightening her as he kicked one of the wooden chairs beside him across the gravel. The two prop men looked up from their game. 'Fuck, fuck, fuck Ella!!!'

'I was under the impression you already had,' Rosemary said very quietly. Ben went quite rigid and stared at her.

'Rosemary, your cab's here.' Betsy had appeared. She looked bewildered and a little scared at the sight of Ben on his feet, his face fierce, his body tense.

'Fuck off, Betsy. Tell them to wait.'

The runner scuttled away, tears starting already down her cheeks.

Rosemary stood up. 'That's enough. Enough. Get me out of here. Right now. I've had enough humiliation to last me a lifetime and beyond.'

Back in the hotel Rosemary phoned the airport. A Business Class ticket was hers to pick up at the BA desk that evening. She phoned Frances. 'I'm arriving at Gatwick at nine-thirty this evening, Franny. Don't ask any questions. Will you be there?'

She left a pile of Spanish money on the bedside table, along with a cheque for the amount she believed would cover her stay. Knowing it would make him angry gave her a small amount of relief. She left no note.

She was at the Barcelona airport by four-thirty and sat in the bar until her plane was called.

She drank champagne on the flight back and smoked almost a pack of cigarettes. Food was unthinkable, and by the time she walked out of Customs and into Frances' arms she felt more than a little sick. Frances took one look at her uncombed hair, her face bare of any make-up and her eyes dead behind her dark glasses and put her into the car with the luggage without one question.

'Get me home,' whispered Rosemary. 'Get me home, and then I'll talk.'

Chapter Thirteen

Frances had arranged to stay the night, and if necessary, the weekend. It was. Rosemary was in a worse state than she herself had realized, unused and incapable of coping with adolescent emotion as she had become after long years of a tidy and seamfree life.

'That's all it is, sweetheart,' said Frances, over coffee that night. 'That's all it is, adolescent emotion. Remember it?'

'Only too well. Why, oh why did I allow myself to get this way ever again? Everything in my life was so, oh God, so smooth.'

'Something had to crack, doll face. Nobody's life can be as neat as you had made yours. But you certainly dived into this one. Blind and stupid. I can say that because I love you.'

'But why, Frances? Why me? What does he want?'

'You my lovely. Under his thumb. Just where he had you.'

Rosemary looked up from the brandy glass she'd been warming in her hands. 'You put that in the past tense.'

Frances looked at her steadily through the haze of her own cigarette. Rosemary lit one for herself from the pack on the table.

'D'you think it's over Frances?'

'Of course it is. You must see that. Leave him to the young ones, gentle heart. Not for us – not all that turbulence. Christ, Rosemary, leave it, please. Don't put yourself through that again. It'll just go on. That's the way he is.'

'How do I forget him? The way he makes me feel about myself? When it's good, it's the best I've ever known. At fifty, that's something.'

Frances shook her head. 'It's sex, my darling. Sex. He's a "zipless fuck" carried on longer than one night. Accept it and get out now before you slip away and vanish.'

Rosemary fell silent. Her friend watched her, wondering how the woman she had known so well for so long could be in a situation so alien to her very nature.

'It's not love, darling face,' Frances said at last.

'What d'you mean? What else?' Rosemary asked. .

'Obsession,' said Frances. 'He's feeding your inadequacies. I bet you're thinking "maybe I over-reacted, maybe this Betsy isn't important".'

A silence fell, short and tense. Then Frances spoke again. 'Am I right? Are you already beginning to forgive him?'

'Franny, maybe I *did* over-react. No, – let me finish. Now, here, at home and at a distance from it all, I'm thinking, maybe she did only take his lunch. He never said he'd be faithful, he just said— Oh Christ, what have I done?' Rosemary stood up and went to the kitchen sink. Too much coffee, alcohol and endless cigarettes heaved relentlessly inside her. There, in her familiar and safe kitchen, Frances held her head while she vomited the day's abuse into her clean, white sink.

The telephone on the wall started to ring and both women stared at each other. 'It's him,' said Rosemary, her throat sore from the vomiting, her eyes red, the skin beneath them blotchy and broken-veined from her retching.

'*I'll* answer it,' said Frances firmly, and leaving Rosemary to wash and disinfect the sink, she picked up the telephone.

'Yes?' Terse and abrupt, she answered without giving the number. Then, 'Oh, sorry. Hello Michael. Yes she's here. D'you need to speak to her?' She said something softly into the mouthpiece which Rosemary couldn't hear over the running water.

'Michael?' said Rosemary once Frances had replaced the receiver. She looked at her watch. 'It's midnight. He never phones this late. And how did he know I'd be home?' She sat down heavily and put her head in her hands. 'God I'm sorry Franny, about all that. Only you in all the world would hold onto me while I was sick.'

Frances went down on her haunches at the side of Rosemary's chair and turned her round to cradle her in her arms. Rosemary began to cry; tired now, the sobs came only with exhaustion. 'I'm so tired, Franny. Tired and foolish. I know you're right.'

Frances wiped her friend's face with a paper towel from the kitchen. 'Good God my darling, this re-cycled stuff is very worthy of you, but it's harsh on the old laughter lines.'

Rosemary laughed. 'It's not meant for mopping faces.'

'If you don't walk away from "Ben the irresistible" your face will need a lot of mopping over the months to come.'

Rosemary straightened her back suddenly. 'You're right. I don't need it. I don't want to be treated like that. We have different ideas about how affairs should be conducted.'

'Good girl.' Frances stood up. 'Now then, you must eat. What d'you fancy?'

'Toast, butter, ice-cream and cheesecake.'

They both laughed. Frances held out her hands and Rosemary stood to hold them.

'You're wonderful, Franny. I'd never manage without you.'

'Oh yes you would. You're the strongest lady I know. Hang onto that. Specially when Ben phones and you ask for that front door key.'

Rosemary put her hand to her mouth, cold still from the ice-cream. 'My God. My key.'

'Don't panic. How much longer will he be in Spain?'

'Another two weeks. They're behind schedule.'

'You'll be over it. Honestly. And if there's any justice in this world, his mother will visit him constantly on the set. Now, enough of the male sex, let's eat.'

Over the food Rosemary said, 'I still don't understand how Michael called.'

'Just eat. I'll tell you in the morning. As Scarlett would say "tomorrow is another day".'

When Rosemary opened her eyes on Friday morning it was almost eleven o'clock. She lay for moments, listening to Pat and the faint conversation she was having with Frances downstairs. The phone rang and somebody picked it up before Rosemary's hand came from under the duvet. She felt curiously empty as she lay there. Neither misery nor bewilderment was any part of her emotions. A vague relief at being home crept in, along with the sunshine that suddenly broke from behind a cloud and poured through her bedroom window. She knew more daffodils would be up in only the few days she'd been away. Soon she would get up and go for a walk in the garden. Now she lay, trying to sort out how she felt. The tears were over, only the foolishness at her own reactions and behaviour remained to haunt her. She clung precariously to the belief that at least she had left with some dignity. She wondered when he would be in touch. Knowing he would, that it wasn't the end, and that somehow there was more to come. But right now, a certain calm crept within her and it was enough. In the respite from the turmoil that had been hers during the last few days, she dwelt on the hours they had spent together in Spain. The good and the bad. This morning, the bad was uppermost in her

178

thoughts. She prayed it would stay that way, knowing that if she remembered how good it had felt to be in his arms and feel his breath in her hair, she would relent and forgive and want him again.

Now the humiliation of Betsy and the news of his son rose within her, and engulfed her once more in a sudden and sharp intake of breath. There was a knock at the door and then Frances pushed it open.

'I'm awake,' said Rosemary, 'come in. I'm fine.'

'D'you want tea? I can bring it up.'

'Could you? I don't quite think I can face Pat yet.'

Frances laughed. 'Don't panic. I'll bring up a tray with some toast. I've told her you had to come back suddenly for some interviews.' She went out again, and Rosemary got up to put on her housecoat. She stood at the window that overlooked the east of the garden and then pushed it open to step out onto the small balcony. There was a stone pot of newly-awoken daffodils by her foot, and she bent to touch them gently with fingers still puffy from her late rising. She stood and watched the cat persistently and patiently sitting, mesmerized, by the small pond. Old Ernie came out of the shed, the cup from a thermos flask held in both his hands as he warmed them round the steaming drink. He looked up and raised one arm to greet her and wandered off down the garden. She wondered for the umpteenth time if she would ever have the nerve to replace him, knowing that he could only potter these days rather than labour with any strength.

Behind her the door opened. 'I made coffee instead, is that all right?'

'Lovely.' Rosemary came back into the room and shut the balcony window, shivering against the sudden cold of the English weather. 'It's a wonderful day,' she said.

They sat at the window, Rosemary on a chintz-covered

bedroom chair, Frances on the chaise. 'I need to tell you something,' said Frances.

Coming out of her reverie, Rosemary turned to look at her friend. 'God you sound so serious.'

'Don't look so stricken, darling heart, it's not really that much to do with you. Just something you should hear first from me. You know us both.'

Rosemary stared at her. Then she said, 'Quite suddenly I know what you're going to say.'

'Do you?'

'You're having an affair with Michael, aren't you?'

'Clever old thing. How the hell did you guess?'

'I didn't until just now. I must admit I'm surprised. He's always been such a faithful sort. Is it something in the air do you think? Does Barbara know?'

'I don't know. I suspect she no longer cares. If what he says is true, she seems more interested in her children.'

'Oh dear. Poor Barbara. They were so happy before Josh was born.'

'So he said.'

'It started at my last recording, didn't it?' and without waiting for a reply, Rosemary went on, 'What about you, Franny? Won't you be hurt?'

'Darling heart, I only want him in my bed occasionally, not in my life for ever. We get on well, he demands little, which suits me fine, because I suspect little is all I have left to give.'

'Will you ever be in love with anyone?'

'I've been in love for years.'

Rosemary's eyebrows rose. 'Who with?'

'Myself, sweet idiot. Myself – life – everything. I never wanted what everyone said I should have. I didn't listen to anyone. I wasn't programmed like you.'

Rosemary sighed. 'I've always envied you that. Except for the children. I'm glad I'm a mother.' She remembered Ella suddenly.

'My God, Ella's first preview's tonight. I could go.'

'No,' said Frances firmly. 'Your love affair with yourself begins now. Ella is fine. She's probably having the time of her life, more than likely in somebody's bed, maybe everyone's bed.'

'Oh don't,' Rosemary groaned. Then, 'She was right about Ben.'

'Now *Ella* is the type to deal with him.'

'I'll phone her.' She reached for the telephone on the table by the bed. 'You can't object to that.'

'If you must.'

'I can't remember the number,' Rosemary said suddenly replacing the receiver again, 'how strange. I've always had a photographic memory as far as the children's numbers are concerned, even when they're away.'

'Then leave it.' Frances was pouring more coffee into Rosemary's cup. 'Leave her be. Once Pat's gone, we'll go downstairs and decide what to do with ourselves this weekend. Phone nobody. Everyone thinks you're away.'

Rosemary smiled with sudden genuine delight. 'My God, so they do. How perfectly wonderful. Let's put the answerphone on. No, on second thoughts—'

Frances looked at her. 'Are you still hoping he'll phone by any chance?'

'Yes.'

'You're mad.'

'I know. But Franny, it's not going to be that simple.'

'All right, all right,' she raised both her hands. 'Mad as you are, I won't say another word. But don't mind me praying that he doesn't get to a phone.'

'Shall I call him?'

'Don't be ridiculous! You will do that over my dead body! Act your age, for Christ's sake.'

Friday passed. For Rosemary that was all it was, a passing day. She unpacked, washed, talked to Frances, went for a walk, and waited for the phone to ring. By six o'clock that evening the only person she had spoken to, apart from Frances, was Michael, and that was because she took his call.

'Are you all right, Rosemary?'

'I'm fine Michael. I'm sure Frances has told you what's happened, so I won't go into it, but I'm fine. Feeling a trifle silly, if the truth be told.' She laughed derisively at herself and handed the telephone to Frances, walking out of the room so that they could talk in peace. It was six in the evening, and she stood in the living-room looking out over the garden and smoking a cigarette. She remembered Ben playing with the cat on that first Sunday when they had had the confrontation over Ella. Three short weeks.

Behind her, Frances had come into the room. 'Shall I make us some martinis?'

Rosemary turned. 'Lovely. You're better at it than me.'

Frances said, 'D'you want to come and talk to me while I do it?' They went back into the garden and Rosemary fed the cat while Frances collected the vodka, martini and ice. 'D'you want olive or lemon?' she asked, her head inside the fridge.

'Both,' Rosemary put the cat dish down and he appeared through the cat-flap with his usual great clatter. 'He has a sixth sense.' She smiled and bent to stroke her old and well-loved pet. 'I'll have to change his name.'

'Why, you idiot?' Frances strained two martinis through ice into slender glasses, and handed one to her friend.

'I want to forget the last three weeks ever happened. I hope he doesn't phone.'

Frances regarded her carefully and thoughtfully over the rim of her glass. 'You lie, my precious, *I* hope he won't phone, *you* hope he'll phone and beg forgiveness and say he'll change for ever.'

Rosemary shrugged. The telephone rang and they both jumped.

'Good grief, I'm as bad as you, you idiot,' said Frances, and picked it up.

'Yes?' and then, 'Hello Ella! What a surprise. Don't you open tonight?' Rosemary put her glass down and motioned for Frances to pass her the phone. 'No, she's here. Had to come back early. Hang on.' Frances passed her the phone.

'Hello darling. How on earth did you know I was back?'

'Don't know, Mum. Are you OK?'

'Yes. Why?'

'I thought you were going to stay for about ten days.'

'Something came up and—' Rosemary shot a glance to her friend who shrugged and began to wander through to the living-room, 'Frances needed me.'

'May God forgive you and wash your mouth out with soap,' hissed Frances, and shut the kitchen door.

'Did you have a good time Mum?'

'Lovely. Never mind about me, young lady. How's it going?'

'It's all smashing. Fucking great, Mum. Look, I really need to see you. Are you coming up?'

'I don't know darling. Nothing wrong, is there?'

'Nothing, nothing. Just something to tell you and a really big favour to ask.'

'What?'

'Shit, shit, shit, my money's run out.'

'Phone me and reverse the charges.'

'After the show Mum, after the show.'

'Good luck darling. Be wonderful.' The line went dead and Rosemary put the phone down. She picked up her martini. Frances was watching the news on television and looked up when she came in.

'All right, is she?'

'"Fucking great" were her actual words.'

'Oh well then, nothing to worry about.'

'She wants a favour. She'll phone later.'

'Let's hope it's only money, sugar plum.'

They went out to eat that evening, to an Italian restaurant round the corner from the house that Rosemary knew well. 'I can't sit and watch you watching the phone all evening,' Frances had groaned. There were no messages on the answerphone when they returned later that evening. They sat with coffee and brandy and a box of chocolates in front of a turned-down television set, put on for moving wallpaper which they could talk through with impunity. 'I'm drinking like a fish,' said Rosemary. 'What's happened to me?'

'Ben Morrison.'

'Don't even say the name.'

'It won't mean a thing in a week. Mark my words.'

Rosemary said after a pause, 'I don't know, Franny. I'm talking and eating and behaving like always, but he's here all the time. I feel as if I'm in shock. How could it have gone so deep in just three weeks?'

'The one affair that hurt more than any other for me lasted one weekend.'

'Good grief. Really? D'you *still* think of – what was his name? Geoff?'

Frances nodded. 'Sometimes I still think I catch sight of him in the street, and when I catch up with him I have to keep running in case this total stranger thinks I've taken leave of my senses.'

'Why Geoff? I don't get it.'

'He was so unobtainable. So arrogant. I don't know.'

'Like Ben, you mean.'

'Right. Like your Ben.'

'He's not *my* Ben.'

184

'How right you are. Sounds to me more like every-one's Ben.'

The telephone rang.

'Will you please stop jumping like that,' laughed Frances, 'you made me spill my brandy!!'

It was Ella.

'Did it go well?' Rosemary enquired.

'For a first preview, or the show in general?'

'Like that, was it?'

Ella sighed. 'Not to panic. The Press are not in until next Wednesday.'

Rosemary said, 'You said you wanted a favour, darling?'

'Can I bring a friend home next weekend?'

Rosemary was surprised. 'Of course darling. But you always can. Why is it suddenly a favour?'

'I didn't want Ben there.'

'He won't be.'

Ella paused. 'Something's happened, hasn't it, Mum? I can tell in your voice. Has that fucking bastard been up to his old tricks?'

'What particular tricks are those?'

'He never learned to control his cock.'

Rosemary couldn't help suddenly laughing. 'Something like that darling.'

'Oh Mum,' Ella groaned, 'd'you feel awful?'

'I am all right. It's over. Now let's not discuss it. Tell me when you're coming.'

'I'm in love, Mum.'

Rosemary took a sharp intake of breath. 'Darling, oh, how wonderful. So – so – well, I can't say fast can I? Bit like the pot calling the kettle black.'

'I just want you to meet.'

'Well I'd love to. Next weekend?'

'Yes, we'll come down on the Sunday morning.'

'You don't mean this Sunday?'

'No. No *after* we open. Is that all right?'

'Of course.'

'I really want you to like her Mum.'

'Pardon?'

'I said, I want you to like her. She's very important to me. Very special.'

Rosemary kept her voice completely level when she answered her daughter. 'I'll look forward to it. See you next Sunday then? Oh darling, good luck for Wednesday.' But Ella had gone, blowing a kiss and calling over her shoulder to someone at the other end of the phone. Rosemary went back to Frances, who had replenished both their glasses. She looked up as her friend came in. Rosemary was convulsed with laughter, tears running down her cheeks.

'What? What!!' said Frances. 'Christ, are you having hysterics? What's happened?'

'Ella's in love,' Rosemary managed to get out.

'She actually said that? "I'm in love." Those were the words?' Rosemary nodded. 'Well,' said Frances, 'I suppose it had to happen eventually. If you window-shop often enough, you're bound to find something you like. It's always amazed me she hasn't picked up a contractable disease. Even crabs would have been some sort of revenge.'

'Oh shut up, Franny. She's serious. She's in love, and she's bringing *her* home to meet me next weekend.'

Frances stared at her. And then they both began to laugh. 'It's all you need. I think it's wonderful. You must tell your mother immediately. It'll kill her off in one short burst, and then you'll be totally free of everyone.'

'Well at least she's safe from contractable diseases,' said Rosemary. 'Here—' She held out her glass. 'That does it. Let's finish the brandy. I think I'll become an alcoholic.'

Chapter Fourteen

Ella's news somehow got Rosemary through the following week. She did her guesting on the radio, called and visited her mother, lying about what a wonderful break Barcelona had been and lunched with Michael.

'Before we both get embarrassed, Michael, I know about Frances. Shall we not discuss it?'

'I wanted to explain. You and I have known each other a long time, Rosemary. It's awkward.'

She toyed with her lunchtime salad. 'Messing on your own doorstep. Frances' words, not mine.' She pushed her barely-touched plate aside and went on, 'Anyway, it's not my business, and Frances has always been more than able to take care of herself. Besides, I'm hardly in a position to advise am I?' Michael touched her hand across the table and said nothing.

'I hope it all doesn't get messy,' said Rosemary, 'for all your sakes. Especially Barbara's. She seems the most fragile.' No more was said of a personal nature, and thankfully Michael turned to business. He seemed to think the TV show would be postponed.

'Have you talked to Derek?'

'He's in the States, but the rumour is that there's no money until November.'

'Is it still going? I mean for sure?' Rosemary asked. At the moment she felt nothing but relief there was no work of any consequence ahead for most of the year.

'Rosemary, I just don't know. Things are bad all round, we know that. However, the radio spot on Sunday mornings seems to be firming up nicely, and I have to talk to someone about a morning game show for the BBC.'

Rosemary shrugged listlessly. She pushed the rest of her food away and picked up the wine. 'I'd like to do nothing for a while, Michael. Let's leave even the P.A.s for a couple of months. D'you mind?'

Michael shook his head, but looked somewhat perturbed as he motioned to their waiter for the bill.

Rosemary drove home. It was Wednesday, and still nothing from Ben. She had toyed with the idea of going up to Nottingham for Ella's press night. The flowers and telemessage had been sent. She sat and watched *Coronation Street*.

Frances rang at eight. 'How was Michael?' she asked.

'The show's been postponed. There's a few other things around, but quite frankly Franny I don't feel any sort of enthusiasm for anything. I could sit and watch re-runs of *Coronation Street* for the rest of the year, if you were to ask me.'

'Listen sweet child, let's go away. I can organize it for next Monday. Can you wait?'

'Where to?'

'Health farm. Shrublands.'

Rosemary stood and conjured up Shrublands Hall. 'Oh Franny, what a wonderful idea. Will you sort it, or shall I?'

'Darling heart. I doubt at the moment you could organize a screw-up in a brothel. Leave it to me. D'you want dinner on Friday?'

'You come here. D'you know it's Easter? I just realized.'

'Right, I'll bring you an egg. Before you start the diet. Please, please sleep well.'

'I am, like a log. Funny, isn't it?'

While she felt better she phoned her mother.

'Well, well,' said Betty, 'first a visit and now a phone call. I feel quite honoured.'

'I'm not working much, Mum.' Rosemary tensed and refused to rise to the bait. She went on, 'I just thought you might like me to take you shopping on Friday.'

'What sort of shopping?'

'Tesco's. Ella's coming for Sunday with a friend, and the cupboard's bare.'

'Oh all right. D'you know she hasn't even bothered to drop me a postcard?' said Betty petulantly.

'She's busy, Mum, be fair. She opens tonight. Did *you* send her a card?' Her mother didn't reply and Rosemary knew she hadn't. 'I'll pick you up about ten on Friday,' said Rosemary, 'is that all right? And if you're very good I'll take you out to lunch. An Easter treat for a good old bunny.'

Easter had always been Rosemary's favourite time of year when the children had been small: organizing the treasure hunt for the eggs, eating too much chocolate and cooking a turkey on the Sunday. She resisted inviting her mother for Sunday lunch, wanting the space to meet Ella's friend – lover – without having to conceal things from Betty. Ella would be inclined to confront her grandmother with the truth immediately. Rosemary knew beyond doubt that it would be a mistake.

Tesco's on Good Friday was packed and, with hindsight, as far as Rosemary was concerned, a mistake. She seemed to be totally forgetting just how famous she was these days. She was stared at, stopped, poked and asked to sign more than a dozen autographs. Even a couple of photographs were taken of her bending over the meat counter searching out a small fresh turkey for Sunday, much to her horror and her mother's ill-concealed irritation.

'How's the toyboy?' one man mouthed at her as he stood by the frozen vegetables and held a trolley, while his wife threw in packets of chips and peas. Rosemary pretended she hadn't heard and marched purposefully towards the Häagen-Dazs ice-cream.

'What's he talking about?' said Betty. 'Why are men so stupid?'

'God knows,' said Rosemary, answering both questions in one.

The girl at the checkout spotted her in the queue and giggled and smirked until it was Rosemary's turn to pass through. The total was over a hundred pounds.

Rosemary said, 'Will you take one cheque?'

'I need proof of identity, Miss Downey,' the girl said.

Rosemary stared at her for a moment, then, laughingly, she dug out her driving licence and credit cards while she wrote the cheque.

She drove her mother back home and unpacked her foodstuff, then took her for lunch in a large Italian restaurant in Streatham High Street. 'Have lamb chops, Mum.'

'Don't let them pile it on my plate. It puts me off.'

Over coffee, Rosemary said, 'I'm going away again on Monday.'

'You've just come back. Where to this time?'

'Frances and I have decided to go to Shrublands. Remember the health farm we went to last year?'

'Goodness me. Another holiday? Well, I suppose it's all right for those who can afford it.'

Rosemary sighed. 'Mum, don't. You know I'd pay for you to go away if you wanted to. You say you hate holidays, that you like sleeping in your own bed at your stage of life.'

Betty didn't answer.

By the time Rosemary eventually got home with her own shopping, the ice-cream was like cold sweet soup. She put it quickly into the freezer and forgot about it. She made a pot of tea for herself, mixing Earl Grey with

Indian and it reminded her of Ben. Still nothing on the answerphone. She had bought Frances an Easter egg just for fun, and put it into the fridge. Then she sat at the kitchen table and drank her tea and lit the cigarette she had looked forward to all day. Next week she would give up. She thought of Ben and wondered what he was doing, thinking, saying. Outside the kitchen window, the birds were busy. Nesting had begun, house-hunting for the tits. Daffodils were everywhere, and another warm Easter heralded in the spring.

Without warning, she began to cry. She hadn't even the energy to get a tissue from her bag, or a piece of kitchen paper. Self-pity washed over her, filling her with anger at herself as well as melancholy. Last Easter she had been so settled. Not ecstatic, not deliriously happy, but settled. Content with the lot she had made for herself. Now the sight of the spring sunshine, the sound of the nesting birds and the thought of not being a couple filled her with everything but joy. She sat for an hour and then got up and wandered through to the living-room and switched on the television.

What am I doing? she thought, but didn't move, and let the Australian soap wash over her and her rambling thoughts. If Ben rang, she knew she would go back, wanting that feeling again more than she wanted his fidelity or her own pride. Why didn't he ring? She watched the news and then read the day's newspaper. The *Guardian* had given Ella's play a good write-up, but her daughter wasn't mentioned.

Frances arrived just after eight. 'Turn that bloody television off and we'll eat in the kitchen. I bought Japanese. I believe it's all raw. Can you credit it? You look like death, sweet face. What the hell have you been up to?'

'I've been with my mother all day, in Tesco's.'

'Did you buy yourself a hairshirt as well?'

*   *   *

On Saturday afternoon Frances left to visit a friend in Brighton. 'Sorry I can't get out of it, sweetheart. I'll miss the brat with lover in tow. How could I have arranged my life so badly? Will you be all right, d'you think?'

'Of course I will, don't be silly. There'll be no time or interest for me to dwell on you-know-who.'

'Don't know what you're talking about.'

Rosemary laughed and Frances kissed her quickly. 'Be good to yourself my lovely girl, I need you always. And I'll pick you up for Shrublands on Monday. I'll drive. We'll be there in time for tea with full cream milk, if my memory is correct.'

'Take care Franny,' Rosemary said, as her friend opened her car door. Then, 'Frances, how d'you feel with Michael at home on weekends like this? Is it awful.'

'I don't think about it. Darling heart, it was my choice. If it gets unbearable I'll walk away, I've done so before.'

Rosemary closed her front door and leaned against the back of it. She felt as if she was in a bad television soap. All it needed was for her to slide down the door in floods of tears to remind herself of an old episode of *Dynasty*. 'Pull yourself together girl,' she said out loud, and went upstairs to shower and wash her hair and put towels out in Ella's room. *I guess they'll sleep together*, she thought, looking at her daughter's double brass bed.

She went to bed early that Saturday, and when the sound of the doorbell rang at one in the morning, accompanied by knocking and Ella's calling through the letter-box, she had been asleep for over two hours.

'Mum, I'm sorry,' Ella flung her arms round her dishevelled and sleepy parent as they stood in the hallway.

'I forgot or lost my key. We decided we couldn't wait till tomorrow.'

'You mean *you* couldn't!' the girl standing behind Ella said with a laugh. She put out a hand to Rosemary, direct and friendly, a smile that spread to every feature of her round and mobile face, brown eyes screwed delightfully when she laughed. 'Hello Mrs Downey. Ella always gets her own way, I'm afraid. We obviously disturbed you.'

Ella turned and flung an arm round the girl's shoulders. 'Mum this is Joanna.'

'Hello Joanna. And please call me Rosemary.'

'OK. And I'm Jo.'

They moved through to the kitchen, knapsacks and carrier bags left in the middle of the hall. Ella switched lights on as she made her way through the house. With the kettle set to boil for coffee, Rosemary said, 'D'you *want* coffee Jo? Or would you prefer a drink?'

'Coffee'd be great Rosemary. Please go back to bed, you must be exhausted, it's gone one. We can look after ourselves.'

Rosemary liked her, immediately and warmly. Jo was a large woman, in height and width, hair long and curly. They both wore jeans, Jo in black, Ella in her usual knee-torn apparel. Rosemary left them to fend for themselves and took herself back to bed. 'We'll talk in the morning Ella. Good night Jo.' Visions of bread being cut directly onto her kitchen table, knife edging into the pine veneer in her daughter's usual way, followed Rosemary back to bed. She bit back the criticism, for Jo's sake if not her own.

Both young women were in bed until mid-day, so Rosemary postponed Sunday lunch until the evening. They all sat around in the afternoon, Jo read the papers and then offered to help with the meal. Rosemary and she were alone in the kitchen while Ella stayed in the living-room. Rock music filled the house and the familiarity that settled over Rosemary made her feel better than she had for the last month. She found herself relaxed and laughing with Jo while they peeled potatoes and carrots together over the sink.

Jo said, 'Did Ella tell you about us?'

Rosemary, unsure she wanted confrontation of her daughter's sex life, nodded, and moved to put the potatoes in the oven.

'Is it difficult for you?' Jo said.

Rosemary faced her. 'A little. I'm sorry.'

'Don't be. My mother pretends it's not happening.'

'Have you, well, always—?'

'Been gay?'

Rosemary nodded.

Jo leaned against the kitchen table. 'Always,' she said. 'Not like Ella. But I am serious about her. Does that embarrass you?'

'I don't know. A little.'

'She told you rather brutally, didn't she?'

Again Rosemary nodded. 'Is it too early for a sherry?' she asked Jo.

The girl laughed. 'I'd rather have wine. White, if that's all right.'

Rosemary moved to the fridge and removed the bottle of Frascati.

'Here, I'll do it,' said Jo, and took the bottle from her. Rosemary handed her the opener and watched her capable hands pull the cork from the bottle in one easy movement. Rosemary put three glasses on the kitchen table and Jo poured.

'It's lovely to meet you,' she said, still smiling at her. 'You too,' said Rosemary, and meant it. There was a feeling of serenity about this thirty-something young woman. Something appealing and strong in the best possible way. Her smile was constant, as if she had the world and her place in it well sorted out.

They ate in the kitchen. Conversation was lively and entertaining. The play was going well, the second one would start rehearsing on Tuesday, and Joanna seemed confident of her cast. 'She's a brilliant director,' said Ella, through mouthfuls of roast potato.

'Oh shut up,' Jo retorted. 'I just cast well.' Rosemary learned that she had had an enormous amount of experience with fringe theatre, had begun in her early twenties as an actress, 'a very bad one,' laughed Ella, and now at the age of thirty-four had been thrilled to be offered three plays at Nottingham. Rosemary envied their energy, and remembered her own. Before Ben arrived in her life.

Eventually, and much later that evening, Ella asked her about him. Rosemary glanced across at Jo, nibbling at one of the Easter eggs Rosemary had succumbed to in Tesco's and given to them after the meal in a state of maternal emotion. 'I'm twenty-five for fuck's sake,' Ella had said, but none the less delighted to be treated at times like the spoiled child she had once been. 'You can talk in front of Jo,' Ella said. 'She knows about Ben. We have no secrets. I tell her everything.'

Rosemary squirmed at the thought of explaining to either of them about her four days in Barcelona. Most of it was becoming like a too-easily remembered nightmare.

Jo said, 'Don't Ella, it's your mother's business. She doesn't ask about ours.'

Ella turned to her, 'I feel Ben's my fault. I brought the cock-happy bastard here in the first place.'

Jo laughed and Rosemary winced. Ella went on, 'He's in love with his own prick, Mum. Lovely man, smashing actor, but off-stage his brain's between his legs.'

Rosemary said quickly, 'Ella, please. I'm still your mother. I've been a fool. Let's forget it.' She got up to pour herself a brandy. Sitting down again, she said,

'Tomorrow I leave for Shrublands and in one week from now I hope to have shed a few pounds and every lingering memory of Ben Morrison.' *And his rather beautiful penis,* she added to herself, and wished with all her heart she could believe it.

Chapter Fifteen

The girls left before Frances arrived. 'We need to get back to go through the script again. Rehearsals start tomorrow. Chekhov beckons!'

Rosemary waved them off.

'The roads'll be clear,' Jo had said, kissing her hostess enthusiastically on both cheeks and hugging her with a certain loved and new familiarity. 'Take care of yourself, Rosemary,' she said, and bounced her voluptuous form round the car and into the passenger seat.

'Come on, come on,' yelled Ella, impatient as always, wanting to move on rapidly to every event in her life. One hand moved off the steering wheel and out of the window of the departing car, 'Bye Mum, I'll phone soon. Love to Frances.'

The house was gloomy and quiet when Rosemary went back inside. Easter Monday meant no Jennie or Pat. She packed a small bag for the week at the health farm.

'Oh hell they've gone,' said Frances, pulling up in front of the house a little while later.

'Ella sent her love. And before you ask, Joanna Tristram is absolutely lovely and probably the best thing that's happened to my daughter.'

'Well, well,' smiled Frances and threw her friend's case into the boot next to her own set of three matching pieces of luggage.

They arrived at Shrublands in time for tea. Shown to their room, they unpacked, weighed and attired themselves in towelling dressing-gowns. 'I intend to stay like this for the entire week,' said Frances, as they made their way to the conservatory and the large silver teapots and jugs of milk straight from the farm.

Rosemary sipped her tea sitting, surrounded by palms and two banana plants, in the humidity of the large old conservatory. Women in track suits and housecoats chatted blissfully around them. The air hummed with relaxation.

'This is the highlight of the day,' said Frances, on her third cup. 'I'm only doing the light diet to keep you company, honey child. I may well sneak down to the pub for steak and chips while you're being massaged.'

'Think of the toxins leaving your body,' said Rosemary as they climbed into their twin beds early that night to watch television. Frances sipped her honeyed lemon hot drink and tried to banish the thought of vodka martinis.

As usual, in that rarefied atmosphere generated by a group of people focusing for a brief time so thoroughly on nothing else but self-improvement, casual meetings promised friendships that would die later in the cold world of business. Two young actresses came over and introduced themselves to Rosemary on the second day of her stay. The four women gathered together between treatments, found conversation easy, and sought each other out most times after that.

They shared headaches and hunger pains, and kept each other away from the public house at the bottom of the drive. Having them around was good for Rosemary. It stopped her talking about Ben. And when thoughts of him overwhelmingly invaded the space around her, she walked. The grounds were enormous, and lambing was not yet over, filling the emptiness in a corner of her heart with a melancholy that was too sweet to distress her.

After aerobics and steam baths, and the 'blitzing' of the ice-cold water spray, the women always met for that special tea at four on the dot every afternoon. It was as inevitable as their aching muscles and their rumbling stomachs.

'Women are quite awesome all together like this, aren't they?' The four of them were sitting, as usual, in the conservatory, the only place where smoking was allowed. None of them had managed to give it up.

'Powerful, we are,' said Mandy, one of their new friends. 'That's why men are so afraid of us and have done their level best to keep us apart from each other for centuries.'

'A need to control us,' Frances threw in, 'and it sickens me how often we mistake it for caring.'

Rosemary shot her a look. The conversation was dangerously near the subject she most wanted to avoid.

Mandy said, 'I have a friend who lives with someone like that. She's been out of love with him for years but he's made her believe she's useless without him. I think she's almost as much in love with his penis as he is!'

'Impossible,' laughed Frances, 'that's the longest and most powerful love affair a man ever has.'

'Franny don't. That's not true of them all,' Rosemary rebuked her.

Mandy spoke again. 'Poor Gill, she's obsessive. She's so worried where he is all the time. That's all she thinks about.'

Rosemary turned to her. 'Gill?'

Mandy said, 'My friend.'

It couldn't be. Coincidences like this didn't happen. *And do I want to know and discuss this?* she asked herself.

Mandy went on, 'Good actress, too. Not that she thinks so any more. We all pray he'll leave, but he's so bloody charming, she always takes him back.'

'Jealousy is the best aphrodisiac in the world,' said Frances.

Rosemary looked at her. It was true. She remembered

the feelings and thoughts she had had on the trip back from Barcelona. Images of Ben and Betsy had aroused her sexually in a disturbing fashion. Was that it? Was that all it was? Sexual obsession. She still remembered and lingered over memories of his hands and tongue on her. The words in her ear, the sound of his heart against her body, still damp from their love-making. It was always the sex she remembered. There suddenly seemed to have been little else. The thought cheered her somewhat. It was the gleam of light at the end of the tunnel she had dug for herself. There was a life to be lived without sex. She'd done it before. It was easier as well.

'Can you really believe that anything this awful is good for you,' Frances groaned as they lowered their bottoms into the cold water after the first session in the steam cabinet.

Rosemary said, 'D'you think Mandy's friend could be Ben and Gill? I didn't dare ask.'

'Don't even think about it. And *don't* ask.'

'I feel better Franny. I really do. If it was all just sex, then I can cope.'

'Hooray! God I need a drink, shall we sneak to the pub this evening?'

'No, you're just the biggest succumber I know. I can feel my hipbones again, and that's the best thing that's happened to me in weeks.'

'How easily we're pleased, innocents as we are. No wonder men always get us where they want us.'

Rosemary wanted to ask about Michael, but Frances always managed to steer the conversation in another direction. 'Early days, early days!' she said to any of her friend's queries. And there it was left.

Rosemary mused on her friend's casualness, the ease with which she handled each sticky situation as far as men were concerned. Now Frances would never have parted with a front door key. 'Oh my God,' Rosemary said suddenly. They were side-by-side in twin steam cabinets again.

'What?' said Frances, unable to turn her head.

'He's still got the key.'

'Oh dear. When's he due back?'

'This weekend.'

'Change the locks. Next Monday. And if you've got that look of "maybe he'll turn up" on your face, I'll turn the heat up in this terrible thing!'

Rosemary started to laugh. 'We go home on Sunday. It'll be all right. God, Franny, I really am beginning to feel better. Maybe I wasn't in love.'

'You just needed a reason to have sex my sweet,' said Frances. 'Most women do. Men just need a place.'

Michael had phoned a couple of times, but mainly to speak to Frances. Any business with Rosemary was short. 'No news on the September slot for the series, I'm afraid. But I'm still talking about the other thing.'

Rosemary wondered for the first time in years where her career was actually going. The lifestyle she had set for herself and her dependants needed a healthy income. It was the first time in years that she had been unsure of the work ahead. 'Do I need to worry yet?' she asked Michael.

'I don't think so, Rosemary. Things are bad all round. There's a trip coming up to L.A. in August. You could come with me, people to meet. Could be some openings there.'

America. The thought was frightening and exciting at the same time. On Saturday night, the first hot meal of the week was served in the sumptuous dining-room at Shrublands Hall for the guests who were leaving the following day. Wine was served.

'Leave the bottle, sweetheart,' said Frances to the waitress who was pouring them a glass each. She grabbed the bottle from the girl's reluctant hands and smiled so sweetly at her that the waitress grinned back and shrugged her shoulders before walking away. The conversation centred on how much weight they'd lost. Rosemary had shed her seven pounds, Frances only two, but as she said herself, 'I did cheat, my darling. I brought chocolates with me.'

Rosemary's mouth opened. 'You little toady. You never mentioned them once! And I could hardly sleep from hunger some nights.' Rosemary took her friend's hand across the table. 'Thanks for this week Franny.'

'Don't get sloppy. I needed it too. Now for Christ's sake let go of my hand so I can get this fork to my mouth! This lentil bake or whatever they call it tastes like caviar, I'm so hungry!'

They stayed for lunch on the Sunday and then went to the shop and stocked up with 'lots of organic foodstuff', as Rosemary read out from the notice on the wall.

'Fibre and fart food,' sang out Frances clutching a hundred-per-cent recycled plastic bag.

'The cottage cheese is good,' said Rosemary.

Frances shuddered. 'God, I hate cottage cheese.'

'Me too.'

'You eat it all the time!'

'It's not fattening.'

They loaded up the car.

'Now,' said Frances, as she turned the car to drive away, 'do we stop on the way for a drink, or wait until we get to your place?'

'Nothing's open, you fool. It's Sunday. Let's go home.' They waved and tooted to the two young women they'd befriended, telephone numbers already exchanged that would never be used. Rosemary had longed to ask questions about Gill, but the fear of confronting what could turn out to be more of Ben's lies and other dents in her own pride, kept her silent. Ben's Gill was a teacher surely? So he'd said. Better left unsolved. She would never know now.

They drove back feeling pampered and relaxed, but ruining it all slightly by stopping for a cream tea at an hotel.

'That's the two pounds back on,' said Frances, looking pleased with herself.

Rosemary, feeling rather self-righteous, only drank the tea and ate one digestive biscuit. 'I feel beautiful again,' she said. 'I *like* myself again. I refuse to spoil it all. No more cigarettes. I've decided. And I'll only drink at weekends.'

Frances groaned. 'You're going to be fun. Thank God Michael's a boozer.'

'Is he?'

'Well he is now.' Frances smiled, more to herself than Rosemary. 'D'you know, I'm looking forward to seeing the man. All that self-imposed abstinence has made me feel quite – I don't know – can't think of the word.'

'Raunchy?'

'That always makes me think of cowboy boots and whips.'

'For God's sake, Franny, you *are* raunchy! I've envied you for years for that very quality. Well, not envied exactly, more admired.'

'Well, well, raunchy eh? I must run that past him later tonight.'

Rosemary looked surprised. 'D'you see him at weekends?'

Frances shrugged. 'He said so. Barbara must be away. I don't ask, he just appears. If I'm there it's great, if I'm not, well, I guess he goes home.'

'I don't know how you stand it.' Rosemary's spirits dropped a little. Maybe if she'd been that way with Ben, it all would have lasted much longer.

'Don't start, Rosemary. It's old ground. Michael and I laid down the rules. If one of us becomes a loser, I'll just make sure it isn't me. Come on sweetness, let's get you home. And don't forget to phone the locksmith first thing in the morning.'

As they pulled into the front gate at Wimbledon, Rosemary said, 'All the tulips are out. It's beginning to look like a May garden.'

'Does that mean Ernie will emerge from his shed at last?' Frances asked.

They got Rosemary's luggage out of the car. 'I never seem to come back from anywhere without the ubiquitous plastic bag,' groaned Rosemary as they trundled through the kitchen door and threw everything on the table. 'I give them to my mother when she comes. She folds them up obsessively and keeps them. God knows what for. D'you want a drink or tea?' She moved towards the kettle.

Frances looked at her watch. 'One drink darling heart. Then I must go.'

Rosemary went to the fridge for the ice. She stopped at the draining board. One mug, remnants of coffee at the bottom, stood in solitude in the middle of her white sink. 'That's not like Pat,' she said. They both heard the footsteps coming down the stairs simultaneously. Wordlessly, they both turned to face the kitchen door that led to the rest of the house. It opened. Ben stood with one hand on the open door, the other on the door frame. He was smiling.

'Hello Rosie. Hello Frances.' His eyes were on Rosemary, his words aimed towards her friend, standing, open-mouthed, lighted cigarette in outstretched hand, smoke curling through suddenly tense atmosphere. 'Nice to see you again.' He moved towards Rosemary. She couldn't speak.

Frances, after what seemed an age, said, 'I'll do the drinks.'

Ben put his hand out to touch Rosemary's arm. 'I got back at lunchtime. Have you been away? I phoned twice.'

Still unable to move, she said, 'Yes. Shrublands.'

'Where?' He laughed. 'Don't I get to kiss you? Have you missed me?'

Frances put three glasses onto the table. 'D'you want the same as us young man?' she said grimly.

He turned to her. 'What?'

'Us grown-ups are having martini. If you prefer Coke I'm sure Ella's left some in the larder.'

Ben paused to digest her words, then smiled at her disarmingly. 'Make it a martini. It's time I joined the grown-ups.'

'Good idea,' said Frances. 'Excuse me, I need the fluffy girls' room. Rosemary, move yourself and pour the drinks.'

With Frances out of the room, Rosemary stared at Ben. He bent to kiss her, eyes on her mouth, his hand moving to the back of her neck. 'Don't.' Her voice sharp, she turned her head.

'Haven't you forgiven me yet?'

Looking back to him she said, 'For what? Let me hear you say it.'

'Shouting at you.'

She started to laugh, then, seeing his sudden frown, stopped and turned to look out of the window, hoping by not seeing him that her shaking would stop.

Ben said, 'Whatever you thought, nothing happened between Betsy and me that day.'

She watched Ben the cat begin to stalk his way through the tulips outside, an unsuspecting blue-tit pecking at the earth between the still-leafless shrubs. She felt Ben, the man, move up behind her and was trapped. He put his arms round her, she, unable to move in any direction closed her eyes against the panic and stood still.

Against her hair he said, 'She brought me lunch Rosie, nothing else. You didn't give me a chance.'

Feeling his breath on her, the heat of his body, to her dismay she realized more than anything she wanted him still. Frances came back into the room and Ben turned towards her smiling. 'We didn't get round to the drinks,' he said. 'Shall I have a go?'

'No thank you. You need years of experience and a certain amount of class to make a perfect martini. I doubt you have either.'

Ben frowned, and then, after a thought, threw back his head and roared with laughter. 'What makes me suddenly feel I'm public enemy number one? Doesn't anyone want my side of the story?'

'Just Rosemary. Wait till I've gone. Tall stories turn my stomach. I've lived to an age when I've sat through so many.' She handed Rosemary a drink and propelled her into a chair at the kitchen table. 'Haven't you got any nuts?' she said. 'Or crisps even? Anything to help keep the bile down.'

Ben smiled, 'Who wrote your scripts?'

'God,' she said, and knocked back the martini. She bent to kiss her friend's cheek. 'I'm going to make my drunken way home now, darling child. Take my venom out on Michael, poor soul, get him all of a dither. I'll phone later.'

She put her hand out to Ben.

'Goodbye you. You'd better make it good. Over forty, you can smell bullshit a mile away.' And she was gone, roaring away down the drive.

Stay, stay, thought Rosemary, *don't leave me with him. He has me and my common sense in a corner.* They sat in silence for moments. Rosemary finished her drink and poured another from the jug that Frances had made up and put in the fridge. Moving back to the table, she said, 'I'm sorry, d'you want a refill?'

'I'll help myself.'

'I've noticed,' she said and sat down again, waiting now for the scene between them to play itself to its inevitable conclusion.

Ben said, 'Rosie, Rosie – please believe me. There's no-one else. It happened with Betsy once. And that was only because you didn't arrive on that Friday when I asked you to. I was upset. Remember?'

She stared up at him as he stood by the open fridge door. The cold air touched her briefly and she shivered. Letting it go, he moved to her immediately, knelt down and put his arms around her. She didn't move away. 'I'd no idea something so trivial would upset you,' he whispered. 'Betsy was just trivia. I told you before.'

'Ben,' she said, looking at him now, 'Ben I don't want this. *You* I want, but not all the rest of it.'

'There is no rest. Promise.'

She said, 'Where's your luggage? Did you go to Gill's?'

'I came straight here. The bags are upstairs.'

She stared at him, powerless in her desire for him, needing more than anything to believe him, unable to move away from the knowledge she wanted his hands on her, the heat of his body against her, his mouth on hers, the centre of him inside her.

'Are you staying?' she whispered. 'What's happening?'

'Will you have me my darling?' He outlined her mouth gently with his finger, his eyes on her lips.

'Oh Christ Ben,' the tears came too easily. 'Take me to bed. I've missed you so much.'

Chapter Sixteen

May was hot. Suddenly early summer was upon them, driving people into gardens and towards the sea – the ocean still cold with memories of winter.

Ben brought a few clothes to the house, going back to Hackney one day, and returning in the old Metro that evening with a suitcase. Rosemary asked for no explanation. His car sat outside the garage in Rosemary's drive. The cat found a place under it, delighted with the new source of shade. A kind of different normality settled on the house.

Pat and Jennie were told she had a house guest. 'In her bedroom,' sniffed Pat one morning to Jennie, when she had gone through to pick up the coffee at eleven. Jennie remained silent about the whole affair. Her employer had become more erratic in her working hours, not always appearing until well after Jennie had arrived, leaving her secretary to make decisions they had always made together. Some days she disappeared into town early to meet Ben who had left in the morning for a voice-over or interview, and then phoned and cajoled her into lunch.

There was little for Rosemary to do that May except concentrate on Ben. Negotiations were going ahead for a permanent radio spot on one of the commercial channels, the television show had been postponed and no definite recording date ahead had been set.

Ben's interviews were for films abroad, in Europe or America, and many television dramas were being cancelled at the last moment.

But for Rosemary, there was no depression. Life with Ben had taken on some kind of glorious daydream. He came back to her every night. They ate out a lot ('On your gold card I bet,' said Frances grimly) or else they stayed at home, sitting in the sunshine-filled evenings on the terrace outside Rosemary's conservatory, drinking white wine. She cancelled several personal appearances when he found himself free and wanted her at home. Michael said nothing, except to Frances, who then reported back to her friend, refusing not to let her confront what she was doing to her life and career.

'What career?' said Rosemary. 'You can't call being a celebrity a career. It's merely work.' They were sitting one afternoon in the garden lunching for the first time in ages on their own. Ben had gone to see his son. It was Sunday, and Michael was at home with his family. 'That's Ben speaking,' Frances replied grimly. She looked at her friend. They had carried their lunch out to sit under the Portuguese laurel tree in the middle of the garden. The cat lay under the white, wrought iron table, pretending to be asleep but whiskers a-quiver at the sound of newly-born birds. To his fury, Rosemary had put a bell on a collar round his neck which tinkled its warning to the house martins as he stalked his way through the long grass in the wild part of the garden.

'You talk like Ben a lot,' Frances said.

Rosemary smiled. 'I'm happy, Frances. Don't spoil it.'

'Darling child, I wouldn't dream of it. If you're happy that's fine. Does he talk of what's-her-name? Gill? And his son?'

Rosemary shook her head. 'He misses James. That's all he says.'

Frances lit a cigarette. 'Have you still given up again?' she said.

Rosemary said, 'He hates me smoking. And dieting.

As you can probably tell from my waistline.' She laughed and clutched at the handles at the top of her hips.

'Isn't it difficult to live with a man after all this time?' Frances asked.

'A little. Certain things have gone from my life. But he makes up for so much. I miss him as soon as the front door closes behind him. I wait all day for the key in the door.'

'Christ.'

'I'm mad aren't I? Ella thinks so, I know.'

'Is *she* still in love?'

'Yes.'

'I think I preferred this family when it wasn't so cosy.' Frances squirmed. 'There's a feeling in this house at the moment that I find vaguely irritating.'

Rosemary laughed. 'Oh Franny you're impossible.'

Frances said, 'Has he met your mother yet?'

Rosemary looked uncomfortable for the first time. 'No. It's got to happen. I'm going to organize it this week.'

'Hooray!' Frances clapped her hands. 'Can I come too? Let me come, let me come.'

'Definitely not,' said Rosemary. 'I'll phone you the next day. I'm going to bring her here for tea and then we'll all go out for dinner.'

'It's the most delicious idea I've encountered for weeks, my precious. It'll see one of them off, that's for sure.'

Having talked to Ben when he arrived home that Sunday night Rosemary phoned her mother the next day.

'I have to be in town for a second interview for that American film at three,' Ben had said. He had made the coffee for them both, and as usual it was too strong for Rosemary, but she kept silent. It was the way he liked it. 'Let me phone her. Maybe she's free today,' she said. She stood and called her mother, using the wall phone in the kitchen. 'Mum, it's me.'

'I'm in the middle of *Neighbours*,' her mother said.

'Sorry. Shall I phone back?'

'No. The accent irritates me anyway.'

Rosemary smiled to herself. 'Mum, do you want to come for tea?'

'Today?'

'Yes. Then I thought I might take you out for dinner. Somewhere nice.'

Her mother hesitated. 'Well, all right. What a surprise.'

'She never sounds gracious,' moaned Rosemary when she'd put the phone down and turned back to Ben.

'I'll meet you later Rosie. Where shall we take her?' He had stood up.

'Aren't you nervous?' Rosemary asked as he pulled her forward into his arms.

'No. Should I be?' he said, kissing her neck and making her squirm.

'Don't, you idiot, I'm ticklish there.' She pulled away and held him at arm's length. 'You *should* be nervous. She's going to have a fit.'

'Don't tell her I'm living here.'

She looked steadily at him. 'Would you rather she didn't *know* you were here?'

He shrugged. 'It's just easier for you.' He popped a black, oil-soaked olive into his mouth from the bowl on the kitchen table. 'I'm going to shower and look at the script for this afternoon. I'll see you in the restaurant round the corner. About eight?'

'Seven-thirty,' she said. 'She'll want to be home by nine.'

He groaned and disappeared upstairs. Rosemary turned to clear away the remnants of their lunch. She wondered what she was going to tell her mother. Ben was right about not mentioning he was living there, but somehow he had disappointed her. She was suddenly overwhelmed with the knowledge that their relationship was still tenuous, and probably temporary. Panic entered her heart for the first time that May. Confronting it was difficult, and it was all she could do not to rush upstairs and face Ben with that same panic and emotion. She had realized now that the only phone calls he ever got were from his agent. He made the others himself, and never offered the number in Wimbledon. She might have felt for the last few 'ten-feet-above-the-ground' weeks that they were living together, but as far as Ben was concerned, Wimbledon was just his present port of call.

I'll make him never want to leave, she thought grimly. And putting the dishwasher on, she went upstairs to get ready to pick up her mother.

'You're putting on weight,' said Betty as Rosemary put her into the car.

Rosemary secured her into the passenger seat and went round to get into the other side. 'Thanks Mum,' she muttered before she opened the door and put a smile on-to her face. It was warm enough to have tea in the garden and she pulled the lounger out for her mother before she went inside to make the tea and cut some cake.

'No lemon sponge?' said Betty, eyeing the Marks & Spencer very best fruit cake with suspicion.

'Sorry, I forgot. No cake then?'

Her mother took the offered cup of tea. 'Just a small slice. Too rich for me. Especially if we're eating later on.'

'We'll go to the Italian round the corner. Is that all right?' Rosemary placed the slice of cake onto a plate and then put it on the table she had placed beside her parent. 'There's a serviette by the plate,' she said.

'Italian?' Betty sniffed. 'I can't eat pasta.'

'You can have fish.'

They ate in silence for a while. The air was so still, they could hear a lawnmower some distance away. The perfume of the early roses drifted teasingly into their faces. The last of the tulips, splayed out to show their black centres, looked like gypsies in their red-and-gold splendour. The cat came from nowhere and lay between them.

'That gardener of yours has put no stripes on the lawn. You should see the Browns' at the corner of my road. Stripes look nice on a lawn. Your father could never get them right.'

Rosemary said, 'I have a – *had* a friend staying with me. Didn't like the stripes. I thought I'd, well, I quite like just the green.' She finished feebly, caught suddenly between Ben's loathing of striped suburban gardens and wanting her mother's good humour on this particular day.

Betty shrugged.

Rosemary looked up as a plane flew loud and low over the house. The cat stood and stretched, then moved to lie under the nearest tree. From the corner of her eye, she caught a shower of petals from the climbing rose fall onto the bed of dying tulips below. She felt sad. Sunshine and melancholy sat between them. Eventually, 'I've a friend joining us for dinner tonight, Mum. Someone I want you to meet.'

Betty looked sharply at her daughter. She held out her empty teacup and Rosemary filled it in silence. 'Thank you.' Her mother stirred her tea. 'What friend?'

'A man. We're seeing a lot of each other at the moment, and I thought it would be nice for you to meet him.'

'Well, well. D'you have a serious boyfriend at last?' Her mother smiled across her teacup, the steam from the hot liquid making her eyes water.

'Hardly a boyfriend. Not at my age. *Man* friend sounds better. And yes, I am serious about him.'

'Will I like him?' her mother asked.

Rosemary paused. Would she like Ben? It would depend totally on what sort of mood he was in, and whether he decided to play the right game. That much she knew about him by now. She prayed he would be at his most charming. 'I hope so,' she replied. She said no more about Ben. The evening would be upon them soon enough.

And as she led her mother into the restaurant at seven-thirty that evening, Ben was already there. One look at his face and Rosemary smiled. He would play the game. He stood up as they approached the table. Her mother looked up at him, dwarfed quite suddenly by his large and powerful presence.

'Mum, this is Ben Morrison. Ben, this is my mother, Betty Dalton.'

He smiled and put out his hand to take hers. It remained limp within the size and strength of his hand-shake. 'Mrs Dalton. It's good to meet you. Where d'you want to sit? This chair will be the best, with your back against the corner.'

'Thank you. Yes, that's nice. Thank you.'

Rosemary realized her mother had gone into some sort of minor shock. The reality of Ben was obviously nothing like she'd imagined. She stared at him, her face expressionless. Rosemary accepted his kiss on her cheek and smiled up at him as he held her chair.

'I've ordered some wine,' he said, 'I hope that's all right.'

'That's fine. Mum, I think, will probably have a sherry. All right Mum?'

Betty tore her gaze away from the man across the table from her and turned to her daughter. 'What?'

'D'you want a sherry?'

Ben suddenly put his hand out to cover Rosemary's. 'Hang on. I bet I know what you'd like, Mrs Dalton. Did you drink "gin and it" when you were a girl?'

Betty stared at him again. She took in the two hands on the table in front of her. Ben played with the ring on her daughter's finger. She said suddenly, 'You'd

214

better call me Betty, young man. Especially if you're going to buy me a "gin and it".'

Ben laughed. And then Betty laughed. Rosemary stared at her mother. She could scarcely remember her mother drinking gin, let alone with sweet vermouth.

Once the drinks arrived, Ben was talking and leaning into Betty, who actually sparkled at him across the rim of her cocktail glass.

My God, thought Rosemary, *she's flirting with him. She looks like a girl.*

When the wine was poured, her mother holding tight onto her 'gin and it', Ben raised his glass. 'My idea of a perfect evening,' he said, 'is two beautiful women to spend it with.'

Betty giggled and sipped her drink. 'That takes me back,' she sighed at the once familiar taste.

She is pretty, thought Rosemary, *all she needed was attention.*

The evening was Ben's. He was charming and seductive, and by the time he drove Betty home in Rosemary's car (Rosemary was put in the back, Betty strapped and wrapped into the seat beside Ben), she knew her mother was almost as bewitched by him as she was.

'How was I?' he asked, after they had seen Betty into the house and he had checked each dark room for intruders.

'I'll see you again Ben,' her mother had said, and offered one flushed, and by now powder-free, cheek up to be kissed. 'I've had a lovely time.'

'You were quite wonderful,' said Rosemary, answering his question as they drove away from the sight of her mother waving at the front door. She turned and watched Betty squinting through the dark to see their departing car.

'You're a genius Ben. She absolutely adored you. I've never seen her like that – not with a man.'

'Mother and daughter eh? Am I clever or am I clever?'

'You're clever.' She kissed his arm while it rested on the steering wheel as they waited at traffic lights.

He smiled, looking pleased with himself and as they drove away he put his hand out to touch her. 'Feel me,' he said. 'Feel me Rosie. I'm hard for you.'

Still too full of food and wine, they took each other quickly and greedily as soon as they got back to Wimbledon. Standing against the kitchen door, he was insistent and aggressive with her, pulling her old-fashioned silk cami-knickers to one side, holding her head hard against him, forcing his tongue into her mouth.

'I want you, I want you, oh Ben I want you.'

He stayed silent, his orgasm quiet as it usually was, he didn't wait for her, but left her still wet and hungry for him, breathing hard against his chest, crying and laughing, her eyes still closed.

'I love you, I love you,' she said, tears on her cheeks.

He pulled the belt of his jeans tight to him again and put one hand under her chin. She was shaking so much, she could hardly stand. 'Let's go to bed Rosie,' he said. 'It's been a long day. I could sleep for a week.'

He was snoring lightly by the time she had finished in the bathroom. He stirred slightly when she got into bed. 'Put the light out,' he muttered without opening his eyes.

She reached a hand out and switched off the light by her side. She longed to read like she had all her life in bed. But Ben hated the light on, so she lay now staring up at the ceiling where the moonlight was shooting shadows from the clouds across the white surface. The elation of the evening had gone. She felt alone. *This is silly*, she thought. *Relationships work like this.* But it was three a.m. before she fell asleep. Then it was suddenly morning, and she woke to hear Ben singing in the shower next door.

Chapter Seventeen

'It was that evening that it all started to change,' she said months later to Frances. Something had shifted, something she couldn't quite put a name to.

Ben had gone into town with his car and a small holdall that morning. 'Taking some cleaning in,' he had said when she gave a quizzical look towards the bag.

She had followed him to the back door, avoiding Pat, who was cleaning in the living-room. 'Are you back for dinner?' she asked. He blew her a kiss and frowned angrily as the Metro was lazy in getting started.

'Don't know!' he shouted above the sudden noisy springing into life of the old car. 'Don't wait for me, Rosie. I'll see you.' And he left.

She spoke to her mother who phoned to thank her for the evening. 'He's a very nice young man,' Betty said.

'I'm glad you like him, Mum.'

'He's a bit young for you, isn't he?'

Rosemary said, 'Probably.'

'Now don't get too involved Rosemary. You'll only get upset if he meets someone Ella's age. Just go out for dinner sometimes. It's nice to have young friends.'

'Yes Mum.'

The headache that had started after Ben left stayed with her all morning. She phoned Michael. 'Can I cancel our lunch today?' she spoke as soon as he took the phone.

'Something wrong?' he asked.

'No, I've just got one of my headaches. I'm afraid it could become a migraine. I don't really think I'd be much good at talking "business".'

'We must meet some time this week,' he said, 'if you want to discuss this radio series.'

She closed her eyes. 'I'll phone later. I must go out and get some of those migraine tablets.'

'Talk to me before five, Rosemary. All right?'

'Yes, all right.'

By the time she got back from the chemist it was gone twelve, and Pat had gone. Ella had left a message on the answerphone. 'Can Jo and I come home this weekend, Mum? I'll even put up with Ben.'

I'll phone her later, decided Rosemary, and swallowed two tablets with the glass of water that she had carried through to the conservatory. June had brought rain and a certain English, summer-like chill was in the air. She shivered and went upstairs to get a cardigan.

In the wardrobe, some hangers hung empty amongst the few clothes that were Ben's. She frowned and put one hand to her head as if to stop it throbbing.

'He seems to have taken some clothes,' she said to Frances, deciding to phone her after persuading herself one small glass of sherry couldn't possibly make her headache much worse.

'To the cleaners?' queried Frances.

'His jeans. They don't go to the cleaners.' She longed for a cigarette. 'Has he gone, Franny? It all feels ominous. I don't know why.'

'I shouldn't think so for a moment. Gone, I mean.' Her friend paused at the other end of the phone, and Rosemary heard the rustle of cellophane.

'God, I need a cigarette,' she said.

'Darling, don't go to pieces again.' Frances sounded concerned.

'Sorry.'

'And for Christ's sake stop apologizing. You do a lot of that lately. Look, I'll come over tonight. With Michael.'

Rosemary spoke quickly. 'No, oh no, that's not necessary. I'm sure he'll phone. I don't understand why I feel so off-balance. What's the matter with me?'

'Not enough sleep. Go and lie down. We'll phone you later. Darling child, look after yourself. Bless you.'

She looked without interest into the fridge for something easy to eat, and saw a sausage left uncovered on a saucer. The fat around it had congealed, white and hard. She picked it up and began to eat, leaving the empty saucer alone in the fridge. She wondered how long it had been there. Ben was the sausage-eater. *I'll probably be sick*, she thought. As if being physically ill would cover the sudden emptiness left by Ben's strange departure.

Lying on the bed upstairs, she watched the rain against the window, her headache throbbing in time to the relentless drumming on the glass pane. Summer rain. Warm. Cotton dresses under fancy umbrellas. Scuttling feet searching for shelter. Hearing the house martins feeding their young under the eaves of the house, she drifted into a distressed and heavy sleep.

She dreamt of a three-year-old Jonathan screaming for her through the night. Panic. Feet too heavy to climb the stairs. Must get to the children. Screams silenced. No movement from their rooms. His blond, smiling head asleep on the pillow. Nothing to fear. Nothing to panic about. Reaching forward to cradle his small, warm-smelling body. His smile, his head, severed from that tiny frame. Blood, sticky hands on soft fair hair. God help me, God help me – my baby!

She woke crying and sweating. Sitting upright, her stomach ached from the rot she had put inside herself. The rain had stopped. It was dusk. The phone rang.

'Mum?'

'Ella? Oh darling, I've just been asleep. I dreamt about you. No – about Jonathan.'

'You all right, Mum?' Ella said. The line from Nottingham crackled.

Rosemary pushed the hair out of her eyes. 'I'm fine darling. I had a migraine so I lay down.'

'Can we come this weekend?'

'Of course.' She realized she still hadn't been to Nottingham to see any one of the plays. 'When d'you finish, Ella?' she asked her daughter.

'Two weeks. Are you coming up?'

Rosemary made up her mind. 'Yes darling. Next week. Is that all right?'

'Great. We finish with *Macbeth*.'

Rosemary's heart sank. 'Oh good.'

'We'll be there late on Saturday, like last time. See you then.'

When she put the receiver down, Rosemary realized that it was the first time for years that she'd had an entire conversation with her daughter without the expletives. She phoned Jonathan in Birmingham. A young female voice spoke.

'Sorry Mrs Downey, they're not here. I'm the baby-sitter.'

'Just say I'd phoned would you? No message. Just my love.' She undressed and put on a dressing-gown, pulling the warm towelling around her aching stomach. Her face was bare of make-up. She brushed her hair hard back from her face, and looked at herself in the bathroom mirror. Her eyes were puffy from sleep, her skin seemed grey and slack. 'Christ,' she muttered, and wandered downstairs to the kitchen, leaving the bed rumpled.

She made herself hot milk: nursery fare, to bring the comfort of childhood. There were no messages on the answerphone.

She sat and watched the ten o'clock news on ITV, listless with uninterest. Time was when she kept abreast of what was going on in the world. Time was when she wasn't in love. She could scarcely remember feeling so inert. He wasn't coming home. Not to Wimbledon. Not to her. Had he merely got bored with her? Felt the handcuffs of permanency with the words, 'you must meet my mother'? One step ahead of him was not where he wanted her.

The doorbell rang suddenly, making her jump. Frowning, she made her way to the front door. Frances called from outside. 'It's us darling girl, open up. I have cigarettes and champagne.'

Rosemary opened the door and smiled at the sight of her friend with Michael.

Frances said, 'God, you look dreadful,' and strode in, kissing Rosemary quickly.

They sat at the kitchen table. Michael, quiet and sipping his drink, watched her. Frances gave her a cigarette. 'Give up when you feel better,' she said.

'Again?' said Rosemary. 'You always make me succumb.'

They stayed until after midnight. 'Barbara's away,' said Frances by way of explanation. Michael looked away at the mention of his wife's name. Not able to catch Rosemary's eye, he went for more wine from the fridge. *Drowning his guilt*, thought Rosemary. Her agent looked thin and worried. She realized she had been so wrapped-up with Ben for the last month that her friends' problems (which were all too obvious) had been ignored, not noticed, not listened to.

After they left – 'a night together!' said Frances as they got into Michael's car – she left the mess in the kitchen and went back upstairs to bed. She fell asleep within thirty minutes, the television at the bottom of the bed still on.

The breakfast show woke her up in the morning, and she lay listening to Pat downstairs. It was almost nine. Ben was absent from her bed, and she wished she could stay where she was, safe and muggy under the strangely uncrumpled duvet.

The following Sunday afternoon, her mother was there for tea, and Joanna and Ella were in the garden, playing croquet on the lawn.

A certain order descended into her life during Ben's absence. There was little excuse not to meet with Michael and discuss business. Her agent had settled for the radio series, and plans were going ahead for the morning television slot to start in October. A game show. She hated the whole idea, but money, or the lack of its regular arrival, worried her. It had been a non-productive summer, and despite protestations about green shoots, there were scant signs of improvement.

'Times are difficult all over,' Michael had said.

'Accept the panel game,' she told him. 'I should complain? Anyway, I can't turn down work in this climate. I'd feel guilty. Ella's home soon, and even Jonathan is facing redundancy. I'll leave it all to you. OK?' And, dispirited, she had turned away, leaving her suddenly wilting career in other hands. The gap in her private life closed a little, worry about money creeping in to fill the corners of her personal misery.

They sat in the conservatory, her mother and Rosemary watching the girls on the lawn, laughing and hitting the ball aggressively with their mallets. 'Joanna seems nice,' her mother said.

'She is.' Rosemary was firm in her response. She heard the front door open and turned her head. Her mother sipped her tea and ate her lemon sponge.

Ben's voice called from the hall, 'Rosie?'

'Who's that?' said Betty.

'I must have left the front door open. It sounds like Ben. Wait a minute, Mum.' She went into the hall.

He stood awkwardly, the door still open behind him,

the key in his hand, his small bag at his feet. 'Hello Rosie.'

She stared at him. Heart beating frantically, butterfly-like in a constricting throat. She searched for words. This was not the scenario she had prepared. Her voice found, it was deceptive in its normality. 'A phone call would have been better.'

'Don't give me a hard time,' he groaned. 'I know I'm out of order, but I really needed to see you.' He followed her through into the kitchen.

'We're all having tea,' she said. 'D'you want some?'

He put out his hand to touch her.

'Don't,' she said, 'not now. We can't talk now. I've people here. You can either join us or come back later. But I'll need an explanation.'

He stared at her for a moment. Then, 'I'll stay. Get me a mug. Who's here?'

She turned to the cupboard to get him a cup and saucer, ignoring what she always thought of as 'his' mug. He must be treated as a guest. 'My mother.'

'Oh good.'

'And Ella and a friend. Joanna.'

'Shit.'

She looked at him. 'I'm sure you'll cope. D'you want some lemon sponge?'

'Ouch.'

'There then followed the most bizarre tea-party I've ever given,' she related to Frances the following week. Betty had been delighted to see him. Offering her cheek to be kissed, fluttering her eyelashes and accepting a sherry as the afternoon wore its way into evening. Ella was cool, obviously desperate to have a go at him. Joanna got quieter and quieter, keeping her head down, shifting her eyes away every time Ben addressed a remark to her. Once he realized his usual flirting didn't work on either of them, he concentrated his efforts on Betty. Rosemary steered the conversation through the rocks, and by five-thirty felt it was a reasonable time to open a bottle of wine and uncork the sweet sherry lurking in the back of a kitchen cupboard.

'I'll take Gran home,' whispered Ella as she helped her mother prepare the drinks.

Rosemary was desperate for a cigarette, had actually stood behind the kitchen door at one time during the tea-party, just to light up in haste and drag on the Silk Cut with so much speed as she staggered back to the conservatory feeling quite giddy. 'Only have one glass of wine, then,' Rosemary whispered back. 'Mum'll go on about it if it's any more.'

'All right, all right. Fucking hell, talk about the Mad Hatter's,' hissed Ella, putting the glasses onto a tray. It had been the first time her daughter had sworn all weekend.

Once Ella had left with Betty, and Joanna had disappeared upstairs, Ben and Rosemary remained in the conservatory. Rosemary lit a cigarette and stared out at the evening shadows. The girls had left the croquet set outside. The weather was cooler, and a sudden breeze caught the leaves on the full trees and lifted them to the fading sun.

Ben sipped his wine, looking glum. 'Can I come and sit beside you?' he said eventually.

She shrugged and turned her head to look at him. He didn't move. Coming to the end of her cigarette, she lit another immediately. 'What happened?' she asked, wondering if he was going to sit there in silence for ever. It was his turn to shrug. 'Where've you been?' she said. 'Am I allowed to ask? Do I have at least that much clout?'

He stirred. 'Don't give me a hard time, Rosie. I had things to do – sorting out. I can't move in here. It was getting too cosy.'

She stared at him. He had managed to make *her* feel guilty. 'I didn't ask you to.' She pushed herself to speak, trying to find some anger. But she felt nothing. Only a slight amazement at his arrogance, and also a horror of herself for still wanting him. 'What now?' she said at last.

'That's up to you.'

'So what happened?' asked Frances over the phone, two days later.

'What do you think?'

Her friend groaned. 'No Rosemary, you didn't take him back? Tell me you didn't, darling heart.'

'Just on a different arrangement, Franny. I promise you. He's not living with me. We're just seeing each other.'

'In bed.' Frances' reply was a statement.

Rosemary hesitated before she answered. 'He didn't stay on Sunday. Joanna and Ella were there. He didn't like Jo. He bought me dinner last night.'

'And he stayed?'

'Yes.'

At the other end of the phone Frances sighed. 'I give up. How d'you feel?'

'Better.' Rosemary brightened. 'This is good. We have dinner occasionally. It's better for me.'

'No, treasure. It's better for him.'

'He's not sleeping with anyone else, Franny. I asked him and he said no. I said I couldn't have an affair with someone who slept around.'

'Dear God, what does he have? The biggest cock in Christendom?'

It was impossible to explain to anyone why she had given in to Ben again. All she knew was that she felt unable to function without him in her life some way or other.

Ella and Joanna had left on Monday morning, to complete the last week of their engagement in Nottingham. There was no work ahead for either of them.

'Are you coming home to live next weekend?' Rosemary asked her daughter, watching while she packed her few weekend belongings haphazardly into the holdall.

'Yes. Is it all right if Joanna comes?'

Rosemary frowned. 'You mean to live? Permanently?'

'No Mum, just till we can find somewhere together.'

Rosemary paused, then feeling churlish she said, 'Of course, darling. But please, please, no nastiness when Ben comes for the night.'

'We promise,' Ella raised her arm with a salute. 'Guide's honour.' She zipped up her bag and flung it round her shoulder. 'You know I think you're mad, don't you?' she said.

'Yes. But only because you've never seen me like this.'

'This is true, Mother.' Ella started to leave the room.

Rosemary looked around at the chaos all about her that had resulted in the packing. 'Are you going to leave it like this?' she asked.

Ella looked briefly over her shoulder. 'Something has to remain the same,' she quipped.

Rosemary knew she had settled for less as far as her relationship with Ben was concerned. Knowing this, the doubt entered her heart and filled a corner she couldn't erase.

She had gone to see Ella in *Macbeth* the following week. She had been playing Lady Macduff. 'You were wonderful,' she had said to her in the bar afterwards, before taking them out to dinner.

They both beamed, at each other and her. 'Have you booked a hotel, Mum?' Ella asked. They were eating Chinese. Rosemary was picking over a stir-fry with noodles. The return to cigarettes had diminished her appetite.

'No darling, I'm driving back. I've things to do in the morning. You'll be home on Sunday, won't you?'

'Yes.' Ella screwed up her eyes and scrutinized her mother. It was Thursday, and the previous weekend and Ben's return seemed a lifetime ago. Rosemary had seen him twice since then, Monday and Wednesday. The second time he hadn't even phoned, just arrived when the nine o'clock news had started. He had seemed so delighted to see her, and loving in the extreme, that she forced herself not to make any sarcastic remarks about telephoning beforehand. Their lovemaking had been frenzied. Still hungry for each other, she had made herself believe that he was everything she had ever wanted, whatever shape or form he came in. She didn't tell Ella why she was going back the same night, that she hoped Ben would be there again. The drive in front of the house was empty, and annoyed with her sinking heart she went inside to the dark and solitude.

'You're not happy,' Frances said to her over lunch one day.

'Neither are you,' retorted Rosemary.

'Oh I see,' said Frances, 'you tell me yours and I'll tell you mine now, is it?'

Rosemary sighed. 'Oh I don't know, Franny. He just arrives. And after something to eat and drink we go to bed and in the morning he says, "Darling Rosie, you're all I want!" and goes again.'

'Where's he living?' asked Frances.

'He says he has a room with some cousins of his.'

'D'you believe him?'

'I have to.'

'D'you have the phone number?'

'Yes.'

'D'you phone him?'

'No.' Frances threw back her head and groaned loudly.

'Oh my darling girl, you can't confront anything, can you? I'll say one thing for him, he knows you very well. Is sex really enough?'

'I keep hoping I'll go off him. It seems to be all we have in common these days.'

Frances said, 'You know you're not in love with him don't you?'

Rosemary frowned. 'Of course I am. Why else would I allow myself to be used like this?'

'You're in love with his penis,' Frances said deliberately. 'You're obsessed with the sex, my little puritan.'

Rosemary stared at her. 'No. Don't be silly. I'm fifty, for God's sake. And I've never been obsessed with sex, you know I haven't.'

'Not before. Face it, stop trying to turn him into something he's not.'

Rosemary looked down at her coffee, her eyes screwed up against the smoke of her cigarette resting in the ashtray. 'Whatever is he?' she said.

Her friend searched for words. 'I can't find a way to say it politely, my darling,' she said eventually. 'He's a delicious and delectable "cock-on-legs". There's quite a few about, it's just that you've never met one before. Only Ella would know how to deal with them.'

'Not any more,' answered Rosemary with a smile.

'Still in love?' asked Frances.

'Yes. And still out of work.'

'And *still* living with you,' stated her friend.

Rosemary shrugged. 'I don't really mind,' she said. 'I find it quite – I don't know, what's the word? Comforting.' And she did. Joanna had settled without a murmur into the routine of the house. It had been clear from the start that she had no time for Ben, but if and when they were around at the same time she always disappeared, either into the garden, where she had taken to pottering around with a delighted Ernie, or upstairs to read and play music.

Ben disliked her because he knew by instinct he held no mystery for her, and it obviously threw him off-balance whenever she appeared. Ella and he had developed a kind of mutual and slightly sarcastic distance between them. 'Sad really,' Ella had said. 'We were always such friends.'

'No you weren't,' Joanna had chipped in, 'he just made you laugh, and performed well in bed.'

'I've grown very fond of Joanna,' Rosemary told her friend. 'She's like another daughter. I dread them finding a flat. The house will be so quiet. I don't think I could cope with the Ben thing on my own.' She leaned across the table and took her friend's hand. 'What's with you and Michael?' she asked.

'He wants to leave his wife.'

Rosemary's eyebrows shot up in surprise. 'My God. You've taken my breath away. Does Barbara *know*? What about the kids?'

'She suspects, and yes, that's what I asked him. What about the kids?'

'Does he want to live with you?'

'So he says.'

'And you?'

Frances shook her head and sighed deeply. 'I never wanted it to get this far. Cohabitation on a permanent arrangement is not my bag, as you well know.' She laughed, short and brusque. 'Maybe I should be with Ben.'

'You'd never put up with him,' said Rosemary.

'If he's as good in bed as you say, treasure face, I would. The years are going by and I'm not getting younger. Things drop off or get nearer the floor practically every hour that passes.'

Rosemary laughed, and wished with all her heart that,

just for once, she could have that part of her friend's nature. Ben would be no problem.

'I'm in a mess,' said Frances. 'I think I might go to Europe for a while and let them sort themselves out at home.' They left the restaurant and got a cab. It dropped Rosemary off at her car that was parked at the South Bank. She hated the idea of Frances going away. *Who will I talk to?* she wondered to herself as she drove home.

Chapter Eighteen

Frances disappeared to Europe in the middle of July. 'Business can't be worse there at the very best,' she said to Rosemary the day before she left. She would be away for a month. Michael remained quiet about the whole affair, and when Rosemary wasn't immersed in her own emotional problems, she wondered how he was coping at home.

'Don't ask,' said Ella. 'Stay out of it, Mum.' She didn't add, 'you have troubles enough of your own,' but her look implied just that.

The relationship with Ben was predominant in her mind, both waking and sleeping it was all that held her attention. She longed to start work. At least that might get her back into some sort of equilibrium, to the order of her life before Ben eluded her completely. He arrived when he felt like it, and disappeared for days without a word.

'How d'you put up with it?' Frances had asked from Paris one night.

Rosemary didn't know. She clutched the crumbs he threw her, no longer mistress of any sort of destiny, let alone her own. They had days together that were wonderful. At times she imagined everything was fine, she could cope. But then the disappearance again, the lack of explanation. The euphoria when he arrived, and most of all the efforts she made to keep him with her, dominated her whole being.

'Why Mum, why?' moaned Ella.

It was the end of August. Frances would be back soon, and Rosemary was due to go to the States with Michael in a week. She hadn't told Ben. He had not phoned or shown himself for over a week, and that had been the longest time without a word from him. She got herself to Martyn for a long-overdue hair appointment.

'Your ends are terrible,' he moaned. 'Where have you been? Get that dye-pot out. Grey hairs everywhere.'

She went to meetings for the morning show, which started at the end of September. Michael said, 'You look better.'

'Today's good Michael. Not only have I finally done something about my roots, but I'd lost three pounds on the scales this morning.' Michael looked blank. She laughed. 'Frances would understand,' she said.

He shifted his eyes across his office restlessly. 'She phoned,' he said eventually. Then tentatively, 'Rosemary, I think I ought to tell you that I'm leaving Barbara.'

Rosemary stared at him. 'Oh no Michael. Why?'

'It's just a trial separation. Not irrevocable.'

She said, 'I know it's not my business, we've never talked about it, but does she know about Frances?'

'She knows there's someone.' He opened his telephone book. 'I'll let you have my new number. For the time being.' He handed her the card he had scribbled on. 'I've taken a flat for six months. Things should be clearer then.' He said no more about his personal life, and Rosemary was unable to ask. The privacy he treasured made him close down, and it showed on his face.

Ben walked back into the house at eleven o'clock one Friday night. Rosemary was making coffee in the kitchen. Ella and Joanna were watching the television.

'Thought you'd gone for good,' she heard her daughter say. Ella had gone into the hall when she'd heard the key in the door.

'I'm working,' he said. 'Where's Rosie?'

'In the kitchen.' She called out to her mother, 'Another

232

house guest, Mum. More than one night?' she had asked him and walked back into the living-room.

Ben laughed, and Rosemary waited for the kitchen door to swing open, conscious that her heart was beating overtime in the usual way it did when she heard his voice. This time it made her angry. With herself as well as him. She turned as he came in, and refused to meet his smile with one of her own. 'Don't,' she turned abruptly from him when the familiar embrace started.

'What?' he said. 'What now? Don't I get to explain?'

'No, Ben.' She put the table between them, sipping her own coffee, not offering to make him one. 'You can't walk in after a week of silence and just expect to go to bed with me.'

'I'd thought we'd got past the candlelit dinners,' he said. 'I thought our relationship was stronger than that.'

'What relationship? Where have you been?'

'Busy.'

'Me too.' She found her cigarettes and sat at the table. He made himself a coffee, finding the mug he always used. His presumption rose in her throat like bile. Her fingers shook and she lit the wrong end of her cigarette in her haste.

'Oh Rosie,' he turned and watched her confusion. 'You're so silly. Look at you.' He moved towards her, taking the wrong-ended cigarette out of her mouth and putting it in the bin. He placed a new one between her lips and lit it for her, cupping his hands round the shaking fingers as she drew the smoke into her lungs.

'Thank you,' she said.

He kissed the top of her head and pointed to the chair opposite. 'Shall I sit there?' he said mockingly, and before she could answer went and sat. 'So what's new?' he said, after a silence.

'I'm going to the States next week. With Michael.'

He stared at her. 'What for?'

'Just to look around. Meet some people. Talk about work. That sort of thing.' She didn't look at him, closing her eyes against the steam from her coffee.

'How long will you be gone?' he said eventually.

'About ten days. I have to be back for the show by the end of September.'

'Oh yes, of course,' he smiled, 'the somewhat dubious panel game.'

'It's my career,' she said angrily.

'No, my darling. Hosting a panel game cannot be called a career. It's just a job you happen to get paid for.'

She stood up, pushing back her chair. 'Damn you, Ben Morrison! It's *my* work. It's what I do.'

'What are you getting in a state about?' He raised his hands. 'Sorry. You know how I feel about it.'

'I'm good at what I do,' she said. She could feel the familiar lump in her throat that heralded tears, the downward pull of her mouth that was so hard to control.

He rose steadily. 'You look good Rosie, that's why you got the job. How many unattractive women d'you see doing that job? Don't kid yourself. It'll only make you unhappy when it comes to an end.' He had taken her breath away.

She said, 'I want you to go away. Please. Just go away.'

He looked up at her. 'If you go to the States you'll only regret it. They like them young over there.'

'Like you Ben? Like the way you do?'

'Oh shit, not that old story. Is that what all this is about? Have I been with anyone else? Is that what you want to know?' He stood and faced her, suddenly aggressive. The chair behind him clattered to the floor. She heard Ella's bare feet pad hurriedly through from the living-room.

'You all right, Mum?' she said, standing in the doorway, looking from one to the other of the two people facing each other across the kitchen table.

Rosemary picked her coffee up again. 'I'm all right Ella. Go back. It's just an argument.'

'Your mother's jealous,' said Ben, not looking at Ella, his eyes fixed on Rosemary's slowly crumpling face. 'Never had that problem with you,' he went on.

Ella said, 'Jesus Christ, you've turned into such a shit since you got your feet under this particular table.' And she turned and walked out.

'Now she hates me,' said Ben. 'You've turned all your friends against me. Do they all think I'm a shit?'

She couldn't answer. She knew if she forced any words she would cry. They stood and watched each other. 'I'm sorry,' he said eventually. 'I shouldn't have said those things. I just can't bear the thought of you going away.'

'My God,' she gasped, incredulous with his audacity. 'My God, how dare you?'

'I love you Rosie, I don't want you to get hurt. They'll eat you alive in the States and I won't be with you.' He came round the table to her and took the coffee from her hands. He began to kiss her face, her eyes, nose, hair and then her lips. Gently, his mouth closed against her lack of response and with that unexpected gentleness she began to cry. He held her in silence, rocking her in his arms, whispering against her hair. 'Forgive me, forgive me. Don't be angry. No-one looks out for you like I do. I love you Rosie, I love you.'

Too weak now, her anger with him forgotten, only her own insecurity rose up inside her to bludgeon out her depleted determination.

He sat and took her on his knee, holding her to him, waiting for her sobbing to die down. At last he said, 'Let's go upstairs. We can talk later.' He took her hand and led her out of the kitchen and up the stairs.

She heard Joanna and Ella laughing in the living-room. Drowning in confusion, her head beginning to ache, she stood while he undressed her and kissed each part of her body as it became exposed.

'All mine,' he whispered. 'Are you all mine?'

She nodded, glum in a misery she could never have explained, feeling her treacherous body respond to his kisses, wanting him on the only grounds he understood.

They didn't talk. 'Tomorrow,' he said, placing a hand over her mouth when she started to say something, 'I'll be here tomorrow all day. Show me how you love me now.'

Unable to cancel, she left for the States with Michael.

'I'll be back in the second week of September,' she told her daughter. 'The freezer is packed. Have you enough money?'

'Don't worry about us. I'm doing a radio play and there's the possibility of a documentary. The wolf is well away from the door. Joanna's working on a project. We're both fine.'

'What if Ben turns up?' Joanna's voice was bright and clear when she came into the kitchen behind Ella.

'He won't,' said Rosemary. 'I'm not sure we're talking. He's extremely cross I'm going. Says it's a waste of time. I'm too old for America.' Both girls laughed and Rosemary smiled. 'Give the cat lots of cuddles,' she said, while Joanna put her luggage in the taxi. She was meeting Michael at the airport. 'And don't shut him in the living-room at night by mistake. He wrecks the plants if he's trapped anywhere.' She kissed them both and looked miserable. She hadn't seen or heard from Ben since Tuesday, and this was Saturday morning. She felt unattached and hated it, forgetting how once she had languished with delight in her single state. 'I'll phone from L.A.,' she said.

236

'Enjoy yourself Mum. Find yourself some rich American plastic surgeon, and we can all go and live in Hollywood.'

Joanna grimaced at Ella's words. 'Yuck,' she said. They both waved, and Rosemary watched them from the window at the back of the taxi as it pulled away out of the drive. She saw them turn and put their arms around each other before going back through the front door, and envied their delight at the prospect of playing house for ten whole days on their own.

The plane was delayed and she sat with Michael in the British Airways first class lounge. Michael phoned his estranged wife, and obviously spoke to his children, because he came back to Rosemary white and rather shaky.

'D'you want to talk?' she asked.

He shook his head and opened the Arts page of the *Telegraph*. She flicked through *Vogue* and watched the robot-like smiles of the hostesses as they dealt with irate businessmen who would be late for appointments. She wondered if it was better to be a man and not be able to cry when confronted by misery, or herself and wallow night after night on tear-soaked pillows over silent phones.

Los Angeles was hot and the airport busy. A car had been organized to pick them up and take them to the hotel. Michael's partner on Sunset Boulevard had arranged it, along with the bottle of Californian champagne that awaited them in their rooms. Michael was blasé, he had been there several times. It was Rosemary's first visit. It always took her by delighted surprise when she encountered the hospitality and indulgence of the Americans.

Michael phoned her from his room. She picked up the telephone in the bathroom of her suite. 'D'you want a drink before you crash out?' he said. She looked at her watch. 'We should stay up,' he went on, as if reading her thoughts, 'it might be two in the morning to us, but let's do it on L.A. time. We'll be better for it.'

'Let me shower,' she said. 'I'll meet you in the bar.'

'I ordered you a vodka martini,' he greeted her when they met thirty minutes later.

She had changed into trousers, but still felt over-dressed in comparison with the track-suited Californians sitting round the bar. A young woman with a towel round her neck came in behind her and threw herself onto a bar stool. She'd been running, and was breathing hard.

'Diet Coke,' Rosemary heard her say. Michael smiled across the table at her. 'How's your room?' he enquired.

'Amazing.' She started to sip the most perfect vodka martini she had ever had, except maybe once in New York. The miles had put Ben out of her mind more firmly than she'd hoped. 'I think I'm going to enjoy myself,' she said.

'Good. About time.' Michael touched her hand briefly as she scooped some nuts into her mouth. 'We can confirm meetings over lunch tomorrow,' he went on. Then, 'Can you amuse yourself until about one?' he said.

'Are we near shops?' Rosemary asked.

He shook his head. 'You're never near anywhere in L.A. I'll get you a driver. Glen will organize it. Someone will pick you up at about ten-thirty, take you shopping, then bring you to the Valley for lunch just after one. How does that sound?'

'Bliss. But I don't mind finding a cab.'

He shook his head. 'It's difficult here. Cabs are scarce and expensive. Glen'll sort it. You'll meet us for lunch.'

She slept well and woke at nine to leave a message on the answerphone at home for Ella. She called Frances, who'd been back in London for several days already.

'I just spoke to Michael,' her friend said. 'He said you were already impressed with L.A.'

'It's wonderful, Franny. I may never return.'

Frances laughed. 'You have shades of the hedonist in you sweetheart,' she said. 'I guessed it years ago.'

'It's a country made for people,' said Rosemary.

'Rich people.' But Frances was smiling as she spoke.

'I'll see you in about ten days,' Rosemary said. 'This call is just to tell you I'm fine and not even thinking of Ben. Not much, anyway.'

'Good. Find yourself a nice rich American divorcee. Maybe a heart surgeon. For God's sake not an actor.'

'That's what Ella said,' laughed Rosemary. 'But she suggested a plastic surgeon. Is she hinting d'you think?'

'Now there's an idea. I love you precious. Phone me when you get back.'

Glen's driver arrived promptly at ten-thirty and drove her, without a word, to a large open-air shopping mall. 'Mr DuPont's instructions,' he said.

The sun was relentlessly hot. The department stores were cool. The coffee at the food market was served in large plastic mugs. For over two hours she shopped. No-one approached her in recognition, and no scraps of paper or old cheque books were pushed under her nose for a signature.

'It was blissful,' she said to Michael and Glen when she met them later for lunch. 'I realize I should have insisted on the Paul Getty Museum, or at the very least an art gallery, but the shopping was just what I needed.'

'It's the American hobby,' said Glen. 'The way we relax. You should have arranged to meet my wife. Now with her, it's an olympic event.' They laughed, and Rosemary took in the restaurant around her. They were sitting at a marble-topped table on an Italian tiled terrace under an umbrella, sunshine finding spaces through vine-covered walls. The people at every table were talking loudly, drinking iced mineral water and eating salad. Glen continued, 'I've about six meetings set up for you, Rosemary. It's a thought you know: a British talk-show host. How d'you feel about it?'

She loved the way he said her name, rolling it off his tongue like a caress. She shrugged. 'I haven't thought. Not really. Let's wait and see what happens.' How could she leave home? Home. Ben. For a while that morning, she'd forgotten. The pain of him hit her suddenly, overwhelmingly, catapulting her out and away from the sunshine and the clinking of ice on the sides of tall glasses. Back to late summer in Wimbledon. Who was sleeping in her bed? Under the summer duvet, between the pink flowered sheets? Leaving them crumpled and thrown aside every morning with little regard for Pat. Was he quarreling with Ella? Was he there at all? Would he be there when she got back? Or had her disappearance to the States been just that bit too wilful, too disobedient? Too much beyond control.

She shivered, and pushed aside the remains of her lunch. The ice in her glass clanked against her teeth and made them ache, as if to distract her from the empty fear that had come from nowhere, that fought its way through the vine-dappled sunshine and settled unasked in the pit of her stomach at the thought of losing him.

'Tonight you come to us for dinner,' Glen said, seeing her back into the car before disappearing to another meeting with Michael.

'The hotel,' she told the chauffeur, and leaned back against the sweet smell of new leather to close her eyes and shut out the fearful panic of being eleven thousand miles away from all that seemed to hold her together.

She met Glen's wife that night. Marlene. She was tall

and slim, with the wide hair and matching smile of a successful American middle-aged woman. Pulled and tucked, she looked much younger than Glen, but they had been married for twenty years. Marlene was a writer. 'I have several projects I'm working on at the moment,' she confided to Rosemary when she led her upstairs in their big Spanish-style house in Beverly Hills. Glen was obviously one of Hollywood's successful agents. 'I may well go into production,' Marlene said picking up a wide-toothed comb and expanding her hairstyle even more. 'We must meet for lunch Rosemary and toss some ideas around.'

'That'd be nice,' said Rosemary, beginning to wonder whether people actually got paid for just having ideas these days. Whatever happened to actual graft?

There were ten people for dinner and a maid to serve. 'She lives in,' whispered Marlene, 'drives me crazy. Weeps all the time, but won't tell me why. I ought to tell her to go but she's so honest.' She turned to the man on her left who was toying with some sort of colourful starter, set in front of him by the maid. Rosemary thanked her and smiled when her hors d'oevre was put down. The maid refused to meet her eye, and refrained from smiling back.

Marlene spoke to the man still frowning at the food. 'Is this raw fish, Marlene?' he said at last.

'It's Japanese,' Marlene said.

'Raw fish.' And he put his fork down. Holding his glass out for Marlene to pour white wine, he smiled across at Rosemary who was biting delicately into what looked suspiciously like a raw prawn cocktail. 'Rosemary you don't have to eat it. You English are so polite.'

Rosemary had forgotten the man's name, and was grateful when Marlene slapped this particular male guest gently on one outstretched brown, hairy wrist as it protruded from the crumpled white sleeve of his linen jacket.

'You're incorrigible Tom. The English love Chinese food.'

'Marlene my love,' Tom leaned into her, 'Chinese food is *not* Japanese. Not all Orientals live in one big clump somewhere outside this paradise, you know.'

Marlene's laugh tinkled like a girl's. She rang a small bell and the surly maid came in to clear the table.

'Most Americans are very ignorant,' said Tom, confiding to Rosemary in a loud voice across the table. Marlene slapped his wrist again.

'Behave, Tom. It's time you found a wife to keep you in order.'

His eyes matched the blue of his shirt. His grey hair had whitened in the Californian sun.

'What d'you do?' Rosemary asked Tom.

'When?' he teased her, pouring more wine into her glass.

'Work. You know.'

'I'm a plastic surgeon. You see around you the spoils of my work and the reason for my success.'

Rosemary threw back her head and laughed. A plastic surgeon. Tom watched her.

'It wasn't that funny,' he said at last.

'I've never met a plastic surgeon before.'

'It doesn't show.'

'Is that a compliment?' Rosemary smiled at him. When he smiled back it was her eyes he watched.

'Where are you staying?' Tom asked her when they were having coffee later in another room.

She hesitated, then gave him the name of her hotel. 'I'll call you,' he said. 'Maybe we could have lunch one day? Or would I be intruding?' He motioned to Michael, talking and laughing with Glen and Marlene.

'He's my agent, not my lover,' smiled Rosemary.

'I'll call you.'

She found the thought of telling Frances she had actually met a plastic surgeon very funny.

In bed that night she thought again of Ben. His face swam up in front of her. She felt detached from him at that moment, and, confused with herself, she fell asleep and dreamed disturbing dreams filled with inexplicable and forgotten terrors. Her tears woke her at three in the morning. 'Oh Ben,' she said out loud, 'what a mess you've made of me.'

Chapter Nineteen

Tom Woods, Marlene's unattached plastic surgeon, phoned her five days later. She had by the time met three independent production company executives and two others from the main networks. Glen had even, to her horror, organized two meetings with casting advisors from a couple of the main studios.

'Good grief, Glen, I'm not an actress! Whatever for?'

Glen put out his hand to cover hers lying across the top of the large desk in his fourteenth floor office. He had to stand to reach her.

'Episodics, Rosemary. You'd be wonderful in soap. You have the look.'

'Suppose they ask me to read?'

'Then *read*. What harm? Think about it. It's good to get your face around in this town.' She giggled. Glen stood up, releasing her hand and smiling at her. He drank his coffee.

'I've seen flats smaller than this desk,' she said.

'Flats?' he queried.

'Apartments.' The irony was lost. She thought of Ella. 'It's a joke, Mum,' she had once said after a particularly tiresome remark she had made during an equally tiresome argument. 'Joke. Remember them? They were big in the Sixties.' Rosemary giggled again, then turned it into a smile for Glen, who was obviously trying to work out why it was funny to have an apartment smaller than a desk.

'Oh all right,' she said eventually, wondering if at least a visit to a casting advisor would be amusing, if not productive.

244

She met a lot of charming people who all made her feel she was the one person Hollywood had been waiting for for years.

'They're round the lightbulb,' she relayed to Michael, one evening in the bar before dinner. 'I'm exhausted. Five days of such enthusiasm. I almost long for a dose of old-fashioned British apathy.'

Michael laughed. 'Wait till you've been home a week. Even a day. You'll miss "have a nice day" even if they don't mean it.'

'Has any of this made any impression?' she asked.

'One independent is seriously enthusiastic.' Michael put his hand up.

'No, I mean it, *seriously* enthusiastic about a talk show. Let Glen pursue it. We can put it on the back burner for a while. Think of next year.'

She thought of Ben. He'd be surprised. 'Furious, more like,' she said, smiling at herself in the magnified vanity mirror in the bathroom that night before cleaning her face for bed. She looked better than she'd looked for months. Confidence showed in her eyes and her carriage. Tom had phoned that same evening, while she was enjoying her first martini. Michael motioned for the bar waiter to bring the phone to their table.

'Rosemary? Tom here. Tom Woods. We met at Marlene's and Glen's the other night. Is this a good time to call?'

'Hello Tom. Yes, it's fine. Michael and I are just sitting here and having one of your wonderful American martinis.' She mouthed the name 'Tom Woods' to Michael's whispered query.

'Are you free for dinner tomorrow?'

'Hang on Tom.' She put her hand over the mouthpiece. 'Could you bear Marlene and Glen on your own tomorrow?' Her eyes smiled across at her agent.

'Go ahead,' he said.

'Yes, that'd be lovely.' She spoke again into the phone.

'I'll pick you up. Seven OK?'

'I'll look forward to it.'

'Have a nice evening.' And Tom rang off.

'I have a date,' she said. 'Don't tell Frances if you call her. Wait till I get home. I want to see her face when I mention plastic surgeon.'

Michael laughed.

She arrived at exactly seven that evening to meet Tom in the bar. He was waiting for her.

'I'm sorry Tom. The elevator took ages. Have you got a drink?'

He had stood up when she hurried towards him. 'I was early. We'll have a drink where we're going. Is that OK with you?' He took her elbow and led her solicitously out through the lobby and into his car. They drove for what seemed like miles.

'Where on earth are we going?' she asked after about twenty minutes.

'To the beach,' he smiled round at her. 'You haven't tasted martinis until you've tasted the ones you'll get tonight. I hope you like lobster.'

'I love it,' she said.

They arrived at the dimly lit and busy restaurant just before eight o'clock. Rosemary peered around her, adjusting her eyes to the gloom.

'They say De Niro eats here. I always seem to miss him.' Tom said after the barman had taken their order. They sat up on high stools at the bar. Rosemary wished she'd worn a longer skirt. Young women, ones with hair as shiny as their long, long bronzed legs, chatted and squealed all round her. Sleek-haired men, well-gelled and gleaming in the dim lights raised their hands for drinks, or in greetings to other diners.

'Are they all actors?' asked Rosemary.

'Only the waiters,' said Tom.

'They're all so good-looking.' She stared around her.

'And young and tanned and rich,' smiled Tom. 'Our table's ready.' He led her across the room, steering her gently between the table-hoppers and laden waiters. 'We have a view of the ocean. Can you see?'

She nodded and took the enormous menu. 'Where do I start?' she groaned.

'Can I suggest?'

'Please.' She put down her menu and let him order. Her eyes, accustomed now to the lighting, took in the ocean through the fairy-lighted windows. Reflections of the diners moved between the white foam from the waves through the window panes. 'It's beautiful,' she said. 'Thank you Tom.'

He smiled at her. 'Los Angeles drives me crazy most of the time,' he said, 'but there's beauty amongst the madness. Just don't get poor here.'

'All cities are the same these days,' Rosemary said seriously. Tom smiled. 'But being America, we have to have more of it. Even poverty. Private wealth and public squalor. Anyway, enough, here we have grilled radicchio. Eat and enjoy. I hope you have a large appetite.'

'He's delightful,' she told Michael the next morning. 'So polite.'

Her agent raised his eyebrows. He looked suddenly like Frances. 'Polite?' he said. 'That's exciting.'

'Michael,' Rosemary said patiently, 'the last thing I want in my life at the moment is excitement.'

'Are you seeing him again?'

'I don't know. He just dropped me at the hotel. I'm not really sure there were actual sparks. Anyway, what's happening today? Can I sit by the pool please? I'm tired out.'

★　　★　　★

The day before they left, the telephone rang in her room while she was getting ready to go downstairs for breakfast. It was Ella.

'Mum?'

'Hello darling. What a surprise! Anything wrong?'

'I don't know. I thought I'd better warn you. Unless Michael knows already. What time is it there?'

'Breakfast time,' Rosemary's heart began to beat rapidly through her cotton shirt.

'Ella darling, what's happened?'

'You're all over the tabloids. You and Ben.'

Rosemary held her breath.

'Mum. Are you still there?'

'Yes. I don't understand.'

'Photographs. Toyboy and all that load of shit.'

'Photos? How?'

'From Spain apparently. Must have been on that film set.'

Rosemary remained calm. 'Is it nasty?' she said eventually.

'Not really. Gran phoned and went on and on in hysterics. Ben rang.'

'What did he say?' Rosemary's voice cracked suddenly and her knees trembled within her Californian new white denims.

'Wanted to know when you were coming back.'

'Is he angry?'

'Just sounded the same.' Ella sounded bored at the very mention of Ben's name.

'Did you tell him?' said Rosemary.

'I said I didn't know,' Ella answered. 'Is that all right? He can find out, anyway,' Ella went on. 'He can phone Michael's office. He knows one of the typists there.'

'Good God,' was all Rosemary could find to say. Then, 'Ella, I'll deal with all this when I get home. I must go and see Michael. Tell him what's happened. Thanks for preparing me. It'll help no end.'

'It's no big deal, Mum. Terrible fucking picture of you in the *Sun*, anyway.'

'Oh thanks darling,' Rosemary laughed, 'that's cheered me up no end.'

'I'd better go.' Ella was suddenly restless. 'I've got an audition. Joanna sends her love. Oh yes, I nearly forgot. Somebody called Gill phoned. Wanted to talk to Ben. I gave her that number in the book by the phone. Is that all right?'

'That's his cousin's.'

'That's right. She said she had that, but he wasn't there. She rang off.'

Rosemary placed the receiver gently back after the final 'goodbyes'. Where the hell had Ben been staying? And how did Gill get her number? London was another world. Had been for the last ten days. Now it was upon her again, threatening her with claustrophobia after the space of Los Angeles. Quiet and immediately-remembered misery settled once more into the corner of her heart. Real life beckoned. Her life waited with an aggressive patience to be sorted out. Waiting for the old order to be imposed. Maybe the confidence of America would rub off. Maybe she could erase the instinct to close her eyes against the whole mess, hoping it would go away. She made her way to Michael's room. He would know what to do.

'I've heard!' her agent's voice called out to her as soon as she walked through the open door of his room. He was in the bathroom. 'I'm on the phone. Frances. Pick it up in there.'

'Darling girl,' Frances' voice came warmly across the miles to her. 'Michael tells me you're having a wonderful time.'

'I *was*. What about the tabloids?'

'Just a pain, angel.'

Michael interjected, making it a threeway conversation. 'It's not drastic, Rosemary.'

Frances said, 'She's worried about Ben's reaction.'

'I'm still here you two,' Rosemary retorted into the phone. '*She's* still here, you know.'

Frances laughed. 'Treasure face listen. Ben phoned me. Wanted to know what plane you were arriving on. I said it would be foolish for him to meet you anyway.'

'Did you tell him? The time I mean?'

'I said I didn't know.'

'Good.' Michael said.

'Who's running my life?' Rosemary asked.

Frances spoke again. 'Longing to see you. Both of you.'

'Thank you,' Michael's voice smiled.

Rosemary said, 'I'll put the phone down, Franny. I'll call you after the jet-lag.' She rang off and waited on the sofa for Michael to join her. His office had called him early with a business matter and told him about the photographs and story in the tabloids.

'Somebody on the film set in Barcelona,' Rosemary said. 'Oh well, I just hope Ben isn't furious.'

'Why should he be?'

'You don't know him.'

Her agent began to outline his last day in Los Angeles.

Rosemary went shopping for presents. Then they both lunched again with Glen. Both men seemed delighted by the feed-back from Rosemary's meetings. Glen suggested she came over and stayed for a while. She wondered if L.A. was somewhere she could live.

'I'll think about it,' she said, but knew it was only politeness on her part. Her mother, Ella and Ben loomed, *almost grimly*, she thought, as they made their way back to the hotel after lunch.

She packed that evening, and Michael and she dined

alone. Glen was taking them to the airport the following afternoon. In the morning she could have a final swim.

'And get my hair done,' she smiled at Michael. 'Just in case the world and his wife are waiting at Gatwick.'

She slept late, hoping to store some hours up, knowing how difficult it was when it came to shutting her eyes on long flights.

Marlene came with Glen to pick them up for the journey to the airport. The four of them met in the lobby.

The man at the reception desk said, 'Ms Downey?' Rosemary turned, smiling and nodding at him. 'A delivery for you,' he said, and handed her a larger-than-life bunch of beautifully packaged yellow and white roses.

'Oh how wonderful,' Rosemary smiled. 'Thank you.' She searched for the card. Marlene found it, unpinned it, and handed it to her.

'Rosemary, you must have an admirer here. Tell us, I can't wait to know.'

Rosemary studied the card. 'I'm sure we'll meet again. Have a safe journey.' she read. 'It's from Tom.' She smiled. 'Tom Woods. How sweet of him. I must phone when I get home.'

'I *knew* he was smitten,' said Marlene companionably in the back of the car as they made their way to the airport. The flowers stayed in Rosemary's arms. 'He usually loathes on sight everyone I introduce him to. And he's such a great guy. I feel delighted and responsible.'

Rosemary protested with a laugh. 'Don't get enthusiastic Marlene, I may never see him again.' She looked again at the flowers in her arms, while Michael checked in their luggage and the other three had coffee. 'It's such a big bunch. What will I do with them on the journey?'

'Someone will whisk them away and put them in water,' Michael said, coming back towards them. 'D'you want to go through Rosemary? Duty-Free might be beckoning.'

'Good idea,' she said, standing up to say her 'goodbyes'.

'Next year,' said Glen.

Marlene kissed her. 'We'd love you to come back, Rosemary. We miss you already.'

'Next time stay with us,' Glen said.

She left the flowers in the First Class lounge with Michael and headed for the Duty-Free and the perfume. 'Let me try some "Red",' she said to the girl at the counter. 'I've never had American perfume.'

'It's Georgio,' the girl smiled at her.

'And it lasts all day!' An English voice behind her made her turn. Jessica, the actress from the film in Barcelona, was standing behind her.

It took a moment for Rosemary to place her, then she smiled. 'Jessica! What a surprise! What are you doing here?'

They kissed briefly on the cheeks. 'I'm on my way to New Zealand, darling. Some minor part in an Antipodean TV series. Never been, so it seemed like a good idea.'

'Would you like a drink?' Rosemary asked.

'What a wonderful idea. Let's go to a bar.'

They ordered white wine and sat up at high stools. Around them the airport buzzed and milled with international voices, and frequent loud interruptions over the busy tannoy system. Rosemary put some of the new perfume at the base of her neck and then put it away in her handbag. The wine arrived.

Jessica said, 'You are looking absolutely wonderful! You get younger every day. How d'you do it?'

Rosemary laughed. 'I've had almost two quite wonderful weeks in L.A. Does that explain it?'

'Not a lot. Are you on your own?'

'My agent's here. He's in the First Class lounge. Our plane has been delayed for an hour, and it's the middle of the night in London, so he can't phone his office. He has withdrawal symptoms and an irate look on his face.'

Jessica laughed with her. 'I'm glad darling, that you said a rapid "goodbye" to the lovely Ben Morrison. His kind of behaviour should only be visited on the young and hopeful. It's character-building when you're twenty, disastrous over forty.'

Rosemary opened her mouth to speak, to say, 'I'm not sure I've said "goodbye",' but Jessica went on, relentless in her confidences. 'When I bumped into him last month so lovey-dovey with that little creature from the film, I thought well, at least the delectable Ms Downey saw the light.' She looked Rosemary up and down, and then continued. 'And, by the look of you, giving him the boot was the best thing that could have happened.'

Words failed Rosemary at that point. She listened to Jessica leading the conversation from Ben to all the young men who got involved with much older women, and just when Rosemary began to let her mind drift and dwell on the idea of Ben and Betsy, Jessica threw in something about 'perhaps it fulfils the fantasy of screwing their own mother.'

'I believe you've lost me there.' And Rosemary managed a smile as she spoke.

Jessica covered Rosemary's limp hand with her own, and leaned towards her. 'Did he try to see you again after Barcelona?'

'No.' And dredging up a degree of deceptive pride she had summoned from God knows where, went on, 'I realized Betsy was much more his style.'

'Delicious though, isn't he? I think I might have dabbled if I'd been twenty years younger. Would you like another glass of wine darling. D'you have time?'

'Thank you.' Rosemary stirred herself into a sort of animation. She needed facts, however slight, to arm herself with some kind of ammunition for Ben's inevitable reappearance in her life. 'When did you meet him?' she asked, smiling, drinking, fumbling in her handbag for a cigarette.

Jessica offered her an open packet. 'Have one of mine, darling,' she motioned to the barman and put up her hand for two more glasses of wine. Rosemary drained her glass and started the next.

'God knows. About July, I think. Betsy – that was her name wasn't it? – anyway, she suddenly appeared in front of me, dragging him by the arm. She was obviously immensely pleased with herself. I got the distinct impression, darling, she was delighted with her success at landing such a prize. Someone told me in Spain she was a star-fucker. She's getting in early with young Ben.'

Rosemary joined in with the short brisk laugh that came from Jessica. The older actress coughed and spluttered over her drink.

'God I must stop smoking. And drinking come to that. Still, at our age, what other pleasures do we have?'

Rosemary bit off the desire to point out there was at least ten years difference in their ages. She wanted to know more about the relationship of Betsy and Ben. 'You said they were lovey-dovey?' she asked, as casually as her trembling would allow.

'Oh yes. He smiled and kissed her hand. She held on for dear life. I think they were living together. Hadn't you heard?'

'No.' Rosemary prayed the smarting behind her eyes was only the smokey atmosphere around them. She

254

went on, 'I don't mix in those circles.' She did some time arithmetic in her head. July. Ben and she had only just put their relationship onto a more casual level. He was either a liar or an extremely fast worker. She remembered June, the passion and the closeness. She heard herself ask Jessica, 'Have you got Betsy's number? Someone tried to contact Ben the other day.'

Jessica frowned. 'Let me see. I'd have it at home. Tell you what, you give me yours, and I'll give you a buzz when I get back.'

Rosemary knew she would never be able to wait that long, but she smiled and scribbled her own number on the back of an old envelope that Jessica found in the bottom of her handbag.

An announcement came across the tannoy.

'That's my flight,' said Jessica. Both women stood up. They kissed each other on both cheeks, or rather they kissed the air above each other's cheeks.

'We must get together,' muttered Rosemary. 'Come over for a drink when you get back.'

'Love to. So glad we met. You must tell me all your youthful secrets darling. I could do with them!' The actress laughed, loud and deep, raised her hand with the handbag in it, shook her hips in pretended sexuality. 'Tell me how to get myself a toyboy please.' And, blowing Rosemary a kiss, she disappeared into the crowd, leaving the other woman standing alone, small and suddenly vulnerable in the centre of the huge airport, wanting someone to pick her up and put her somewhere safe.

Michael appeared at her side, smelling now of expensive cologne and tweed jackets. Smoke and the taste of Californian wine rose with the bile in her throat.

'Oh Michael,' she said. He took her arm.

'I wondered where you'd got to,' he said, frowning. 'Are you all right? They've called our flight.'

'I met a friend,' she murmured, and they made their way back to the lounge to pick up their airport bags and Tom's flowers.

'Did you keep the sleeping tablets Marlene gave us?' she asked when she was snapping herself into her seat belt once on the plane. Michael nodded. 'Can I have two?' she said. 'I'd like to sleep on this trip. I can't face the depressed state of the British Isles without at least a few hours of rest inside me.'

Michael gave her the tablets. He had asked her nothing about her encounter at the airport, and for that, Rosemary was grateful. She needed to think and mull it over. She took the two sleeping pills and washed them down with a glass of champagne handed to her while the plane was being loaded. Three glasses of alcohol with tranquillizers was not the wisest of actions, but at the very least, it guaranteed sleep. Twelve wakeful hours to dwell on the words of Jessica would have been more than she could face.

The air stewardess smilingly took the flowers from her. 'I'll put them straight into water,' she said, and buried her nose into the cellophane around them. 'They smell beautiful, Ms Downey.'

'Nothing to eat for me,' whispered Rosemary, when they started to bring the dinner around. 'Wake me an hour before we get in,' she said to the same stewardess. 'Can you do that?'

'I certainly can.' The girl put a blanket round her. 'Hope you get a good night's sleep Ms Downey. Nice to have you aboard.'

The pills had begun to work. A feeling of euphoria swept over her. 'Like a pre-med,' she muttered up to Michael who was peering over his reading glasses at her, putting down the papers he had been studying.

'What did you say?' he leant towards her.

She giggled. 'Not important,' then 'we must always travel British Airways. It's so nice to be recognized. I think I missed it.'

The last thing she heard was Michael saying, 'Can I have that in writing?'

They flew towards Britain and into the dawn. Rosemary slept.

Chapter Twenty

A warm September day greeted them when the plane landed. Rosemary had breakfasted, washed and made-up in the final hour of the journey. 'I must phone Marlene,' she said to Michael while they waited for their luggage. 'I've never slept so well on a long flight. Her pills were magic.'

'Somebody from the office is picking me up,' he said, making his way towards 'Nothing to Declare'. 'We'll drop you first.' He pushed the trolley with their luggage, and Rosemary carried Tom's flowers, almost unseen behind the size of the bunch.

She saw Ben first and felt herself grow smaller with a desire to stay hidden. 'It's Ben,' she said, knowing that Michael had already seen him.

And then the three of them met. The two men, tall and imposing, standing awkwardly, their eyes searching each other and then towards her.

'Hello Ben,' she smiled and lowered the flowers so he could bend to kiss her cheek.

He had his hands behind his back and once their greeting was established, he brought them up towards her. He was holding a single rose. White with touches of gold. 'Bit pathetic really,' he said. The solitary bloom trembled in her outstretched hands as she took it. Tom's flowers, forgotten now, hung by her side.

'Oh Ben,' she said, 'how lovely.'

A flashbulb went off nearby. Michael turned, followed rapidly by the faces of Ben and Rosemary. Photographer.

Just the one. He flashed again. A man came towards them, smiling.

'Miss Downey? Mr Morrison? Can we take some photos? We're from the *Mail*.'

Michael stepped in, one arm up across Rosemary. Ben frowned, suddenly unsure of himself. He held on to Rosemary's arm. They heard Michael say, 'Listen chaps, we've had a long flight. Miss Downey would like to go straight home. I'm sure you understand.'

'And *you* are, sir?' the reporter said.

'Miss Downey's agent,' Michael said briefly.

The photographer snapped again. Ben stirred beside her and Rosemary felt his tension turn to anger.

'Leave it Ben,' she said, restraining him now with only her voice. Her hands were full of flowers. 'Michael will handle it.'

Michael turned to them. He looked tired and cross. 'Can you get her home?' he said curtly.

Ben looked at him. 'I have the car. How do we get there?'

'Just take her. I'll handle this.'

Ben turned and took Tom's flowers from her abruptly. She held onto the single rose, her face held down towards the gold-tipped bloom.

'A foolish move Ben,' Michael said quietly. 'Meeting us was a foolish move.'

'Patronizing shit,' Ben muttered as they dashed towards the car park exit.

The photographer raised his camera for one parting shot. Ben, in return, raised the middle finger of his right hand in mock salutation. Michael grimaced, shook his head, then took the journalist's arm to lead him politely and persuasively towards the coffee bar.

The small crowd that had gathered now dispersed; one or two people called out for an autograph. Rosemary ignored them and followed Ben.

'My luggage,' she said. 'Michael's got my luggage.'

'He'll bring it, for Christ's sake,' Ben said over his shoulder as he pulled her along. 'Don't panic.'

The whole episode had taken moments. Once in the car, Ben threw the bunch of flowers into the back, and they drove in silence out of the airport.

'Why are you so angry?' Rosemary said eventually. 'It was bound to happen after the story broke.'

'I didn't think,' Ben said grimly. He glanced at her. 'I missed you Rosie.'

She turned and looked out of the window. Even after her sleep, she felt suddenly exhausted and could find nothing to say. 'I met Jessica at the airport,' she said eventually, not looking at him.

'Jessica? Who's Jessica?' He tooted his horn at the man in the car in front of him. 'Fucking idiot,' he muttered. 'Forty miles an hour in the middle lane.'

'Jessica,' Rosemary said firmly, and turned to watch his face. 'She was on that film with you in Spain. Remember? And what was that little runner's name? Betty? Bessie?'

'I don't know.' Ben's face remained impassive.

There was a long silence. He drove too fast and too close to the other cars for Rosemary's liking, but she said nothing, deflated now about being home and hurled once more into the same atmosphere she'd run from in the first place. 'The rose was a nice thought,' she said, amazed at her weakness at still wanting to please him. He shrugged. He was not to be placated. Once again she was confused, finding herself so rapidly in the wrong and totally unaware how she got into such a position.

'Who sent the funeral bunch?' he asked.

She hesitated. He turned then and looked at her, taking his eyes dangerously away from the busy road ahead. 'Watch it Ben!' He braked quickly. Her heart beat loud and fast.

'Well?' he said. He had pulled now into the inside lane and reduced his speed to a steady fifty miles per hour.

'Well what?' She refused to play his game.

He laughed. 'I see. You had a good time then?'

'I had a wonderful time. Thank you for asking.'

He pulled suddenly into a layby, the abrupt swerve of the car flinging her against the door making her cry out as she hit her shoulder. The car stopped. He turned off the ignition and put his arm out towards her. Without warning, she felt herself flinch and draw back from him. He looked surprised. 'For Christ's sake Rosie, I wasn't going to hit you.' He looked hurt. 'I wanted to kiss you. I wanted to see if you missed me. I never thought you'd leave me in the first place.'

She watched his face. He was like a small boy. Hating herself, she started to cry.

He groaned. 'Oh no. *Now* what have I done?'

Confused beyond belief with his erratic behaviour, unsure of her feeling, she let him draw her into his arms and start to kiss her. He touched her breast, her neck, her stomach; kissed her face, her eyes where the tears still fell, and then excited by her exposed vulnerability, put his hands down the front of her jeans, undoing the button and then the zip. She struggled against him. 'No Ben, no, don't. Not here, not now.' He didn't listen, he didn't hear, his hands held her firmly, tightly, touching her, feeling her excitement building within her, her legs trembling, kissing her protests away, almost hurting her with his fierceness.

'Enough,' she said eventually, weak, disgusted. 'Enough - please. I'm sorry. Take me home, please.'

Satisfied with her pleasure abated, he smiled down at her. She lay quietly against him. He did up her jeans, straightened her shirt as if she was a small child. His child. 'My Rosie,' he said.

She couldn't look at him. Her body shook. Her mind closed against the pleasure he'd given her. Cars on the road beside them went by relentlessly. The sun shone. Ben put on a Miles Davis tape. Rosemary wiped her eyes and repaired her make-up and her hair. Ella and Joanna would be home.

'Can we go now?' she said at last.

He smiled at her. 'Just a minute my darling,' he said, and reaching into the back seat he picked up Tom's flowers, opened the door of the car and threw them as hard as he could. The sun glinted on the cellophane as they flew into the brightness. She watched them fall into the blackberry bushes, the berries ripe now for picking. She thought irrationally and ridiculously, *I haven't made jam for years*. Ben smiled at her.

'Goodbye L.A.,' she whispered.

He didn't hear, or at least, did not respond, but turned the engine on and pulled out onto the road again. She closed her eyes and prepared herself for Wimbledon.

For four days, and four nights, Ben stayed with her. And other events fell around her so fast and in such a devastating manner that she was glad at least for the solidarity of his physical presence.

'I'm afraid I've fallen out with Gran,' Ella said when she'd been home only an hour and scarcely unpacked.

Ben had left her almost immediately, kissed her tenderly, and said, 'I'll be back by five. I promise. I'll make supper.'

And unable to find the time or the energy to ask about Betsy or Gill or anything, she had nodded and listened to the car pull out of the drive, trailing its usual noisy exhaust.

'He must get that car fixed,' she'd muttered.

'Did you hear me, Mum?'

Rosemary looked up from the coffee she was stirring

with some double cream she'd found in the fridge. 'What did you say darling?'

'I've rowed with Gran.'

Rosemary frowned. 'What about?'

'I told her about Joanna and me.'

'What d'you mean?' In her jet-lagged state, she found the conversation confusing. Ella said patiently, as if to a child, 'Sorry Mum, I meant to leave it and tell you later, but I wanted to get the info in before Gran. She'll phone soon enough.'

Rosemary stared at her and then laughed. Ella looked relieved. 'Why on earth did you tell her?' said Rosemary. 'More to the point *how* on earth did you tell her? I wouldn't know where to begin!'

Ella sat down opposite her, wiping the surface of the table with a clean tea towel she had in her hand. Rosemary remembered a time when it would have irritated her, and a J-cloth would have been thrown in her daughter's direction. She stayed silent and waited for Ella to explain.

'She phoned a few days ago, furious about the photos in the newspaper. I tried to be patient and explain it would blow over, but you know what she's like. More worried about what her neighbours would think than any humiliation you might feel.'

'She's not that bad.' Rosemary's protest came weakly, more due to tiredness than lack of agreement.

'She *is*,' Ella retorted and took a deep breath. 'Anyway, because I didn't commiserate with *her* humiliation, she started asking whether that fat friend of mine was still living here and when was she going to find somewhere to live and stop sponging on you!'

'Bloody cheek!' Rosemary said quickly.

'That's what I said.'

'Those *exact* words?' Rosemary raised her eyebrows.

Ella shrugged. 'Well, one of the words might have been different.'

'You'll give your poor grandmother a heart attack one day if you keep saying "fuck" in front of her. She'd be happier if you robbed a bank. She hates swearing.'

Ella went on. 'So she said. Hates swearing I mean, not robbing the bank. Anyway, I told her I loved Joanna, that we were lovers, that you didn't mind, and she should stop interfering in *all* our lives.'

'Then what?'

'She put the phone down.'

Rosemary stood and took her empty coffee mug to put in the sink. 'That's my mother,' she said, 'never confront anything unpleasant. Just replace the receiver.'

Ella stood and came over. She put an arm round Rosemary's waist. 'I'm sorry, Mum. Can you handle it? She's bound to phone. You've got until three – I told her you'd be home then. Gives you a few hours. She got *that* information before the row.'

'It's all right darling. I'll tell her you were being provoking.'

Ella took her arm away and stepped back. Her voice was suddenly raised.

'Fuck it Mum, no! Don't be your mother's daughter. Just for once, *you* confront her. You're both the same, for Christ's sake!'

Rosemary turned to her, surprised, almost shocked at her outburst. 'What d'you mean? My mother's daughter? I'm nothing like her.'

'Yes you are! Just tell her straight. For fuck's sake just *tell* her. If you'd said you were actually sleeping with Ben she wouldn't have been quite so shocked when she saw those stupid newspaper photos of you both gazing into each other's eyes!'

Rosemary sighed. 'OK, I'll try,' she said. 'And you're right. I'm a coward. Anything for a quiet life.'

Ella had calmed down. 'If you could actually face

anything properly, you'd have got that key back from Ben by now,' she said.

Rosemary's eyes narrowed. 'Don't push your luck.' Her voice was low and edgy.

Ella grinned and raised her hands in surrender. 'Your business,' she said.

'Now,' said Rosemary, 'have you anything else to tell me before I sort my cases out? Any more bad news?'

'Ben's shitting all over the house.'

'What?'

'Not him, the cat! He's shitting everywhere. The vet says it's old age, he can give him something, but it might not work for long. He does it a lot when Ben's here.'

'Now I'm completely confused.'

'Your lover stayed *twice* while you were away,' Ella spelt the words out carefully, 'and both times Ben the cat messed all over your bedroom!'

'Good God. Ben must have been livid!'

'He was. He bribed me into clearing it up. Said it made him gag. And he kicked the poor cat through the cat door.'

'He hates cats.'

'The cat hates him.' Ella moved towards the fridge. 'Can't say I blame the creature. Men are pathetic when it comes to cleaning up.' She opened the fridge door. 'I'm starving. When are you going shopping?'

Rosemary laughed. 'Let me at least unpack first!' She made her way into the hall, calling over her shoulder, 'Hold any more news until I've showered. I'll be able to tackle it better if I'm clean.'

She'd digested the news of Ben's sojourn at Wimbledon while she'd been away, and wondered who or what he'd been escaping from. She found the thought of him sleeping alone in her large bed rather pleasing, *like a homing pigeon*, flashed through her mind. *Suddenly I'm his security blanket.* But it delighted her. She would say nothing about it. She showered, unpacked, ate lunch. 'Where's Joanna?' she asked.

'Oh yes, I forgot you didn't know: she's working on two new plays at a pub theatre in North London. She's going over the script with the writer.'

'Good.'

'The money's terrible,' Ella said brightly, and then more seriously, 'you *don't* mind her being here, do you Mum? It's only money that's stopping us getting a place of our own, and we don't fancy a bed-sit between us.'

'I'm not surprised.' Rosemary looked up from her lunch. 'The thought of sharing a bed-sit with you would fill anyone with horror, even Joanna.'

Ella laughed. 'I'm going upstairs.' She left the conservatory where Rosemary had sat down to eat. 'Call me if you need me.'

The phone rang at exactly three o'clock. It was her mother.

Rosemary took a deep breath. 'Hello Mum. All right?'

'When did you get back?'

'I had a lovely time,' said Rosemary.

'Anyway, you're home.' Betty paused at the other end of the phone. Rosemary waited, refusing to help her mother into the conversation she obviously wanted.

'Yes, I'm home,' she said.

Betty Dalton eventually went on. 'You know, I suppose, that Ella was rude to me? Did she tell you how upset I've been?'

'About the newspapers? Yes, she told me.'

'Oh I'm over that.' Betty's voice was dismissive, then she lowered her tone as if someone was listening. 'It's the other thing. What she said about that girl that's living there.'

'Joanna.'

'Yes. Her.'

'Go on, Mum.' Rosemary was patient, dredging up the courage to be truthful.

'Well,' Betty went on, 'it's what she said. It's silly. I can hardly tell you.'

'They're lovers, Mum. They're in love.' She said it loudly, quickly, and waited for the predictable reaction. She heard the intake of breath from her mother.

'You mean you know? It's been going on under your roof, and you condoned it?'

'Yes. Ella is over eighteen. And Joanna is a nice girl.'

'*Nice* girl? It's what they *do* that worries me.' Betty's voice began to rise in near hysteria. 'A granddaughter of mine indulging in God-knows-what. We never had anything like this when I was a girl. They should never have made it legal.'

'It's just legal, Mum, not compulsory.'

'Don't be smart with me Rosemary.'

'Look, Ella is gay. And between two women it has never been illegal.'

'Of course not, it never used to happen. *You're* to blame, you know.'

Rosemary was taken back at that remark. 'How?' she said.

'Having that boy, that Ben there. I suppose you've been sleeping with him. The whole house is just a mess. Well you didn't get it from my side of the family.'

'Mum,' Rosemary interrupted her, 'Mum, I'm still jet-lagged and I think I'll put the phone down. I'll call you tomorrow, or maybe the next day.'

'Are you going to let your daughter carry on like a pervert?'

Rosemary felt herself begin to tremble. It reminded her of childhood misdemeanours. Just the tone in her mother's voice was enough. She said firmly, 'I don't want this conversation Mum. Listen – Ella is gay. It is not a crime. You must just face it. I know it's difficult for you, and I'll be patient, but she's still the same Ella.'

'And don't use that silly word,' her mother said.

'What silly word?'

'Gay.'

Rosemary laughed. 'Mum, I'm too tired to dodge all these clichés. I'll phone tomorrow.'

'I'm very upset.' Betty began to sound suspiciously near tears.

'I know. You'll get over it.' And she replaced the receiver.

Ella was standing behind her. 'You were wonderful,' she smiled broadly at her mother.

'I'm still trembling,' Rosemary said. 'Is it too early for a drink?'

'Yes.'

'You're right. Put the kettle on. We'll have tea.'

The phone rang again. Ella picked it up. 'Who's calling?' she said, looking across at her mother who was about to move into the kitchen. Then, 'Oh hello Barbara. How are you?' She put her hand over the mouthpiece and mouthed across to her mother, 'Michael's wife.' Rosemary frowned. 'She's here,' said Ella into the phone again, 'hang on!' And she handed the phone across.

'Hello Barbara,' Rosemary spoke tentatively. Ella pulled a face and backed into the kitchen in mock horror.

'Rosemary.' Michael's wife's voice was tense. 'Please be truthful with me.' Rosemary's heart sank, but she remained silent. Barbara went on, 'I know you've been to L.A. with Michael. I just want someone to tell me what's going on.' Her voice cracked.

'Surely Michael's said something?' Rosemary's tone

was gentle, her heart going out towards the tears in the other woman's voice.

'Said something?' Barbara came back, shrill, sharp, 'Said something? Of course he's said something. He's left us. You must know that.'

'Yes I do.'

'Well. What have *you* got to say?'

Rosemary paused, surprised at what sounded like accusation in Barbara's voice. '*Me?*' she said. 'It has nothing to do with *me*, Barbara. However sorry I feel, however much I don't want to take sides, I can't interfere.' She heard the tears start at the other end of the phone. Eventually she spoke again. 'Barbara, listen, there's nothing I can do. What d'you *want* me to do?'

'Leave him alone.' The woman at the other end of the phone spoke now in a whisper, her tears subsiding, her words spoken with obvious difficulty. 'Please leave him alone. We need him.'

It took moments for the truth of Barbara's belief to sink in, then Rosemary said, 'It's not *me*, Barbara. For Christ's sake, whatever made you think that? He's not with me!' She spoke vehemently, horrified that Barbara should have come to such a conclusion.

Faced with an obviously truthful and immediate denial, Barbara spluttered, 'Oh God, oh God, I'm sorry Rosemary. It's just that he always seemed to say he was with you, and when he mentioned about you being in the States with him and everything . . . Oh God, I'm sorry. Please, just forget I phoned.' She started to cry again and just as Rosemary had decided to interrupt, Barbara put down the phone.

'It's like being in a bad B movie,' Ella remarked as they drank their tea and Rosemary related the conversation.

'I must phone Michael.' Rosemary stood up and went back into the hall to find his new number on the pad by the

269

phone. There was no reply from his flat so she dialled the office.

'He's not back until tomorrow,' his secretary said efficiently. 'Would you like to leave your number?'

'You're new,' said Rosemary.

'Yes I am,' the girl said.

'He knows my number. It's Rosemary Downey.'

'Oh Miss Downey. I'm sorry.'

'It's all right. I'll probably track him down before tomorrow anyway.' She rang off and dialled Frances' number. The answerphone was on, so she left a message. 'If anyone's there, can you phone me?' she said. 'It's Rosemary.'

By five-thirty Ben had returned, coming through the front door at the same time as Joanna.

'D'you want tea or a drink?' Rosemary asked him when Ella and Joanna had disappeared upstairs. She got a bottle of wine from the fridge door. 'I want a drink,' she said, not waiting for his reply.

'OK.' Ben flung his hold-all into the corner by the door.

She eyed it. 'You staying for a while?' she said.

He smiled. 'D'you mind?'

'No, I've had a dreadful day so far. Nothing you could do could make it worse.'

'Maybe it'll get better,' Ben said, his arms round her while she poured the wine, his lips against her hair.

Chapter Twenty One

She was too tired to confront him about Betsy properly that night. They both drank too much. Ben cooked and the four of them ate in the kitchen. Even Joanna laughed at his jokes. He was again the man he'd been when he'd first appeared in her life.

She fell asleep half-way through the spaghetti, and Ben walked her upstairs and put her to bed.

'Was it my cooking or my jokes?' he asked, and tucked her too tightly under the duvet.

'Don't tuck it in,' she started to say, but sleep overcame her, a jet-lagged, coma-like unconsciousness coming upon her swiftly. Ben left the bedside light on and went downstairs.

It seemed only moments later when the phone woke her suddenly. She sat up. The room was dark, Ben was asleep on his back, snoring softly and in a way she often found rather endearing. For a moment confusion engulfed her. Then she remembered. She was home. She picked up the phone and spoke softly.

'Hello.'

'Rosemary?' It was Frances.

'Franny! What is it? What's the time?' She peered down at the illuminated clock by the side of the bed.

'Two-thirty,' Frances said.

By now Rosemary's eyes had focused and her confusion cleared. 'What's wrong?' she asked, panicking too quickly.

'A crisis darling. I need an ear and maybe a shoulder. Barbara's overdosed. Michael was here until half-an-hour ago and then went home. The eldest son was on his doorstep. Michael hadn't left his answerphone on.'

'I know.' Rosemary, fully awake, sat out of the bed and felt around for her slippers. 'I tried to get him earlier. Barbara phoned me in a terrible state. She thought I was the affair he was having.'

'Oh Christ.' Frances, sounding tired, sighed.

Rosemary heard her light a cigarette. 'Is she in hospital?' she asked.

'Yes. Stomach pump. Michael's at the house now. With the children.'

'D'you want to come over here?' Rosemary asked, reluctantly looking down at Ben, still asleep.

'Is that OK?'

'Yes,' she agreed firmly.

'I told Michael I'd be with you, I guessed that's what you'd say. See you soon.' And Frances was gone.

Ben stirred as she found her dressing-gown and left the bed.

'What is it?' he said. 'You all right?'

'Go back to sleep,' she whispered. 'Problems with Franny. She's coming over.'

He turned away from her and closed his eyes again. She went downstairs. The house was chilly. She could smell autumn in the night air, and closed the small window in the downstairs cloakroom. Fully awake now, she went into the kitchen and put the kettle on for tea. Somebody flushed the toilet upstairs. She heard Joanna's plump feet padding comfortably back to Ella's room and the murmur of conversation as the bedroom door opened and then closed. The hall clock struck a quarter to three. The house fell silent again. She made tea and sat waiting for her friend.

'Who found her?' she asked Frances later.

'She phoned the hospital herself.' The pile of cigarette

ends in the ashtray was growing fast. They were still sitting in the kitchen. Rosemary, hungry after only half a dinner had made some toast. Frances just smoked. 'It was simply a cry for help,' she said, looking at her empty tea-cup.

'Poor woman.' Rosemary moved to put the kettle on again. 'D'you want more tea darling?'

Frances looked up at her. 'Do you blame me?' she said.

Rosemary shook her head. 'I can't,' she answered. 'I'm too close to you. I think I blame Michael.'

'Shit, shit, shit!' Frances stubbed out her cigarette. Some debris from the overfull ashtray escaped onto the table. Frances' voice was loud. 'I *told* him not to leave home! How the hell did I get into this mess?' She lit another cigarette.

Rosemary could stand it no longer and emptied the ashtray. 'Michael's in love with you,' she said lamely.

Frances looked at her. 'It's not a reason to turn your life upside down.'

Rosemary said, 'It is for some people, Franny. Michael's one of those people. He just chose badly. I mean, at this point in his life.'

'Is that an accusation?' Frances' voice was sharp.

Rosemary came across and put her arms round her friend. She spoke with passion. 'Good God, no,' she said. 'I'd love to be like you. I envy your ability to enjoy without commitment. Look at the mess *I'm* in.'

Frances said, 'What mess? You're not in a mess. For Christ's sake – *Barbara's* in a *mess*. All you've done is fall in love with a young man who's a good lay and is giving you a good time in bed, and you've convinced yourself he's something he's not. That's all. Anything else is your own making. Your silliness. Like Michael. He wouldn't listen to me. *You* don't listen to Ben. Don't see what he is. The truth doesn't fit into your particular upbringing that matches sex automatically with love.'

273

The two women drew apart. Frances smiled. 'Sorry. I shouldn't take it out on you.'

Rosemary said, 'No, you're right. I've been accused twice today now about not confronting things. I'm so tied up with my own problems that the rest of life seems to have become peripheral.'

Their hands touched. Rosemary rose to make more tea. They watched the sun come up and smoked, ate cornflakes and listened to the birds outside. Morning had come, and sleep had evaded them. Frances bathed and went to work. Rosemary went upstairs to shower. Joanna padded to the kitchen to make coffee. And Ben stayed. The day took shape, and Rosemary wondered what else would make its turbulent way to her door.

The day that Michael went home was a time for contrition all round.

Ben was filming in North London, a night shoot, so he disappeared for work at teatime. By then, Rosemary had phoned her mother and apologized, accepted the acceptance with gritted teeth, and spoken to Michael, who had collected Barbara that afternoon from the hospital, cleansed and drained of both emotion and sleeping tablets.

'Forgive me Rosemary,' she had said when taking the phone from a husband still stunned and ill-at-ease with the chaos his loins had created.

'I understand,' was Rosemary's reply.

'Sorry,' said Michael. 'We're all sorry.'

Too right, thought Rosemary, and out loud, 'I'll speak to you at the office tomorrow, Michael.'

'I'll be here,' he said. 'Just sorting things out. You know.'

She phoned Frances, still at work. 'It's over,' said her friend, still exhausted from their sleepless night. 'I've told him it's over. I can't cope with all that in my life.'

274

'She's as selfish as you,' muttered Rosemary to Ella that evening. She hunted in the freezer for some remembered left-over meat sauce for pasta, tucked away in Tupperware during more organized times.

'We ate it,' said Ella, answering her mother's query and ignoring her first remark.

Ben the cat messed in the spare room. Someone had locked him in by mistake.

'It just old age,' said Rosemary, cleaning it up with a mixture of pine disinfectant and washing-up liquid.

'Hope it won't happen to you,' Ella retorted.

Rosemary ignored her. 'We'll get Chinese,' she said. 'Is that all right? I can't stomach the thought of cooking. It'll have to be all right.'

They ate with plastic forks, the food straight from the foil-covered containers, the monosodium glutamate sticking to their tongues, overwhelming the taste of warm red wine. Joanna, bright and enthusiastic still with life, chatted about the new play. Ella was depressed about the lack of work. Rosemary would start the radio series the following week.

The phone rang that evening four times. Once from Frances, apologizing.

'Not you, for God's sake,' groaned Rosemary. 'I never want to say or hear "sorry" again. Even the cat seems contrite. He's not left my side all evening.'

'I'll phone in a couple of days,' said Frances. 'I must sleep for about twelve hours and then go up to Edinburgh tomorrow.'

The producer of the new television series called, young and eager. 'We'll get together next week,' he said, 'just a chat.'

'I start in four weeks,' Rosemary told Joanna as they loaded the dishwasher. 'I'll be glad to be busy again.'

Ella, behind them, finishing the ice-cream straight

from the half-empty cartons, sighed deeply. 'It's all right for you two,' she muttered.

'Go and get a job,' said Joanna. 'Any old job. Waitressing. Anything.'

Ella sighed again and wandered upstairs. Moments later they heard the familiar sounds of Madonna drifting down into the hall and through the left-open door of the kitchen.

Joanna grinned at Rosemary. 'She'll be fine,' she said, 'don't worry about her.'

Left alone, Rosemary went into her study to sort out her diary. The phone rang for the third time. She heard breathing and then the dialling tone again. She went to bed. One more night's sleep and then she could tackle Ben about Betsy. She was tempted not to bring it up. They had been comfortable together since she had come home. Maybe if she ignored it, it would go away.

He made love to her when he crept into bed the following morning. Took her without speaking, without waking her first. She lay in his arms when they had finished. The hall clock struck four. Convincing herself that his actions were matched with a loving heart, foolish in the security of believing the lies she told herself, she said, 'Can I ask you something?'

He kissed her hair. 'What?'

'You may not like it,' she said. She stroked his arm, wishing she could see his face, feeling his sleepiness now creeping through his body. The room was dark, the moonless sky unseen through the open curtains.

'Ask me Rosie,' he muttered, 'but make it fast, I'm falling asleep.'

'It's about Betsy,' she said. Quickly, before her courage evaporated. He said nothing. 'Are you seeing her?' she spoke again.

'No.' It was all he said.

She pulled away and sat up, peering through the darkness, desperate now to see his eyes and the expression in them. She put out one hand to find the bedside light.

'Don't,' he said. 'Leave it.'

She brought her hand back to touch his cheek. The room stayed in darkness. 'Were you?' she asked.

'I bumped into her. We had coffee. We met what's-her-name. That's all.'

'Jessica.'

'Yes.'

She waited. 'I don't believe you.' Her words were whispered. They were out without thinking. Instinct had won the day.

'That's tough,' he said. She shuddered. 'I'm joking Rosie,' he said, 'Just joking.'

'It's not funny.'

He groaned. Sat up with her. Turned the light on. 'I slept with the girl,' he said, taking her hands, his face close to hers, his brows heavy now with a frown. 'I can't just ignore her if we meet unexpectedly.'

'All right.' She didn't want him angry. 'Don't be cross,' she whispered, 'don't be cross with me.' Childlike, afraid of losing him again, she felt herself slipping once more into his power, his web, his arms.

'Be like this,' he murmured. 'I like you like this.' He mouthed his words against her hair. Aroused by her weakness, he made love to her a second time that night. Feeling distressed, soiled, excited by his sudden and sleepy passion, she asked no more questions. This was how he wanted her. This was how she'd be. This was the way to keep him. Powerful at work, she would be a child at home. Could it be that this was right for them as a couple? Happiness came in different forms, and was not always matched with peace of mind. She understood that he had tapped a need for domination in her that both frightened and excited her. It suited him so, without question, it suited her. Comforting in the short term, she clung to him. Her need was his need. So what if she spent some of her time pushing the days uphill? He would come and make it fine, because it was what he wanted.

I'll divide my life, she thought as she began to drift towards sleep. *This way he'll always come back.* And telling herself it was what *she* wanted as well, she dismissed the thought that it was all he had to give.

Her life once again swung into workman-like action. Jennie greeted her return gladly and cheerfully, accepting the presents which Rosemary had brought back for the children with much delight. Pat moaned persistently about the mess created by Joanna, and in particular, Ella. Her mother was organized to come over for lunch the first weekend.

Four days after her return from Los Angeles, Tom, Marlene and Glen were almost forgotten. For four nights Ben had come back to Wimbledon. She asked nothing more of him. She had mentioned about Gill phoning. He said he'd deal with it. 'I'm seeing James on Sunday.' He kissed her when he spoke. It was the only way she ever knew whether he would be there or not. He came and went. She wondered at the self-indulgent way he lived his life. She dwelled no longer on her own complicity with his behaviour.

Frances was coming back on Sunday and coming to lunch at Wimbledon. 'I'll pick Betty up,' she'd said.

Michael went back to the office, and on the phone to him, after a visit to the supermarket, Rosemary finally broached the subject of his personal life. 'Tell me how Barbara is. And the children.'

He answered tentatively, 'Better.'

Rosemary doubted it. His voice betrayed the tension he must be feeling. *The house must be hell,* she thought. Barbara always cried a lot without reason, so at a time with good reason, the atmosphere must be more than a little moist.

After a pause, Rosemary, desperate to get the ice-cream she'd just bought into the freezer, Michael said reluctantly, 'I can't get hold of Frances. And there's no way I can just leave a message on her answerphone. D'you know where she is? When she'll be back?'

She toyed with the idea of saying 'no', but knew he wouldn't believe her. She ran her finger round the lid of the carton of ice-cream. It had begun to melt. She licked her fingers. Chocolate chip. Joanna's favourite. And Ben's. 'I'm not sure she thinks it's a good idea to contact her, Michael.'

'We can hardly just leave it.' He sounded tired. Obviously too embarrassed to question her further, he said instead, 'Will you ask her to phone me next week? I'll be in the office Monday morning.'

She wanted to say, 'Don't! Look after your wife. Make a clean break.' But she didn't. 'I can ask her,' she said, 'but I have to be honest, I don't hold out much hope.'

Michael sighed. Two days of marital disharmony loomed ahead of him. 'I'll be at home if you need me urgently, Rosemary. Have a nice weekend.'

'Love to Barbara,' she said, but he had already gone. She would have liked Ben to take her out occasionally but he never suggested it. She prepared dinner. She had no idea if and when he would return. She merely waited.

'The cat's messed on the landing,' said Ella, coming into the kitchen and poking around in the Tesco's plastic bags. Rosemary slapped her hand away as she took out the bread and started to pull off parts of the crust. Ella ignored her with a laugh, ate the crust and put the tattered loaf into the bread bin.

'Clean it up, then,' Rosemary said.

'Think I'll wait till it gets hard,' Ella puckered her nose, 'it'll be easier then.'

'You're disgusting.' Joanna had come in and was helping to put away the shopping. 'I'll do it Rosemary.' She went upstairs with kitchen paper and disinfectant.

'What's the matter with that cat?' Rosemary said, frowning, her voice a mixture of worry and irritation.

Ella shrugged. 'He's been scraping up all the earth in the plants as well,' she said, and left the room to watch Joanna.

'Please God send her some work,' muttered Rosemary, 'she's driving me mad.'

The three of them ate on their laps and watched the television.

'Can't miss *Coronation Street*,' Ella said, curling her legs underneath her.

'Leave some for Ben!' Rosemary shouted as the two girls went into the kitchen for second helpings.

'Too late,' Ella yelled. 'He can make something for himself. What time's he coming in?'

Rosemary didn't answer. Annoyed with Ella, herself and Ben, Rosemary slipped into the trance-like repose of the television addict. At eleven, she tipped the cat off her lap, said good night and went upstairs to bed. He'd said, 'See you later,' when he'd left earlier. She tried not to imagine where he was, but ideas flooded into her over-active mind. Pictures of tangled limbs and open mouths and Betsy's young, taut, boy-like figure lingered in her thoughts, and to her utter disgust she began to get excited. Sexually aroused, she longed for his hands to be on her, and once in bed she did what she hadn't done for years and masturbated. It was a practice she'd found more thrilling in her teens. Now it merely induced dissatisfaction, and the sleep she fell into was troubled and filled with eroticism.

Ben arrived much later. She woke briefly when he kissed her. Then he turned away. 'Sweet dreams Rosie,' he said, and was asleep five minutes later. She lay awake now, staring into the darkness, eyes wide, stinging with tiredness, wondering if she was only imagining the smell of perfume and sex that came from his warm and naked body.

Ben slept late the following morning. It was Saturday. His part in the film had finished. She'd brought him tea, and that much information had been muttered just about intelligibly from under the duvet.

'D'you want some toast?' she asked, longing to talk to him, desperate now to find out whose perfume he smelled of.

'Wake me about eleven,' was all he muttered.

She went downstairs, depressed, wishing she had the courage to demand.

Joanna and Ella went off early to the market.

'Come with us, Mum.'

She shook her head. Joanna stared at her as if wanting to say something. But she turned away, remaining silent. She remained in her dressing-gown, and watched the clock, longing for it to be eleven. At ten to the hour she put the coffee machine on and got out Ben's special mug. Standing by the sink, looking out across the garden, watching suddenly the first leaves beginning to change colour and fall, she saw the cat outside. She tapped the window. He looked old and bedraggled, wet from the rain that had fallen during the night. The stones on the patio were still damp, the sun weak and autumnal. She shivered and wondered about turning on the heating. She tapped the window again. Ben looked up, his amber eyes stared at her, then he turned, tail upright, and disappeared with what looked distinctly like high umbrage into the wild part of the garden. Frowning, she turned to the back door, surprised that he hadn't come hurtling through the cat-flap in his usual erratic state when he saw her. He was always so hungry in the morning. She looked down. The cat-flap had been covered with a piece of hardboard which was nailed in a haphazard fashion to the door.

Heart beating, lips tightened in hot and sudden fury, her eyes watered with a mixture of tears and cold air as she flung open the back door and ran to the spot where the cat had disappeared. She whistled, called his name, went back through the open door to pick up his still-full food bowl, and outside again to cajole and tempt him home. There was no sign of his wet and bedraggled feline body. No answering purr, no familiar damp fur twining and rubbing seductively round her cold, bare legs.

She went indoors, her nose running from the cold, her pity for the cat overwhelmed by her anger with the man asleep upstairs, tears already stale on her cheeks, skin reddened in the autumn weather.

Down on her knees, she tore at the cardboard across the cat-flap, breaking her nails as, bit by bit, it came away in her hands. 'There darling. Now come on home.' She wiped her face on the kitchen towel and waited for the beating of her heart to steady itself. She would deal with this. The coffee percolated, and she filled a mug, half with the hot milk already boiled. Hands shaking, she went upstairs to chastise the unloving lover in her bed.

'It's eleven o'clock Ben.'

He opened his eyes reluctantly and looked at her.

She spoke quickly. 'Did you nail up the cat-flap?'

'What?' He put out his hand for the coffee. She ignored it.

'I said, did you nail up the cat-flap?'

'Yes.'

She fought the desire to tip the coffee onto his sleepy arrogant face.

He sat up and picked up the mug from the bedside table where she'd now placed it for safety.

'Why?' she asked him.

'That fucking cat had shit in the kitchen.' He started

282

to drink his coffee, noisily and with too much speed. 'Jesus Christ!' The coffee spilt, the mug smashed back onto the table, hot liquid spilling onto white lace. 'Jesus Christ that's hot!'

'I put hot milk into it for a change,' she said quietly, frightened of the sudden violence, watching the brown stain spread relentlessly across the table covering.

'What the fuck for? You know I like cold milk. What's this? Some stupid American idea you picked up?'

She stared at him, withdrawing into silence, then finally, 'What's wrong? Why are you so angry?'

'Fucking stupid bitch.' He got up and out of bed, pulling back the duvet. Coffee on white cotton, brown and ugly. She drew back, retreating towards the dressing table. He turned rapidly and watched her sudden movement. 'I'm not going to hit you,' he said.

'You frighten me.'

They stared at each other.

'I've got to go,' he said.

'What?' She was incredulous. 'What d'you mean? Go? I asked you about the cat-flap. What have I done? What's going on?'

'Here we go,' he sighed, then turned and started to put on his jeans.

Confused, angry, she moved up to him. 'Ben, don't go. I'm sorry about the cat mess, the coffee, whatever. What's made you so mad?'

He spoke without looking at her. 'I loathe this cosiness you insist on. Hot milk, shitty cats, you're like my fucking mother. Why do all women start putting up lace curtains once you've screwed them?'

'You bastard.'

'Right,' he said. Dressed, he went into the bathroom to splash his face and clean his teeth, taking his tooth-brush from his denim jacket.

He lives his days and nights prepared for flight, thought

Rosemary. 'I don't want you to go,' she said, not quite believing she could mean it.

'I have to be somewhere.'

'Where?'

'Hackney.'

'Are you going to see your son?'

'No.'

'Then who?'

'What is this?' He stood upright, towering over her. She had followed him into the bathroom, standing close now behind him. He turned and took hold of her elbows, forcing her onto her toes. His face was close to hers. She could smell the toothpaste from his breath. He was still frowning. 'Don't do this Rosie. I don't want it. It's all these little things that pull us apart.'

'What things? What things?' Desperate, her voice a whisper, she forced herself not to cry.

'Forgetting how I like my coffee. Coming here and finding cat shit everywhere.'

'The cat's old. It's not his fault.'

Ben stood up, letting her go so suddenly that she staggered back. 'I'll call you later,' he said. He picked up his hold-all and put his hand on her shoulder, his anger gone, disappearing as fast as it had arrived.

Her stability rocked beneath her, the room whirled, she began to cry. 'Please, please don't go. Please Ben.' It was like listening to someone else's voice coming from her, so much did she shock herself. Her pride fell like a stone, evaporated into her desperation to keep him there, not wanting to be alone, feeling now stupid and inadequate.

'Don't beg,' he said, then, 'I can't take this Rosie.' And he went.

She sank down onto the floor, her knees hard against the carpet. She heard the front door slam. 'Explain to me, explain to me,' she said over and over again, rocking herself, her tears falling and mixing with the mucus from her nose. Twenty minutes earlier she had stood in her conservatory watering her plants, had placed coffee into a percolator, put milk into a saucepan. Out of nowhere anger and confusion had sprung up, engulfed her and left her shaking, crumpled, lying now on her bathroom floor, feeling more and more foolish as the tears subsided.

He'd wanted a fight. He'd got one. She remained where she was, too weak to get up and clean up the bed. No-one could ever deny he always got what he wanted.

Chapter Twenty Two

She didn't know how long she sat there, her head hard against the pedestal of the wash-basin. There were hardened toothpaste spills on the carpet by her side. As the crying fell to silent tears, she scraped the white stains with one broken fingernail: Mint-flavoured toothpaste under her nails.

Eventually Ella's voice came from downstairs, the front door flung open. 'Mum! Mum!' Distress, crying, Joanna saying, 'Calm down, calm down. I'll phone.' A telephone was picked up in the hall, Ella's footsteps sounded in the kitchen, Joanna's low voice spoke into the receiver. Rosemary tried to move. Emotionally drained, it seemed that immobility had set in.

Ella came upstairs. Still crying, her daughter opened the bedroom door. 'Mum, Mum, are you in here?'

Rosemary found her voice, got to her knees, then to her feet. 'What is it darling? I'm here.' Words voiced from a dry throat, rasping, painful, eyes swollen from weeping and rubbing.

Then Ella flung herself in the direction of the bath-room. 'It's Ben, Mum, Ben's been run over. Oh Christ, I've brought him in. He was in convulsions.'

Rosemary's heart stopped, then loud in its beating. Her hands flung to her face, covering a mouth ready for screaming. No sound came. Then, strangled, unable to move, holding onto the basin, water still running which she'd set to rinse her face. 'Ben? Ben?'

Joanna came in behind them. Calm. 'It's all right Rosemary. She means the cat. I've called the vet.'

The room spun. One of them took her to the bed. Somebody screamed. The sound was hers.

'I'm sorry, Mum. I didn't think.' Ella's tears mixed with hers as the two of them sat on the still-stained and dishevelled bed.

Joanna spoke again, squatted down on her haunches in front of them. 'You OK Rosemary? Something else happened?'

She breathed normally at last, pushed uncombed hair from her eyes. 'I'm all right. I'm all right. Where's the cat?'

'In his basket. The vet's coming.'

'Let me see.'

The three of them went downstairs and into the kitchen. Ben lay in his small, material-covered wicker basket, ragged from long years of busy feline claws. He didn't move. There was blood from his mouth. His breathing was so shallow that Rosemary had to lean close to feel his body. The two girls watched. Joanna put the kettle on for tea.

Ella sat at the kitchen table, her distress visible on her drawn face. 'He never goes in the road,' she said. 'Why wasn't he in the house? He hates the rain. It's raining again.'

Rosemary kept one hand on the silent bedraggled body of the old cat. The blood continued to trickle from his mouth. His eyes stared into the side of the basket. He was seeing nothing. She knew he was going to die. All she could do was be there, one hand gently, quietly stroking his ear. He'd always loved his ears being touched, had squirmed and yelped with delight as a kitten, then bitten, the hand that had delighted him. 'His way of saying thanks,' she'd told the children, confused with the feline violence. 'What happened?' she said.

'The car didn't stop.' Joanna put tea on the table. Three mugs, three teabags.

'It happened right in front of us,' said Ella. 'We were

287

just coming into the drive. Why was he in the road, Mum?'

Rosemary turned her head to look at her. 'He's been out all night,' she said, her voice small, a feeling of guilt spreading through her. 'The cat-flap was nailed up.'

The two girls turned to look at the back door. Ella spoke. 'What the fuck was *that* all about?'

'He was messing. Ben did it. Last night. To teach him a lesson.' She began to cry again, silently, her cheeks still wet from the morning's tears. 'I'm so sorry,' she whispered.

'I'll fucking kill him!' Ella banged the table. 'I will! That interfering, fucking—'

Joanna put an arm round her shoulder, placed her tea in front of her, and in silence stirred in two teaspoons of sugar.

Ben, the cat, died five minutes before the vet arrived.

'There was nothing I could do, Mrs Downey. Internal injuries.'

Rosemary nodded.

'Shall I take him?' he said.

She shook her head. 'We'll bury him in the garden. He's been with us so long.'

The two girls put him carefully in a shoe box and then into a plastic bin liner. He had stiffened already, his spirit long gone.

'He'll catch all the rabbits he wants now,' muttered Rosemary. She had put herself hastily into jeans and an old shirt of Ben's that she'd found in the wardrobe. The three of them stood under a tree where Joanna had dug a grave.

'You always told us that when we were kids,' said Ella. Mother and daughter smiled at each other. The autumn rain had chilled the air even more. Rosemary shivered. The afternoon was half-way over.

The girls went to their room. Rosemary went to her study. By the phone was a number that Ben had given her for his cousins where he'd said he was staying.

A woman answered.

'Is Ben there?' Rosemary said, afraid he would be and feeling unprepared.

'No,' the voice sounded surprised. 'We haven't seen him. Who is it?'

'Just a friend.' She thought again. 'It's about work actually. Do you have Gill's number?'

'Hang on.'

She waited. The woman spoke again, 'I'm terribly sorry, but I can't find it. I have another one. Somewhere in South London, I think.' She gave Rosemary the number. Rosemary thanked her and said 'goodbye'. She looked at the scribbled numbers in front of her. She couldn't bring herself to make the call. As she stood there, the telephone rang. It was Frances.

'Thought I might come over and stay the night, sweet one. Is that all right?'

'Yes please. We've had an awful day, Franny. The cat got run over. He died.'

'Oh darling, I'm so sorry. How awful for you.'

She went back upstairs and stood in the shower for a long time. The smell of Ben had lingered on her body, impregnating her from the old shirt she had been wearing. She could still sense him in the bedroom. The very air seemed angry.

Going through the wardrobe she found his briefcase, opened it, and tipped the contents onto the bed. Scraps of paper, old underground tickets, car park receipts tumbled against white lace. An address book, characteristically and predictably black, some photos. She held them at arms length to study them, too tired to move and find her glasses. A woman and a small boy, smiling at the photographer, then Ben with the boy, holding him aloft, the child's head flung back in delight, Ben's face full of the game of 'playing at fathers'. Then snaps of Ben in costumes, taken on location, a Chinese girl smiling up at him while he stared straight ahead. Then Betsy's face, then both of them, entwined, heads turned to smile into the lens, then another, just Betsy, head and shoulders, written words across the collar of a shirt at the bottom of the picture. 'To my darling, from your own Betsy.'

She stared at the bed, the briefcase empty now. A frenzied look through the address and phone book. Where to start? What was Betsy's surname?

The phone rang. It was Jonathan. With shaking hands still clutching scraps of paper, she spoke as normally as she could. 'How are you all darling?'

Her son's voice came quickly to her, sounding like his father, words tumbling too fast in that familiar way. 'Mother, I'm in London next week. Shall we meet?'

'Lovely darling. Are you all coming?'

'No. Just me,' then after a pause, 'Are you OK? You sound odd.'

'The cat died, Jonathan. Just today. We're all a bit shocked.'

'He'd had a good innings.'

She gritted her teeth. 'What day shall we meet?' she said.

'How's Wednesday?'

Standing there, Ben's address book held in shaky hands, she caught sight of herself in the mirror. The strange reflection stared back at her through red and tired eyes. Could she meet her son at this time of crisis in her life? Wasn't it bad enough to have Ella involved? She said, 'Can I phone you darling? Tomorrow? I'm not sure I'm free on Wednesday.'

'OK. There's a little girl who wants to speak to her granny.' Putting down the phone ten minutes later, she began immediately to look again at the contents of Ben's briefcase, glad to be back to the pain and addiction of her own life, distancing herself quickly from the childish innocent chatter of 'Barbie dolls' and 'little ponies'.

Ben and Betsy. Ben and Gill. Ben and a Chinese girl, looking up at him with the same look on her face she recognized in all of them, herself included. She gathered everything together and re-filled the briefcase. She shut the wardrobe door. His lies filled her thoughts, obsessed her with wanting to know the truth. She looked at her watch. It was five o'clock. Frances would be here at six. Somehow, dinner must be prepared, Ella and Joanna taken care of, the kitchen cleaned and life continue.

'Just leave it,' Frances said when she'd told her about the morning's events. 'Change the locks on the doors. Forget him.' They drank brandy and ate chocolate-minted fingers in front of the living-room television, the sound turned down so they could talk.

'I can't,' Rosemary said.

Frances raised her eyebrows. Unsmiling. 'How long have you had this death-wish darling?' she asked.

Rosemary shrugged. 'I'm so tired Franny. So confused with what's happened to me.'

Her friend made no move to comfort her. 'D'you realize how quickly you'd forget him?' she said.

Rosemary shook her head.

Music from Ella's room pounded above them. Bursts of laughter came from both young girls.

Frances smiled. 'I wish you had your daughter's ability to shrug off misery instead of so thoroughly enjoying it.'

Rosemary frowned.

'She has Joanna,' she said.

'You have you,' Frances' voice was loud and firm, 'and me, sweetheart, if push comes to shove.' She moved to the brandy bottle and filled her own glass, then offered it to Rosemary. 'Let me see him off,' she said.

Rosemary looked up at her. 'What d'you mean?'

'Let me see him off,' Frances repeated emphatically. 'It would give me the utmost pleasure. I've been writing the speech for weeks.'

'I don't know where he's gone,' Rosemary said quietly, wanting now the whole situation taken off her hands.

Frances paused, thinking, then she said, 'Give me the number his so-called cousin gave you. Let me have some fun.'

'We don't know who lives there,' Rosemary said.

The two women sat by the phone, the receiver at Frances' ear, the number at the other end ringing out. 'Sssh,' Frances hissed.

Somebody picked up the phone and Rosemary gasped, then clapped her hand over her mouth. The voice at the other end was young and female. 'Hello?'

'Oh,' said Frances, holding back laughter now, ignoring Rosemary's frantic signalling to replace the receiver, 'I know this sounds ridiculous,' Frances said into the phone, her voice over-loud and arrogant, 'I haven't a clue who I'm ringing. I found this number on a scrap of paper in my husband's pocket, and rather than let the private investigator have it, I thought I'd do my own dirty work. Who *exactly* am I speaking to?'

The voice at the other end of the phone spoke without hesitation. 'My name is Tejero. Betsy Tejero. Who the fuck is your husband?'

Rosemary heard her, pulled away from Frances and suppressed her laughter.

'His name is Drew. Andrew Canon-Smythe.'

'Sorry madam, his shoes aren't under my bed. Hope you find the bastard.' The phone went down before Frances could say any more.

Rosemary exploded into laughter. Frances smiled at her. 'That's *the* Betsy I presume?' she asked. Rosemary nodded. 'Now will you change the locks?' her friend said. Then, 'Are you getting hysterical?'

'Slightly,' said Rosemary. 'What on earth are we doing? We're behaving very badly.'

'Good. About time. Let's finish these chocolates and put the chain on the front door, by way of rounding off the evening.'

'He won't come back tonight,' Rosemary said. Her laughter stopped. She longed to know whether Ben had been there when Betsy's phone rang.

She put the chain on the front door that night, but Ben didn't come back anyway. Hope lay despairingly but silently in the pit of Rosemary's heart. She remembered the locksmith, but the phone call was never made.

Ella suddenly got a job. She would go to Glasgow, rehearsals in October, and not be back until Christmas. 'Can Joanna still stay?' she asked her mother.

'Yes please,' Rosemary said, wanting the company of the round, serene, and smiling girl.

Betty visited, refused to speak to Joanna, and never mentioned Ben. After two weeks, Rosemary was working again, and found herself almost glad of his absence. Almost. She had met Jonathan after all, but came away from the lunch amused and irritated. He had seen the newspaper when she'd flown home from Los Angeles.

'And I spoke to Gran,' he said, eating lunch in the Caprice where Rosemary had taken him.

'Did she phone you?' Rosemary asked, furious.

'*I* phoned *her*,' he said. 'I knew I'd never get a straight answer anywhere else.'

Rosemary tightened her mouth. 'I won't discuss my private life with you Jonathan. And I really don't want *you* discussing it behind my back with my mother. She knows very little.'

'She's told me what's going on.'

'She's told you what she *thinks* is going on. And don't use that tone to me. You sound just like your father.'

'I'm surprised *he* hasn't called. Or has he?'

'He has more sense.' She ordered more wine, knowing she'd feel dreadful later on. Jonathan covered his wine glass with his hand and shook his head. 'I can't drink the whole bottle,' she snapped.

'Then send it back,' he retorted.

She had laughed then. He was suddenly ten years old again, his bottom lip stuck forward in petulance. 'You'll trip over that,' she smiled, touching his mouth. He moved his hand in irritation. Rosemary sighed. 'Oh Jonathan,' she said, 'I'm so sorry. I embarrass you. Anyway, the affair is over. All right?'

'Not my business.'

She laughed again. '*Now* you tell me,' she said, and much to his fury she had leaned forward and ruffled his hair.

He had gone back to Birmingham as irritated as she was.

Rosemary related the story to Ella. 'Fucking typical,' her daughter said, and took the bottle of unfinished wine that Rosemary had taken home with her from the restaurant, which had embarrassed her son even more. He had been pleased to kiss her 'goodbye' and put the miles between them.

'You could always change your name,' Rosemary had teased him.

He sighed. 'Oh Mother,' he said, 'sometimes I know exactly where Ella gets it from.'

At the end of the two weeks, when there had been no word from Ben, she began to wonder whether she should try to phone Betsy, ask for her address, and send round the few belongings he'd left at Wimbledon. She thought of him constantly, but the unhappiness over the cat's death had turned some part of her against him. She invented scenes and dialogue in her head, preparing herself for his next entrance into her life. Too much had been left undone and unsaid. No-one at home mentioned him. And she waited. Next time she would be prepared. There would be no scene, just a lot of things said that she had planned, and then she would send him away. This time for good.

But every night she listened for his car to turn into the drive, starting up sometimes when she thought she heard a key in the door, her heart still beating fast as it always had done. But there were no tears. She smiled, and joked with friends, and only Frances watched her carefully, wondering just how long this present calmness would last.

'I *want* to finish it,' she said once to her friend. 'I long for him to be here one night when I come home, just so that I can tell him to go.'

Frances doubted her resolve, but said nothing. 'I hope the bastard has gone for good,' she said.

Rosemary smiled to herself. She knew better.

Then one night she had gone to bed early and been asleep by ten-thirty. The phone rang just after midnight and she sat up too quickly in bed. The room swam. She picked up the phone, knowing, feeling sure it was him, and suddenly hating the excitement she felt in her loins. 'Yes?' she said.

'Is that you Rosemary?' The American voice came back to her. Disappointment. 'Tom?' she said. 'Tom Woods?'

'Hi! I realize suddenly that it's late there. Were you asleep?'

'How nice to hear from you. No, I was reading,' she lied easily, her heart still again beneath the white cotton nightgown.

'I'm coming to London tomorrow,' Tom said. 'I'd like to see you. Is it convenient?'

She hesitated. Then, 'Yes, of course. It would be lovely.'

He sounded pleased. 'I have a package to bring you, from Marlene. Something you said you couldn't get in England.'

'Butter-Buds!' she said quickly, and laughed.

'Right,' his voice smiled and she remembered all at once how easy it had felt to be with him.

'I'm looking forward to seeing you again,' she said.

'Me too. Can I bring anything else?'

'No thank you,' she said firmly.

'Will you come to the hotel? Saturday?'

'Where are you staying?' she asked.

'The Savoy.'

Her heart sank. 'Shall we meet in the bar?' She hoped her hesitation didn't show in her voice.

'I'll be in the lobby, Rosemary. I'll be the one holding a jar of Butter-Buds.'

She laughed again. 'About eight?' she said.

'Sounds great.'

'Have a safe journey, Tom.' Unable to sleep again straight away, she turned the television on and plumped up the pillows behind her. If Ben turned up between now and Saturday she wondered what she'd tell him, or even what he'd say. Frances would be delighted. Finally feeling slightly foolish, she fell asleep toying with the idea of buying a silk blue shirt. 'Fool,' she muttered, and closed her eyes.

Chapter Twenty Three

She bought the shirt.

'Great colour,' remarked Ella.

'Like your eyes,' smiled Joanna.

The three of them were standing in the kitchen drinking coffee, Rosemary showing the girls her purchase. Ella said, poking through the carrier bag, 'You've bought perfume as well. Who is this guy? Is he rich?'

'Probably.' Rosemary took the empty bags and started to fold them neatly. She reminded herself of her mother, so half-way through the task she changed her mind and threw them in the bin. 'He's staying at the Savoy,' she said. Then, without pausing and as casually as she could, 'No phone calls?'

'No he didn't,' Ella said, and pulled a face.

Rosemary took herself and her new belongings upstairs. She put Ben and another day without a phone call out of her mind. She'd got through the last two-and-a-half weeks. She'd survived, she'd slept, she'd even eaten sensibly. No crumpets and butter for comfort this time round. She was quite proud of herself. Except. Well, sometimes she would wake very early in the morning and think she heard a noise. Sounds of his feet on the stairs, the bedroom door opening. And she would wait, eyes closed, expecting to feel the warmth of his body slipping in beside her, feeling his leg placed over hers, drawing her to him, kissing her hair and moving his lips down fiercely to her mouth. Then she would fall asleep again, one hand pressed between her thighs, waiting for the creek in the floor-board as he crossed the room.

Then suddenly it would be morning. And no-one lay beside her. And disappointment filled that open corner of her heart. She would get up quickly, do something, go early to the studio, eat breakfast in the BBC canteen, meet friends, buy clothes she could ill afford. By teatime she would feel fine, drive home and wait with bated breath to hear Ella's voice as she fumbled at the back door: 'Ben phoned, Mum,' or even find him there, standing again, J-cloth in his hand, turning and saying, 'Forgive me Rosie, I missed you, I've been a fool.' But only the girls were there, Ella saying, 'Hi, did you get to Tesco's?' or Joanna, smiling in that gentle fashion, saying, 'You look tired Rosemary, shall I make some tea?' And disappointment would be mixed with a certain relief, which she didn't always understand. She wanted it to be over, yet dreaded the opportunity to make that happen.

She spoke to Frances about it. 'I still love him but don't miss him,' she'd said, 'can you understand that?'

'Yes.'

'Will it stop?'

'You know it will.'

'And with you and Michael?'

'I miss him, but I don't love him.'

Rosemary nodded.

It was one of those evenings when nothing went wrong. The blue shirt tucked easily into a black silk, short skirt she had been unable to squeeze into only two months ago.

'I lost weight,' she said to Frances, who'd phoned while she was putting the finishing touches to her hair. 'And why are you phoning? I've no time to chat. You only just caught me.'

'I'm checking up that you're going. Don't quite trust you yet.'

'Well I am, and before you say it, no he didn't.'

Rosemary knew her friend had dreaded Ben turning up once again on the Wimbledon doorstep, and Rosemary pushing all thoughts of 'that much more suitable plastic surgeon' right out of the window.

'What *do* you mean?' Frances said, pretending aloofness over the phone. Rosemary laughed. Her friend went on, 'Have a truly wonderful time, darling girl. Maybe you'll get laid at the Savoy. I've always rather fancied that. I did the Strand Palace once, but I was young and easily impressed.'

'Get out of here,' Rosemary was still laughing, 'you're incorrigible. I have no intention of being laid anywhere. We're having dinner, that's all. He's just a nice man.'

'Hmm, mm, m.'

'I'm going to ring off Frances, so don't make those sounds. I'll phone immediately I can tomorrow morning. I'd hate to keep you curious all day.' Still laughing, she rang off.

Ella drove her, in Rosemary's car, to the Savoy.

'Darling, I'll get a cab,' Rosemary had protested.

'No you won't, I've always wanted to drive up to the Savoy. I wish you'd let me take my old banger, I'd love to see those doormen's faces if I asked them to park it.'

'You're not coming in?' Rosemary's voice went up a notch.

'Don't panic, Mother. We'll go straight home.'

They got into the car, Joanna in the back.

'They wouldn't let me in, anyway, not in jeans. Did you know, Jo, that you can walk about in jeans at the Savoy, but you can't actually sit anywhere and be served?' She sounded amused more than peeved.

As Rosemary stepped out of the car, Ella said, 'We'll go to McDonald's on the way back. Save cooking.'

Rosemary bent back into the car. 'Did you put the answerphone on?' she said.

'No!' retorted Ella. 'We're not expecting any calls, are

we?' And before Rosemary could answer, they had gone. She saw Joanna's bottom as she clambered from the back seat and threw herself next to Ella when the car stopped at the lights then turned left into the Strand.

'I hope they don't drop chips,' she muttered irrationally, and went through the revolving doors of the Savoy entrance to meet Tom.

'No Butter-Buds in your hand?' smiled Rosemary when she saw him. Tom was standing patiently in front of the kiosk that sold theatre seats, watching the people milling around. He turned with a smile at the sound of her voice.

'I'd forgotten how beautiful you were,' he said by way of a greeting. 'Shall we go straight in?' He looked first at his watch, then took her gently by the elbow and led her into the Savoy Grill. Motioning to the hovering head waiter, he ordered two champagne cocktails.

The Italian maitre d' greeted her. 'Miss Downey,' he smiled, 'we haven't seen you for a long time.'

'It's nice to see you Alfredo.'

'D'you know everyone?' Tom asked once they'd been left alone.

'Everyone knows *me*, I'm afraid. I'm quite famous in England. Is it a pain, or are you used to starry dates? Living in Hollywood I mean?'

He laughed. 'I work on the famous. I date shop girls.'

'Now you're teasing me.'

'Just a little.'

The waiter appeared again. They took their drinks and toasted each other.

'Are we celebrating?' she asked.

'Just seeing you. Isn't that enough?'

'Were you this smooth in L.A.?'

'I doubt it. I'm more nervous here. You're on your home ground, so I feel I must work harder to impress.'

'What makes you think you have to impress me?' she asked, realizing she was enjoying the flirting.

'I didn't say I had to,' Tom replied. 'I just want to.'

She'd forgotten how pleasant it was to sit at dinner with a man you could flirt and converse with, without sex being in the air between them.

'Where are my Butter-Buds?' she asked when they got to dessert.

'In my room. I won't forget. Trust me.'

The evening had been wonderful. He had made her feel beautiful, intelligent and pleasant company without invading her sexuality. She wondered briefly if he was attracted to her as a woman or only lightly aroused as she was to him. She realized how seldom she sat to eat with Ben and didn't play sex games. How foolish she was. Had been. There was a grown-up world out here and in the last few months she'd forgotten the pleasures of her past life, so involved had she become with what seemed now just lust.

The Savoy Grill hummed with polite and sophisticated glitter. Unreal, yet easy. The familiar smell of wealth had begun to convince her what she'd been missing while wallowing at home in her own obsessive misery. 'I am so enjoying myself, Tom,' she said impulsively. He stretched out across the table and took her hand. 'Now everyone's looking at us,' she smiled.

'They've been doing that all evening,' he said, 'or don't you notice any more?'

'I don't catch their eyes,' she said.

'How clever.' He took his hand away and lowered his voice. 'There's a lady coming over. D'you know her?'

Rosemary looked up and saw Jessica heading towards them. Tom stood up as she approached their table. Jessica was just slightly the worse for drink. 'Darling how lovely. I was going to call you. You look wonderful. Who's this delicious new man with you?'

'Tom, er—' her mind was a blank.

Tom put his hand out. 'Tom Woods,' he said. They shook hands.

Rosemary squirmed at the realization she'd forgotten his name for the moment.

Tom offered his chair to Jessica.

'No thanks darling. I'm with some people. We've been to see the new play at the *Vaudeville*.'

'Good?' asked Rosemary automatically, and with no real interest.

Jessica pulled a face. 'Terrible. That Ben was there, Rosemary. My God, what is his last name? Oh yes, Morrison. That's it. Ben Morrison.'

Rosemary's heart began to beat loud and fast. *Thanks Jess*, she thought, *you've just ruined a beautiful evening. Now please go away.*

But Jessica chatted on for a few moments. Tom remained standing, and Rosemary watched the actress' mouth moving, and tried to concentrate. 'Sitting two rows behind us, darling. The previews have been packed with thespians, hoping the American company would fall flat on its arse, no doubt. Waiting like vultures to take over all those dreadful parts. Precious little work around as it is. Mind you, it'll only run a week, if *that*. American black comedy is not what we need right now.' She clapped one hand to her mouth and smiled gaily at Tom. Rosemary saw he was trying politely not to cough as the smoke from Jessica's cigarette drifted relentlessly into his blinking eyes. The ash fell unheeded onto their table as she waved her arms around.

'I realize I'm being frightfully rude, darling,' Jessica said. 'Tom here is an American and I'm on the edge of insulting him!'

Tom smiled gently. 'Not at all,' he said. 'I'm in oil, not the theatre.'

Rosemary stared at him.

Jessica was obviously impressed. 'Where d'you find them?' she threw over her shoulder to the woman sitting down. 'All of them sexy, and now rich.'

Rosemary blushed and Tom laughed out loud.

'Oil?' said Rosemary after Jessica had gone back to her friends and was quite obviously talking about them.

'I knew it would impress her and yet not encourage.' Tom pushed his dessert away. 'Shall we sneak into that small, private-looking lounge off the lobby and order coffee?' he whispered to her.

'Yes please,' she answered immediately.

He called the waiter, tipped him generously and ordered the coffee to be sent through.

They sat alone in the comfortable lounge. The waiter brought petit-fours with the coffee. 'Shall I take these home for my daughter?' mused Rosemary.

'Why not? Treats for the children!'

'She's twenty-five. Lives at home still. With her gay lover.'

Tom raised his eyebrows but didn't reply. *Now why did I tell him that?* Rosemary thought. She'd drunk too much champagne. 'If you had told Jessica your real job, she'd have joined us for the evening,' said Rosemary.

'I know that. I only tell women I want to encourage that I'm a plastic surgeon. To everyone else, I'm in oil, or plastics. And if I really want to frighten them off I tell them I'm a dentist or an arms dealer.'

Rosemary threw back her head and laughed out loud.

Tom leaned forward. 'Is Ben Morrison someone I should know about before I make another move in your direction?'

She stared. 'Why d'you ask? I mean, why should you think that?'

'I saw your face when Jessica mentioned his name. You looked like a lady who was desperate to ask if he was alone.'

She could find nothing to say. He leaned back, watching her face, then spoke again.

'I'm sorry. Let me back off with dignity.'

'I'm not sure that's necessary any more. I think my relationship with Ben Morrison is drawing to an inevitable conclusion, if it hasn't done so already.'

'I can only say I'm glad. For my sake, anyway.' He smiled across at her but made no move to take her hand. 'Why don't I go and get your Butter-Buds and then drive you home?'

'I'd like that,' she said, and watched him leave the room. How glad she was she hadn't had to refuse him anything.

On their way to Wimbledon, Rosemary sat drowsing in the passenger seat beside him.

'Shall I call you tomorrow?' he asked.

'Yes please. I'll be home all day.'

'I could come for tea.' He turned quickly to smile at her and then looked back at the road.

'With my mother there?' she teased.

'I love old ladies. They all find me vastly amusing and very young.'

'Yes. I don't doubt it.'

'Then shall I come for tea?'

'Phone me at lunchtime. I'm sure I'll say yes.'

'Right you are.'

She laughed at the awkwardness of the English slang that sat uneasily on him.

'I'm trying to be very English just to impress you,' he said. 'I've never met anyone quite so British as you.'

Before she could reply they had arrived in her road. 'It's the next drive,' she pointed with her left hand. She was about to ask him in for another coffee but, as they turned into the drive, she saw Ben's car, arrogant in its shabbiness, in front of the door. She glanced upwards. Her bedroom light shone behind the lace nets, the curtains undrawn. The rest of the house was in darkness. It was one o'clock in the morning. 'D'you mind if we say good night here?' Her voice was shaking.

Tom looked at her carefully. He kept the engine running for a moment and then, as if he had second thoughts, turned it off abruptly and bent over to kiss her briefly on her unresponsive mouth.

'No,' was all she said to him. 'No, Tom.'

'Don't panic, Rosemary. It was the friendliest of kisses, I assure you. No requests on my part.'

'Thank you. And thank you for a really lovely evening.'

He came round and opened the car door for her. She sat for a moment, not wanting to get out of the car, summoning a courage that had deserted her along with the frivolity of the champagne. He asked no questions, but watched her fumble for her key, held her bag while she opened the door.

'Good night Tom.'

He got back into his car, raised his hand, and pulled out of the drive, gravel spluttering against the wheels. She wanted stupidly to call him back, to tell him to go upstairs and confront the man in her bedroom, but this was her battle, her scene, her dialogue.

There was no cat waiting to twirl round her ankles, as she checked the kitchen. McDonald's cartons overspilled from the rubbish bin, coffee mugs stood in the sink, chairs were pushed away from the tomato ketchup-stained table top.

'Oh Ella,' she muttered, and turned the light off again. She turned to face the stairs, slipped off her high heels and, holding onto the bag and shoes in one hand, the other on the bannisters, began to creep upstairs, half-praying her daughter would wake and stand by her side during the confrontation with Ben Morrison.

Chapter Twenty Four

She opened her bedroom door. The bed, facing her, held Ben sitting upright with a script in his hand. A mug with the remains of coffee stood on the table beside him. Just the light on his side shone across the room. He looked as if he belonged there. As if she was the intruder. He didn't smile; and her mind was blank of things to say.

'Had a good evening?' he asked. His eyes stayed on her face, his voice so low that she could barely catch the words.

She threw her bag on the chair, her jacket she took across to the wardrobe and searched for a hanger. Her hands and knees were shaking.

'Leave it,' he said. 'Just leave it on the chair Rosemary. I want to talk to you.' He sounded irritated and it made her angry. The evening with Tom had given her a certain courage, and she turned now to face him across the bed, her jacket discarded on top of the handbag.

'What are you doing here?' She spoke softly and hoped she sounded firm and sure of herself.

'I have a key,' he smiled now, 'and I thought that was fine by you.'

'Well it's not,' she said. Her eyes shifted briefly away from him. She had heard Ella's door open and somebody moving to the bathroom. Then again, 'Why are you here Ben? You can't just walk into my house after almost three weeks and expect to be welcomed back without a word. Where did you go?'

He began to say something but she stopped him. 'No, don't speak. Not now. Let me say this.' He shrugged, watched her, stayed silent, then smiled. And waited. She went on, 'You should have phoned. We had a fight. Things have happened since you left that time.'

'So I see.' He nodded towards the window and she realized he'd seen Tom bring her home.

'He's just a friend.' The words came out without thinking and she was angry he'd made her feel defensive. She spoke again, quickly, with confusion, 'No, I don't mean that.'

'He's not a friend?' smiled Ben.

'Yes, of course, but not just – for Christ's sake it's not your business. My life's my own. Why, why, why are you here? Go away.' The scene she had planned in the last weeks was not unfolding. She sounded distraught. 'Go away,' she said again. Lamely. Unsure.

He was still smiling. She stared at him.

'I missed you,' he said again. He patted the bed beside him. 'Come to bed.'

She stayed where she was. She wanted him to see her pain, understand her rapidly-disappearing fury, but she could find no words. 'The cat died,' she said eventually.

He stared at her mouth. He patted the bed again. Threw back the duvet. His nakedness confronted her, erect, available. 'Come to bed,' he said softly.

'I don't want to.'

'Then why have you undressed, Rosie?' he asked. And she had. While she'd stood there. Automatically. And her clothes lay across the chair behind her. She couldn't remember disrobing and she stared down at herself, the treachery of her own body confronted her passively.

'Go away,' she said again. Childlike. Afraid. Out of control. 'Please go away.'

'Who's the man?' he asked after a moment of complete stillness.

'What man?'

308

He sighed. 'Don't play games with me Rosie. Who brought you home?' He reached across now and took her arm. His grip was tight, restraining her as she reached to pick up her dressing-gown and cover herself.

'Let me go Ben, I want to put something on.'

But he ignored her. She remained naked and vulnerable and his grip tightened. Fear came suddenly and locked itself into her breathing and the clamminess of her hands.

'Just tell me,' he said.

'You don't know him.' She struggled faintly against his hold on her and he reached up to take her other arm. Her legs widened to keep her balance. He had pulled her forward to lean towards him.

'I want to know him,' he said softly, his face now close to hers as he pulled her nearer. His eyes on her mouth, his smile moving nowhere except on his lips. 'I want to know everyone you know Rosie. Don't you realize you're mine? You belong right here. I'll always come back. You know I love you.'

'No. No.'

Then his smile went and something different came into his face. And her fear erupted inside her. She struggled to stand up straight, pulled away from him, took him by surprise and found herself free to go for her dressing-gown. In silence he moved across the bed, tore the dressing-gown from her hands and picking her up bodily, flung her face-down onto the duvet. And pinning her arms, her face pushed into the pillow climbed onto her, and into her, and took her. Invasion. Forced entry. War declared on her body. In silence, without love or even lust. Merely control – possession. And though she struggled, she couldn't cry out. The humiliation of Ella maybe answering her call was enough to keep her silent. The only sounds were of his breathing, the soft noises of her struggle murmuring uselessly against his strength.

Then it was finished. Over. He turned and pulled the duvet up to cover them both. Nothing was said.

She turned away from him, onto her side, rigid with degradation, wondering, hoping it was merely fear that kept her in that bed, by his side, head next to his, the pillow cool against the heat of her cheek.

He fell asleep. One hand on her back. Staking ownership. He had said one thing as he closed his eyes. 'Good night Rosie.' That was all. And she lay, foetus-like, wanting to put her thumb now in her mouth, to curl her hair frantically round her finger in desperation, as she did when a baby. His hand remained on her back. She didn't move, too debased to get out of bed, dress, find her daughter, turn him out, yell and scream with anger. And then she fell asleep. Lying there beside the man who had merely taken her as a matter of course. His right. When she woke after only a few hours, he still slept. The sun came through the window and threw speckled light across his placid, handsome face. She watched him, his mouth half-open, his eyelids flickering as if in a dream. And she wanted to kill him. She understood now all those stories of vengeful women. There was no sign on her body of the struggle that had taken place in her bed just a few hours previously. Because his strength had made her fearful, keeping her from crying out. No bruising showed on her, not really, just a little across the top of her arms where he had held her.

She did the one thing she'd seen in all the movies. She went and stood in the shower, to let the water wash away the smell of him and the aroma of her fear and capitulation. She wondered again about killing him, but knew she couldn't. She toyed with the thought of maiming, picked up her nail scissors from the bathroom cabinet and held them tentatively in one shaking hand.

He stirred in his sleep. Turned and touched the empty

pillow beside him. Murmured something, kept his eyes closed, then spoke again, louder. 'Put the kettle on Rosie.'

And she replaced the scissors, and went to the wardrobe for another dressing-gown, staring with disdain at the one he'd torn from her grasp the night before. As if it had betrayed her. Irrational.

Downstairs she put the kettle on to boil and stared from the window. Outside held the promise of a beautiful day, an Indian summer. Where was she? Who was she now? Nothing of what she'd once been came now to fortify her at this moment. She'd liked herself once, but no longer. She merely belonged to someone. She was his thing. Not by the usual and clichéd physical violence of a man to a woman. That she would have walked away from months ago. That would have been too easy a form of control for him. This was real power. What he had was the strength of will to be in her bed after the invasion and ask for attendance to his needs. 'Put the kettle on Rosie.'

Too late now, the protest would be too late, ineffectual, and even more humiliating. She made tea, longing for the useless cat-flap to swing open and reveal her old friend hurtling into the room as she took something from the fridge. She put the milk into her cup, poured tea, took a spoonful of honey and watched it melt into the orange liquid before she stirred. *I should poison him*, she thought briefly, and it made her laugh. She sat and drank her tea. She had no desire to fill his mug and take it to him. She would just sit and see if she could muster just a small piece of Rosemary Downey so that that once-strong lady could face him when he eventually appeared in the kitchen.

She must have sat there, without moving, until the kitchen door opened and Ben stood there. The clock on the wall showed eight-fifteen. She looked up at him and pulled back a little, her hands tightened round her now empty cup. He was dressed and smiling.

'What happened to my tea?' he said, and moved to the table and the teapot. She put her hands in her lap now, pressing them together in their sudden clamminess. His audacity gave her courage and a cold anger settled somewhere inside her.

'I drank the whole pot,' she said.

'OK.' He moved without tension and filled the kettle again. 'Nice day,' he said, over her head, nodding at the garden through the large window.

She stood up and went to the bread bin; toast would stop her feeling sick.

'You making toast Rosie?' he asked, still looking at the garden. She didn't reply. 'Put a couple of pieces on for me. I had nothing to eat last night. Your fridge was empty.' He smiled, as if unable to believe his own cheek.

She had picked up the bread knife to cut the bread and turned towards him, the knife held in one shaking hand a little away from her body. 'Why don't you just leave?' she said quietly and found herself staring into his brown eyes and still smiling face. He looked at her. Then the knife. She spoke again. 'I am speechless at your audacity. Why don't we decide not to discuss last night and you just leave, before anyone else gets up.'

He was silent. The smile wavered just a little. He nodded towards the bread knife. 'Why don't you put that down? Something nasty might happen. By accident.'

'I can't even begin to tell you what I'd like to do with this knife, Ben. But you're not worth it. I want you out of my life. I swear if you make one move towards me I'll kill you. I've had enough.'

He paused. Then shrugged. 'I was jealous,' he said. 'You're mine.'

'And you're living in another time. Those ideas went out fifty years ago, Ben Morrison.'

'Yes, well, that's your era, not mine.' He turned away and got a teabag to put in his mug, and poured the now boiled water onto it.

Her resolve began to wilt a little. He knew she would never use a knife against him.

'I seem to have ballsed it up again, don't I Rosie?' He spoke with his back to her.

She lowered the knife. 'Yes,' was all she managed.

Then he turned. 'D'you really want me to go? Think about it. It's good between us. I'll try harder.' That smile again.

She just stared at him. And then felt an irresistible urge to laugh begin inside her. 'There's more to life than sex,' she said.

'Don't kid yourself Rosie. To most men, women are just cunts on legs. Believe me, they're all trying to lay you. Stop imagining it's your mind they're after.'

Then she did laugh. 'Christ, you are unbelievable! Did you learn all this bilge at your mother's knee or what?' She saw the anger on his face and raised the knife again.

He turned, quickly, viciously, picked up his mug of tea and flung it across the room, splattering it against the door. China pieces and hot liquid spilled and fell against wood, then stone. The spoon clattered onto the floor. She kept the knife still in her hand, and a steady calmness came over her.

Ben picked up the small hold-all he'd brought into the kitchen with him and flung it over his shoulder. His anger had gone already. The show was over. She watched him and their eyes met. Blank faces, showing each other nothing. Expressionless in their misery. 'I'll call you when you calm down,' he said eventually. She didn't answer. 'I suppose this whole scene will be related

313

to Frances?' he said. She remained silent, longing for him to leave, afraid to hear Ella's or Joanna's footsteps coming downstairs. 'You know Rosie, at your age, you should consider yourself lucky that I always come back.' And he was gone, opening the back door and then closing it quietly behind him, so as not to have to pick his way through wet and broken crockery.

She heard the car start on the third attempt. She listened to the familiar splutter of the engine as it picked up morning strength to carry him away. Then there was silence. And she put down the knife, carefully placing it beside the brown, uncut bread. Then she buried her face in her hands and started to cry. She didn't hear anyone on the stairs, and then there was Joanna, holding her, placing her in a chair.

Ella stood behind her. 'What's happened? Mum, what's wrong? Fucking hell, look at the mess in here!' She started to pick up the pieces of china, afraid to tread on the stone floor with bare feet. Joanna was on her haunches in front of the seated Rosemary, cradling the older woman's head against her while the sobbing went on. 'Make tea Ella,' Joanna said quietly.

Rosemary's daughter, silent now, moved and made tea. The clock in the hall struck eight-thirty.

'Put honey in it,' Joanna said and, still in silence, Ella obeyed her, suddenly afraid for her mother. 'Drink it Rosemary.'

She sipped the hot liquid, felt the strength from Joanna's large hands stroking her hair, massaging the back of her neck, pulling down her shoulders, forcing the tension away. And then the tears stopped and she merely sat there, unable to find words to explain her behaviour. Then eventually, looking at Joanna still squatting at her side, seeing above her Ella's worried face while she sipped her tea, she managed to speak.

'I'm all right,' she said. 'I'm all right. I'm sorry, did I wake you?'

At the normality in her mother's apology Ella sighed with relief and sat down. 'We heard the crash,' she said, 'then you crying.'

'Are you feeling better?' Joanna asked.

Rosemary smiled weakly. 'I will be,' she said. 'I promise.'

'Has he gone?' Joanna's voice was very quiet.

Ella said, 'What did you say?'

Rosemary smiled and put one hand out to touch Joanna's face. 'Yes, he's gone,' she said.

'Thank Christ for that,' Ella said loudly, and got up to make toast.

'Promise?' Joanna remained close to Rosemary, her face and voice insistent.

'Promise.'

'I'm glad.' Joanna stood and pulled a chair away from the table and sat down.

'Understatement,' said Ella. 'I'll never invite any of my friends to your parties again.'

Rosemary closed her eyes against the memory. She felt dead inside. The calm that had by now settled on her felt almost worse than the misery of the moments before. At least then she had felt alive, at least you *know* you're alive when you're that unhappy. But she felt and thought nothing. The day ahead held only artifice: Tom and her mother were coming to tea. No-one to tell what had happened last night. No-one to recognize the final death of self, or so it felt at that moment, as she sat and drank more tea. She couldn't think of one reason for living, and that frightened her more than Ben had ever done.

Chapter Twenty Five

It was easy, that Sunday, to keep busy. Joanna had a technical rehearsal at the theatre and disappeared at nine-thirty. Ella said, 'What're you doing, Mum?'

'Gran's coming to tea.'

Ella pulled a face. 'Think I'll join Jo for the day.'

To her surprise her mother made no comment, merely shrugged, and continued cleaning the kitchen which she had attacked almost immediately after breakfast had broken up. She washed the floor, the tiles, the stove and then started on the windows.

Ella watched her. 'Is all this for Gran?' she said eventually.

'No.' Rosemary spoke without stopping. 'This is for me.'

'You don't mind me leaving you in the lurch then?' Ella said to her mother's back.

'You must do what you want.'

Ella left by eleven. Rosemary finished the kitchen. She took off her dressing-gown and flung it straight into the washing machine then walked into the hall and started up the stairs quite naked. She toyed with the idea of turning out the cupboard under the stairs, but decided to make scones instead. 'Cheese scones,' she found herself muttering.

She showered again and then put on her jeans and a shirt. She put all of Ben's few belongings that were still in the wardrobe into a pile and removed them into the cupboard in the spare room. 'There,' she said.

The telephone rang. It was Frances. 'Hoped you'd still be at the Savoy,' her friend said.

'He's coming for tea. Why don't you come over? Mum'll be here.'

'All right. Shall I pick Betty up?'

'Yes please.'

There was a pause, then Frances said, 'Are you all right?'

'Yes. Why?'

'You sound strange, my love. You never readily agree to anyone offering to take a chore from you. Usually the dialogue is "are you sure you don't mind?"'

Rosemary could think of nothing to say.

'Rosemary—?'

'I'm still here. I'm fine. Really. Will you pick Mum up about three? I'm going to make some scones.'

'I'm sure there's a connection there somewhere darling, but I'll leave it for now. Just one thing, did you have a good evening?'

'When?'

Frances was exasperated. 'Last night! With what's-his-name. Dear, dear, was it that bad? Or even that good?'

'Oh! You mean Tom. Yes, he's fine. We had dinner and he brought me home. Nice man. Look, Franny, I'm rather up to my neck. Shall I see you about half-past three then?'

'You are definitely strange,' Frances said firmly. 'I'll see you later. Take care.'

She rang off and almost immediately the phone rang again. Rosemary jumped and then picked it up. 'Who is it?' she said.

'Rosemary?' Tom's cultured East Coast accent spoke softly.

She relaxed and sat on the bed. 'Oh Tom.'

'You OK Rosemary?'

317

'Everyone keeps asking me that,' she laughed. 'I'm just busy, that's all. And I wanted to get into the garden before the sun goes in.'

'I won't hold you up. Am I still expected for tea?'

'Yes. About four. Er, yes. Um, any time really.' Her voice trailed off. She wondered about clearing some leaves away in the garden before she made the scones.

Tom spoke again. 'OK, I'll see you at four. With your mother.'

She smiled. 'You're a brave man,' she said. They said goodbye and she replaced the receiver.

She decided to tackle the garden. 'I'll do the scones after sherry,' she said to herself, and smiled as if in total surprise at such a decisive idea. The autumn garden stood at peace with all its majestic colours. Gold and amber and red tumbled around her and under her feet as she walked. She stood for a moment and watched two flies absorbed in copulation on one slender stem of a still-flowering rose bush. She flicked them away. 'Not even spring,' she said under her breath, and then drew the sudden, chilly breeze into her lungs. Not many birds were left to sing. They'd done their practice gathering for several weeks, now they'd gone. She bent down and touched the earth where Ben the cat had been buried. 'I miss you,' she said. Soon she would get another one, a kitten, but not for a while. The space in her heart was still full of memories.

She worked on the fallen leaves until one-thirty, enjoying the feel and colour as she piled them high into the wheelbarrow. Her hands and nails were a mess when she finished, so she poured herself a sherry and went upstairs to shower again.

Then she made scones. Cheese ones. Thirty-six of them. 'I'll keep them warm,' she said and put them gently into the bottom of the oven. Then she changed her mind and removed them again. She stood now, two plates of scones in her hands and tried to decide what to do. The decision suddenly seemed monumental and she frowned, bit her lip and then was saved from confusion by the doorbell.

Her mother stood, with Frances, at the front door. The sun had gone in. They kissed, exchanged greetings, banalities, and then went through to the living-room, where Rosemary had lit the fire. She made tea, then decided it was too early and threw it away. 'I'll wait for Tom,' she said to herself. She could hear Frances and Betty chatting in the living-room as she stood in the kitchen and set the things on a tray.

Tom arrived at ten-to-four. 'Am I too early?' He stood, his arms full of crysanthemums.

'No. Thank you,' she took the flowers, smiled at him, put her cheek out to be kissed and led him through to introduce him, knowing that Frances would entertain while she went once more into the kitchen.

She found vases, three of them, to hold all the crysanthemums. They were gold and amber, like her garden. She buried her face in them, stopping the cutting of the long stems for a moment to level them up. 'They never smell,' she said out loud again, 'I hate crysanthemums. I hope I don't die in the autumn.' She made the tea, re-heated the scones, put out butter and jam, and carried them into the living-room, then went back for a second tray with the crockery.

'D'you want some help in there?' called Tom.

She didn't answer, and returned almost immediately and began to pour tea. She longed for them all to go. Tiredness swept through her body relentlessly. Her legs ached, the tops of her arms felt sore, conversation died on her lips.

Frances watched her while she talked to Betty and Tom. 'When I take Betty home,' she whispered to Rosemary as she followed her into the kitchen where more tea was made, 'I'm coming straight back. Something's happened. Is it that dreadful man again?'

'Who?' Rosemary looked at her, genuinely confused suddenly.

'Who?' Frances hissed at her. 'I'm talking about Ben Morrison, for Christ's sake! How many dreadful men are there in your life?' She nodded into the hall and touched Rosemary's arm. 'I like *him*,' she whispered.

Rosemary drew back from her touch and Frances frowned.

It seemed hours before Tom stood to go. He looked at his watch and sighed. 'Rosemary, I've gotta leave. I don't want to, but I have a dinner engagement.'

She stood up to join him, hoping she didn't look too relieved. It was six-thirty. Soon the clocks would go back and it would be long, dark nights again. 'What a shame,' she smiled at him.

'Will I see you again before I leave for the States?' he asked softly after his 'goodbyes' and when they stood alone at the front door.

'I don't think so,' she looked sorry, or so she hoped, and lied, 'I have to go away tomorrow.'

He pulled her suddenly towards him and kissed her on the nose. She stiffened and threw a glance towards the living-room.

He smiled and let her go. 'Wouldn't your mother approve?'

She laughed with him.

'I'll call you from L.A.,' he said, and with one hand raised, got into his car and drove away, tooting his horn as he left the drive. She stood politely, middle-aged and middle-class, one hand waving, smiling a little ruefully so he would believe she missed him already.

'Don't shut the front door until the guests can no longer see you,' she muttered as she shivered and went once again into the house.

Frances was on her way to the kitchen with dirty crockery. She stopped and said, 'What did you say?'

Rosemary looked up. 'Just something my mother used to tell me,' she said.

'I'm going to take her home,' murmured Frances.

'Oh dear, so soon?' Rosemary began to load the dishwasher.

Frances looked at her and screwed up her eyes with suspicion. 'Well don't sound so pleased,' she said. Then went on, 'I'm coming back. I want to talk to you.'

Rosemary looked up. 'I thought I'd have an early night,' she said lamely.

'It's half-past six sweet child! You're a big girl, you're allowed to stay up until at least eleven.' She left with a protesting Betty, who wanted to stay and watch television and have a drink, but didn't quite know how to ask, so she allowed herself to be shuffled into Frances' car.

'I'll phone tomorrow,' called Rosemary, and closed the door on them. 'Perhaps she'll change her mind,' she said to her reflection in her dressing table mirror, when she'd gone to cream her face and get into her night attire, while remembering Frances' promise to return before nine that evening. She put on her electric blanket, more for comfort than warmth, and then remembered that she hadn't eaten all day, not even to taste her own cheese scones, so she went downstairs again in bare feet to make herself a sandwich. She made one with cheese and pickle and the other with raspberry jam. Two rounds of sandwiches in Hovis bread. Then, taking a knife, she scraped out the cheese and pickle, and put it in with the raspberry jam. She stood back and surveyed her culinary effort and smiled. 'There.' It was something she'd wanted to do so often when she was a child. All the things you wanted most at the same time.

She opened a bottle of dessert wine and drank a glass between mouthfuls of sandwich.

The house was as quiet as a grave. She sat very still, so as not to spoil it, and concentrated on the sound of her own breathing. This occupied her until all at once the hall clock struck nine and the doorbell rang.

It was Frances. Rosemary looked surprised.

'I did say I was coming,' her friend said, and then, as Rosemary didn't move, 'are you going to let me in?'

'Oh,' she stepped back from the door, 'I'm sorry, come in. I forgot. I've been busy.' They walked into the kitchen and Rosemary sat down again. 'D'you want some wine?' she said, nodding at her own glass.

'Lovely.' Frances went to the fridge. She looked at the bottle. 'Are you drinking this?' she asked.

'Yes. It's very good with cheese and jam sandwiches.'

Frances laughed. 'Too exotic for my taste. I think I'll have a gin.' She watched Rosemary, who stared into her wine and drummed her fingers on the table. The two women sat facing each other.

'It's so quiet,' Rosemary said softly.

'What's happened?' Frances tried to take her friend's hand, but Rosemary pretended to misunderstand and finished the wine in her glass instead.

'When?' she said, 'what happened when?'

'I don't know. You tell me.' Frances' voice was very gentle. There was a long, long silence. Frances waited. The ticking of the hall clock was loud through the dark house. Only the moon lit up their faces through the large kitchen window. Frances moved to switch on the lights over the kitchen units.

Rosemary said, 'Franny, I think I'm going to have a nervous breakdown. I'd like to have one. I want to go to bed. Will you put me to bed?'

'Tell me what happened. Just tell me.'

After moments, Rosemary began to talk. Frances held her friend's hands when she once stumbled over the words. Just the once. Otherwise she told it all, without emotion or fear or confusion. And when she related about the mug shattering on the floor, she laughed. There was quiet again when she finished, and then Frances spoke. 'The bastard raped you.'

Rosemary shrugged.

'Did you tell Ella, or Joanna?'

She shook her head.

'Did you get the key?'

'No.'

'I think *I* might kill him, never mind you.'

'I don't want Ella to know,' Rosemary said. 'And I want you to do me some favours.'

'Anything.'

'I want you to phone Michael and tell him I'm ill and I can't do the radio show next week.'

Frances stared at her. 'All right,' she said eventually. 'What else?'

'Tell Jennie to cancel everything and not to come next week. Put Pat off as well, and then tell Joanna and Ella I'm ill. She goes to Glasgow soon, anyway.'

'What about *you*? Where are you going?'

Rosemary looked up, surprise in her voice. 'Nowhere. I want to go to bed. I just want to go to bed. And I don't want to talk to anyone. Will you do all that?'

'Yes. But one promise.'

'Go on.'

'You must never, ever let him into your house again. And this stays just here – this horrendous episode. I'll stay with you this week.'

'No.'

'Yes. Otherwise—'

'All right.' Rosemary moved one hand vaguely, tired now with all the talking. 'Can we go to bed now?' she said.

Frances took her upstairs. She went back to her own

house and made several phone calls, one of which was to Michael at home. She could imagine what consternation that caused, but felt obliged to let him know straight away.

'Does she need a doctor?' he said, worried.

'Not at the moment. She's in shock, but please don't ask me what about. She'll get over it. She just wants some peace.'

'It's that blasted boy, isn't it?'

Frances hesitated. 'That's over. I'm sorry, Michael, about phoning you at home. I had no choice.'

He laughed. 'It couldn't be worse here anyway, Frances.'

'I'm sorry.'

'Let me know if I can do anything. It was nice to hear your voice again.' He replaced the receiver and took a deep breath before the explanation to Barbara. It was so unlike Rosemary to suddenly disappear and turn over all responsibility to others. He wondered what had happened to disturb her so utterly.

When Frances got back to Wimbledon Joanna and Ella were there. She went round to the kitchen door and found them opening tins of soup and baked beans.

'Weren't you supposed to come earlier?' Ella said brightly. 'It's a bit late for afternoon tea.'

'I'll have a large gin, then,' said Frances, and put her small suitcase down on the floor.

'I think Mum must be in bed.' Ella tipped some cold beans onto a slice of buttered bread. Frances shuddered.

'She is. She's not well. I'm staying the week. Do either of you want a gin while I've got the bottle in my hand?'

Ella stopped eating, and Joanna turned from the stove where she'd been heating up the soup. 'Mum's ill?' Ella

324

said. 'What's happened? Did that fucking Ben come back?'

Frances shook her head. 'No. She just wants to lie low for a while. She'll be fine.'

'They had a big fight this morning,' Joanna said softly.

'I know,' Frances sank into one of the kitchen chairs. 'She's just in pieces at the moment. But he won't be back.'

'Did she get the key?' Joanna asked. Ella went back to her beans.

Frances shook her head.

'He'll be back,' said Joanna sadly.

'Over my dead body.' And Ella began shovelling the cold baked beans into her mouth.

'Not this time,' said Frances.

Joanna drank her soup. 'Poor Rosemary,' she said, 'fancy loving someone who makes you feel so bad about yourself.'

Ella smiled at her.

'Some men just have that talent,' Frances said, and stood up to go to bed, taking the glass of gin with her and blowing a kiss to both girls.

'Do have some cheese scones with your beans,' she said, 'your mother made enough for an army. I hate the thought of eating them all week, and she never throws food away.'

'I *hate* cheese scones,' said Ella vehemently, and she shuddered as she always did when a child, remembering her mother trying to disguise the parsnips in mashed potato.

Frances laughed and went to bed. She looked quietly into Rosemary's room and seeing her friend asleep, moved to turn her bedside light out.

'Leave it,' said Rosemary, her eyes opening suddenly.

'I thought you were asleep.' Frances sat on the side of the bed. 'It's late.'

'Did you sort it all out?' Rosemary asked.

Frances nodded. 'I'll do Jennie and Pat in the morning,' she said.

'Early.' Rosemary closed her eyes again, 'Before they leave home would be best.'

'All right. Can you sleep?'

'Yes. For a week, I hope.' She took Frances' hand. 'Thanks.'

'It's the least. Shall I leave the light on?'

'Yes please. I don't like the dark.'

Frances kissed her on the cheek and stood up. 'The chains are on both doors,' she said.

Rosemary nodded. 'Good. Keep the burgulars out. That's what Jonathan used to say.' She smiled to herself and closed her eyes. 'I'm so tired,' she said. 'Wake me next Sunday.'

Frances went to bed.

Chapter Twenty Six

Joanna's show began with four days of previews. Ella started rehearsals, saw the opening night of Jo's play, then left for Glasgow. Jo would follow on the Sunday, and stay for a couple of weeks. Frances stayed at Wimbledon, going to work during the day, and sitting with her friend in the evenings. They would sit downstairs and eat too much and talk. Rosemary stayed in a dressing-gown, her face naked of make-up, her hair lank, the dark roots showing through dull blonde.

'Looks quite trendy, Mum,' Ella said one morning when she took orange juice into Rosemary's bedroom before rehearsals.

'That's nice, dear.' Rosemary was looking out of the window watching the wind and rain hurtling through the rapidly disrobing trees.

Ella was confused and unhappy. 'It's so unlike her. Something's happened that she's not telling us. No-one takes to their fucking bed because of a fight.'

Joanna punched her arm, gently.

Frances said, 'That's an unfortunate adjective,' and raised her eyebrows.

Ella sighed. 'At least she talks to *you*,' she said to Frances.

'You pack for Glasgow, I'll stay till she's on her feet, precious brat, which won't be long.' The older woman tried to sound reassuring. Ella and Frances had declared quite a friendly truce during the four days before the younger woman left for Scotland.

Joanna's show had opened to very good reviews. 'It might get a transfer,' she told Frances.

'Is that good? Excuse my ignorance. Good for *you* I mean?'

Joanna laughed. 'Probably.'

Michael had managed to convince the BBC radio department that Rosemary would be back for her usual spot after only a week, and they put in a replacement while she was away. A certain young disc jockey decided on wishing her well again over the air-waves, which meant that flowers appeared from fans, sent on to her from Michael's office and the programme producer.

In the first show of emotion during the whole week, Rosemary screwed up her face and looked embarrassed. 'What am I supposed to have?' she asked Frances.

'Flu.' Her friend threw the flowers into various vases. It made Rosemary laugh for the first time that week. They were both in the kitchen on the Friday evening, Ella packed and gone, Joanna at the theatre.

'I loathe flower arranging,' Frances said, laughing with her, 'but if it's going to make you smile again I'll take it up as a hobby.'

'Please don't. Let me, you pour the gins.'

Later on the same evening Frances asked her if she was feeling better. Rosemary thought before she spoke. Then, 'I don't feel anything. Just safe in the house.'

'You'll have to go out sooner or later, darling one. Next Tuesday for instance, the BBC are expecting you back.'

Rosemary shrank into herself and shivered. 'I'm terrified,' she said.

'Of Ben Morrison?' Frances asked.

Rosemary shook her head.

'Then who?' Frances leaned forward.

'I don't know Franny. Everyone. Myself. I'd let him back, you know. If he came here again. I miss him.'

Frances stared at her. 'For Christ's sake, Rosemary,

the man declared war on you! What d'you miss? What did you have? Except sex?'

Rosemary closed her eyes briefly, then opened them slowly to take in the anger on her friend's face.

'I can't explain,' she said, 'or even expect you to understand.'

'Try me.'

'He made me feel as if he's all I have. All I'll get. That I'm lucky to have him. I don't know. My intelligence tells me one thing, my body the opposite.'

A silence fell. Then Frances spoke. 'Will you see someone?'

'You mean a psychiatrist?'

'He's a counsellor. A good one. And a friend of mine.' Frances took her hands. 'You're appallingly depressed. He could help. Get you on your feet at least.'

'I don't know. I don't want to get into all that. I've managed so much of my life up till now.'

'For Christ's sake Rosemary, you can't languish on your bed like Camille because you're besotted by some thug's penis.'

Rosemary threw back her head and laughed. 'You do have a way with words, Franny.'

'That's twice this week,' Frances smiled.

'Twice what?'

'Twice you've laughed. I was beginning to think I'd lost my touch.'

'Never.'

Frances leaned forward. 'Will you see this counsellor? Please.'

Rosemary took her hand from her friend's grasp and ran it quickly through her tangled hair. She sighed deeply.

'And would Martyn come and do something with your hair at the same time?' asked Frances.

Rosemary shrugged. 'I can't make the decision.'

'Well then, I will. My friend will be here tomorrow,

and I'll talk Martyn into coming on Monday. Before the BBC on Tuesday.'

'It's radio, Franny. Who cares what I look like?'

'It's for you, you fool, that's what it's about. Your self-esteem, your own worth. Listen to me—' She pulled her friend round towards her. 'You have to forget Ben Morrison. He hasn't, and he mustn't, destroy you. You can't go on laying down your affection like a doormat, letting him make you believe eventually in your own worthlessness.'

Rosemary forced her gaze away and stared into the fire. She said, 'I believed my passion for him made me indispensable to him.'

'You *are* indispensable to him. All the women he lays are indispensable to him. It's all he has to make him feel his own worth.'

'I'm told he's a good actor, that he has a wonderful career ahead of him.'

'It's obviously not enough. He needs your weakness. Makes him feel strong.'

'He'll change. The other girls, they're temporary. Our relationship is different, more permanent, I'm sure. He was jealous, that's all. I ought to hang on to that. He'd never been jealous before, it made him vulnerable, so he hit out in the only way he can. If I'm patient and find out what he wants from me, I know he'll change.'

Frances leaned back in her chair and shook her head. 'I can't believe I'm having this conversation with you after what he did to you.' There was no answer. Frances waited and then eventually spoke again. 'He won't change, Rosemary. You'll see that if you just hang on. Some men's love affair with their own penis lasts well into old age. You can tell by the way they hold onto it the older they get, jiggling their money against it, hands in their pockets, wondering miserably why it gets smaller with age, afraid to stand shoulder-to-shoulder in public lavatories in case of comparison. Ridiculous! Give me the men who can take it or leave it and walk tall swinging their arms away from their own bodies!'

Rosemary smiled at her. 'You sound quite passionate about it,' she said. 'All right, phone your man. If he can get me back on my feet, maybe I'll decide what to do.'

The counsellor arrived the following morning at about mid-day and listened for a long time.

'No tranquillisers,' he said firmly, writing on his pad. 'You're depressed, let's get you out of that first.'

'Anti-depressants,' said Frances when he'd gone.

Rosemary looked surprised. 'You seem to know. I thought it would be just a tonic.'

'I've been on them.'

'You've never said.'

Frances shrugged and kissed her friend before going to the chemist. 'Martyn's coming tomorrow, not Monday. OK?'

'OK.'

The anti-depressants arrived, and Rosemary started the course straight away. She had enough for three weeks. 'Then what?' she asked Frances.

'You'll start feeling better in about five days. But you must start work on Tuesday. Will you?'

Rosemary nodded tentatively. She said no more about Ben. She longed to ask if he'd phoned, knowing Frances wouldn't tell her, but not daring to answer the phone herself. She could hardly believe that she had already begun to forgive him. But by Tuesday, on the way to the studio by taxi, watching the people wandering down Regent Street and up to Oxford Circus, she knew that she longed to see him. To say to him, 'I forgive you', to hear him say, 'I'm sorry Rosie, it's because I love you'. And she would understand, and put her arms round him, and a whole new depth in their relationship would start. She kept all these fantasies, dreams, ideas, to herself, fearing the derision of others, knowing how foolish she would seem to them. She let them think she was getting better, had put the whole idea of Ben Morrison behind her, was getting on with life as she always had done.

So Frances went home and, with both girls in Glasgow, she had the house to herself. And she stopped putting the chain on the door and waited every night in case he came. When the phone rang once at three in the morning, she picked it up and no-one spoke at the other end, she convinced herself it was him and that he was too afraid to speak. She began to feel gentle towards him, seeing him now as vulnerable and hurt, longing for a love that only she could give.

The week before Joanna was due back from Glasgow, she literally bumped into a young woman in the salad queue at the BBC canteen one lunchtime. They both apologized and smiled. And Rosemary thought the face was familiar.

The girl said, 'It's Rosemary Downey, isn't it?'

Rosemary searched the face, and her memory, to try to put a name to the dark, straight hair and blue eyes.

'Yes,' she said, and then, 'I'm sorry, but I can't quite remember?'

'Oh, you don't know me, Rosemary. I'm Gill, Gill Spencer, Ben's friend. I'm sure he's mentioned me. I'm Jamie's mum.' Rosemary wanted to sit down suddenly. Her appetite disappeared. Gill Spencer looked around at the busy canteen and then pointed quickly to an empty table. 'Can we talk? There's a table there. Would you mind?'

Rosemary shook her head and the girl led the way across the room. She was taller than Rosemary, very tall in fact, and quite thin. She looked bright and smiling.

Rosemary suddenly wanted to be any place but where she was. They sat and faced each other.

Rosemary said, 'I didn't realize at first. That it was you, I mean. I saw a photo of you and your son.'

Gill smiled, 'I didn't realize Ben flashed it around. Thought it cramped his style.' She laughed.

'It doesn't seem to bother you,' said Rosemary, and then, 'Did he tell you about me or—'

'Good God no, that's not his style. He likes you to believe he's a loner. Sort of like Clint Eastwood disappearing into the sunset, leaving everyone satisfied but missing him!' She laughed again and Rosemary shook her head, confused. 'D'you really find it funny, or are you pretending? For my sake I mean? I realize you and he split. He told me—'

'Well he would, wouldn't he?'

Rosemary stared at her. Gill looked suddenly serious. She sighed. 'What I really wanted to ask may be difficult for you. But it's for Jamie's sake as well as mine. We don't see so much of him. Ben I mean – his dad. He's always gone off, but just lately, I can't seem to track him down at all. And when I saw you, remembered the photo in the paper a few months back, it just seemed fate that I should get this radio play and bump into you.'

'I didn't know you were an actress.'

'Well, when I can get the work. Ben's not too bad with money. It's just him we'd like more of.'

'I don't see what it's got to do with me. What d'you want?'

Gill had finished eating. Rosemary had long since given up on her own meal. 'D'you smoke?' Gill held a packet of Marlboro across to her. Rosemary took one and lit it from the girl's large, old-fashioned lighter. The flame went out and she cursed, shook it and tried again. 'Hold on, it's always doing this.' She stood and went

333

over to another group of people she obviously knew and leaned forward to light a cigarette. She chatted to them for moments. Rosemary watched her. Lively and fast talking, jeans faded from age and frayed where someone had taken scissors to shorten them. They were much too large and a man's belt pulled them in to fit her tiny waist. *Ben's jeans*, thought Rosemary, and felt sick with jealousy.

Gill came back and sat down again. 'Sorry about that,' she nodded towards the table she'd just left, 'they're in the rep here. I asked about auditioning.'

'What did you want to say to me?' Rosemary wanted the meeting to be over, wanted the seclusion of her own small recording studio in the bowels of the building.

'I don't want to embarrass or even upset you. But you look like a nice lady,' Gill said and gave her a quick smile.

Rosemary looked at her watch. 'I don't have much time,' she said, 'perhaps we could meet later for a drink?' She felt she might have been able to cope better with a gin and tonic in her hand. The Marlboro made her cough. Gill pushed the ashtray towards her and Rosemary stubbed out the half-finished cigarette. 'Bit strong for me,' she said.

'Will you share him with me?' Gill said it quickly, as if otherwise her courage would leave her.

Rosemary stared at her. 'I beg your pardon?'

'I think you heard me the first time.' There was a pause. Gill said quietly and intensely, 'Ben won't mind, you know. As long as we both let him know *we* wouldn't mind.'

Rosemary could find no words, and the silence stayed between them, the chatter around them swirling in and out of Rosemary's consciousness. She found a voice at last. 'I can't do that. And I don't know where he is. I haven't seen him. We had a fight.'

Gill said, 'Did he leave of his own volition?'

Not really wanting to go into details of that last confrontation between herself and Ben Rosemary answered, 'Well, sort of. I'm not sure. But it was, I don't know, about two weeks ago.'

'He'll be back.' Gill pushed her chair away from the table and looked at her watch. Ash fell from the end of her almost-finished cigarette. She looked down at Rosemary. 'Does he have your key?' Rosemary didn't answer. Gill went on, 'He always comes back. Lets you simmer down a bit and then just when he senses you really want him he turns up.' She laughed. 'Think about what I said. We'd like to see him.'

'Don't you mind about the way he is?' whispered Rosemary, horrified.

The girl shrugged. 'That's Ben. He's always been like that. Likes to spread it around a little. Happiness I mean. Thinks he does us all a favour. I got used to it. D'you have my phone number?' Gill stubbed out her cigarette at last and searched in the back pocket of her jeans. She found the tail end of a blunt-looking pencil, then pulled one of the paper napkins from the pile on the table in front of her and began to scribble on it. She pushed it across to Rosemary. 'If you see him first, tell him what I said. Thanks for talking to me. Give me a bell.' And she was gone, joining up with the crowd from the other table, holding her script in one hand, tucking her pack of cigarettes in the pocket of the man's shirt she was wearing, pushing and clowning and laughing.

Rosemary sat where she was, feeling older and more middle-class than she had ever done in her life. Why, oh why, had Ben Morrison ever become involved with someone so far removed from his own world as Rosemary Downey? What did he first see in her? How did she ever not see him as everyone else did?

She did her show, went across to the Langham Hotel with the producer and had her gin and tonic. She excused herself to make a phone call and rang Michael. 'Can you get me out of that quiz show?' she asked.

'Not unless you want to find yourself another agent,' Michael said firmly.

Rosemary sighed. 'I'm emotionally battered,' she murmured.

'I'm sorry?'

'Never mind. All right.'

In a few weeks she would be on television, but not hosting a show that Ben would approve of. 'Even more puerile than the last,' had been his comment, but the money was good, and Christmas loomed, usually one of her favourite times of the year. She should start making her lists. Her heart sank at the prospect.

The night before Joanna was due back, she and Frances went out to dinner, and she relayed the story about meeting Gill. Frances began to laugh.

'It's not *that* funny,' Rosemary felt and sounded quite peeved at her friend's insensitivity.

'I would love to have seen the look on your face. That prudish bile-like expression that comes over those beautiful grey eyes, that tightening of the mouth and the slight shaking of the head. You must have been the very image of your mother.'

Rosemary was horrified. 'Am I really like my mother?'

'Sometimes,' Frances laughed again. 'Don't panic; Ella has a lot of you in her, and there's nothing prudish about that delectable monster.'

'I thought you were getting on better when you stayed.'

'Love of *you* dear one.' Frances touched her friend's hand across the table. 'I'm joking,' she said. 'My, you *are* sensitive these days.'

'Sorry. The Gill episode shook me. Made me see the position Ben has put me in. I feel like a concubine.' She grimaced and Frances laughed again.

'Well it's over, so forget it. It's all over. Or did you agree?'

'Don't be absurd.'

'I'm teasing. What did she look like?'

'Thin – and tall.'

'Nasty.'

'And she had dirty fingernails.'

'You do notice the most peculiar things about people.' Frances drove her home but didn't come in.

Letting herself into the empty house Rosemary could smell the lavender from the energetic polishing that had taken the returned Pat by storm that morning.

'Nice when it's just you here,' she grumbled to Rosemary, 'I can really get to grips with this house when it's empty.' Rosemary could scarcely see the point or satisfaction of cleaning a clean house day after day, but smiled and agreed.

The next day was Sunday. She took her mother out to lunch as a treat. Betty asked whether she'd heard from 'that nice middle-aged American chap'.

'Once,' said Rosemary.

'I liked him,' said her mother, in a tone of voice that meant she disapproved of practically everyone else her daughter had ever introduced her to.

'Bit young for you,' teased Rosemary.

'Don't be so silly,' her mother retorted, 'you know what I meant. I wouldn't have another man in my house. I was thinking of you. You need someone to take care of you in your old age. Stop you living in a house full of all these weird people.' She sniffed.

'If you mean Joanna,' said Rosemary, 'I like having her around. Anyway,' she filled her mother's glass with more white wine, ignoring the fluttering protests, 'I think she and Ella are looking seriously for a flat now that money's easier.'

'About time. What the neighbours must think . . ?' Her voice trailed off with imagined horror.

'They probably think "well, well, three women living together. They must be lovers".'

'Don't use that word.'

Rosemary laughed and kissed her mother's cheek.

She took Betty home, surprised at her mother's refusal to come to Wimbledon for the evening. 'Stay the night, Mum,' she'd offered.

But Betty shook her head. 'I'm not feeling that good. I think I'll have a day in bed tomorrow.'

Rosemary looked surprised. 'Phone me if you want anything,' she said. 'I've checked the heating. Leave it on all night, don't get cold.'

'I can't do that, it's far too expensive,' Betty grumbled.

'I'll pay the next bill. Don't argue, Mum.' She kissed her and went home. Betty had looked tired and suddenly very much her age. She would be eighty at the beginning of January. 'I'll take her to the Caprice,' she'd said to Ella months ago. 'I can't face an eightieth birthday in the house. She likes the Caprice.' She wondered what time Joanna would get back from Scotland. It was a long train journey, especially on a Sunday. She listened to the answerphone when she got home. There was still no word from Ben. She died a little each time she found no message from him. She wondered if Gill had seen him, or even heard from him. The dark evening set in, and a November fog settled along with the lengthening shadows. She had changed into her track-suit, taken off her make-up and opened some wine to keep her company in the evening ahead. She lit the fire and sat in the silence, thinking and remembering the year behind her. Next week she had the final clothes shopping for the new television show. At least she would be free of Ben's snide comments while she worked. But it was no comfort at that moment. She remembered the feel and the smell of him, his body against hers, and she ached for him with a longing she was ashamed to confront with too much honesty.

At seven o'clock the doorbell rang. She frowned, wondered if Joanna had forgotten her key, and went into the hall, taking her drink with her. Opening the door, letting in the cold and mist, she peered into the gloom, feeling the warmth and security of the house behind her. Ben was standing there, his hold-all on his shoulder, his toothbrush protruding from the pocket of his denim jacket. His breath escaped in cold mists from his mouth when he spoke at last.

'Hello Rosie.'

She stood back to let him in without a word, closing the cold night behind him. He pulled her into his arms and she went to him, still in silence, feeling his heart beat under the cold of his jacket, the hold-all still on his shoulder, the toothbrush sharp against her face. They stood for moments.

'I'm glad you're here,' she whispered. He took her hand and led her back into the living-room.

Chapter Twenty Seven

It had been a long time since they had spent an evening
together alone. She wished she'd been prepared for him,
dressed and made-up. Old habits are hard to forget, like
preparing herself for the man in her life.

He sat on the sofa, away from the fire, his jacket
undone but not removed, his bag on the floor beside
him. He smiled at her, up at her, while she stood
over him, glass in her hand, still feeling the sensation
in her body as she'd stood in his arms.

'Would you like a drink?' The obvious was all she
could think to say now that he was here after all these
weeks. All the prepared dialogue imagined for so long
vanished at the sight of him, dark and imposing, sitting
there against the chintz, his back to the window where
the curtains were still undrawn.

'What you got Rosie?'

'Wine. Opened, or there's whisky.' He nodded and
she went through to the kitchen. The trembling in her
legs unsteadied her as she poured his drink. 'Let it
be all right,' she muttered to herself. 'Dear God, let
it be all right. Put the right words in my mouth. Let
me please him this time.' She took his drink back into
the living-room and then went to put more logs on the
fire. He had drawn the curtains, and now sat once
more in the middle of the sofa and watched while she
manipulated the poker with trembling hands, praying,
searching for something to say.

At last he broke the silence. 'Are you going to stop
pottering and come over so I can kiss you?'

And she went to him. Immediately. He pulled her onto his lap and kissed her, one hand firmly on the back of her head, one holding his glass of whisky.

'Sit beside me,' he said, and when she did, he kept one arm round her and forced her head onto his chest. In silence they sat for a long time. The fire blazed. She could feel his heart, hear her own.

Eventually she said, 'I must sit straight, I have a crick in my neck.'

'OK.'

'Are you hungry?' the question as if to a child home from school.

'What you got?' his eyes twinkled.

'No left-over Sunday best,' she said. 'I was out to lunch. Took my mother. I could make you a sandwich.'

'Great.'

She heard the television go on in the room as she stood in the kitchen and cut bread to butter and fill with cheese and ham, the way he liked it. She had avoided asking him where he'd been. She wondered if she should mention Gill. If they could just talk to each other, maybe then she could make it work.

'I bumped into Gill,' she said at last, once he'd begun to eat.

'I know.'

'You've seen her?' Familiar jealousy rose inside her. But she smiled gaily across at him from the chair she'd sat in, once back from the kitchen. The desire to touch him was so strong within her that she had to distance herself.

He nodded.

'Did she mention our conversation?' Rosemary asked.

He laughed. 'Sharing me out like pass-the-parcel you mean?'

'Well, yes, I guess it did sound like that.'

'I said you'd hate it.' He stood up, 'D'you mind if I take my jacket off?' He did so and flung it on the back of the sofa. Her fingers itched to hang it in the hall, but she restrained herself, knowing how irritated he often was by her incessant tidying.

'I would,' she said as he sat again to finish his food. 'Hate it, I mean. Thank you for realizing that.'

'Well there you are Rosie, I'm not such an insensitive bastard as you thought.' He stood to take the plate back to the kitchen and towered over her, sitting small and looking frightened in the chair by the phone. 'Did you miss me?' he smiled.

'At times.'

'You don't hate me then?'

'No.' The answer came quietly and with some hesitation. She went on, 'I feel I ought to.'

He took the plate out of the room and came back almost immediately with the whisky bottle and replenished his glass. She remained still, almost holding her breath, trying not to show how much she wanted him. How excited she was to see him standing in front of her, his eyes teasing her face, knowledge of her and her body obvious in every move he made towards her, knowing the power of his presence. He squatted down on his haunches in front of her and took the wine from her hand, whispered into her hair as his mouth breathed against her cheek. 'Show me,' he said, 'show you don't hate me. I want you Rosie, I'll always want you.' And he pulled her down onto the floor, undressing her. He turned off the table lamp so that the fire played on her naked body at the same time as his hands. Breathing hard, conscious of the way he took over, she felt all her submissiveness excite him. She stiffened, pulled away, remembering the last time, but he was gentle, insistent and persuasive. Talking her again into believing it would be all right, 'Just here Rosie . . . trust me . . . you're so beautiful . . . so ready for me . . . have you missed me?'

342

And not waiting for answers, he buried himself into her at last until she cried out. He reached up and pulled cushions from the chair above her, and she gave herself again without thought.

They didn't hear the front door, didn't hear Joanna's calling 'Rosemary, I'm back!' nor the door of the living-room opening behind them. Ben stopped, looked up, pulled away and sat up, leaving her exposed to the surprised face of her returning lodger.

'Oops! Sorry Rosemary. Sorry.' And the door closed once more behind her as Rosemary heard the girl's feet hurtling with a certain panic in the direction of the kitchen.

'Oh my God.' Rosemary sat and pulled her track-suit on, stumbling on one leg against the chair, pulling the top back on as Ben had taken it off, without undoing the zip.

'And it was all going so well,' he laughed. He had merely pulled up his trousers, adjusted his belt, and sat now, back on the sofa and picked up his whisky again. The mood had gone. Cold realization settled on her, filled her with a shame that took her breath away, and leaving her shaking from the lack of consummation.

Dressed, she sat and buried her face in her hands. 'Oh my God.'

Ben was merely amused. 'For Christ's sake Rosie, it's your house. You can screw who you like where you like. Your daughter's dykey friend should learn to knock.'

She looked up at him. 'My feelings are beyond your comprehension, aren't they Ben?'

A deep sigh accompanied the raising heavenward of his eyes. 'Are we gonna have one of those conversations again?' he said.

'Ella's dykey friend, as you call her, happens to live here, on my invitation. I enjoy her company. I don't

343

exactly get much of that from you!' she snapped back, offended at last by his casualness.

'Maybe she could supply you with everything else as well,' Ben said quietly, 'then you could let me go for good.' She stared at him coldly. 'But then there's a certain thing she doesn't have, isn't there?' he went on, smiling again now. 'I know you Rosie, a cock is something you'd miss.' He was so genial, so soft in his manner, she realized he probably actually believed he was making her feel sexy towards him again.

She spoke at last, searching for the words, a coldness and detachment creeping through her, filling her once again with the self-loathing he aroused so easily within her. 'I've never, ever, met anyone quite like you Ben Morrison.'

'You must have done. There's more of us around, if you get bored with me, that is. We give a service. You pay for it.'

'I have.'

'I know.' He shrugged. 'That's tough.'

She shivered at the words and drained her wine glass. She wanted him to go so that she could apologize to Joanna. She longed for the easy company of women. 'I'm almost sure I hate you,' she said at last.

'You always have done. From the moment you decided to fall in love with me. You're dependant on me for your pain. It makes you feel like a girl again.'

'I wish I'd never met you,' she whispered, almost to herself.

He stood up and put his jacket on. She made no move to stop him. Her resistance to more humiliation had finally strengthened.

He picked up his hold-all. 'You'll find me easy to forget. I told you at the beginning there's nothing here.' He patted his chest. His eyes were cold now. He said, 'Don't worry about it. Revenge will be the sweetest moment for you, better than even the misery you're so keen on.'

'Why on earth did you bother in the first place?' she couldn't resist asking him.

'You were there,' he said. 'There for the taking. Sometimes it's like that. You asked for nothing at first. It was great. Everything about you said "here I am, unattended, come and get me". So I did. It never crossed my mind to offer you anything except the obvious. You were crying out for it. You were content just to empty yourself into me. Isn't that right?' He bent towards her, his face close to hers, she smelt the whisky on his breath, the familiar smell of his cologne.

'I wasn't aware you had anything else to offer but the obvious,' she said, hoping he would realize the cruelty in her tone.

But he merely laughed. 'Nothing,' he said. 'I have nothing. To offer that is.' He was too close to her. It was probably the longest near-serious conversation they had ever had.

'What?' she said.

He spelt it out. 'I have nothing to offer.'

'So you take.' It was a statement, not a question.

He looked bored suddenly, tired of the game, and stood up straight again, shifting his bag onto his other shoulder, running his fingers through his hair, burping gently, as the sandwich she had so lovingly prepared such a short time ago, was being digested. 'Only from the ones like you. The ones who only know how to give. Ella's a taker. It's why we didn't last. We're alike, Ella and me. You should take some lessons.'

'Never!' she spoke vehemently. 'My daughter's not like you.'

He laughed and went to the door and opened it. 'You should see her in action,' he said. 'Don't see me out. I'll give you a bell, Rosie.' She heard him call 'cheers' to Joanna and then the front door closed behind him.

Joanna's footsteps padded softly across the hall. 'Are you all right Rosemary? Has he gone?'

'Yes, he's gone, Jo. Taken a lot with him, I'm afraid.' She switched the table lamp on beside her and smiled up at the anxious face of the young girl. 'I'm sorry about all that. You must wonder what kind of family you've become involved with.'

'As long as you're OK.'

Rosemary sighed ruefully. 'I've become a mystery to myself over Ben Morrison,' she said. 'I wish you'd met me before he appeared in my life. You might have liked me then. *I* liked me then.' She laughed.

Joanna said, 'I like you now. You're much stronger than you think. You just fell in love with the wrong person. I've done it.'

'Not Ella?' Rosemary frowned. But the young girl smiled at her.

'No. Not Ella. Ella's too like you to be that cruel. You just don't have her cunning.'

'Or perception, judging from the length of her affair with Ben. I should have known. She tried to warn me.' They stopped talking and stared into the fire.

'D'you want another drink?' Joanna asked.

Rosemary held out her glass. 'Please. Will you join me? Tomorrow I'm going on the wagon. Might as well give everything up.' She felt tired, 'I've made a fool of myself once again Jo,' she said. 'Can we keep this to ourselves?'

Joanna frowned. 'I always tell Ella everything.'

'Well then, not quite yet. Right now I can't face the language she'd use!'

They both laughed.

'All right.' Jo went to the door with Rosemary's glass. 'You'll fall out of love eventually, Rosemary.'

Rosemary closed her eyes. 'Christ, I hope so. It must be better than this. As soon as he's gone I want him again.'

'That sort of sex is a difficult addiction.' Jo left the room.

Rosemary stared after her. Would she take him back again? He still hadn't left his key. She still hadn't demanded it.

It felt so unfinished. She waited for the phone call. She started the new job. Confessed to Frances what had happened: Joanna finding them on the floor, her nakedness, her stupidity, her continuous shame.

'He really has got you by the short and curlies, hasn't he?' said Frances. 'Quite literally, in fact.'

Rosemary didn't find it funny. She was beginning to alienate her best friend, knowing her obsessiveness for Ben was beyond Frances' understanding. So she stopped mentioning him. She prepared for Christmas in between both her jobs. She got thin and drawn-looking, brittle in her attempt to show some kind of face to a world that knew little of the turmoil going on inside.

Then one day, about a week before Christmas, she found herself standing in the canteen of the television studio getting some coffee, and, just ahead of her in the queue, she saw Betsy. She pulled back and went out along the corridor to her dressing-room. The dresser was bringing her outfit for the show that evening.

'Julie, could you get me some coffee? The queue's so long and I need to make some phone calls.'

'Of course Miss Downey. Just black?'

Rosemary nodded and the girl left the room. She sat for a moment. Then she picked up the phone to personnel. 'Is Mike Charger there?' she asked. A pause and then Mike came to the phone. 'Mike. Rosemary Downey here. Can you do me a favour? I've just seen an old friend of mine in the canteen – She didn't see me – I'd like to know what show she's working on, and in what capacity.'

'Sure thing, Miss Downey. Just give me the name and details.'

'She'd be in stage management I think. Her name's Betsy, er,' she searched her memory, 'Betsy Tejero.'

Mike laughed. 'You'd better spell that!'

After only five minutes Mike phoned back. Betsy was assistant floor manager on a new situation comedy. She would more than likely be around the studios for at least the next couple of months.

Julie brought her coffee and left her alone. Rosemary rummaged in her handbag, found her Filofax, and then took from it a scrap of paper. Then she dialled the number of the production office for the sit-com that Mike had given her. She recognized the voice on the phone. It was her lucky day. 'Moira? Moira Dayton? Is that you?' Moira had been on the stage management of one of her first recordings at least ten years ago. She was now a director, according to the television grapevine. 'It's Rosemary Downey. How nice to speak to you after all this time.'

'Rosemary! I was going to contact you but we've had problems here. New show and all that. How's things?'

'Fine.'

They exchanged pleasantries for as long as Rosemary could bear it. Finally she said, 'I believe Betsy's with you. A.S.M.'

'Betsy?' Moira thought for only seconds. 'Oh yes of course. She's comparatively new to television. She a friend?'

'Sort of. I have her phone number, not her address. I know it's strictly against the rules, but any chance of you giving it to me? She's with a friend of mine that I want to surprise – a *nice* surprise, don't get me wrong!' Rosemary laughed nervously. 'I'd be grateful if you didn't mention it to her, otherwise all this subterfuge would have been a waste of time! Can you do that?' She had spoken quickly, the words falling without thought from her mouth, winging it, before she lost her courage and wondered what had possessed her.

Moira said, 'No problem, what's your dressing-room? I'll get somebody here to scribble it out and pop it down to you.'

'You're a darling.' Rosemary breathed a sigh of relief. 'Efficient as ever, I can tell.'

Moira laughed. 'My producer might disagree with you at times. We must meet in the bar for a drink. Let me know when you're free.'

'I will. Good luck with the show. And thanks again.' Her hands were shaking when she put the phone down. She didn't quite know what she was going to do once she got Betsy's address. Find Ben? And then what? There was nothing to say. She had no longer known whether she even wanted him back; until the sight of Betsy had tampered with the calm that had fallen on her since Ben's last departure. Maybe, if he was at Betsy's, she could demand the return of her front door key. But then, he might just comply, and then what? No hope for any kind of reconciliation. No door left open for him just in case. He hadn't used the key when last they'd met. But he'd come, wanted her, had said he would phone. It seemed now a lifetime ago. She knew that if she didn't resolve it one way or the other, she just would never get on with her own life, give up this addiction, this obsession, this night and day desire to hold him, touch, feel him. *Why not* love *him?* she thought. But it was no longer a word she used in connection with Ben. Love was not supposed to retard one's emotional growth. Or was it? Maybe she'd forgotten. Her youth seemed to belong to another lifetime, another person. She'd learned nothing. Nothing to help her now with this compulsive, repulsive behaviour.

She was called to the studio. She met the contestants, helped put them at their ease, then went back to her dressing-room. An envelope was on the door. Betsy's address: a road in Stockwell; a flat. *Must be*, she thought, number 12A. A basement? She found her A–Z and looked it up. Easy to find. What now? She had no plans, no ideas, just wanted to know if maybe Ben was there. Send a Christmas card to him? Love from Rosemary. No. Just – from Rosie. That would be better. Maybe even intrigue him a little. Maybe drive him to pick up the phone one more time. *Oh Christ*, she thought, *will this never end? All this silliness?* Furious with herself, she tightened her mouth, her face, in determination, and went to make-up. The laughter, the gossip, the wonderful, delicious, mindless small talk amongst the girls would take her mind off all this wasteful stupidity which passed for her mind.

'If only you realized it,' Frances had said only a few days before, 'you're actually getting better, lovely one. I wish you'd embrace that fact.'

She did the show. No hitches. She went to hospitality. At ten o'clock she looked at her watch and began to say her 'goodbyes'.

'Do you need a car?' the producer had asked. Gone were the halcyon times of a limousine on studio days. Different TV company, less money for fripperies. No longer prime-time television.

'No thanks, George,' she smiled. 'I brought my car today.' She picked up the black sedan in the underground car park, tipped the attendant and without another thought drove towards Stockwell, the A–Z open on the seat beside her.

She found the street. The house was divided into flats, 12A was in the basement. Dead geraniums languished in peeling painted wooden window boxes on the inside of railings, steps led to a half-glassed panel door. She turned the car round and parked down the street, opposite the house, turned off the ignition and the lights, and waited. It was almost eleven o'clock. Joanna would wonder where

350

she was, maybe after a while presume she'd gone out to dinner.

She waited, her eyes on Betsy's flat, watching the steps down, wondering who was inside. There was a light on. She imagined the rooms: cluttered and small, maybe shared with another girl. Would Ben be there now? Did he stay often?

At midnight a taxi drew up. Two girls got out. Rosemary peered across the sparsely-lit street. One of them was Betsy. She paid the fare, the other girl went down the steps. The door opened, somebody called, a man's voice, from inside the flat. Betsy squealed, ran down, the taxi pulled away, the door slammed. Silence again along the street. Music, loud, reggae, sprang up from another house. The moon appeared suddenly from behind a cloud, and for moments the street was alight. Ben's car was there, on the other side of the road, near the flat: the dirty number plate was dusty, hidden by London grime. She stared, rooted to her seat, shaking now, wanting the car not to be his, wanting him to appear from the house, shout 'goodbye', drive away from Betsy, from the basement, go to Wimbledon – 'It's you I want Rosie, only you.'

The moon disappeared again. She got out of her car, went across to the Metro. Stood near it, touched it, smelt it, sensed the aroma of him, even through the locked doors. She peered inside at the untidiness, prayed for some sign that he was still hers – but the car was here, *he* was here. She shivered in the cold December air. Across the street now, behind her car, and in the house windows above her, Christmas tree lights flickered and glowed. No holly wreaths on the doors here – too many stealing eyes and hands, no doubt – She'd remembered her mother putting hanging fuchsias in her terraced porch one May after they had visited the garden centre. They'd gone inside, made coffee, filled a watering can and returned to water the new plant – and it had already gone, the garden gate still open and swinging from careless stranger's hands. Her mother had been furious but resigned.

She shivered again and again, but wanted to stay near his car, willing him to appear, to open the door of the basement flat and feel her presence there, wanting him, 'Do with me what you want Ben, I don't care any more. I'll share you, whatever, just once more. I'm here, can't you sense it, feel it?' But no-one came, no doors opened, only the music, the lights, the cold, the silence and the loneliness behind the murmur of the London suburb. Somewhere, a clock struck one. Music had stopped. People were asleep. Ben and Betsy, making love, were behind that door, maybe in that front room. She stood now at the railings, straining to hear sounds from inside. There was nothing. One light, faint, maybe from the back of the flat. Probably the kitchen. She hoped they were eating, talking, not making love. Not holding and touching and stroking, with Betsy moving beneath him and making noises like hers while he stayed silent. Maybe he spoke to Betsy, mentioned love when he kissed her, mounted her, smiled down at her, their eyes locked together in mutual passion.

She bent down and put a hand, then both hands, through the railings, touched and tore at the cold, dead geraniums. She pulled them up easily, roots shallow and shrunk from the near-freezing earth. She threw them now, one by one, down onto the steps leading to the glassed front door, against the panes at the front window, thudding noiselessly, waking, disturbing, no-one.

Her hands, cold and dirty, passing at last to her chilled face, wet from silent tears, took her by surprise. She had no idea that she'd been crying. She stumbled back to her car, catching one high-heel in a grating as she stepped off the pavement. Shoe pulled from foot. Remained there. She had often wondered what piece of human history was behind one discarded shoe left in the street. Her own story was there now, waiting to be retrieved and then discarded by the infrequent road sweeper, or maybe to be used by a child for dressing up, found on the way to school or church one Sunday. 'Look what I've found Mummy.' 'Leave it, you don't know where it's been.'

She turned back then to Ben's car. What message, what sweet memory could she leave? 'I was here Ben. Feeling you and that girl. Young limbs placed beneath your long and strong legs, where mine were once, where I belong.' Down on her haunches, one left-over shoe in her hand, bare-stockinged and laddered feet on dirty pavement and gutter. She let his tyres down – like a disgruntled schoolboy bored with his life, not even to hang around and see the discovery, home to tea after school, wondering only briefly what chaos his action had caused, then passing on to another mischief to relieve the monotony of a young life.

She drove home. It was two in the morning. Cold, dirty and torn, the numbness in her shivering body suited her mind.

Joanna was in the kitchen, on the phone, obviously talking to Ella. She stopped and gasped when Rosemary walked in. Ella, at the other end of the phone, said, 'What's wrong Jo? What's the matter?'

Joanna, her eyes on Rosemary, who sank now into one of the kitchen chairs, said into the phone, 'It's your mum. She's OK but I think she's fallen or something. Rosemary? It's Ella. Are you OK?'

Rosemary looked up. Took the phone.

'What's wrong Mum?'

'Nothing. I'm fine. I fell, broke my shoes. It's nothing. It's late.' She passed the phone back to Joanna.

'I'll sort it out,' Jo said. 'Call me tomorrow. OK? I'll be up at the weekend. I'll tell your mum what you said, about Ben.' She put the phone down.

Rosemary frowned. 'What did she say? About Ben? What did Ella say?'

Joanna moved across to switch the kettle on. 'I'll make some tea,' she said. Then, after a moment, 'Ella bumped into him in Glasgow. He's filming up there. For the BBC, I think. She'll talk to you tomorrow.'

Rosemary stared at her. 'Ben? In Glasgow? But I thought—' Her voice died away.

'What?' said Joanna.

Rosemary shook her head.

Joanna, true to form, asked no questions. She watched the older woman, made some tea, placed a mug of it, sweetened with honey, in front of her and waited.

'No more,' said Rosemary at last, not talking about the drink. She smiled now at the confused Jo. 'That's it,' she said.

Some unknown man or woman would come from his house, his flat, his castle, tomorrow and try to drive away a car with four flattened tyres and curse some wretched adolescent. Ashamed and chastened, and feeling more foolish than she had ever done, Rosemary went to bed. Ben was in Glasgow. Ella had seen him. Other people drove dirty Metros with the filth of London streets covering the number plates. She hoped she'd see the funny side one day.

Chapter Twenty Eight

Her alarm woke her at seven, without tea. She had been too tired to find teabags and milk the night before. She lay for moments and stared at the ceiling. The bedroom was cold; she would change the central heating clock and see that it switched itself on at six instead of seven. A few years from now, and her body would shiver without twenty-four-hour warmth. The dullest birthday would be upon her in just a few months. There was nothing exciting about being fifty-one. She felt the radiator behind her begin to warm up. The chair opposite her held the discarded skirt and jacket from last night, one high-heeled shoe thrown in the waste basket by the side of the dressing table.

She reached for her dressing-gown on the bottom of the bed and stood up to cover herself. She ran the shower and stood waiting for the water to run hot. Cleaning her teeth over the basin, the shower cubicle steaming up behind her, she looked in the mirror. Remnants of last night's make-up remained decadently on her face. She looked and felt exhausted. Somehow she was to drag herself to the hairdressers. Somehow she was to face a new set of eager contestants, bright-eyed from their overnight stays in three-starred hotels in outer London.

She cleaned her face, showered, dressed and made-up. She went downstairs. Pat was in the kitchen. She looked carefully at Rosemary.

'Shall I make you some breakfast?' she said, moving to the kettle.

'Just tea, Pat, I'll eat a croissant or something later.'

'You look exhausted.'

'Late night.' Rosemary shuddered at the memory and picked up the post from the kitchen table, where Pat had deposited it. There was a letter from Ella to Joanna from Glasgow. She smiled at the familiar hurried scrawl on the envelope. 'Only bills and rubbish for me,' she said. She drank tea. Pat stood and joined her.

'Tree looks lovely,' she said.

'You always say that,' smiled Rosemary, 'every year. I've had those decorations since the kids were small. I don't know why I go on bothering year after year.'

'If it wasn't for us women, Christmas would disappear,' moaned Pat. She went back to her cleaning.

Rosemary heard the sound of the vacuum start up in the living-room. Pine needles would already be falling from the sweet-smelling Christmas tree which stood glimmering by the french windows.

She felt sick now with the memory of last night. She moved to the phone and rang Frances' number. 'It's me,' she said, quietly, privately, away from Pat's acute hearing.

'Hello precious, I'm seeing you tonight, or are you cancelling?'

'No. Come to the bar. I finish by nine.'

'You sound exhausted.'

'I think you were right about the counsellor, Franny.'

'What happened?'

'I'm too ashamed to tell you. I need the whole day to find the courage.'

Frances laughed. Then she said seriously, 'Ben's not shown his face again?'

'No.'

'Phoned?'

'No. He's in Glasgow apparently. Ella saw him. That's all I know.'

*   *   *

At nine, before she left for the hairdresser, Rosemary phoned the counsellor to make an appointment. It would have to wait now until after the holiday. 'Is it an emergency?' the man's secretary asked unemotionally.

'No.' Rosemary hesitated only momentarily. 'January the 4th will be fine.' She felt drained once again of any feeling apart from embarrassment. Driving to her appointment with Martyn, she thought of the flattened car tyres and dead geraniums. She could feel the sensation of earth still under her fingernails, and remembered how she had scrubbed her hands before she went to bed. 'Oh my God,' she said out loud and pulled suddenly into the side of the road beside a kiosk and on two yellow lines.

'Can't stop there.' The traffic warden appeared from nowhere, gleaming with patronizing, delighted authority.

'One second,' she said, 'I'm just buying cigarettes.'

'Sorry madam, soon be in trouble if we all did it now wouldn't we? Just move along, before I get my little pad out.'

'Shit,' she said and moved back to the car. She wondered for the umpteenth time why she was never recognized when she really wanted to be. She stopped again outside a newsagent and ran in, quite suddenly desperate to start smoking again, knowing it would make her nauseous on an empty stomach. She stood in a queue. Morning papers were pressed into hands, coins thrown onto the counter. A smell like wet biscuits wafted from the two old men behind her, unwashed in clothes that had never seen a dry cleaner. 'Twenty Silk Cut please.'

Unsmiling London faces were all around her. Disgruntled, with no Christmas spirit, as they waited anxiously for the holiday ahead. It would provide a brief respite from work, but would hurtle them into either the claustrophobia of distant relatives or abject isolation. Neither option was enticing.

357

'Oh sorry, and a box of matches please.' She smiled, was met with only a sigh, eyes shifting away. She retreated to her car, lit a cigarette with shaking hands and drove to the hairdressers.

'Sorry I'm late Martyn.'

'Everyone is. Not to panic. Christmas is everywhere. Should be cancelled.'

She wondered if there was anyone who really enjoyed this holiday. Apart from children and dedicated Christians. She envied the anticipation and faith of both.

At lunchtime, before the camera rehearsal, she went to the bar for a sandwich. She avoided the canteen, afraid to see Betsy, in case in some extraordinary way her presence in Stockwell the previous night had been noted or even guessed at. *How paranoid can you get?* she chided herself. *Rosemary Downey would be the last thing on Betsy's mind.* The bar was packed. Her producer, George, an enthusiastic and young man quite new to television, bought her a sherry. 'You look exhausted,' he said.

She laughed. 'So everyone's told me since I woke up this morning. Don't worry, I haven't been to make-up yet.'

They chatted about the show. There was little else they had in common. And Rosemary had already begun to tire of hosting this particular panel game. She doubted it would run for more than two series. Only the ratings would decide. George was unstinting in his praise for both her and the show. She listened, hating to dampen his obvious delight. Could he really believe that this would be the start to lead him into producing *Film On Four*?

He left to talk to his personal assistant on the phone. There was a problem with an expected contestant who was either late or had cold feet and stayed at home in Morecambe. Rosemary bought a ham sandwich in white bread, ate the ham and discarded the rest.

'Hello Rosemary, d'you mind if I join you?'

Her heart stopped in panic, she had been thinking again of Betsy and the flat in Stockwell, thought the girl was now here, but when she turned, it was Anne who stood in front of her. Anne from her last show. Derek's Anne, standing with a glass of lager in one hand, holding a plastic handbag, beaming with the pleasure of seeing someone she thought of as an old friend.

Rosemary stood up. 'How nice to see you Anne.' They kissed, pressing cheeks, pursing lips at the air. 'Sit down, what's happening in your life? It's been ages.' Anne sat. Rosemary waved to the barman. 'Have some wine?' she asked.

Anne nodded. 'Lovely. I couldn't believe it was you. You hardly ever come to the bar.'

'Aah,' said Rosemary, 'wasn't I good in those days?' Two glasses of wine were placed in front of them. Rosemary offered Anne a cigarette. 'I can't remember,' she said, 'do you smoke?'

Anne shook her head. 'No. Didn't know you did.'

'Really gone to pot these days,' laughed Rosemary, feeling a lack of mirth sweep through her. She touched Anne's arm. 'I hardly dare ask you. Have you seen Derek?'

Anne's embarrassment restrained Rosemary from asking any more questions. The shifting away of her eyes told her everything. So Derek the vile had failed in his attempt to be a one-woman man and returned to the only pathetic creature in the whole world who would have him and ask for nothing in return? She wanted to say, 'Why on earth did you take him back? Why, after all those years of futile promises and lies, after the humiliation and no future, did you take him back?'

But they talked of other things. Rosemary, in the following thirty minutes, gave the woman more concentrated attention than she had in the previous ten years.

At last she felt she understood her. This once-despised, misunderstood, merely silly woman, drinking wine and laughing at small-talk, gossiping about old mutual acquaintances, could be Rosemary ten years from now. Hanging on to something that maybe thrilled her once or twice a week (if she got that fortunate). Or maybe even the thrill of surrender had gone by now. Maybe long ago Derek, too, had convinced Anne how lucky she was to have him, even if only to share that pathetic, chewed-up little tyrant. They kissed again and said goodbye. Promising phone calls and lunches that would never happen.

Rosemary left for her dressing-room and the studio, feeling defeated and strong all at the same time. Defeated because she empathized with Anne, saw the life ahead if she walked the same path, recognized the look in the eyes, understood the weakness. And because of that feeling of defeat, a strength began in her that she had searched for since March. Her desire to shake the younger woman had all but taken her over. She should have said, 'Leave him. Leave that cruel man, recognize the fantasy he's created that you call hope.'

But she had merely sat and talked and listened and smiled. And then got up and left. Tomorrow she would start the search for what remained of Rosemary Downey.

Frances was already in the bar when she finished the show and left hospitality after only a polite ten minutes. From tonight they were on Christmas break.

'Don't you wish we'd decided to go away now?' said her friend, carrying two coffees from the counter and finding a sofa to sit on.

'Not with Mum on her own. I was hoping Jonathan would have her again, but she simply refused to go to Birmingham. She's not well these days. She's moaned about her bad health for so long, it's taken her by surprise now that it's actually happened.'

'What's the doctor say?'

'She needs a holiday. In the sun.'

Frances laughed. 'And this to someone who's never been out of SW16!'

'Exactly.'

Frances said, 'Well?'

'What?'

'Don't pretend. What have you been up to?'

She told Frances. Relating it made her squirm again. The words came out with hesitation at first, and then fell over each other in her haste to finish the tale. But Frances merely laughed at the end.

'Why, for God's sake, do you find it funny? I feel as if I'd gone insane.' Rosemary's voice rose just by a whispered notch.

'Did you never do anything like that before?' Frances asked.

'Good God, of course not. I'd have told you. How many years have you known me?'

'Before then, as a teenager?'

'No. Never.' Rosemary stared at her. 'I can't believe you're not deeply shocked. I thought you'd take me home and put me to bed.'

Frances threw back her head and laughed. People at the bar turned to look at her. 'I'm not your mother, darling girl! And I once scratched the paintwork on a man's car when he was inside my best friend's flat screwing her! And I left my name, so that the revenge was complete!'

Rosemary looked honestly shocked. 'How old were you?' she whispered.

'Seventeen,' Frances said conspiratorially. 'He was a twenty-five-year-old married man, making his way through all the girls in our sixth form.'

'You make me feel as if I should be pleased with myself,' Rosemary said.

'You should. It's the first sign of life I've seen in you for months.'

They had pasta in a late night spaghetti bar and went their separate ways.

'I'll be over on Christmas Eve,' called Frances, shivering and trying to find her car keys.

Rosemary waved and drove home. Joanna was still up, watching a video in the living-room. Rosemary put her head round the door. 'Hi Jo, any phone calls?'

'Three. One from Ella and two with no-one at the other end.'

'Getting a lot of those.'

Joanna turned the video off and followed her into the kitchen. 'You look much better,' she smiled at Rosemary. 'Glad it's over for a while?'

'I'm quite suddenly looking forward to Christmas.'

Jo sat at the table and watched the older woman potter for a moment.

'What did Ella have to say?' Rosemary asked over her shoulder.

Jo said, 'Sent her love. Will phone on Christmas Day. I'm going up tomorrow night. Is that OK?'

'Fine.'

With cards at last posted, presents packaged and beribboned, tree lights secured and holly picked and into vases, Christmas, as always, was ready. On Christmas Eve, Rosemary picked up her mother and brought her to Wimbledon. Frances joined them.

It was a peaceful holiday, quiet and soul-restoring. 'Just what I need,' sighed Frances on Christmas night. 'It's been a dreadful year.'

The day after Christmas, alone again, the phone rang just as she was leaving for Frances' party. It was Tom from Los Angeles.

'A belated Happy Christmas,' he said.

'It's still going on here,' she laughed. 'Two weeks usually. I'm just off to Frances' for a party.'

'Tell her "hello". And I hope to see her in the spring.'

'You're coming over?'

'Sure am. Some time at the end of February.'

'Make it March 1st for my birthday.'

'That's a promise.'

So the season came and went. New Year's Eve, Rosemary's least favourite night of the year, she celebrated ('if that's the word' she remarked to Frances) with a dinner party at her house. It was the first time since her fiftieth birthday that she had held any sort of large gathering in her own home. This time it was for ten people. She cooked the meal herself, Frances standing by mixing martinis.

'Can we take down these sodding decorations tomorrow, Rosemary child?' she said, picking a card from the floor where it had fallen for the umpteenth time.

'The radiator softens the glue,' said Rosemary automatically. Then, 'My God, I *am* like my mother. I say that every year.'

At twelve, as always, people kissed and said the same old things: 'Well, it can't be worse than last year', or 'This'll be the one, you mark my words', and the countdown on the television heralded in some usually dreadful variety show.

And then it was over; by one o'clock only Frances remained. They loaded the dishwasher, made tea, put out the bottles and sat and yawned over the dying embers of the fire. The Christmas tree rapidly shed pine needles with every movement in the room, the holly was dying in the vase by the fire, red berries shrivelled and fell from the branches exposed on the mantelpiece.

'Christ, it's over.' Frances refused tea, drank brandy.

'You'd better stay,' said Rosemary, 'you're too pissed to drive.'

'Thank you honey child.' She looked at Rosemary, staring now into the fire, her face flushed with the heat and too much food and drink.

'Are you better?' she asked her eventually, her legs outstretched, her shoes long abandoned, twirling the brandy glass in her hand.

'Better?' queried Rosemary, looking up.

'Are you over him? Not unscathed, but over him?'

Rosemary thought for a moment. 'I'm calmer,' she said, 'but I'd prefer him not to appear. I don't think I could turn him away quite yet.'

Two days into January, Ella phoned. 'Belated Happy New Year, Mum. Celebrations go on for ever up here. Jo's coming back tomorrow.'

'Happy New Year darling. Lots of parties?'

Ella groaned. 'Tell me about it. I'm fucking exhausted. Listen, Mum, how are you?' her voice was serious. 'I mean about Ben and all.'

'What d'you mean? Have you seen him again?'

'It's just – oh hell, Jo said I shouldn't tell you, but knowing you, maybe I should.'

The calm that had settled on Rosemary the last few weeks wavered a little. She sat down and changed the phone to the other ear. 'Tell me,' she said, and knew she sounded beguilingly calm.

'There's been an accident. New Year's Eve. He's back in London and in hospital apparently. The eye hospital in the East End.'

'What happened? What sort of accident? And how do you know?' She was thinking quickly.

'It's his eye, apparently. They were doing some studio work on this series for the BBC. He was hit by a boom. He's probably going to lose an eye. I thought you'd like

364

to know. Poetic justice really, roving eye an' all.'

'Not funny Ella.'

'Just a gesture, Mum. Jo's just punched me.'

Rosemary said again, 'How did you find out?'

'He took one of the girls out in the Christmas show up here; she told me because she knows I knew him.'

'I see.'

Joanna came on the phone. 'If you like, Rosemary, wait till I come back and I'll go to the hospital with you. Save you the phone call, I mean, if that was your intention.'

Rosemary smiled. Sensitive Joanna. 'You know me well,' she said.

'I must see him,' she said to Frances.

'No, no, don't, lovely. I'll phone the hospital. Do me a favour, don't go.'

But that next morning, the day that Joanna was returning home, the phone rang at eight o'clock. It was Ben.

'Rosie?'

Her heart dropped. The hairbrush she'd been using and was still in her hand clattered onto the dressing table in front of her. She sat on the side of the bed and held the phone tensely, hard into her ear.

'Rosie?' he spoke again. His voice was very quiet.

'Hello Ben. I thought you were in hospital.'

'I am. I'm calling from one of those wheel-about telephones. I just wanted to talk to you. How did you know I was here?'

'Grapevine.'

'I see.' He paused. She could find nothing to say and was distressed by the effect his voice still had on her.

'Were you thinking of coming to see me?' he asked eventually.

'Would you like me to?'

'I wouldn't have phoned, would I?'

'Are they going to operate?'

365

'This morning.'

'I'm so sorry Ben.' And the compassion was genuine.

'Oh well, I was always better at character work,' he joked. 'It's never done Peter Falk's career any harm.'

She couldn't think of anything to say.

He spoke again. 'Will you come tonight?'

'All right. What time?'

'I dunno. About half-past seven? Yeah. Half-past seven. I'll be the only one with the patch. Oh no, maybe not. Not in an eye hospital!'

'Good luck.'

'See you later Rosie. That'll be great.' The phone went dead. His money had obviously run out.

She had to sit for quite a while before she could get her breathing back to normal. But it was nerves more than excitement. Habitual emotion followed her round all day, curiosity of how she'd feel at the sight of him, pity for the disfigurement of her beautiful Ben. Her Ben? Did she still feel that?

Joanna came home at about five that afternoon. 'I'll come with you,' she said when Rosemary told her.

'No, that's not necessary.'

'I won't come to the ward. I'll drive you.'

Joanna had only recently passed her test. Rosemary was dubious. 'All right,' she said, 'but I'll drive.'

After six outfits had been discarded, she settled for a trouser suit she had purchased in a pre-Christmas sale and which was still unworn. She searched every drawer and shelf in both bathrooms for any sort of tranquillizer, but to no avail.

'What are you looking for?' asked Joanna.

'Valium.' Rosemary pulled a face, mocking her own silliness and panic.

Joanna said seriously, 'Perhaps you shouldn't go.'

'I'd never forgive myself. He asked me. I'd hate him to feel abandoned.'

Joanna snorted with derision. Rosemary raised her eyebrows in surprise. It was unlike Jo to state, even in a small way, any sort of criticism.

They got into the car and drove to East London, stopping on the way to buy flowers.

Jo settled herself into the tea-bar in the hospital with the previous Sunday's newspapers which she carried around for the whole of the following week so that she could read every paragraph.

Rosemary checked the ward. She took a deep breath and went up the three flights of stairs to see Ben.

Chapter Twenty Nine

'Where do I begin to tell you?' she said to Frances much later. 'How can I ever describe how I felt?' It was one of those scenarios that would probably play for ever in her memory. At the beginning, humiliation, hurt pride, immobility. Later, thankfully, a good yarn to relate at dinner parties.

'I had an experience like that once,' Frances said. 'Well, not exactly like that. Just the same humiliation of being rooted to the spot. I was dancing with this fella I was just besotted with, and he with me, according to his big mouth. Said he was going to leave his wife and children, make an honest woman of me. Remember I was a mere twenty-one at the time, a baby. Anyway, there we were, dancing so close together we were welding with self-created heat, and he's whispering things like "I'll never leave you, you're all I want" etc, etc, etc. You know the dialogue. Then he hands me his glass of whisky. I should have known really, any man who dances with a drink in his hand. But he was from Glasgow, so it seemed normal at the time. Anyway, he hands me this glass. "Hold this," he says, still with his tongue half-way down my throat, "and don't go away. I'll be back in a minute. I'm going to the loo." And he went. And there I was. Strange party. All his friends. Holding this sodding glass of whisky.'

'So what happened?' Rosemary said.

'He never came back. I never saw him again. Well, not until about five years later. "I drank the whisky" I said to him. He'd forgotten by then. Thought I'd gone mad.'

'Where had he gone?'

'Where d'you think? Back to the wife and children. "Oh Hamish is a homing pigeon," said one of the other party goers. He had to be a Hamish didn't he?' She laughed.

But Rosemary was once again the innocent when she entered that ward. It was large, with cruel lighting, full of the sound of visitors and the clacking of heels from quick-moving nurses. She stopped a smiling West Indian Sister hurrying past with a delicately-covered bedpan.

'Excuse me, Sister, could you tell me where a Mr Morrison is situated?'

The nurse frowned slightly, then smiled even more broadly. Rosemary knew the look. She'd been recognized. 'It's Rosemary Downey isn't it? How nice to meet you. I'm a big fan.'

'Thank you.'

'Ben's in the far corner,' she said, and pointed to a glass-windowed partition at the far end of the ward. 'He's been awake for quite a while, but we haven't moved him back to the main ward yet. Just as well really.' She laughed and moved away. Rosemary watched her go, her hips moving erotically under the crisp uniform. Rosemary made her way down the ward. Visitors watched her progress, conversation being difficult with some of the ailing patients, they seemed pleased with the diversion she caused with her famous face. Her cheeks grew hot, her hands sticky. She looked not to right or left, her eyes on her feet moving towards the partition, and Ben.

The door into the small, single-bedded recovery ward stood open. She went inside. Ben half-sat against many pillows, his hands resting on the outside of the bed-clothes, the blue blanket clashing with the unfamiliar, green-striped pyjamas he was wearing. Betsy Tejero sat

369

by the side of his bed and held one of his hands. On the other side, Gill Spencer stood arranging some flowers in a vase that stood on the bedside locker. A girl whom Rosemary had never seen before was standing awkwardly at the bottom of the bed, dodging at times a young black nurse who bustled around with temperature charts and various pills and potions that she was preparing.

Ben looked up and saw her. 'Rosie!' he said, and smiled. 'You came.'

'Yes,' she said and stayed rooted to the spot, next to the strange, red-haired girl on her right.

Betsy said, 'Hi Rosemary,' and turned back to speak quietly to Ben.

Gill turned, and smiled. 'Hello. Shall I get a vase and put those in water?' She took the flowers that were now hanging limply in Rosemary's hand. She said to the nurse, 'Is there another vase?'

'I'll get one.'

The red-head on Rosemary's right smiled briefly.

Rosemary searched for something to say. 'How long must you be here?' she asked eventually.

'Just a few days,' Gill Spencer said before Ben could answer.

He nodded. 'Just a few days.'

The red-headed girl looked more and more miserable. The nurse bounced back in and snatched the flowers from Gill's hands. 'I'll see to these,' she said and bustled away efficiently. 'Far too many visitors Ben,' she threw over her shoulder, and stepped back to let in another one.

The Chinese girl in the photograph. She went straight to the bed and bent to kiss Ben.

'Hi Margot,' he said. He put on a wan smile for all his guests.

Betsy said, 'Shall I order more milk for Thursday if that's the day you're coming out?'

Every female eye in the room looked at her.

The red-head said, 'Aren't you coming down to me? To Sussex? Just to recuperate.'

'Diane's a physiotherapist,' Ben said. 'She works in the hospital.'

The eyes shifted now to Diane, who still looked sad. Gill went back to arranging the locker. Diane and Rosemary just looked at each other.

Betsy said, 'Well, let me know.'

'They seem to think I should recuperate,' said Ben lamely.

Margot said, 'What about the film?'

Ben shrugged. 'I think they've got all they need from me.'

Gill said, 'Will you get compensation?'

Betsy spoke quickly. 'Yes. But it'll take for ever.'

Gill sat opposite her, on the other side of Ben and on the bed. Betsy stroked his hand.

Margot bounced with delight at the end of the bed, oblivious to everyone except the man in front of her. 'I'm so pleased it's all over. I thought about you all morning.'

Gill said, 'I think I'm going to the radio rep on a six-month contract, so you won't have to worry about work for a while. Jamie and I can manage on my salary.'

Ben smiled and touched her face. He looked up at Rosemary again. 'How's the show going Rosie?'

She nodded. It was physically impossible to get the words past her lips – Any sort of words, banalities, small-talk, even 'how d'you feel?' She wondered how long it would be before she got the power into her legs to turn and start the long walk back down the ward.

The nurse came back.

'Not too long, ladies.' She looked at the watch on her uniform. 'Just five more minutes.' She bent across to Ben. 'I'll straighten your bed when everyone's gone,' she twinkled at him, 'then we'll wheel you back to the big ward.'

'With all the other eye patches,' he said, 'how will you tell us apart?'

'Don't worry Mr Morrison, I'll always find *you*.'

He winked at her. She laughed and left. Ben caught Rosemary's eye and for a moment they stayed locked in each other's gaze. He shrugged, just slightly, seeming to say 'you see how it is?' Out loud, he said, 'You look great Rosie.'

Female eyes swept over her. She flinched, moved, and finally spoke. 'I have to go Ben. Dinner. With some American friends.' She couldn't resist it. She went to the door. 'Hope the recuperation goes well.' She smiled at Diane, who ignored her and continued to play with the white coverlet at the bottom of the bed. 'Goodbye,' she said. And then, 'Goodbye Ben.' She went. Down the ward, past the watchful eyes. Thanking the Sister, down the stairs, not waiting for the elevator and into the tea-bar to find Jo. Smiling, placid, thoughtful Jo.

'Thank God you came,' said Rosemary, and passed her the keys to the car. 'For Christ's sake take me home. And tell me I don't look as stupid as I feel.'

'Is that it then?' asked Frances. 'Is that finally and irrevocably and positively, please God, IT?'

Joanna had taken Rosemary home. Her teeth were chattering with cold and some sort of extraordinary kind of shock. She changed her clothes, tore off the trouser suit and pushed it to the back of the wardrobe. 'Attire of the final humiliation,' she said to Joanna, who was standing in the bedroom doorway, holding a glass of brandy, looking her increasingly familiar worried look.

Rosemary drank the brandy, touched Jo's cheek, and laughed. 'Don't look so anxious, Jo my love. It's just slight hysteria. I'm not going to have another minor

372

breakdown. It's all so ridiculous.' She'd packed a case and phoned Frances. 'I'm coming to stay, for just a week,' she said.

'That's nice. And surprising. What happened to "I can't sleep in other people's beds"?'

'Forgotten. Along with common sense and survival of self.'

'Fine. You'll find plenty of that here. Stay as long as you want, lovely one.'

So she'd gone to Frances. She phoned Michael and said where she would be until further notice.

'Are you OK? What about the show?'

'I'll be fine,' she said firmly. 'He'll have to phone here,' she said to Frances. 'D'you mind?'

'That's the least of my problems.'

'In answer to your question,' said Rosemary, 'I think it probably is, as you call it, IT.'

'Only probably?'

'I'll have to change the lock on the front door.'

Frances rubbed her hands gleefully. 'Oh how I would have loved to be a fly on the wall in that hospital ward.'

Rosemary shuddered. 'Don't. It's a nightmare. The man has humiliation down as an art form. Do you suppose it was all intentional? When he asked me to come?'

Frances shook her head. 'I don't think it crossed his mind. His arrogance is absolutely supreme. You can't but admire it. I wonder if this eye business will cramp his style?'

'Why should it?'

'You're right. The most important item is still intact. At the moment, anyway. Some lady might set about a nasty revenge some day.'

'Believe me,' Rosemary gritted her teeth, 'it's crossed my mind.'

Frances leaned forward and filled her friend's wine glass. 'Can we be grown-ups again now?' she said with a smile.

'Yes please,' said Rosemary. She stayed just over a week.

'Will he turn up at any time?' Frances asked on the day Rosemary was to go home.

Rosemary shook her head. 'Not this time. He knew. He's too conscious of making a good exit.'

'I hope you're right. And if you once, just once, get the remotest fancy for anyone with the sniff of Ben Morrison's kind ever again, I'll just say "hospital".'

Rosemary smiled. 'He's out of my life,' she said. 'As long as I don't see him or smell him, I'll be just fine.' She went home.

The television series finished. Michael was in negotiations for another of the same. Rosemary sighed. 'Is there *nothing* else?'

She continued at BBC radio, avoiding Gill Spencer in the canteen, and took each day with determination to get her old life back.

One Saturday, at the end of January, she had gone to Streatham to spend the day with her mother. They shopped and went to a matinée.

It was the last scene, almost, to be played with Ben Morrison. Only this time her part was cut, taken out of her hands, played better by Joanna, who was alone at the time in the house at Wimbledon. She was washing a shirt by hand in the kitchen sink, standing by the big window, humming to herself, looking out at the cold, bright day outside. Ella would be home from Glasgow the next day, her contract had finished, and Jo's life seemed good. They had some flats to look at when Ella got back, Jo had started work on another play, and the last one she directed was transferring into the West End. It was the kind of January weather that happened now and then. Cold but mellow, 'more like early April' Rosemary had said before she left that morning. She had brought Ben's belongings, still sitting in the spare room, down to the kitchen.

'I'm going to leave these at Portland Place for Gill Spencer on Monday,' she said grimly.

Joanna smiled, pleased, and waved her off to Streatham. She and Ella were going to buy Rosemary a kitten when they left the house. They would choose it together when Ella came home. She squeezed the excess water from the shirt, too delicate to put in the washing machine. It was Ella's, and Jo had the patience to do any handwashing. 'There,' she said and turned to find some clothes pegs so she could put it, dripping, on the line outside.

She hadn't heard the key in the front door. Or the footsteps across the carpeted hall. Soft-soled trainers below jeans and denim jacket. Ben came straight into the kitchen. Jo, sleeves rolled up, hands wet, soap-sudded nose, stood stock still and stared at him. She found her voice. 'You scared the life out of me.' She grabbed the tea-towel from the rail by the sink and dried her hands. Drips, drops of water were scattered by the sink.

Ben smiled. 'Didn't you hear the front door?' he said. Then, 'I have a key. Remember?'

She looked at him. Not smiling. 'What d'you want?' she asked, trying not to stare at the eye patch he now wore.

'Is Rosie here?'

'No.'

'When will she be back?'

Joanna shrugged.

Ben said, 'You don't like me do you?'

She paused, her natural politeness fighting for supremacy lost out to her instinct. 'Not much,' she said.

'Still, can't please everyone can I?' Ben said, smiling and still, watching her, hinting less than discreetly at her sexuality.

She said nothing. Then at last, 'There's no point in hanging around here, Ben. Nobody here wants you any more. You'd better go.' She couldn't believe what she'd said. She waited, hardly daring to hope that he would leave.

Ben scrutinized her with his one good eye. 'Are you quite sure of that?' he asked.

'Absolutely,' she said, more firmly than she believed. Then, 'I'll get your things. Rosemary put them here just this morning. She was going to get them to you next week.' She got the small pile, including the old briefcase, and pushed it into his arms, forcing him to take it.

'She seems to have told you only her side of the story,' he said.

Joanna felt the anger and distaste grow inside her. 'It's all I need to know. I know your kind, Ben Morrison.'

He smiled again at her, put one hand out and stroked her cheek before she could pull back. 'I hardly think so. Now what would I do with you, babyface?' He turned before she could find words to counter-attack his patronizing gesture. She let him walk again into the hall. 'Perhaps you could tell Rosie I stopped by. I'll pop round when she gets less encumbered.'

Joanna moved forward, fast, light on her feet, her eyes flashing, dark curls spilling from the headband she'd used to control her wayward hair. 'I want the key,' she said.

'What?' There was a laugh of incredulity in the one word.

'I want that fucking key,' Joanna said vehemently, passionately, stiff with anger. Her voice grew louder.

'The fucking key, you bastard! And take one step nearer that lady again, just one fucking step, and you'll regret it for the rest of your life. She has more friends than you've ever imagined, and you've outstayed your welcome, or should I say *use*?'

There was a long pause. Joanna put her hand out. Ben hesitated, then shrugged. He put his hand at last into his top pocket, the one that held the travelling toothbrush, and took out Rosemary's front door key. He held it out to Jo. She took it, said nothing. Ben went to the door without a word, without a sign, and left.

Joanna burst into tears.

Chapter Thirty – Epilogue

March. And of all things it was snowing.

'January looked so promising,' groaned Rosemary to Pat. She held the new kitten up against her cheek.

'It's female,' Ella had said. 'What will you call her?'

'Joanna,' Rosemary answered without hesitation, 'because this little thing is pretty, brave and unexpected.'

Joanna had blushed.

The girls had found a flat. 'The smallest one in the entire fucking world,' Ella had moaned, but she nevertheless looked pleased. 'I think I'm going to play house at long last, Mum.'

'I thought you'd never say it,' Rosemary joked.

They had gone at the end of February, taking everything Rosemary had to offer in the way of linen, crockery, pots and pans and so on, plus a few things that were not offered, as Rosemary found out for several days after they'd left.

'Don't complain,' Frances said, 'be grateful. Your house is tidy again, and it no longer smells of plimsolls.'

'Trainers,' Rosemary corrected her. 'I think they're called trainers now.'

'Funny. They *look* just like plimsolls.'

Ben had not returned. Had not phoned.

'Taken fright,' shouted Ella. 'Turned tail! My big brave girl showed him the door.'

Joanna was embarrassed. No matter how much Rosemary told her she'd done right, that someone had to do it, and that she herself would never have had the courage, Jo still felt she had interfered.

'Nonsense,' said Ella, 'you were the only female he couldn't work his charm on. You were fucking wonderful!'

'Must you be so fucking noisy?' Rosemary shouted back at her.

The girls looked at each other and laughed.

'Really Mother, what has happened to you since you turned fifty?' Ella teased.

Rosemary ignored her. Fifty-one loomed.

Tom kept his word. He had phoned several times, and was now in England. London. It was March, and it was her birthday. He wanted to take her out, but she refused.

'I will throw a dinner party,' she said, 'and you can meet some more of my friends – I mean apart from Frances.'

Their friendship had progressed on his return to London. After the first week, she had succumbed and spent the night with him at the Savoy.

'Well?' said Frances eagerly.

'He's a nice man,' said Rosemary. 'Don't rush me. I don't want to move mountains this time.'

Frances sighed. 'I'm beginning to think it was Ben Morrison's cruelty that kept you interested. You never called him "a nice man".'

'I don't want another Ben. One a lifetime is enough.'

'Balls,' said Frances. 'You just refuse to forget him.'

On the morning of her birthday, Saturday, Michael phoned. 'To wish you Many Happy Returns,' he said. 'And to tell you some interesting news.'

'Thank you. It's Saturday. Are you in the office?'

379

He was. Rosemary realized how often he'd done a six-day-week in the last few months.

'What's the news?' she said.

'They'd like to see you in L.A. again. Glen phoned late last night.'

'I can't believe it. I'd forgotten all that.'

'It means that you could forget the next panel game series.'

'Let's do it.'

Michael laughed. 'Have a good birthday. We'll talk on Monday. My love to Frances.'

'He's unhappy at home,' Rosemary remarked to Frances.

'I can't help him,' her friend replied. 'I can't take the heat in that particular kitchen.'

So Rosemary felt sad for her agent, and for Barbara, who couldn't forgive or forget, and for Frances, who probably felt more than she would ever admit, even to herself.

'You look beautiful,' Tom said, and kissed her as he handed her the present he'd carefully chosen. He'd been the first to arrive, rapidly followed by Frances who had disappeared upstairs to have a bath after a long tedious day. There were just eight of them for dinner. Frances had invited a client she was working with, and was obviously heading for another affair.

'Is he nice?' whispered Rosemary, not too sure.

'He makes me laugh,' whispered back her friend. 'I ask for very little. A few good dinners, the odd orgasm – with emphasis on the odd – and a lot of laughs! And he fits the bill.'

They were on dessert. Rosemary looked round the table. The candles lit up the faces. She felt safe again. Her exposure to all that uncontrollable passion had made her grateful for the peace that had followed. She remembered now only the pleasant part of her affair with Ben, was saddened in some ways that it was over, and still dreaded the thought of him appearing in her life again. 'As long as he keeps away I'm fine,' she said.

She had grown slimmer since Christmas, her hair was longer and softer. Her confidence was growing again. There were times when she thought *oh I wish you could see me now Ben Morrison. You'd fall for me all over again.* But they were thoughts, brushed aside, not confronted.

Tom leaned towards her. 'This could be great news about L.A.,' he said. 'When will you come?'

'Now who do you think would be the first person I'd tell Tom?' she teased.

He touched her face. Stroked her cheek. Smiled with his eyes.

The phone rang. 'I'll take it in the hall,' she said, and looked at her watch. It was eleven-thirty, late for anyone to call. 'Must be Ella,' she said and went through to pick up the telephone.

'Happy Birthday Rosie.'

A feeling of total euphoria swept over her when she heard his voice. Better than the headiness of the first months of being in love. Better even than their first kiss. It was all the good things that had ever happened to her rolled into one.

'Ben?' she said, keeping her voice low. 'Is that you Ben?'

'Meet me somewhere,' he said, his voice so quiet that she had to hold her breath to hear him properly.

'I'm having a dinner party,' she said. 'I have guests.'

'Meet me somewhere,' he spoke again, and there was pleading in that voice. 'Rosie, my love, I'm incapable of going on for one more day without holding you in my arms.'

A pause grew – long and tense. Silence crackled. Breathing, short and heavy from one end of the line.

Falling out of love is like falling out of a window and going up. 'That's tough,' she said. Without a tremor, without fear, without any sort of feeling. And she put the phone down.

THE END

LILIAN
by Jill Gascoine

Jessica Wooldridge was at just about the lowest ebb of her life when the phone call came from Los Angeles.

She had turned fifty, was recovering from a serious operation, and was in the throes of nervous depression. The kindness of husband, sons, and friends in their comfortable Sussex village only served to make her worse. Then came the invitation from Norma – vigorous, vibrant, outgoing Norma who had married a wealthy Californian and upped to live a golden life in a magic world of luxury homes, swimming pools, parties, and shopping. Everyone agreed that Jessica should go to Los Angeles – for a few weeks.

The visit was to revolutionise her life. New people, new friends, new exhilarating experiences, even the bad things – like the murky problems of Norma's marriage – served to startle her into freedom, fulfilment, and ultimately a deep and profound happiness as an unexpected love affair exploded into her life. The weeks became months – until finally Jessica had to face the dilemma of her future.

COMING FROM CORGI IN DECEMBER – *LILIAN* – EXCITING, POIGNANT, AND PULSING WITH ENERGY – THE NEW NOVEL FROM THE AUTHOR OF *ADDICTED*.

A SELECTED LIST OF FINE NOVELS AVAILABLE
FROM CORGI BOOKS AND BLACK SWAN

THE PRICES SHOWN BELOW WERE CORRECT AT THE TIME OF GOING TO PRESS. HOWEVER TRANSWORLD PUBLISHERS RESERVE THE RIGHT TO SHOW NEW RETAIL PRICES ON COVERS WHICH MAY DIFFER FROM THOSE PREVIOUSLY ADVERTISED IN THE TEXT OR ELSEWHERE.

☐	99564 9	**JUST FOR THE SUMMER**	*Judy Astley*	£5.99
☐	13648 4	**CASTING**	*Jane Barry*	£3.99
☐	99537 1	**GUPPIES FOR TEA**	*Marika Cobbold*	£5.99
☐	99593 2	**A RIVAL CREATION**	*Marika Cobbold*	£5.99
☐	99488 X	**SUGAR CAGE**	*Connie May Fowler*	£5.99
☐	99467 7	**MONSIEUR DE BRILLANCOURT**	*Clare Harkness*	£4.99
☐	99387 5	**TIME OF GRACE**	*Clare Harkness*	£5.99
☐	99590 8	**OLD NIGHT**	*Clare Harkness*	£5.99
☐	13872 X	**LEGACY OF LOVE**	*Caroline Harvey*	£4.99
☐	13917 3	**A SECOND LEGACY**	*Caroline Harvey*	£4.99
☐	14284 0	**DROWNING IN HONEY**	*Kate Hatfield*	£4.99
☐	13737 5	**EMERALD**	*Elisabeth Luard*	£5.99
☐	99449 9	**DISAPPEARING ACTS**	*Terry McMillan*	£5.99
☐	99480 4	**MAMA**	*Terry McMillan*	£5.99
☐	99503 7	**WAITING TO EXHALE**	*Terry McMillan*	£5.99
☐	99325 5	**THE QUIET WAR OF REBECCA SHELDON**	*Kathleen Rowntree*	£5.99
☐	99584 3	**BRIEF SHINING**	*Kathleen Rowntree*	£5.99
☐	99506 1	**BETWEEN FRIENDS**	*Kathleen Rowntree*	£5.99
☐	13756 1	**AN ORDINARY WOMAN**	*Susan Sallis*	£4.99
☐	13346 9	**SUMMER VISITORS**	*Susan Sallis*	£4.99
☐	14296 4	**THE LAND OF NIGHTINGALES**	*Sally Stewart*	£4.99
☐	99529 0	**OUT OF THE SHADOWS**	*Titia Sutherland*	£5.99
☐	99460 X	**THE FIFTH SUMMER**	*Titia Sutherland*	£5.99
☐	99574 6	**ACCOMPLICE OF LOVE**	*Titia Sutherland*	£5.99
☐	99470 7	**THE RECTOR'S WIFE**	*Joanna Trollope*	£5.99
☐	99492 8	**THE MEN AND THE GIRLS**	*Joanna Trollope*	£5.99
☐	99126 0	**THE CAMOMILE LAWN**	*Mary Wesley*	£6.99
☐	99495 2	**A DUBIOUS LEGACY**	*Mary Wesley*	£6.99
☐	99591 6	**A MISLAID MAGIC**	*Joyce Windsor*	£4.99